EVEN BETTER THAN THE REAL THING?

MARTINA REILLY

HACHETTE
BOOKS
IRELAND

First published in 2012 by Hachette Books Ireland

1

All the characters in this publication, except for those historial and contemporary figures who are clearly in the public domain, are fictitious and any resemblance to real persons living or dead is entirely coincidental.

A CIP catalogue record for this title is available from the British Library.

ISBN 978 1 444 72593 3

Typeset in Constantia by Hachette Books Ireland.
Printed and bound in Great Britain by Clays Ltd, St. Ives.

Hachette Books Ireland policy is to use papers that are natural, renewable and recyclable products and made from wood grown in sustainable forests. The logging and manufacturing processes are expected to conform to the environmental regulations of the country of origin.

Hachette Books Ireland
8 Castlecourt Centre, Castleknock, Dublin 15, Ireland

www.hachette.ie

A division of Hachette UK
338 Euston Road, London NW1 3BH

Praise for Martina Reilly

'Clever, frank and funny' *Bella*

'We love Martina' *More*

'Has all the elements of an excellent read: mystery, drama and romance' *Woman*

'A rollicking good yarn' *Irish Evening Herald*

'Like Marian Keyes, Reilly takes a cracking story, adds sharp dialogue and buckets of originality' *Scottish Daily Record*

'A top holiday read' *Closer*

'Martina has the wonderful knack of combining sensitivity for a serious subject with a big dose of humour'
Irish Independent

'Martina Reilly's characters are so well observed . . . a substantial read'
She

'Hard to put down, laugh-out-loud funny . . . perfect holiday reading' *Woman's Way*

'Reilly has a wonderful comic touch, both in the way she draws her characters and in her dialogue . . . a brilliant read' *U* Magazine

'A cracking read – warm, splutter-out-your-tea funny, and unputdownable. I loved it' Sarah Webb

'Compelling, heart-wrenching . . . will keep you riveted until the end'
Colette Caddle

'*A Moment Like Forever* is a shining example of why she is adored by her fans . . . it's captivating, heart-warming and heartbreakingly sad in equal measures' *www.sassysaysbooks.com*

'I absolutely loved it. Her books are consistently good and I adore her story-telling abilities' *www.chicklitreviews.com*

Also by Martina Reilly

Flipside
The Onion Girl
Is This Love?
Wish Upon A Star
Wedded Blitz
Something Borrowed
All I Want Is You
The Summer of Secrets
Second Chances
The Wish List
A Moment Like Forever

Fast Car
Dirt Tracks
Livewire
Freefall

This book is dedicated to all my friends – the ones I know and love, and the ones I've met through Facebook and Twitter
Thanks for all your support x

And to Van Gogh, who was the most fascinating and brilliant man

Prologue

'OK.' The man strode into the premises, obviously impatient to be gone as quickly as possible, 'What's the big secret?'

John Cole flinched at the abrupt tone and wondered yet again how on earth he'd been persuaded to do this. It was madness, complete craziness. If he got caught, he'd face prison, his reputation ruined. Then again, he supposed, by the time the trial came up, he'd be long gone. And, as Robert had pointed out to him, he could always plead ignorance and get away with it and then Robert would take the rap. But John knew he'd never do that to his friend and it was his daughter that had ...

'Well?' The impatient man, Harry Collins, a renowned expert, glanced at his watch with irritation. 'Come on, John, I don't have all night. You told me this was special.'

'It is.' John was surprised at how normal his voice sounded. 'I'll just go and fetch my friend. He has something to show you.' Knees trembling, he sauntered as confidently as he could towards the back of the premises. 'Pierre,' he called, 'come and meet Harry Collins, the man I told you about.'

John's best friend, Robert, gave him a nervous smile as he got to his feet. Dressed in black trousers and a dazzling white shirt, which accentuated his dark looks, he appeared more like a continental European than a man born and bred in Dublin. Rolled up, under his arm, was a canvas measuring roughly twelve by eighteen inches.

John marvelled as Robert, abandoning his normally apologetic stooped manner, swaggered confidently from the back room into the blinding light of the gallery. Head up, his whole frame looked more powerful and John, hurrying behind him, wondered why Robert never adopted that persona in his real-life dealings. He'd known Robert since they were kids knocking about together on Dublin's southside, and having the same interests in art and history, they'd clicked and been friends ever since. John had never realised how deep this friendship went until his life had taken this terribly unexpected tragic twist.

Robert came to a stop in front of Harry Collins and looked at John expectantly.

'This is Pierre,' John introduced Robert awkwardly, his heart beginning to thump hard. 'He's an old friend of my family,' which at least was true, he thought wryly, 'and he contacted me last week about a painting he'd found in his late grandfather's belongings.'

'*Great* grandpère,' Robert corrected in a pretty good French accent. 'Dis bee-longed to my great-grandpère.'

John nodded. 'Yes.' He turned back to Harry. 'Pierre's grandfather inherited a number of paintings from his own father so technically this painting belonged to Pierre's great-grandfather. Pierre?'

Very slowly, Robert, aka Pierre, unrolled the canvas. As it flapped open, revealing the sombre portrait, John had to admit that it looked great. She was an amazing little painter, he thought in admiration, pride filling him up. He glanced quickly upward, tearing his eyes away from the painting and realised, with a quickening of his heart, that Harry wasn't in such a hurry now.

Harry had paled. He moved nearer the painting and reached a finger out and touched it. 'Is this what I think it is?' he breathed, his voice hushed.

John nodded. 'Eighty per cent certain,' he swallowed hard.

'It iz,' Robert nodded vigorously. 'I can guarantee it.'

As Harry poured over the painting, Robert managed to wink at John, who scowled hard at him.

It had taken two years to get to this point and as of right now, they couldn't back out.

Ten years later . . .

1

'D'you smell that, Eve?' Olivia, my friend, says. She's sitting in the passenger seat of my car as I drive down a gorgeous, tree-lined road. Massive Georgian houses line each side of the street. I'm peering out the window looking for an address.

'Smell what?' I ask distractedly, pulling up outside the most impressive house so far.

'Money,' Olivia announces, sniffing wildly. 'Loads and loads of money.'

I giggle and tell her to shut up. Then I glance at my piece of paper, on which I have written the address of Della Sweeney, eminent art collector. 'OK, this seems to be it,' I say as I hop out of the car. 'Wish me luck.'

'Good luck,' Olivia waves at me and gives me the thumbs up.

She's more excited than I am.

I'm not so sure I'll even need luck. Della Sweeney contacted *me*, so she obviously wants me to do a mural for her. I walk up Della's enormous driveway which is cobble-locked in black and grey. There is enough room for ten cars, but only one enormous vehicle takes up space in front of the door. Skirting around it, I ring the doorbell which jangles on and on inside the huge house.

The door is opened some moments later by the tallest woman I have ever seen.

'Hi, Eve Cole at your service?' Smiling brightly, I push my green cap back on my head.

I hadn't expected Della Sweeney to look like this. Her online pictures, ones that show her buying various expensive and sought-after canvases, are just portraits and don't highlight the fact that she must be at least six foot tall. In truth, now that I'm in front of her, I'm a little nervous, but excitement at maybe getting a glimpse of her art collection bubbles up inside me and I grin like a lunatic.

'You're Eve Cole?' Her tone does not inspire confidence. She purses her lips and narrows her eyes as if she believes her eyesight has gone wrong somehow.

'Yes.' Another smile. I've been told my smile is charming despite the fact that my bottom teeth are a bit crooked. I head her off at the pass. 'I know you probably think I look young, but actually I'm twenty-eight.'

'Twenty-eight?' She pauses. Pats her greying hair and stands upright. She is the tallest old woman I have ever seen. 'You look about fifteen.' It's like she's accusing me of robbing her.

'So I've been told,' I grin. 'You should have seen what I looked like when I was fifteen.'

Not even the ghost of a smile. 'And,' she stresses, 'I thought you'd be better dressed.'

Ouch. I'm wearing a pair of dungarees and a stripy T-shirt along with a pair of green Converse trainers and my trusty green cap. 'These are my old clothes,' I explain politely, 'you asked me for a quote for a wall painting. I'm not auditioning for secretary.'

'"Interviewing" is the word I believe you're looking for,' she says imperiously. Then she stands back and opens her door a little wider. 'Well, please come in.'

Gee, thanks, I feel like saying, but I don't. This woman wants to offer me a job and I want a job. Especially here. Olivia had been agog when I'd told her that I'd got an e-mail from Della Sweeney. In fact, she was so agog that she'd insisted on coming with me to see where the woman lived and find out what she wanted. What does Della want? She'd just said a wall painting, so I'd assumed she meant a mural, which is good news as things have been slow in the mural-painting business recently, though, surprisingly, I can make a steady living from selling my canvases online. Loads of people love Van Gogh and I'm only too happy to paint replicas of his most popular paintings for them. But murals are what I love best. Huge paintings on walls or ceilings or floors. Because the job is so much bigger, it takes so much longer and it's nice to lose myself in something like that for a while. Of course, I don't only paint some Van Gogh, I copy all the Old Masters but I'm best at him. I find his style easy, his brush strokes come naturally to me. I like his choice of colours and his use of light. I'm not familiar with his lesser-known works but give me the sunflowers or the starry night stuff and I'm as happy as he must have been when he sold his first piece. Which I can also paint.

'Come on,' Della says to me as she leads me through an enormous hallway which I can't help but gawk at. This place, situated in one of the richest areas in Dublin, is bigger than it appears from the outside, and even that's massive. In fact, my whole apartment would fit into this hall and there'd be room to spare. I'd even bet when she bought this house that she didn't pay as much as I did for my dog box. My negative equity dog box, as it happens. My negative equity dog box in a ghost apartment block. Well, except for the Party People downstairs and the gorgeous Larry, as Olivia has christened him, across the hall from me. The only upside of the whole mess is that I have a great social life.

I wonder if Della gets lonely living in this place by herself. When I did a quick search on Google, it revealed that she has no family. Her footsteps echo in the marble, tiled hallway while my trainers squeak like a newborn chick. I catch up as she leads me into a massive dining room that smells of old oak. The ceiling is high and the walls have that charming unevenness that is lovely in period houses but not so cool in negative equity apartments. I can't help gasping at some of the paintings on her walls and wonder if they are the originals. There appears to be some le Brocquys and a Turner. 'This is where I was planning to have the painting,' she says, indicating the wall behind her massive oak table.

I nod. 'That should be fine, the light in here is good, so there should be no problem. Now tell me, what would you like done?'

'I'm not quite sure. Anything once it's original,' she says.

'Original?' I shake my head. 'I only really do copies. I don't paint original stuff.'

'Why not?' This woman does not seem to like me at all. Her tone is sharp. 'Why on earth don't you paint originals? I never heard of anything so ridiculous.'

No one has ever asked me that before. I've never really thought about it. 'Well,' I match her tone – I'm not going to get the job now anyway – 'I happen to be very good at what I do, people really like my copies.'

'I'm sure they do, I've bought one, it's very good but I don't want a copy. What would you charge for an original Eve Cole painting?'

'Twenty thousand euro,' I name an outrageous amount.

'Fifteen and you've got a deal.'

I wonder briefly if I'm on one of those TV shows where they set you up. I glance around but can't see any cameras. Turning back to her, I ask suspiciously, 'What did you say?'

She looks calmly at me. 'I collect art,' she says, her hand encompassing the fantastic work on the walls. 'I spend money on good quality art as an investment. I happen to think you have potential. Your copies are fantastic, so I thought I'd ask you here to discuss an original.'

'Well,' I say less cockily now, feeling a little flutter of pride, 'I'm really not an original sort of artist.' For fifteen thousand euro, my mind says, you just could be.

'Nonsense,' the woman dismisses that comment with a wave of her hand. 'Even though you paint the Old Masters, you do have a certain style that's your own. I've noted it in your work. What is it they say? Oh, yes, just think what you'd like to express and say it through your art.'

'Most things I want to express, I just say straight out,' I attempt a joke, but she still refuses to smile. 'I'm not one of those mysterious people,' I add, 'I don't think I have much to say.'

She looks at me in some disbelief. I suppose she thinks it's a bit sad that I've admitted to not having original thoughts, but I'm not a deep thinker.

'Seventeen thousand euro and that's my final offer. 'She folds her arms and I admire her exquisite bracelet as it jangles with the movement. 'You must have been interested in my offer,' she raises a sceptical eyebrow, 'I mean why else would you have come here?'

'I thought you wanted me to paint a mural.'

'And what good would a mural do me? No, I stated in my e-mail to you that I wanted an original canvas. Didn't you read your e-mail message?'

Obviously not. I'd read hers as far as 'I'd like you to come to my house', and just assumed it was a mural she wanted as that is always what people want when they get me to call out. After that, I'd skimmed to her address, seen her name and almost had a heart attack with excitement. Then I told Olivia. 'Obviously I didn't read it properly,' I admit. 'I just assumed—'

'I can give you an advance to get you working,' Della says, cutting me off, 'if that'll help.'

Seventeen thousand euro would help a lot, I think. I could get my mortgage down for a start. But an original?

'Most people would be flattered,' she says.

'Well, I am,' I say. 'I mean a painting of mine hanging beside that.' I point to a le Brocquy and, for the first time, she smiles.

'Yes, it's wonderful, isn't it?'

'It is.' I venture towards it and see the tiny little sensors she has fixed onto it so it can't be stolen. For a brief second, I imagine my painting here and impulsively I nod. 'All right then.' I immediately wish I hadn't.

'Fantastic. You'll do it?'

'I'll try. I'll pay you back if I can't manage it.'

'You'll manage,' she says. Then adds, 'And I'll know if you're faking it, so don't paint me a blue line and tell me it's some sort of cerebral thing.'

I wonder if she spoke to Louis le Brocquy like that.

'I'd never do that,' I say indignantly, whilst thinking, damn.

She writes me a cheque for three thousand euro and I have to sign a receipt for it. Twenty minutes after I walked through the front door, I'm back on the street, climbing into my dingy old car, that's only worth about a hundred euro, and thinking that I must be mad.

'Well?' Olivia demands the second I sit behind the wheel. 'What did she want?'

Dumbly, I hand Olivia the cheque. 'An original,' I stammer, as I fire the engine.

'No way!' Olivia squeals and I only hope Della Sweeney has gone back inside. 'From you?'

'No, from my cat,' I sneer at her, grinning.

'You don't have a cat,' she smart asses back before thumping me on the arm in delight. 'Eve, this is fantastic. OK, lunch. Now.' And then, before I can stop her, she plucks out her phone and dials our friends to tell them that we have big news and to meet us now.

I groan. Trust Olivia to tell everyone.

2

The thing about my friends is that we all have flexible lives. By that, I mean we can meet up for lunch whenever we like. There's me, a painter of Van Gogh fakes and, unless I'm in the middle of a painting, I can down tools whenever the call comes. There's Olivia, a potter, self-employed and doing quite well thanks to her dad's investment in her talent. She is the most successful of my friends and had taken the day off in honour of me seeing Della Sweeney. Next up, there's Eric, Olivia's boyfriend. He's a student, twenty years old to Olivia's twenty-eight and she likes him because at twenty he won't be thinking of 'settling down or any of that rubbish'. Then there are June and Laura, both unemployed, but both living at home and drawing the dole, so they have enough money to go to a pub in the middle of the day. They were at art college with Olivia and me, but left before they finished because they both got jobs, which they've now lost. Finally, the fifth member of our gang is David, a personal trainer with a body as rock hard as, well, a rock, I suppose. He's a friend of one of Olivia's old boyfriends and while the old boyfriend left our group, David stayed on. I was quite glad because David is a nice guy. Besides the rock hard physique, he's funny and has a face like an action man. Olivia reckons that he fancies me, though I'm not so sure because he's never asked me out. Anyway, David's personal-training business took a nose dive with the recession, so now he's running boot camps for unfit people and doing quite well, thank you very much. He's the last to arrive and he slides in beside me, a pint of orange juice in his beefy hands.

'So, what's this exciting news?' he asks.

He smells of the shower and fresh soap. Yum.

The others all look eagerly at me. I open my mouth to tell them but am interrupted by Olivia announcing dramatically, 'Eve is only poised at the cusp of the big-time.'

I snort out a laugh. 'I wouldn't quite put it like that.'

'So how *would* you put it?' David asks, looking at me with his brilliant blue eyes. His soft, gentle tone belies the tough-looking, shaven-headed exterior. My heart flips like a pancake.

'Now surely that's a conversation for you and Eve to have in private,' June giggles as Olivia snorts loudly.

I ignore the innuendo and David's blushes as I explain what Della Sweeney wanted with me. I underplay it a lot, not wanting to make it into a big deal. I have serious doubts about whether I can produce the goods and, if I fail, I do not need everyone's pity. As I finish telling them about the commission I have to paint, there is an awed silence.

'Seventeen grand,' Eric whistles impressed. 'That's, like, all my college fees paid.'

'That's a year's dole, almost,' June says.

'It's at least two boot camps,' David nods. We all gawk at him. 'Joke,' he holds his hands in the air. 'More like four,' he deadpans.

Eric tosses a beer mat at him as we laugh.

'Well, I think it's brilliant you're going to paint your own stuff,' Olivia pronounces when the laughter dies down. Eric wraps his arm about her shoulder and they remind me suddenly of Ashton Kutcher and Demi Moore, a boy and a woman. 'I mean,' Olivia continues, appealing to June and Laura, 'wasn't this girl fantastic in college? And what does she do? Instead of being original, she copies other people's paintings.'

'Van Gogh is hardly "other people",' I laugh.

'Well, it's a waste,' she leans across the table and jabs her finger on it emphatically. 'A waste,' she says again.

Olivia has never said this to me before. I'm taken aback. 'Well, thanks,' I attempt a grin, 'it's nice to know that I've wasted the last six years of my life.'

'Ah,' Olivia waves her hand in the air, 'that's not what I mean. But you're better than being a copier. I reckon you just sort of drifted into it because of your dad.'

'My dad?' I swallow, uneasy talking about him in any company. My dad died five years ago, wasted away to nothing by motor neurone disease, and even the mention of him causes a massive lump to form in my throat. He was such a great man. It was such a hard time.

'Oh don't get me wrong,' Olivia shifts her position on the seat, shaking Eric's arm off as she leans even closer, 'he was a lovely man, but you and he were too close. He was a copier and I don't think he saw beyond that, not even for you.'

'He was not just a copier,' I say. 'He was an art dealer too.'

Olivia's raised eyebrows tell me what she thinks of this. 'Mm.'

'I know what Olivia means,' Laura, who has been quiet up until now, says. 'Your dad was cautious, maybe too cautious and it was limiting. And you became cautious too. And then when he got sick' – she places a hand on my arm to let me know that she's not trying to upset me – 'it was easier for you than trying to go it alone. I'm sure you couldn't even think straight at that time. But even your copies, they have a certain style that's most definitely yours.'

That's what Della said. It's a nice thing to hear.

'Well, I'm still not sure that I can do it,' I say, expressing the fear I've had since leaving Della's house and diverting the subject away from my dad.

This is met by a chorus of 'of course you can' and 'you're brilliant'.

And so lunch turns to tea and tea turns into way past supper time. And at that stage, it's taxis home for all of us.

And as I stagger out of the taxi, David helping me to my door, his arm about my waist making me feel all melty and safe, I feel so happy just to be me, crappy apartment in the middle of a south Dublin building site and all.

3

To most people, my apartment would not be seen as the most desirable of properties. From the outside, it's in the middle of a half-finished estate. Whatever green spaces there were meant to be have morphed into massive muddy mounds of clay. Bricks and blocks and pipes litter the streets, if there were any streets. It's an obstacle course just to get to the main road. There is, however, a nice view of the Dublin Mountains from my white functional kitchen, which is fitted with some cool space-saver presses. I have one bedroom and a big sitting room. This room is the reason I bought the place four years ago. It's large, airy and bright and makes the perfect studio. Facing south, it has floor-to-ceiling doors of glass which lead onto a small veranda that you'd have to be anorexic to sit out on. But these doors flood the room with the most beautiful light, summer and winter.

The concrete floor is perfect for my needs and though I sometimes pine after a sofa and some comfy cushions, I know that beggars can't be choosers and I am one poor, just-about-making-the-mortgage beggar. For comfort, I have two bean bags or I sit in the kitchen on my wooden chairs at my small wooden table and whenever my mother calls over, that's where she sits too. She has long ago given up on me as the daughter she can boast about down the local Tesco as having her own lovely place and a man and kids. Instead, she has to satisfy herself by telling the neighbours of my special talents and the fact that I'm a free spirit who doesn't want to be tied down. Which to be honest isn't true at all. I don't mind admitting that I would love to have a man in my life, one who is the owner of a comfy sofa preferably. I've had one or two relationships which have fizzled out like damp fireworks that never quite got going. But I have never found 'The One'. In fact, I've never found even half a one. But I live in hope. In fact, I've more hope of finding The One than I have of ever producing an original artwork for Della Sweeney. Two weeks later, I am still struggling to deliver.

I've sat on my kitchen chairs and I've tried to think deep thoughts – on the economy, on politics, on my own single state. I've tried to think about what makes me tick and what my hopes for the world are, big thoughts and, so far, I haven't managed to get interested in any of them. I'm desolately doodling on a sheet of paper when my gorgeous neighbour Larry raps on the glass door of my studio. Larry is a walking work of art. He never crosses the hall to knock on my door, preferring instead to hop from his veranda onto mine, risking his life in the process. He says it gives him a small buzz which helps him cope with the fact that collecting the dole is the highlight of his week.

I don't know if Larry will ever find a job because he's been in prison. That's where he did drama and, because of that, he's decided that the life of an actor is for him. I don't know if he's any good, I think he must be because he can mimic all the Party People who live downstairs. He's a laugh and he's really sorry for whatever he did that landed him in Mountjoy, which wasn't murder or manslaughter or anything like that, he assured me, though he's always very mysterious whenever the subject of his misdemeanour is broached and he's never told me what it was. Something like that would normally make me wary, but Larry is strangely compelling. He's the kind of guy you listen to, you laugh with, his eyes, a mesmerising silver grey, pull his audience into every tall story he tells, his mouth always seems to be about to break into a smile and his whole lean, fit body fizzes with energy. All that and he has the face of an angel. Big innocent eyes, long curly eyelashes, lean jawed and clear skinned. His short shaven hair is sinfully black and shiny. Larry, despite being an ex-con, is too good to miss out on. He's like the extra cream on the strawberries – you know it's bad for you, but you eat it right up anyhow.

'Hi,' I open the door and he bounds in. He's dressed in an old pair of jeans and a green sweatshirt with a picture of an apple on it. He's wearing Doc Marten boots. 'Want a cuppa?'

'I'd prefer tea, ta.'

It's a joke we have. It's not very funny, but it's the way he says it. I smile. 'Come on out to the kitchen so.'

He follows me and on the way has a look at my latest efforts to create an original painting. 'What's this meant to be?' He holds up a page where I've drawn a circle and inside it lots of shapes.

'You tell me,' I say glumly.

Larry grins. 'Well, I'd say it was a picture about how trapped you're feeling having to do this original picture. This here,' he indicates all the swirly bits on the page, 'is your anxiety.' He straightens up and, doing a fair impression of the art critics I remember coming into my dad's gallery when I was younger, he says pompously, 'And these erratic shapes are the artist's suppressed hopelessness and insecurities. Note the yellow colour, this has been long associated with cowardice, so the artist is feeling a bit of a coward about it all.' Then he winks at me. 'Am I right?'

'Fantastic,' I grin back. Then I sniff loudly, my nose in the air. 'What is that smell? Oh yes, it's bullshit. That' – I indicate the picture – 'was just a doodle, to free my mind so I could think deep and profound thoughts.'

'And those thoughts haven't yet materialised?'

'Nope. The only thing I could think was that the next time I plan on sitting on my kitchen chairs for long periods, I'm going to have to buy a few cushions.'

Larry laughs loudly. 'Well, you sit down on your cushionless chair and I'll make the tea, how about that?'

'Go on so. There are biscuits in the press.'

'Brilliant.'

I watch him as he potters around my kitchen, unable to tear my eyes away from his perfectly formed backside, his broad shoulders and his smooth neck. He has rolled up the sleeves of his sweatshirt to reveal brown muscular arms and, for the first time, I notice that he has a tattoo of a silver fish on his inner wrist. I can't believe I'd never noticed it before. It's actually pretty impressive.

'Liking your art,' I say.

He turns towards me questioningly.

'On your wrist?'

'This?' he holds his arm towards me and I catch it, glad of the chance to examine the tattoo. It's perfect. Every scale seems to shimmer. I trace my hand over it and look up to see his eyes studying me intently. There's a funny look in them. Sad or resigned, I'm not sure which. It makes me a little wary though.

'Where'd you get it done?' I ask, dropping his hand quite abruptly.

He doesn't seem to notice. 'Place in the city centre,' he says tuning away and filling up the mugs with hot water. 'I got it done with my first dole cheque.'

'What made you choose a fish?'

He places the tea in front of me and shrugs, 'It's a salmon actually. And I dunno. I just liked it.' He doesn't look at me as he answers it so I think he *does* know, only he doesn't want to say, which is fair enough.

'It's a nice job. I've got a tattoo too, on my ankle. See?' I pull down my stripy sock and, lifting my leg, I show him a tiny little ankle bracelet tattoo. 'I kept losing my own ankle bracelets or they kept breaking and so I thought, here's the solution. My mother went mad.'

Larry grins, showing his white teeth, nice and straight and even. 'What age were you?'

'Eighteen.'

'D'you regret it?'

'Nah. Maybe when I'm about eighty and hobbling along in my old lady sensible sandals sporting a tattoo, maybe then I might think it was a mistake.'

'Aw, that's not so bad. You'll have forty good years to enjoy it between now and then.'

I hit him for that. 'I do *not* look forty. I am still in my twenties, thank you very much.'

'So what happens when you lose your earrings or your necklace, d'you get them tattooed on as well?'

'That's exactly what my mother said!' I laugh a little and so does he. Finally, biscuits on the table, he sits opposite me. 'I really only called in to invite you to a party tonight. Downstairs in Ed's. Bring your own drink.'

'Do I have a choice?' I ask wryly. 'It's either go to Ed's party or stay up all night listening to it.'

'That would be an accurate assessment of the situation all right,' Larry agrees, smiling. 'But if it's any consolation, they said they'd like you to be there. You and that big fella that always hauls you home when you go drinking with your mates.' He quirks his eyebrows.

'His name is David and he doesn't haul me home. He helps me to the door.'

Larry grins and goes on, 'And, as I have an audition tomorrow for a small part in a film and I've to be dishevelled, I figured a bit of realism wouldn't go astray. So I'm going.'

'A film?' I'm seriously impressed.

'It's only a small part. But the pay is good, so my agent says.'

'An agent,' I snort, 'get you!'

'You should get an agent,' Larry says. 'Especially if this auld wan is right and your original paintings will make a fortune. You need someone looking after you.'

'You could do it,' I bat his comment away with a joke. 'You'd convince anyone I have deep thoughts.'

For some reason, Larry flushes and looks away and doesn't manage to come back with any sort of a quip, which surprises me.

'Have I said something wrong?' I venture after a silence that can only be described as unnaturally long.

'No,' his eyes don't quite meet mine though, so I know I must have. Draining his cup, he stands up and looks down on me.

'Don't beat yourself up about this painting,' he says then. 'You'll find enough people will do that to you without doing it yourself.'

'Wow.' I jab his arm. 'Aren't you the philosopher? Can you tell me what to think so I can paint it?'

His answer is a smile, and I follow him back into my studio where I watch nervously as he leaps back onto his own veranda. Then with a mock-salute, he's gone.

Back to my deep thoughts.

4

Later that evening, just as I am about to head out the door with a twelve-pack of beer, my mobile rings. It's my mother. I flirt with the idea of ignoring the call, but I know I'd feel guilty all night if I did. Flipping the phone open, I utter a breathless 'hi' in the hope that she'll get the hint that I'm about to go out.

'Are you going somewhere?' she asks.

'Yes.' I don't elaborate. She is deeply suspicious of Larry. Oh, she loved him when she met him in my apartment one evening, but that was before she found out he'd been in jail, then she started advising me to sleep with knives in my bed and told me to invest in a personal alarm. She even got a security firm to post their brochure to me.

'Please wait,' she sounds a little tearful and my heart quickens.

'Why? What's happened?'

'I can't get Robert on the phone, he's the only one that could explain this. I mean, maybe it's good news, I don't know. But I don't think it is because if it was, they would have told me earlier, before John died, but they didn't so I know there is something strange about it. I—'

'Mam?' I interrupt before she gets herself into a complete state, 'What is wrong?' I don't like the fact that she mentioned my dad. My mother and I tend to steer clear of that awful time in our lives.

'You'll have to come and see for yourself, if I told you you'd think I was reading it wrong, but I'm not, I know I'm not. I know what my eyes are telling me. I know that there is no way your father could have—'

'Mam, take a chill pill.' She's mentioned him again. Now there's a lump in my throat.

'*Take* a chill pill! Take a *chill* pill. Take a chill *pill*.'

Oh dear, I think. 'Right,' I say, 'I'm on my way. You sit tight and calm down.'

'I don't want to ruin your night out,' she says then, knowing full well she's done just that.

'Well, you have,' I grin, 'so get over it.'

'You'll see why when you come over,' my mother predicts ominously. 'You'll see why.'

Half an hour later, I pull up outside my mother's apartment block in Donnybrook. Even though it's only about eight miles from my own very humble abode, it might as well be on another planet. I have unfettered muck and weeds, she has cobble-lock and fountains. I have a corner shop that closes at eight because of wild, roaming youths; she has high-end restaurants and shopping malls. I have a ten per cent occupancy rate and a dangerous stairwell; she has classy neighbours and a carpeted lift. She bought the apartment after Dad died, not wanting to stay in a house on her own. She wanted something with more security, a place where they – whoever 'they' were – would have to scale the walls to rob her. My mother is a bit neurotic like that.

She's on the fifth floor and she still has money left from the sale of the house for a nest egg. Even the auctioneer was amazed at how much our old house sold for; someone really wanted it, he said. I miss the house though. It wasn't a mansion, just a four-bed semi about ten minutes walk from the sea in Dún Laoghaire. The back garden was one of those large overgrown wildernesses that kids love and right at the end of the garden, my dad had built an artist's studio. When I was a kid, he and I would paint for hours in there. He'd find old canvases and ask me to paint over them and I would. Sometimes, he even made his own paint from oil and pigments, but mostly we used oil from tubes. I miss that studio, the smells in it, of oils and freshly cut wood. I miss the comfort of standing at his old easel and the sound of him pottering around and telling me how great I am. I miss the silence of being so far down the back garden that not even the sound of traffic from the road outside permeated the calm. I miss him, I miss his quiet dignity, I miss his soft humour – and I miss his passion for art. Mam tries her best but we both know that she hasn't a clue.

Hopping out of my car, I slam the door and the whole vehicle shakes like the rattling wreck it is. Then, pulling my bobble hat on – it's pouring rain – I make a dash for the front door. My mother buzzes me up and, as I cross the gleaming, white-tiled foyer to the lift, Paddy the porter bounces up like a jack in the box to bar my way. He's about sixty with a face like Clarence, the angel from *It's a Wonderful Life,* innocent and kind and smiley. It's a sadly deceptive face though because he is a bit of a letch. In order to pass him, I have to compliment him. I try my best to keep it clean.

'What's today's compliment?' he asks, his brows lifted expectantly.

'Hmm,' I purse my lips and look him up and down. 'Paddy is the coolest guy I know.'

He feigns devastation. 'I'm in my' – a hesitation – 'fifties,' he pronounces. 'I don't do cool.'

'Gosh, I thought you were only about forty-five.'

'Much better.' He stands aside. 'You may pass, madam,' he indicates the lift. 'Tell Iris I was asking for her.'

'I'm sure she'll find it easy to contain her pleasure at that,' I answer, hopping into the lift before he can say any more. As the door slides closed, I hear him laugh and it makes me smile.

My mother has her door open before I even get a chance to knock. She drags me inside, looking furtively left and right before slamming the door closed. 'Oh, thank God you're here. I still haven't been able to reach Robert.'

Because my mother is not the most self-reliant person and tends to panic a lot over the smallest things, before Dad died he asked Robert, his best friend, if he'd keep an eye out for me and my mother and, to his credit, Robert has been brilliant. But now he's got a new woman friend and she has managed to draw the normally reserved Robert from his shell. Right now, they are on holidays together and I'm sure the last thing they need is panicky phone calls from my hysterical mother.

'Robert is on holiday,' I remind my mother as I follow her into her sitting room, which is a world away from my own shabby, though light-filled, affair. My mother has fabulous taste and her apartment is a shrine to diversity. She's got some lovely pieces from our old house mixed in with IKEA staples. Surprisingly, nothing jars and it's all very relaxing. I think that maybe if I could unwind into my mother's big brown leather sofa, I'd have some deep thoughts. But, nah, I'd probably just fall asleep.

'You sit there,' my mother, who hasn't even dressed or brushed her hair, pushes me gently down onto said sofa. 'I'll just get the letter, it arrived today. It was addressed to me but I didn't know it was a bank thing because it was in a nice envelope. And Robert wasn't here to open the post—'

'Robert opens your post?' God, I had no idea that she was that helpless.

'Well yes, your father always did it and now Robert does. I save it for him unless I know it's a card for me or something, and I thought this was a card so I opened it by mistake.'

'Well if it was addressed to you, you hardly opened it by mistake.'

She bats my comment away with a toss of her hand and leaves, her dressing gown flapping after her. I wonder, with a growing sense of unease, what crisis has taken place. Normally, I don't take her that seriously which is usually the best course of action, but my mother not getting dressed is something to be concerned about.

She arrives back, like a mini tornado, flops down beside me on the sofa and shoves an innocent-looking white envelope into my hands.

'Open it,' she says. 'You read it and see if you come to the same conclusions as me. I'm afraid to look again.'

'OK.' Then before I pull the slim-looking paper from the envelope, I add, 'Mam, calm down, OK? Please? For me?'

She nods but continues to hyperventilate as I withdraw the white page. Unfolding it, I see that it's a bank statement from a bank I don't recognise.

'It's just a bank statement,' I say. Then, I look again, 'Oh, it's a statement of interest earned on the account.'

Mam says nothing.

And then I see what she must have seen. I peer at the page more closely this time. Maybe it's not in euro, my mind says. But then, at the top, I read, 'currency: euro'. And I swallow hard.

'Does it say that I have almost eleven million in a bank account?' my mother whispers. 'In a bank I've never heard of?'

'I'm not that great with banking stuff,' I stammer out.

'Eve?'

I shrug. 'OK, yeah, I think so.'

She lets out a tiny, hysterical shriek.

'Mam, calm down, there has to be a mistake.'

'I don't think there is.' She hops up and begins frantically pacing around. 'Where on earth did I get that kind of money? All I can think of is that it was your father's money. I vaguely remember Robert sorting out the bank accounts when John died,' she finally coughs out.

I wince a little.

'I keep wondering if John was robbing banks or blackmailing some mafia man or something?'

Despite myself, I start to giggle.

Mam glares at me before smiling a tiny bit too. She lets out a deep sigh and flops back on the sofa. 'If only we could get hold of Robert,' she moans.

'He's away with his . . . ' – I don't know what to call Denise, his woman friend – ' . . . girlfriend,' I eventually manage. 'He'll be back on Tuesday. We'll ask him then. It could be a banking error.'

A brief look of hope illuminates my mother's face before it vanishes to be replaced by gloom. 'And it might not be.'

'Which means that you are a millionaire,' I say. 'Wouldn't that be nice? Maybe Dad made some shrewd investments or something.'

Another look of hope, this time sustained. 'Oh,' she says, 'I never thought of that, your dad was a businessman after all.'

'He was.' I know both of us are thinking 'hopeless businessman', but neither of us say it. I fold the statement back into the envelope and say, 'Let's not worry until you talk to Robert, OK?'

'Yes. I suppose.' She pauses, then reaches over and squeezes my hand in hers. 'Sorry for ruining your night, pet.'

'It's OK.' I give her a gentle push. 'Now, go shower and dress and I'll treat you to dinner.'

'You can't afford that,' she exclaims. 'Let *me* take *you*.'

'Nope, I offered first so hop it.'

Smiling again, she stands up. 'All right.' Then she looks at me. 'You look very nice, Eve. I like your dress. Are you sure you can't salvage something from your night.'

'It was only a party, so it wasn't a big deal.'

'In your block?'

'Where else?' I joke.

She frowns slightly. 'Well, if we are millionaires, the first thing I'm going to do is buy you a nice place to live.'

'I have a nice place to live.'

She looks in exasperation at me before leaving and I soon hear her pottering around her room, pulling out clothes and getting the shower ready. Whilst she is gone, I surreptitiously call Robert, figuring that he might be more inclined to answer to me, but it goes straight to his voicemail, so I leave a message. 'Hey, Robert, it's Eve. Can you ring me back when you get this message? Make it after eleven. Mam has probably rung you, but ring me first, OK? Hope Denise is behaving herself.' Clicking off, I sink contentedly into the sofa and flick on the telly.

Three hours later, I'm on my way back to my apartment, having just dropped my slightly drunken, relaxed mother home, when my phone rings. Robert's number flashes and I immediately pull into the side of the road and earn a 'you stupid bitch' from an irate motorist behind. I wave an apology and get the finger in return.

'Hi,' I say to Robert, 'thanks for ringing back.'

'No problem,' he says cheerily. In the background, I can hear the sound of people chattering and glasses clinking. 'Dee is just gone to the bar so I thought I'd give you a call. We've seen a wonderful play tonight, the French version of *Tartuffe*. Dee said she could see me in the main part.'

I smile. What I know of Tartuffe is that he's a ladies' man, a world away from shy awkward Robert. But Dee thinks he's wonderful, which is all that matters. Their bumbling, fumbling, blushing love affair is really quite cute. They met at their local drama group. Robert, despite his shyness, always fancied himself as a bit of a thespian and has been in plays for years. He's actually not bad, just a bit wooden sometimes. One night, Dee, a skinny, mousey woman who wears enormous glasses and clothes that are so old fashioned I have never seen them in any shops, approached him and asked him to sign her programme because he was just wonderful in his portrayal of whoever he was portraying at the time. Robert's performances tend to blend into one another a little. So Robert signed her programme and then, sometime later, offered to trace Dee's family tree for her. It was his idea of a date; he's a history professor slash genealogist. They spent their days in the national archives, wearing white gloves and whispering to each other before finding out that Dee's parentage was not so great at all, having as she did two convicts in her family. But love triumphed and now they are officially an 'item'.

'What seems to be the problem?' Robert asks, 'Iris must have called me about ten times.' He laughs a little. 'Dee thinks she's jealous.'

'Well, tell Dee that she's not. She's delighted to see you getting your groove back, old timer.'

Robert laughs again.

'Anyway,' I continue, 'my mother's a bit confused. She opened a letter from a bank today.'

'And?' Robert suddenly sounds very cautious.

'Apparently, she's a millionaire to the tune of eleven million.' As I utter the words, I realise how absurd it sounds and I break into a giggle. 'Can you imagine?'

There is no sound of reciprocal laughter from Robert's end, and a sudden feeling of unease worms its way into my body making my stomach clench tight. 'Robert?'

'Yes. Well, Eve, she shouldn't have opened that. I normally deal with her banks.'

'It was addressed to her.'

'Robert, here's your drink. It's so cheap here.' Denise's light, fluttery, nervy voice floats down the line.

'Just gimme a minute, Dee,' Robert says.

'Oh, yes, of course,' Dee says hastily. 'I'll meet you back at our seats.'

'Eve, I'll be back on Tuesday. I'll, eh, explain it all then, OK?'

'Explain what?' I say, suddenly breathless. 'Will we be happy about it?'

'He never meant you to find out.' Robert pauses then amends, '*We* never meant you to find out.'

'Find out what?' I feel like I should be shrieking, but my voice has morphed into a terrified whisper.

'I'll call you on Tuesday and we'll talk to your mother, OK?'

'Robert—'

The line goes dead. Robert has cut me off. He never does that. I stare in disbelief at my phone before flipping it closed. I sit in the car for a long time.

5

The meeting with Robert is set for five o'clock on Wednesday evening. Between the weekend and Tuesday, I have fielded anxious call from my mother, speculating about what it could all mean. She figured, as did I, that if it was good news, Robert would not be holding a meeting, nor would he be taking twenty-four hours after his holiday had ended, to, as my mother put it, 'come up with a good story to paint it all in a nice light'. This was ironic, considering that my dad had been a very respected, if not exactly rich, art dealer. Over the past few days, I've thought about my dad more than at any other time since his death, wondering what he might have done to amass such a large amount of money. Laundering and drug dealing did occur to me but I immediately dismissed those ideas. My dad had been a gentleman to the end. Even the disease that took him did not change his sweet demeanour. I never heard him moan or complain, though at the end, he could barely talk. Or paint. I used to sit with him as he lay in bed and I'd draw pictures for him and 'Van Gogh' them with sharp strokes of yellow and ochre. I smile, in bittersweet remembrance at the way his eyes would crinkle up.

Pulling up outside my mother's, I see that Robert is here already, his Nissan Micra huddled into her parking space like an interloper at a party, I park my own excuse for a car beside his and trot over to the foyer. Paddy beams at me as I enter.

'How's things, Eve?' he calls. 'What're the magic words?'

'Paddy is a seriously sad man, but he's hot.'

'Paddy is not sad anymore,' he chortles.

I roll my eyes and because the lift isn't available, I decide to do the healthy thing and I make for the stairs.

Four floors later, I'm almost on the floor. Yet again, I've reneged on my New Year's resolution to go out for a nightly jog. Larry has even offered to go with me but not even the thought of him in a nice tight pair of running shorts has been able to tempt me. I've told him I'll wait until the weather improves.

'It's bloody France you should be living in,' he said to that. 'This, honey, is as good as it gets.'

It was pouring rain at the time, so he was lying.

Breathing heavily, my heart fit to burst, I let myself in to my mother's apartment. She is in the kitchen with Robert, and he is showing her his holiday snaps. It all looks so perfectly normal, except that Robert hasn't taken off his red jacket. Robert is the sort of man that always takes his jacket off when he enters a house. He thinks it's rude not to. He's dressed in jeans and a blue shirt, his feet sporting a pair of horrendous brown brogues which spoil the casual look he's obviously aiming for. Though Robert must be in his mid-fifties, he looks younger. And acts older.

'And this was Denise in the ruins of an old monastery,' Robert is saying proudly, jabbing at a photo. I peer over his shoulder. 'I showed her where the monks' quarters would have been and the remains of the chapel that they would have prayed in.' Denise in her long brown skirt and white frilly short-sleeved blouse looks as if she'd have fitted right in with the monks as their resident nun.

'She looks very tanned,' my mother says politely.

'She gets a great colour,' Robert nods, 'browns up like a sausage in a pan.'

There's a small silence. Now that I've arrived, I suppose I've sort of spoiled the normality they'd been pretending existed.

My mother pulls away from his photographs and glances at me. 'Tea, Eve?'

'No, let's just see what Robert has to say about the money,' I go straight for it. There is no point in prolonging the inevitable. Robert drops his pictures and they scatter over the floor and, as he bends down to pick them up, my mother raises her eyebrows at me. The man is nervous, she seems to be saying. Apprehension forms a lump in my throat.

'Shall we sit inside?' my mother asks.

'Let's.' More confidently than I feel, I lead the way. I sit on a chair, by myself, not wanting my mother to distract me from whatever it is that Robert has to say. I think my mother would like to believe any sort of good news and Robert, while a great friend to us, is adept at painting everything in a more favourable light than it actually is. It's something I normally love about him. Today, though, we both need to hear the absolute truth.

My mother sits opposite me, obviously she's going to look at me for clues as to how I'm taking the news of whatever mystery Robert has to reveal. Robert, worryingly, doesn't sit down. He stands, his back to my mother's ultra modern fireplace. His hands are clenched behind him but he bravely attempts a reassuring smile. 'Now,' he says expansively, 'the money.' He laughs a little, attempting a joke, 'can we all just pretend that you never opened that letter?'

'Oh,' my mother looks at me. 'Well—'

'No,' I say sharply. 'We can't. Now Robert, just tell us. Go on. How hard can it be?' I flash him a smile.

'You do have a lovely smile,' Robert winks at me, but I don't smile back. Then he sighs, and massages his head and says on a groan, 'This was never meant to come out. He was only trying to look after you both.'

I ignore the quizzical look Mam is throwing across at me. 'So, go on.'

There's a pause as Robert clears his throat. Then, his voice shaking a little, he says, 'John discovered he was sick about two years before he told you both,' Robert looks from me to my mother. 'He was understandably devastated.'

Oooo-kay, I think, shock number one. And it knocks into me like a bowling ball. 'Two years?' I croak out.

'Two years?' my mother says, fingers pressed to her mouth.

Robert nods. 'Yes. He told me that he'd been feeling a little off. Said his hand felt weak. I didn't think much of it and neither did he until he dropped a valuable painting he was hoping to make some money on. So he went to the doctor, got some tests and was told he had a three-to-five-year life expectancy, maybe a little more. Meantime, he lost about fifty thousand on that painting he dropped.'

'Oh, poor John.' My mother blinks back some tears and I wish I'd sat beside her. 'He should have told me.'

I can't say anything. Two whole years and he didn't say a word to us. I'm sad and confused, and then sad again.

'Why didn't he tell us?' my mother asks tearfully.

'He didn't know how,' Robert says gently. 'I suppose he wanted to feel in control, to be able to do something for you both before he died.'

I recognise, through the shock, that an even bigger revelation is coming. I recognise that Robert is soft soaping us. But I also realise that what Robert is saying is probably true. My dad would have wanted to do something for us. But he should have told us ...

'John was a great man,' Robert says sincerely, his voice breaking into my scattered thoughts, 'but as you both know, he was not the best at business. He was respected, sure, but he undersold some of his paintings because he wanted them to hang in such and such a place or he bought artists that he believed in and no one else did. At least not then. He was untainted by money really.' Robert sounds as if he finds it hard to believe himself. 'So,' he bites his lip. 'That's where I came in.'

'You?' My mother looks at him. 'What do you mean?'

'John knew that his financial future was uncertain. He was worried what would happen after he left. I told him I'd take care of you both, but he wanted to see you financially secure. He started scouring the place for paintings, actively seeking out new artists and wearing himself out. The stress was bad for him, so I presented him with an idea.'

A long pause. In the apartment next to my mother's, a

telephone starts to ring. Someone answers.

'Which was?' I prompt.

Robert looks at me and in his blue eyes I see ... what? I'm not quite sure. Regret? Sadness? Apology?

'It, eh, centred on you,' Robert gulps, nodding at me. 'You and your brilliance.'

Soft soap, I think.

'Her brilliance?' my mother says. 'What brilliance?'

Gee, thanks, I almost giggle, but I don't. A strange sort of dread has replaced the apprehension. I half think I know what Robert is going to say, but no. No way. They'd never have—

'She can paint like Van Gogh,' Robert states as if it was the most obvious thing in the world.

My thoughts go skittering all over the place again.

'So?' my mother says, puzzled.

Robert is gazing at me as he continues softly, 'The first time John showed me something you'd done, I truly believed it was real.'

'You know nothing about art,' I splutter out. 'You always said that.'

'I learned,' Robert nods, sounding a little ashamed, yet defensive. 'I learned about canvas and how it should be from the same era as the artist. I learned about pigments and brushes and all of Van Gogh's paintings and where he painted them and his life—'

'What are you saying?' I stare at him, dismissing what I'm thinking as preposterous.

'I learned all about paintings and lost paintings . . . ' his voice trails off.

'Oh God,' I say softly, 'You faked a painting.'

Robert bows his head. 'Yes, we faked a painting,' he confirms.

'Faked a painting?' My mother looks from me to Robert. 'I don't understand. Eve, what does he mean?'

I'm still not quite sure. I mean how could he have done it? Jesus. It can't be true. 'Robert,' I stammer out uncertainly. 'Are you saying that you and my dad sold a fake Van Gogh?'

'Yes I am.'

His words run together as if, by saying it quickly, it'll sound better.

'A fake Van Gogh that ... that,' now the words are choking me, 'that I painted?'

'Yes.' Then adds, 'Sorry, Eve.'

I think I'm going to be sick. I have to sit back further in the chair. 'When? What one?' And then, unexpectedly, I remember a tiny little thing from when I was about eighteen. Out in the studio in the back garden. My father coming in with an old canvas. There was a painting on it already, partially scraped off. He said it was something he'd unearthed in a skip. Now I wonder if he'd found a painting from the 1880s, scraped at it and then presented it to me to paint over. I remember him asking me to copy a portrait Van Gogh had done from his time in Saint-Paul hospital. A painting of a fellow patient. 'I think that would suit this canvas,' he'd said. That wasn't unusual, my dad had a thing about canvas, about what paintings could be held within its size and shape and make. I do too. I saw at once what he meant. And so, like Van Gogh, I treated the canvas and sketched onto it. I drew the picture, and then in rapid, quick, short sharp brush strokes, my mind emptying of everything, I painted quickly. On that canvas, I'd copied, but not exactly, the painting Van Gogh had done of one of the patients. It wasn't a nice painting in the traditional sense, but it had a piercing power that was a little scary. It was my interpretation of the original. My father had admired it, though not overtly, and I remember being disappointed because I'd been quite proud of it.

'Which one was it?' I ask, just to be sure.

'It was a copy of the painting of one of the mental patients at Saint-Paul with Van Gogh,' Robert swallows hard. 'I'd wanted to do the sunflowers one, but John had said they were too high profile. And so ...' his voice trails off again.

'Oh Jesus. Jesus.' I'm incapable of saying anything else.

'What is going on?' my mother asks. 'Eve, darling, are you OK?' She comes over to me and, surprisingly, she wraps an arm about my shoulder. She's normally the panicky one. 'Robert?' she looks questioningly at him.

He crouches down beside us. I notice that he's had a haircut, obviously Denise's influence. It's not a fashionable haircut but it's a style nonetheless. 'It was all my idea,' he says. 'John didn't want to do it but he knew if it worked you two would have money and he could die in peace and, if it didn't work, I told him I'd take the rap, though he'd never have stood for that, I'm sure. But I knew it would work.'

'Can someone please explain what is going on? What is this thing about a fake painting?'

And so Robert explains again to my mother what he and my father did.

'But they must have had tests done on it,' my mother is pale now. Her hand seeks and finds mine and she clenches it hard. 'They don't just accept things like that.'

'And the provenance?' I stammer out. 'How did you manage that?'

The provenance is the history of a painting. Who it belonged to, how long for, where it sold and for how much. A good provenance tells the true worth of a painting. A good provenance is almost as valuable as the painting itself.

'Well,' Robert gives a stilted smile and holds out his hands, 'I'm not a history professor for nothing. I don't have a keen interest in genealogy for nothing.'

I stare blankly at him.

'The painting you did,' Robert says, 'and the original painting that Van Gogh did were of a patient who was in the hospital at Saint-Paul with him, right?'

I nod.

'A patient that has never been identified. A patient who could be anyone.'

'And?'

'Well,' he attempts a smile, 'meet his great-grandson!' And he does a sort of semi-bow and at my lack of response, he immediately looks shame faced. 'We planted evidence to say that this unidentified man had received a sort of 'thank you' painting from Van Gogh as a token of his appreciation for sitting for him. I mean Van Gogh tended to paint a number of portraits of the same person, didn't he? And even though his brother Theo had a catalogue of his work, who's to say he didn't give the odd painting to friends and sitters? The man was in an unstable mental state after all.'

'But I still don't understand – how did—'

'Well, it wasn't as hard as it seemed actually.' Robert sounds as if he's trying to stop pride from creeping into his voice. 'It just meant inventing a few new French citizens.'

'What?' I'm beginning to get a slight headache and a feeling that I'm in some sort of a dream. This is forgery on a grand scale. These sorts of things do not happen to normal people like me and my mother.

'It's a little complicated,' Robert says, 'and hard to explain, but, basically, because I'm a renowned professor of history, I got access to the French archives, found a family who suited my needs and added an extra family member. Your father forged the documents, he was good at handwriting. This extra family member got married, had a son. When he was in his forties, he was admitted to Saint-Paul around the same time as Van Gogh, sat for a Van Gogh portrait and received a painting as a thank you from Van Gogh. This person died there, his son went off and got married and had a son, Pierre, who was me. I inherited the painting.'

I blink. My mother looks bewildered. 'But that would have taken ages,' I stammer out.

'Two years or so,' Robert confirms. 'We had to alter census records; they take one every five years in France. We had to get into the birth, marriage and death records and, to be honest, there are probably a couple of holes in the whole thing, for instance no gravestones for the family, but we reckoned nobody would ever investigate that far. We faked letters from my' – he makes quotation signs with his fingers – 'great-grandfather, to his wife. Just one or two letters with a vague reference to a painting given to him by a strange artist. The thing about the art world, Eve, is they see a new Van Gogh, they want to believe in it. Money in it for everyone.'

'And did you have any photos of this great-grandfather?'

'We did. It's amazing how everyone looks the same in the old black and whites.'

I can't believe that he's actually smiling. A slow sort of fury is building up in me. 'But they must have tested my painting?'

Robert nods. 'They did to a point. The canvas was old, the painting underneath which we had scraped off might or might not have been Van Gogh, they couldn't be sure that it wasn't one of his lost paintings, though we knew it wasn't, the materials used were authentic, the varnish was good, we baked it to age it and then we rolled it up to make hairline cracks appear in the paint. Then we added dust. And the *pièce de résistance*, it wasn't signed.'

'Van Gogh didn't sign a lot of his stuff.'

'Exactly, so if we were trying to fake a painting, we would have had it signed so there would be no doubt, but with this one, there was doubt, so it couldn't have been a fake, do you see?'

I sort of did. 'So you sold it?'

'We got it authenticated and an auction house took it and put it in its catalogue, but just before the auction a private buyer expressed an interest. And so we sold it to him. The idea was to get the entry in the catalogue anyway. More provenance.'

I don't know what to say. My mother is very quiet too.

'Was it not all over the news that a new Van Gogh had been located?' I ask faintly. 'I should have come across it.'

'Yes it was on the news, but they weren't obliged to reveal my identity and John chose to remain anonymous. We just had to make sure you never saw it.'

It's like swallowing what you think is a sweet and for it to turn out bitter and horrible. I can't believe my dad would have done that to me. 'That's why I went to France for a few years and only came back when John was dying,' Robert said. 'I had to keep up the pretence of being a French citizen just in case questions were asked, but they never were.'

His words fall into silence. The enormity of what he did seems to fill the whole room. I realise that my hand is aching from my mother's grip. She has also begun to hyperventilate.

'It's OK,' Robert says soothingly. 'It all happened about eight years ago now and if it's any consolation, your dad never spent the money. He just lived off the interest and he made me promise not to spend it either. You just thought the money he had was from the proceeds of the paintings he sold in his gallery. D'you know, the interest even bought this apartment?'

'No,' my mother says faintly, 'I bought this place out of the proceeds of the sale of our old house.'

Robert winces, realising that he should have kept his mouth shut. 'I bought your house for an inflated price,' he says. 'Then sold it later for what it was really worth. You'd never have afforded this place otherwise.'

'Oh!' my mother lets out a little yelp and clutches her chest.

'I put the house money back into the account,' Robert says, trying for lightness. 'Not that anyone would know. You'd be amazed at the interest millions makes.'

My head is reeling. I blurt out, 'What you both did was robbery. You robbed some poor guy of eleven million—'

'Ten.'

I glare at him.

'He wasn't poor, believe me,' Robert attempts a laugh, which doesn't quite come off.

'You robbed him.'

'No, he and everyone else believes he got a Van Gogh. If he goes to sell it, he'll probably make a profit.'

'You robbed him.' I eyeball Robert until he drops his gaze.

'I just can't believe John would—' my mother says softly.

'Well, believe it, because it's true,' I snap. I pull my hand from hers and glare at Robert. The anger I feel frightens me. My dad used me, he used my gift, he wanted to make himself feel better about leaving us, and so he and Robert took one of my paintings and – I can't stay here anymore. I'll either cry or hit him and I want to do neither. Instead, I make my way to the door.

'Eve, come back,' my mother says. 'Eve.'

'I'll go,' Robert offers swiftly. 'You stay, Eve.'

'I need to be on my own,' I don't turn back. 'I'll call you, Mam.' I don't bother saying goodbye to Robert.

It's as if someone has shattered a mirror that I'd been using all my life and what I can see now is all twisted and broken.

I have to get away.

6

I drive around for a while, not quite sure where I'm going. I find myself in a car park looking out to the sea in Dún Laoghaire, minutes from our old house. I spend a few moments listening to the constant roar of the sea out beyond the pier and I think I'd like to get out of my car and walk to clear my head, but I realise that I can't. Walking will only allow me to think too much and so I reverse out of the car parking space and drive on. Past the sea and upward into Dalkey, onto the Vico Road where all the millionaires live. And onto Shankill. Thoughts skitter in and out, weaving and knotting themselves together, so that my head is all over the place. Throughout the drive, my mobile keeps ringing. I fish it out of my jeans, turn it off and throw it in my bag. After a few more miles of aimless driving, I realise that I just want to go home. It's almost eleven. And so I turn back onto the motorway.

Thirty minutes later, I'm climbing the stairs to my deserted apartment block. A half-naked blonde girl scuttles out of the Party People's place on the ground floor. She scurries on by without meeting my eye. Ed is half dressed too, his shirt open to the waist, as he waves the girl off. Then he grins lazily at me and I nod a greeting, unwilling to engage him in conversation. I envy him his casual lifestyle. Behind him, the beat of party music continues.

I trudge upstairs, unlock my apartment and, as I step inside, I am suddenly bathed in the most glorious moonlight as it pours in through the balcony windows. Its beauty and purity remind me suddenly of what I've lost and I have to bite back a sob. I have lost my certainty. The certainty of who my dad was. The certainty and safety of my easygoing life. I'll be on tenterhooks in case my painting is discovered as a fake. Forever, I'll be living in fear of prison and of people thinking that I did something that I didn't. No matter how much I want to, I can never go back to the person I was this morning. Eve who painted Van Gogh and loved it. Now when I look at my work, I'll only see fakery and scam.

A small tear ekes from the corner of my eye and I brush it away.

I will not cry.

No, I will not cry.

I had been happy with my life. I really had. And now it's gone.

And it's the deception that hurts most. The betrayal. How could my dad, whom I trusted, have put me in this position? What would have happened to me if they'd been caught? Would I have been implicated? Probably not. They would have protected me, and Robert would have taken the rap. Would probably still take the rap if it was ever discovered that the painting was a fake. But the problem is, even if I let him, which I couldn't, who would believe him? Hey, my surrogate uncle sold a fake Van Gogh, I paint fake Van Gogh's, but no, I had nothing to do with it. Yeah, right.

I shake my head, not wanting to confront it. There is only one remedy here, I decide, as I pull out a bottle of wine from the bottom of the press, where it is languishing among the chickpeas and the lentils that I'd bought about a year ago in the mistaken belief that I might actually cook with them. Locating the corkscrew, I twist and twist until the cork comes up with a tiny 'pop'. I pour a generous glass and take a grateful swallow.

It's corked but I decide to persevere. At least it will relax me. It will take the edge off the painful truth that, from now on, I will be living in fear of exposure. And my poor mother . . . I suppose I should give her a call. I shouldn't have left her the way I did, but it was as if I could see my life crashing down around me and I had to get out. But my mother must have been feeling like that too. I'd better give her a call.

I locate my phone, switch it on and see that Robert has sent me a text. A sad face with the words: *Ring me. Sorry.*

Sorry? I think in disbelief. What use is 'sorry'? He and my dad embezzled millions from some poor sucker who's now stuck with a fake painting. OK, a very good fake as it happens, but a fake that's probably worth only about two hundred quid. On top of that—

My mobile rings loudly and I jump, red wine sloshing everywhere. It's my mother.

'Hello?' my voice shakes.

'Oh, Eve,' my mother sounds relieved. 'Thank God you're safe. I had visions of you doing all sorts of nasty things to yourself.'

'To myself?' I try to joke, but I sound as if I might cry again. 'I'd rather do nasty things to Robert.'

A pause. 'Hmm. Yes, well, we have to talk about what we're going to do. Robert thinks we should all just sit tight until there is something to worry about.'

'Easy for him to say, it's not his painting hanging on some art collector's wall.'

'I know that Eve. But what choice do we have?'

'I can't leave my painting out there.' That's it, I realise suddenly, my own words echoing back to me. I can't leave it out there. Once I get it back, I can start over. 'I have to get it back.'

'Oh, Eve, how can you do that?' She sounds despairing. Eerily, I'm reminded of the time when my dad was dying and expressed a wish to go to an art exhibition. I'd told my mother that I intended to take him and her response had been exactly the same. I'd been so angry at her that day. So angry at her inability to take charge. At her ability to make me feel so helpless. And, of course, I hadn't been able to take him on my own and it was one of my big regrets. But her attitude is not going to deter me this time. 'I don't know yet. But that's what I have to do.'

My mother doesn't answer.

'Where's Robert?' I ask, 'Did he leave soon after me?'

'No, he's still here. He didn't want to leave me on my own.'

I can't believe that there is a faintly accusatory tone in her voice. As if I'm the one at fault.

'He really wants to talk to you, love. To explain. He's explained it all to me. He says they were desperate, well your father was and he—'

Robert and his positive spins. Well, he won't do it to me. 'I don't want to talk to him, not just yet. Have you any idea, Mam, what they've done?'

'Yes,' she says and she sounds remarkably calm. I wonder if she's drunk. 'They committed a crime, put themselves in danger so that you and I would be safe. There are lots of things that money did for us over the past few years that—'

'Mam!' I'm shocked. I cannot believe she is talking like this. 'It doesn't make it right.'

'I know that,' she says. 'I know that, Eve, and I don't want that money any more than you do, but your dad being so sick does make it understandable, eh?'

'No. No, I don't understand why my father used a painting of mine and implicated me to make himself feel better about dying. I don't understand that.'

'Oh, Eve!' her voice trembles and I picture her with her hand to her mouth. In the background, I hear Robert saying something to her.

I click the phone closed and burst into tears.

7

In the days that follow, I attempt to lose myself in my paintings. Most of my work comes from orders on the internet and I've two *Sunflowers* and a *Self-Portrait with Bandaged Ear* to get ready by the end of the month. I can never understand why someone would want a self-portrait for their room, especially one of Van Gogh with half his ear missing, but it pays the bills. Normally, I'd enjoy the pressure of having to do three paintings in the space of four weeks, but things have changed. My joy at producing accurate reproductions has waned in direct proportion to how much trouble I'll be in if I ever get found out. Just as I feared, every time I pick up a paintbrush, I see myself as a criminal and I know instinctively that unless my attitude changes, I can't keep doing this job. If I don't enjoy it, it'll show in the paintings, despite the brilliant and joyful yellows.

I finish a varnish on *Fifteen Sunflowers* and know in my heart that something vital is missing from it. Then, not wanting to start into another copy in case I ruin it, I decide to turn back to my ideas board for Della Sweeney. Doing a painting for her might be my only hope, diversifying to survive. But I still have nothing to say, not because my mind is its usual blank but because my mind can't settle on anything other than the words, 'I have to get the painting back, I have to get the painting back.' Every time I try to distract myself, I keep flitting back to that phrase. My thoughts are like a butterfly on a flower, not able to settle anywhere for very long.

Right then, my mobile rings. I approach it cautiously as I haven't spoken to my mother or Robert all week, not sure of what to say to either of them, not sure that I even want to talk to them right now. But it's Olivia. Damn, I suddenly remember I was to meet her for lunch. Just the two of us for a change.

'Hey,' she says, 'are you on your way? I'm standing at the corner of the road and I feel like a prostitute. I'm all dressed up for a change and men driving by in cars keep looking at me.'

Men driving by in cars always look at Olivia. It's her tall, slender frame and her vibrant red hair. It's the reason I talked to her all those years ago in primary school. I fell in love with the colour of her hair, I'd never seen anything like it.

But, I think, I'm not going to be good company for anyone. And I feel that I can't go dragging Olivia into my dramas, not until I have a plan of action at least. And I can't meet her and not tell her either. 'I'm so sorry, Ol,' I feign a hoarse voice, 'I completely forgot, I'm dying here.' I give a cough for good measure and a bit of a sniff.

'Oh,' her concerned tone kick-starts the guilt. 'Oh, do you want me to come over?'

'No, you'll only catch something. I'm so sorry.'

'Not at all, you take care. I'll give Eric a ring, he's in college, so he's always available.' She gives a dirty laugh which makes me smile.

'Have fun,' I say.

'Oh, I will,' Olivia sniggers, then adds, 'And you get that scrummy neighbour of yours to mop your brow, no point in letting him go to waste.'

'Yeah, right, I'll keep that in mind,' I say in a tone that implies eye-rolling.

'Or if he can't oblige, I'm sure cute little David will.'

Olivia still thinks David fancies me, although I don't see any evidence of it, unless buying me loads of drinks and giving me a massive hangover is his way of wooing me. It might be nice to go out with David, I think, he has a great sense of humour and his easygoing charm is infectious, but he has to ask me first. I'm really old-fashioned like that. 'Haven't you a lunch to go to?' I change the subject before she can go on about how shy David is beneath his muscle-bound exterior.

'He's just shy—'

I start to cough again and Olivia takes the hint. 'See you soon, I hope,' she coos and I can tell she's smiling. 'Take care, honey bee.'

'You too.'

Talking about lunch has made me hungry but, as usual, I've nothing to eat in the place so, pulling on my parka, I lock up and head to the shops.

8

I've just entered the car park of the apartment building, having eaten in the local cafe, when I spot Robert standing beside his car. He's obviously been waiting for me. I groan quite loudly and a person walking by glances in my direction. Robert makes no attempt to approach me, choosing instead to watch as I walk towards the front door of the building. As I near him, he fixes me with a pleading stare and I'm reminded of a kid begging for sweets. Ignoring his look, I pass by and punch in the code to my block. I'm not completely surprised when he bounces in front of me, saying, 'I've been waiting here for the past hour and a half, would you not talk to me?'

I pretend to think about that and finally say with mock-regret, 'Eh, no.' I realise suddenly how mad I still am at him and my dad. And it's hard to be cross with a dead man, so I suppose I'm punishing Robert on the double for this. 'I'll talk when I'm ready,' I continue sullenly, attempting to push past.

But he doesn't move. Instead, he plants himself more firmly in the doorway. I become aware of how tall he is. How lanky. How he has started to use strong-smelling aftershave. 'Eve,' he spreads his hands wide, a beseeching look on his face. 'What do you want me to do? It happened years ago, we thought it was for the best—'

'The best?' I splutter indignantly. 'The best? Are you joking me? That wasn't for the best.'

Robert swallows nervously. For the first time, I notice wrinkles around his eyes and mouth. Today, in the harsh light of an April afternoon, he looks pale despite his tanned complexion. It's not helped by the beige shirt and the cream jacket, two colours that have never suited him. 'Can't we discuss this in your apartment?' he pleads, 'I promise—'

'Robert,' I interrupt firmly, 'I'm not ready.' Now it's my turn to swallow hard. 'I just can't. Not yet. I need to make a decision about what to do.' And you'll try and influence me, and muddy the waters, I think to myself.

'There is nothing to do,' Robert hisses. 'Come on, Evie, there's—'

'Don't call me Evie!' At this moment, I resent his pet name for me. It represents all the innocence of my childhood. 'You might have persuaded my mother it's all cool, but it isn't her painting that's sitting waiting to be uncovered as a forgery, is it?'

'It'll be fine.'

'And you know this, how?' My voice rises. 'Have you taken some sort of tarot-reading course? Did you consult your crystal ball this morning?'

'Aw, now, Eve, don't be sarcastic—'

'Do you know what my crystal ball tells me?' I am shouting, I realise, but I don't care. 'It says that you and my dad have just ruined the next fifty years of my life.' I swallow back a sob. 'Nothing is the same now.'

'Aw, Evie, don't.' He attempts to touch me, but I pull away. 'Look,' he says softly, 'I'll take the rap, you know I will. I promise. I'd never—'

'Eve?' It's Larry. Neither of us had noticed him. He must have come from the corner shop because he's carrying a bag that appears to be filled with ready meals. His eyes flick from me to Robert, warily. 'Is everything OK here?'

Larry has got a good three inches on Robert.

'Everything is fine,' Robert placates. 'Me and Evie were—'

'I was asking Eve,' Larry snaps, and I have to say that despite my distress, his commanding presence is a bit of a turn-on. His grey eyes rest on me, 'Well?'

'We were just finished,' I answer and then think how like a film I sound. That's what the good guys always say to the bad ones if someone comes to rescue them. *We were just finished*. What a cliché. But, then again, you can hardly expect anything else from someone who spends her life copying others. 'Bye, Robert.'

'Aw Evie—'

'Stop calling me that!'

'But I just—'

'You heard her,' Larry says, positioning himself menacingly between me and Robert. God, it *is* like a film. Larry even looks like a film star, all broad and handsome and brooding. He's wearing an old denim jacket and faded black jeans.

'This is ridiculous,' Robert says. 'Eve, can you call your Rottweiler off? She's my godchild,' he tells Larry. 'We were just talking. Eve, come on.'

'I'll ring you, Robert.' Larry's bulk is blocking Robert from view, so I move my head slightly. 'I will,' I add.

Robert gives a huge sigh, his shoulders slumping. 'See you do,' he says, 'Your mother needs to hear from you too. She's very upset.'

'So am I.' I can't help it, my voice wobbles and a big tear plops out of my eye, so I turn and, pushing past both of them, I run inside, ignoring Robert as he shouts anxiously after me. The lift is broken, as usual, so I take the stairs, two at a time, hardly able to see because I'm crying and I realise that aside from the first night when I heard about the scam, I haven't actually cried over it since. Instead, I've held this huge lump inside but now, actually admitting out loud that I am upset, sets it all off. Behind me, I'm aware that Larry is pounding up the stairs and he's better at running than I am. His hand on my arm jerks me to a stop in the stairwell and I turn around to find him looking at me. Then all of a sudden, he pulls away as if I've burned him. He shuffles awkwardly from foot to foot before saying, 'Stop crying, Eve, hey? I'm shit in a crisis.'

And I hiccup out a laugh which turns alarmingly quickly into a sob and then he looks a little panicky before hesitantly holding open his arms and I throw myself into them and cry and cry and cry. And even as I'm doing it, I'm wondering how on earth I'll explain it to him. I'm wondering why he suddenly seems so trustworthy. He was the one in prison, not Robert or Olivia or anyone else I know. But maybe that's the reason Larry is the person I'd prefer to talk to. And I also know that I like the smell of his clean shirt and the feel of his awkward embrace and his muttered 'there, there' as he attempts to pat me on the back without touching me too intimately.

'Come on,' he says eventually, pushing me gently away, his hands on my arms, 'I'll take you home.'

'I don't want to go home,' I sniff. The thought of walking into my apartment which is stuffed full of finished and half-finished fake paintings fills me with dread. 'Not just now.'

'Oh.' He doesn't know what to do. He stoops down and retrieves his shopping bag, which he must have dropped when I threw myself at him. I notice that a tub of coleslaw seems to have dislodged its contents over the majority of boxes in his bag.

'Sorry,' I nod at the coleslaw. 'I'll buy you some more.'

'Don't be daft,' he glances up at me and smiles. Then adds, 'Come on into my place, I'll do you a coffee or whiskey or whatever.'

I have never been into his apartment before and, as he pushes the door open, I can see why he has never invited me. It's more spartan than my own place though there is an old brown sofa occupying space against one wall. Aligned along the opposite wall are copious fishing rods and other fishing paraphernalia. A lot of books are piled higgledy-piggledy on the floor.

'Make yourself at home,' Larry says. 'I'll put on the kettle unless you want a whiskey?'

'D'you have any beer?'

He nods.

'A beer would be good.'

'Liking that idea a lot,' Larry winks at me as he disappears into the kitchen. 'I'll just unpack this stuff and wipe it down and be right back.'

'OK.' I watch him leave before having a little look around the room. I'm drawn to the books on the floor, an eclectic collection ranging from history tomes to popular thriller novels to lavish photographic books. Some of them look really expensive.

'Where'd you get all the books?' I call out.

'You don't wanna know,' he shouts back. I smile, not knowing what to make of his comment. I flick through a couple before having a glance at his fishing rods, which are also quite diverse, being of varying sizes and widths. I wonder if his obvious love of fishing is why he got the silver fish tattoo.

Beside the rods, there is a small cheap table with some fishing magazines scattered on top and, about to topple over, a small wooden photo frame containing a picture of a little girl. She looks to be about two and she is smiling gummily at whoever is taking the photo. It's winter and a red bobble hat is pulled right down over her ears and little wisps of brown hair peep out from underneath it. She's laughing. The photograph was obviously taken on a cold day. Her pale face and red-tipped nose contrasts well with the bright blue and yellow of her scarf. Her coat is red and yellow and the sun is a white disc in a clear blue sky. She's cute and the happiness in her face is stunning. I pick it up, loving the contrast of colours in the photo, when a noise from behind startles me. It's Larry, two cans of lager in his hand. His eyes drop to the photo, which I'm still holding.

'It was about to fall off the table,' I explain blushing. 'I just picked it up.'

I busy myself fixing it in place, conscious of his eyes on my back.

'Lovely photo,' I say, turning back to him.

He ignores the comment; instead he hands me a can and breaks the tab on his. 'Cheers.'

'Cheers.' I open mine and we clink them together.

'Sit down,' he indicates the sofa.

I sit at one end while he sits on the other. We both take a long drink.

'So,' he eyes me, 'are you feeling better now?'

'Sorry about that,' I mutter. 'Thanks for coming along when you did.'

'Is he really your godfather?'

I nod. 'Yeah, that's Robert, my dad's best friend.' And then the tears start up again and I clumsily wipe my eyes with the sleeve of my jacket. 'Sorry about this.'

Larry angles his body nearer to me. 'Is he hassling you? Are you scared of him? You should report it if he is.'

'No, no, nothing like that.' I place my can of beer on the floor fearing it will spill all over his sofa, though to be honest, there looks to be a lot of stuff spilled on his sofa anyway. I wipe my face clean of tears. 'No, nothing like that,' I repeat.

'So, what's wrong?' Larry asks. Then adds, 'You don't have to tell me if you don't want to.'

But I do want to. I have to tell someone. An objective someone. And if anyone knows what jail is like, it's got to be Larry. Not that I plan on going to jail.

'I do want to tell you,' I say, 'but if I do, you have to swear you won't tell anyone else.'

A small grin lifts the corners of his mouth. 'Are we ten?'

'I mean it. You will not believe this when I tell you.' Then I wonder if I should. Am I making him an accessory to a crime? But, no, I don't think I am. 'Please.'

'Swear,' Larry still looks amused. Then adds, 'I don't exactly have a wide circle of people I can tell anyway.'

So, as best I can, I tell him. As my story progresses, he looks first disbelieving, then astonished and then, I notice uneasily, he looks impressed. 'And so here I am,' I finish up, 'with a fake painting out there somewhere that could be uncovered any time.'

It's a couple of seconds before he responds, and then it's with a most unsatisfying, 'Wow.'

'What do you mean, "Wow"?'

'The fact that they thought of it, that's genius, the fact that your painting fooled a load of people, that's genius too. The fact that they forged provenance, that's neck and the fact that they actually got away with it. Holy Christ.' He gawks at me. 'And you say that the guy in the car park organised it.'

'Larry, I think you're missing the point—'

'No, no, I'm not.' He shakes his head. 'Honest.' Then he whistles, 'But I wasn't expecting you to tell me that.'

'What were you expecting?'

'I dunno. That you'd had a fling with Robert, that—'

'What? Ugh. What do you think I am? I think I'll go.' I hop up from the sofa feeling foolish for thinking I could depend on him to be what I needed. Was I mad? He'd been in prison. Prison, for God's sake. My mother is right. And to think that I've just entrusted him with my biggest secret ever.

'Aw, Eve—'

I turn to leave and my foot tips my unfinished can of beer across the floor. It spins right across the room, spilling its contents everywhere. 'Shit.'

'You did that on purpose,' Larry says.

'No I—' But I see he's grinning so I stop.

'I'll wipe it up,' Larry's grin fades as he hoists himself from the sofa and stands facing me. 'Look,' he says, sounding a little embarrassed, 'I think you're a top girl, I do, honest. And I understand how you must be feeling and I won't tell anyone. Swear.'

His apology, if that's what it is, works its magic. The indignation goes out of me as quickly as money from my bank account. 'OK, thanks,' I mutter.

'No prob. D'you want another drink?'

'No, thank you.' I have to hold on to some annoyance.

'I'll just wipe this up, right, and we can talk about it, if that's what you want.'

'That would be nice,' I answer meekly.

'Good.' And he smiles and leaves.

What just happened there, I wonder? One minute I was annoyed, the next not so annoyed. Still, I trust him so I sit back down and wait until he comes back with a large amount of kitchen paper and proceeds to wipe the floor.

'D'you want help?'

'No, ta. You sit tight.'

More silence before I ask, 'So what would you do if you were me?'

'Oh, believe me, you don't wanna know that,' he sort of laughs before sitting back on his hunkers and studying me. 'But you want to get that painting back, don't you?'

'Obviously. I mean, I know what my dad did was wrong, but he was a good man,' my voice trembles as I add, 'I couldn't bear for people to remember him as a criminal.' I pause and admit, 'And I guess, I really, really don't want to spend the rest of my life living in fear that it'll all come out. Better to get the painting now.' I heave a sigh. 'But I don't know how.'

'You could buy the painting back,' he says, 'providing it hasn't gone up too much in value.' Then he laughs. 'Imagine if it has.'

I ignore his laughter. 'That's what I'm thinking, only I'm afraid they'd recognise me, or my name.'

'Use a fake name.'

'No!'

'Why not? What would the big deal be? A name is just a name.'

'I wouldn't know how to go about lying and pretending to be someone else.'

'Good for you.' Then he stands up abruptly, the floor not very well cleaned at all and walks into the kitchen.

'Larry,' I call out, but he doesn't respond. So I walk cautiously towards his kitchen. He's standing at the sink, his back to me, staring out the window, his palms flat on the worktop, his head bowed.

'I'm pretty stressed over all this,' I attempt to explain. 'Up to now, I've had an OK life. Except for,' I pause, swallow, 'well, except for my dad dying, that was hard, but, overall, I've had a good time of it. Nothing much bothers me, but this . . . ' I don't finish. I can't finish.

'Tell me,' Larry asks, his back still towards me, 'Why did you tell me this?'

'Huh?'

'Why tell me about this? You've got friends, did you tell them?'

'No.'

'Why?'

'I don't know.' And I really don't. Except maybe that Olivia would blab it, but perhaps I'm being unfair to her, she's been a great friend. When Dad was dying, she was there every day to help out. She even made him a special cup to drink from, one that he could hold, that wouldn't spill its contents everywhere. It gave him dignity. But there was that time in college when I confided in her about a guy I liked and the next day everyone knew, including the object of my desires. It was mortifying. If I told Olivia, I'd worry she'd let it slip.

'Did you happen to find out what I did that landed me in prison?' Larry startles me with the question as he turns to face me.

'What you did?'

'Uh-huh. Let me ask you one question, OK?'

'OK.' I'm confused. I have no idea what he is on about.

'Did your dad or Robert ever pull a stunt like that before or since?'

'No!'

A wry grin. 'Well, then, they did it for you and your mother like they said. You should be grateful they loved you so much.'

'Oh right. Thanks. And you figured that out, how?'

'I figured that out because most guys who pull this kind of thing do it time and again.'

'And you would know, how?' And then, quite suddenly, I know. 'Oh,' I say, feeling a little mortified. My eyes flick from his face to my feet and back to his face. 'Oh,' I say again.

His smile this time is devoid of any sign of laughter or fun. 'I was the best in the business at one time, Eve. I could charm money from a bankruptcy hearing.'

'You could?' The words are dry as they leave my mouth. I feel I have to cough.

He nods, 'I could.' A pause, before he adds without any arrogance, 'If I wanted, I could get you to give me every penny in your bank account.'

'That'd be a waste of your time,' I try to joke, though I'm feeling a little uncomfortable. Maybe I'd never asked Larry why he'd been in prison because I wanted to hold on to the nice guy I thought he was.

'Wouldn't matter,' he returns the smile, 'I loved a challenge. I conned money from almost everyone I came across. It started out as . . . ' he shrugs, coughs and says, 'well, a sort of hobby but I was good at it. You probably told me because you think I'm a straight up guy, trustable, dependable, honest. That's what all my marks thought too.'

'Marks?'

'The ones I conned.' He pauses. 'I got caught eventually, though. So, your dad and Robert are decent men as far as I can tell. Well, they tried to be.'

I don't know what I'm supposed to say. This was not how I saw the afternoon panning out. I thought he'd be shocked, that he'd offer some advice. But he hasn't. Instead he's applauded their ingenuity and told me that they were good men. 'I still need the painting back,' I gulp out. 'I don't care if they tried to be decent.'

'Do you have to be so self-righteous?' Larry asks.

That's the final straw. More tears spring into my eyes. God, I hate the way they seem to keep doing that today. 'I'm not being self-righteous. I just can't live with uncertainty, Larry. I want a worry-free life or at least as worry-free as is in my control. I just want to be back to where I was last week.'

'I want to be back to when I was ten, it won't happen though.'

'Well,' I say softly, 'it mightn't happen for you, but I'm going to do my damnedest to see it happens for me. I am going to get that painting back.' I turn to leave. 'Thanks for listening.'

I am at the door when, from behind, he says, 'Let me have a think about it. Maybe I can help. OK?'

I pause and turn around slowly, 'You think you can?'

He sighs. 'Most probably. Once a con always a con.'

'Oh, I wouldn't want you getting into any trouble. This has to be legal.'

'I'll call in to you during the week. In the meantime, don't tell anyone what you just told me.'

I ignore the fact that he hasn't reassured me on the legal issue. 'OK,' I answer slowly, 'but you are not to get into trouble for me.'

'Bye, Eve.'

'See you.' I close the door softly and take a deep breath before heading into my own apartment.

9

I spend two days waiting with the nervousness of an *X-Factor* hopeful to hear from Larry, but he doesn't call me with any sort of a plan. I decide to give him another couple of days before I hatch my own ideas, but in the meantime, as I'm unable to paint and too depressed to hang around the apartment, I decide that I'd better call in to my mother. This mess isn't her fault and, besides, I'm feeling guilty for the way I've shut myself off from her. I don't ring to tell her I'm coming probably because I'm secretly hoping that she'll be out when I go over. That way, I can avoid seeing her for a while longer without any accompanying remorse.

Just as I shut the door of my place, a man emerges from Larry's. He calls out a goodbye and I hear Larry yelling goodbye back to him. I stand and stare – it's the first time I've ever noticed Larry have a visitor. I suppose I thought I was the only one he really talked to, I never imaged that he had a life beyond mine, which is really odd. Anyway, I suppose I must look like one of those nosy neighbours and even more so when I say, 'Hi, visiting Larry?' Then because I hadn't actually planned on saying that and it had just come out, I flush, mortified.

The man jerks a little and then slowly turns towards me. He's tall, well built and I suppose he must be in his early thirties. His brown hair is long and is obviously let grow with abandon because it hangs down to his shoulders in no particular style. It's the only remarkable thing about him, everything else about his appearance is standard issue, from his pale watery blue eyes to his pale Irish skin. Even his clothes are everyday, a pair of jeans, a navy round-necked jumper, a black biker jacket and lace-up black Docs. He cocks his head to one side and studies me and my very embarrassed face for what seems like an age, before nodding and breaking into a smile. The smile transforms him. It's incredible. He should be in an ad for toothpaste or floss or even one of those ads for a healthy heart or something. His whole faces opens up and his eyes crinkle and sparkle and, when he speaks, his voice is like golden syrup trickling from a spoon. All gooey and sweet and promising. 'Yes,' he says, nodding. 'And you care because?'

But he's not being sarcastic.

'Because I'm Larry's incredibly nosy neighbour, that's why,' I say, zipping my parka up and smiling right back.

'You're also very attractive.'

'And you're very cheesy.'

He throws back his head and laughs. 'I am.'

Together we walk downstairs and out the main door. He tells me his name is Clive and that he's known Larry a long time. 'He's told me about you,' he goes on. 'You've been really good to him.' He pauses. 'It hasn't been easy for him since he came out of prison.'

'I suppose not,' I say.

'Anyway,' Clive points to a big monster motorbike, 'this is me. Nice to meet you, Eve.' He holds out his hand and we shake. His grip is firm.

'Safe travelling on that thing,' I smile as I pull out the keys to my car.

He doesn't answer, and my voice is drowned out by a roar of engine.

*

My mother is in, but she's hosting her book club.

'Come on up,' she says delightedly.

I tell her I'll contact her later, but she is adamant that I call up and say hello to the gang. Entreaties of 'oh do, Eve' echo in the background from her book buddies and so I reluctantly agree that I will, but only for a minute. With relief, I notice that Paddy is not behind the desk that morning. Instead, there is what turns out to be an even worse guy, a glowering, dour man who barks at me, 'Who are you going up to?'

'Iris Cole on the fifth floor. She's buzzed me up.'

'And you are?' He sort of postures menacingly in front of me, his arms folded, his legs apart. He's about ten foot tall. Well, that's what he appears to be.

'I'm her girlfriend.'

That throws him, I see in satisfaction. He shifts about on his feet. Then splutters, 'Yeah, right.'

'Yes, it *is* right,' I confirm pleasantly, suppressing a grin. I quirk my eyebrows, not quite sure what I'm doing and knowing for sure that my mother will kill me if she finds out. 'Do you have a problem with that?'

'Iris Cole, fifth floor,' he splutters out. 'Go.'

'Thank you.' I can feel his eyes on my back as I catch the lift. Seconds later, I'm outside my mother's and, when she answers my ring, I see that she is wearing a royal blue taffeta cocktail dress and high blue shoes. Her hair is swept up and long orbs dangle from her ears.

'Are you going somewhere?' I ask.

'No.' She embraces me and I catch a whiff of strong perfume that makes me cough.

While my mother normally looks well, she seems to have taken her wardrobe to a whole other level of glamour today. 'You look like you're off to the races.'

'Well, I'm not,' she laughs, sounding embarrassed. 'There's nothing wrong with looking well.' Then hugging me again, she says fiercely, 'Oh, I'm so glad to see you, Eve.' Holding me now at arm's length, she scrutinises my face. 'I was telling everyone that I hadn't seen you in a while, that you were a little upset and they assured me that you'd call when you were ready and here you are.'

'Here I am.' I hug her back, glad that I've come now.

'Hey everyone,' my mother calls gaily, as she propels me toward the sitting room, 'Eve is here!'

There's a chorus of 'hello's' as I enter. There are about ten women, all around my mother's age or older, sitting on the sofa or on kitchen chairs. I know most of them. One lone man, also about my mother's age, sits on an armchair across the room. I think he's a neighbour because I've seen him around.

'Well, let me introduce you to everyone, Eve,' my mother says as she rattles off a list of names that I forget two seconds later. The man gets up and enfolds my hand in his, holding it firmly and eyeballing me hard. 'Lovely to finally meet you,' he says with such sincerity that I cringe.

To my amazement, the other ladies sigh dreamily. He's obviously the heartthrob of the group, though fat and balding and buttoned up were never ever in vogue as far as I can remember.

Then my mother bustles about getting me a coffee as I hunker down on the floor beside the coffee table and grab a handful of biscuits. There is an awkward silence but they all smile pleasantly. 'So,' I ask, breaking it, 'what's today's book?'

The man speaks up. 'Oh, it's brilliant,' his voice is cultured and assured, a voice that commands attention. 'It's called *Septus Siberius* and it's by an Indian writer whose name I won't even begin to attempt to pronounce.'

The women laugh, though I imagine he has cracked this joke before.

'I don't think it's that brilliant,' one of the other ladies thrusts a copy into my hands. 'I couldn't make head nor tail of it.'

I glance down at the book and instantly recoil. The cover is gross. A tiger with its stomach ripped out. It's like a 'cruelty to animals' poster. 'I don't think I'd ever buy this, never mind read it.' I push the book away. 'Who chose it?'

'Liam did,' my mother answers as she places a cup of coffee on the table for me. 'And I thought it was good.'

'Yes, the cover and the book are a symbol of the grossness in our society,' Liam goes on knowledgeably, 'and the fact that we have to rip the heart out of it.' He seems to relish saying the word 'rip'. He even does a hand action.

'Well, I happen to think that tigers are lovely animals,' someone else says. 'I wouldn't want to rip the heart out of one.'

'A tiger looks lovely, but it will rip you open first,' Liam pronounces. 'Look at the Celtic tiger in Ireland, that ended in tears.'

'I agree,' my mother says, in her I-don't-actually-have-a-clue voice. 'It was a very well-written novel with a lovely central image that was developed as the story progressed.'

'Oh, well said,' Liam actually claps.

I have to say, I am impressed too. My mother blushes like a schoolgirl.

'Well, I didn't understand the point of setting most of the story in a supermarket,' someone looks at my mother. 'Why do that? You don't see any tigers in supermarkets.'

Everyone looks at her.

'Oh,' my mother says, sounding regretful, 'I could go on and on about that but, and I hope you'll all excuse me, I haven't seen my daughter in ages, so can we?' she looks questioningly at her friends and they all agree that it is getting late and that they should run on. One by one, they pull on coats, stuff their copies of the book into their bags and exit, and my mother and I go to the door to wave them off.

'We never decided on the next book,' Liam, the last to leave, says with concern.

'You decide,' my mother says. 'Your choices are so interesting.'

'OK, I will,' Liam smiles broadly. 'Bye now, Iris, it was lovely. Thank you. And bye, Eve, lovely to see you too.'

My mother waves him off and then turns to me saying, 'Poor, Liam, he was so lonely on his own in his apartment. All his family are abroad and his wife is dead three years and he retired and has no life so I invited him to the book club and he's a great asset.'

I don't know if I'd call reading a book about a tiger set in a supermarket a great asset but I don't get a chance to say anything as my mother hugs me again and then, with her arm about me, she walks me back into the sitting room. The two of us sit side by side on the sofa and she says with feeling, 'I'm so glad you came.

I was getting terribly worried but everyone kept telling me to leave you alone.'

'Everyone? How many people did you tell?' I have a sudden horrible vision of the whole world knowing about the painting.

'Oh loads,' she says airily, and then at my look of alarm she clarifies, 'not about the painting, silly, just about you. I made up a story.'

'Oh.' I don't want to ask what, but I do anyway. 'What?'

'Oh nothing,' she waves it away. 'I can hardly remember what it was now.'

It's a few seconds before either of us speaks again. Her hand rests in mine and I like it. I wish we could stay like that as I feel that no matter what I say, it'll cause trouble and I don't want to just yet. In the end I go for, 'I'm sorry for not ringing you, I had to sort things out.'

'I know you did. It was a terrible shock. I still can't believe it. I'm not even thinking about it, which is probably the wrong thing to do. Have you seen Robert?'

'Nope.' I lie. 'Why?'

'Well, he's devastated, he really is. And he has assured me that he hasn't spent a penny of the money they made, just the interest. Well, apart from the time he bought our old house.'

Her green eyes, the same shade as mine, study me for a second. Then she asks the question that I know will cause trouble, 'So, what have you decided?'

'I have decided,' I begin carefully, 'to get the painting back and give the money back.'

She stiffens. My mother likes to avoid problems. 'Robert says it'll be fine.'

'Well, I would rather ensure that it was fine, Mam. You don't have to get involved. I'll figure it out.'

'But it might be,' she frowns, 'you know, dangerous. I mean, how do you give millions of pounds back to someone?'

'I'd imagine that's the easy part. I have to convince them to sell me back my painting that they think is worth millions first though.'

'And how will you do that?' she gasps. 'Oh, Eve, I don't think you should get involved in all this.'

'I *am* involved, Mam. It's my painting. I don't know how they did it, but Dad and Robert conned a lot of people.' I pause. 'It is OK to give the money back, isn't it?'

My mother looks astounded that I've even asked. 'Of course it is. I don't want it. It might mean that I have to get a job or something but I've told Robert that I'm not happy to spend money that isn't mine.'

Just then, my phone bleeps. Fishing it from my pocket, I read: *U dere dis eve? Lar*

I text back. *Yes.*

He texts that he'll see me then.

A whoosh of relief washes through me.

I can hardly concentrate on the rest of the visit as I wonder what Larry has to say.

10

Am I mad to trust Larry? I ask myself later that evening as I wait for him to show up. Not mad, my brain tells me, just desperate. I peer out my balcony window, wondering when he's going to appear. There's no sign, though the light is on in his place as I can see a sliver of it cutting through a gap in his curtains and slicing out into the early evening. He's probably having his tea, knowing that if he comes over to me, there's a fair chance he'll end up eating burned toast or some other such delicacy. I really have to learn how to cook properly, though I can make a mean spaghetti bolognese from scratch. My dad taught me. And then thoughts of my dad send me back to the balcony window and it starts all over again.

After a while, in order to maintain the energy to keep up my rocketing stress levels, I forage about in the press and pull out a packet of chocolate biscuits and eat all of them while watching the window. At around eight, just as I've polished off the last biscuit, the thump of music starts in the Party People's apartment and just as I'm wondering why I haven't been invited, Larry appears at my veranda, holding a bottle of wine.

'Hey,' I smile, relieved to see him. I'd probably have eaten the remaining contents in my press if he hadn't come. Scrunching up the empty biscuit packet and stuffing it into the pocket of my jeans, I unlock the window and let him in. He follows me to the kitchen where I find two clean glasses and a packet of nachos. We opt to sit on the two bean bags on the floor of my studio as we tuck in.

'So?' I blurt out the minute we're settled. 'What's the story? Can you help me?'

He smiles, amused, but doesn't answer. Instead he draws back from me and appears to scrutinise me, top to toe. His eyes glimmer in the half-light of evening and I shift uncomfortably.

'Well?' I ask again.

'I've been thinking about it,' he says slowly, 'and I've done a little bit of work, which I'll show you later. But I've been reading up a lot of stuff on the internet about buying and selling art. Can I run it past you to see if I've got it right?'

'Sure.' I'm touched that he seems to have gone to so much trouble. 'Though I'm a bit of a novice. I just sell directly to the public.'

'No worries. We'll figure it out. But to start,' he angles his body to face mine, one long leg bent so he can rest his arm on it as he holds his wine glass, the other leg stretched out in front of him giving me a glimpse of a brilliant white sports sock and trainer, 'a lost painting appears. But how do you prove it's a genuine Van Gogh? Number one, the canvas must be from the same era as the painting, the paints too.'

'Uh-huh,' I nod. 'And as far as I know, the canvas was. Van Gogh would have used oil paints from a tube in 1889,' I say. 'They were invented then.'

'Right, so that's that covered. And your brush strokes would have had to be like his—'

'It's what I do best,' I admit, feeling ashamed about it for the first time in my life. 'I can just stand in his shoes and paint like him. I studied his paintings a lot as a kid, I loved them.'

Larry nods and continues, 'Then the painting needs a story of where it has been all these years – provenance, right?'

'Robert is a historian, he also studies genealogy. He was the perfect person to gain access to the French archives. He probably said he was researching. Then all he had to do was slip fake family histories into the files. He said he found photographs in old auctions and pretended they were pictures of his grandfather. Then he faked all the relevant birth, marriage and death certificates, probably using paper of the same era. Well, my dad might have done that, he was good at copying things, just like me.'

'And what else did they tell you they did?'

'Letters from the original owner to his family to say he'd been given a painting, so they would have had to source old notepaper or had it made. I'm sure there was lots of other stuff.'

'And then, selling it? I assume they went to a dealer?'

'Well, my dad was a dealer, you see. I suppose they had to get the painting authenticated first by some reputable people that would strengthen the provenance. And then the word would have gone out that a Van Gogh had been found and either the painting would have been auctioned or sold privately either through my dad or another dealer. It was sold privately as far as I know.'

'Did they run tests on it?'

I shrug. 'I guess. Or maybe the buyer might have after he'd bought it. If it was found to be a fake, he could have returned it and got his money back. Most reputable dealers would give a refund.' But was my dad reputable? I really don't know anymore. It hurts.

'So it hasn't been found to be a fake yet?'

'Probably not. But if they try to restore it at any stage, it might be found out.'

'Is there any record of it on the internet? You never told me what it looked like or the name of it.'

It was the one thing I'd been avoiding. If I never saw that painting again, it would be too soon. 'I haven't checked.'

'Well, maybe it's time you did.' Larry stands up and crosses over to my computer which sits on the floor in the corner of the room.

I can't bear to join him. I sit as if frozen on my little blue bean bag, clutching my glass of wine.

'Come on,' Larry coaxes and pats the ground beside him. 'What are you afraid of? Either the painting is there or it isn't and maybe if it's there, we can find out who bought it.'

'I'd rather not see it.' My mouth is suddenly like sandpaper. Seeing my painting among Van Gogh's masterpieces would be like seeing a loud-mouthed gatecrasher at my wedding.

Larry shrugs and presses a few buttons. 'Now, I've found that this is the best site for viewing all his work.' He seems to be ignoring the fact that I haven't moved. 'I'm going to go into portraits and you can tell me the name of it.'

'I don't know what they called it.'

'Well then, you're going to have to come over here and identify it.' He flicks a glance over at me and when I still remain seated, he says impatiently, 'For Christ's sake, Eve, get a grip. Come on.'

He's right. I have to do this. Wearily, I haul myself up and cross towards him. I crouch down, peering over his shoulder as he flicks down through the computer images. Some of the paintings I know so well, some not so much. Some of them I wish people would ask for just so I can try painting them. All of them are beautiful, well in my eyes anyway. And then, oh God, there it is. A swollen-faced man with a blue neckerchief and yellow shirt. A hint of madness in his gaze and yet a gentleness on his lips. *Man with Swollen Face*. I open my mouth to say 'there it is' but all that comes out is a croak. Instead, I point a shaky finger at the screen and Larry enlarges the image. My computer is a good one. I need it for sending jpegs and stuff, so I invested in one with a good screen resolution. My fake painting looms out at me and I flinch from it. And yet, in the back of my mind a little voice pipes up saying, 'It's bloody good.' Underneath the painting is a catalogue number, the size of the canvas and the words 'private collector'. No information on who has it.

'Nice,' Larry observes. 'Looks real to me.'

'Well it's not,' I take a huge slug of wine. Then another. 'I'll have to talk to Robert and ask if he can find out who has it.' I pause. 'Then what?'

'We get it back,' Larry says grinning. 'We offer to buy it.'

I like the way he has said 'we'. 'Whoever has it mightn't want to sell.' In fact, looking at it, I doubt anyone would let it go for the same price they paid for it.

'Everything is for sale,' Larry says, eyeballing me, and there is something in his gaze that I can't quite fathom. It doesn't reassure me though.

'I don't know what you mean.'

'We agree to whatever price he wants,' Larry smiles.

'I only have eleven million,' I say. Then the absurdity of this statement strikes both of us together and we both begin to laugh.

'It's a start,' Larry chortles.

'But what if the painting costs more?' I say eventually, gloom descending once again. 'How can I buy something if I don't have the money?' More wine is needed. I fill up my glass and take another slug. 'Want some?'

Larry shakes his head, still staring at the screen. 'Let's not worry about that for now,' he says. Then logging out of the site, he keys the name of my painting into Google. Loads of articles pop up. He scans the list and settles on one entitled 'Lost Van Gogh reappears over one hundred years later.'

'Oh, please don't read it,' I groan. 'Please.'

Larry laughs. He's enjoying this, I think, indignantly as he begins to read the piece aloud in his gorgeous hypnotic voice.

'A painting, believed to be worth millions, has been found in the attic of a man who died last year. His son, Pierre, came across the treasure as he was sorting through his father's belongings. 'He left me a lot of junk that his father's father, my great-grandfather, had handed on.' Among this 'junk' was a painting that his great-grandfather had received when staying in a psychiatric facility in France in the 1880s. It was thought for a long time that Van Gogh had only painted one of the patients during his stay at Saint-Paul in France but it later emerged that *The One-Eyed Man with Swollen Face* was also painted there. Now it seems that *Man with a Swollen Face* could be the third. It appears from correspondence held by the owner's family that Van Gogh gave the painting to the patient as a present for sitting for him. The painting is an amalgamation of *Portrait of a Patient at Saint-Paul* and *The One-Eyed Man with Swollen Face*. Van Gogh experts have stated that if this painting proves to be genuine, it is an amazing find, but said they will await the results of tests to determine its authenticity. The owner has opted to retain his anonymity.

'Oh God,' I moan.

Larry goes into another site. This time, the article says that the painting had been bought privately before going to auction and that the buyer wishes to remain anonymous.

'We need to find out who owns it now,' Larry states the blindingly obvious. 'Can you ask that Robert guy?'

'Yep.' Robert has access to all the ledgers of Dad's business so the purchaser should be listed somewhere and, to be honest, I doubt that you'd ever forget the name of a person you sold a fake ten million painting to.

'Right, well, once we find that out, this is what I think we should do.' Larry turns around and faces me. He's uncomfortably close and I can smell the wine on his breath, the scent of his aftershave. I move away feeling slightly unsettled.

'Now, hear me out, this is very do-able.' He pauses to allow me to absorb this before continuing. 'I can pose as a dealer for a rich client. I'll approach various other dealers and owners, asking if they are prepared to sell or source a Van Gogh portrait, that way it won't look as if we're zoning in on your painting in particular. We go to viewings and then we decide. You'll be the rich collector who is happy to pay a generous asking price. We take it from there.'

'Pardon?' This all sounds a bit cloak and dagger.

Larry repeats himself.

'This sounds,' I place my wine glass on the floor and get my brain to think, 'well, a little like, I dunno—'

'You can't go in as an ordinary Joe with eleven million,' Larry explains patiently.

'Well, you can't just be a dealer, no one will know you. Where is your gallery?'

Larry grins. Back to the computer. He spends a little time hacking into his own computer as far as I can tell and then suddenly the screen is filled with a picture of a very posh building. The words 'Shanagher Gallery' appear over the red-painted door. Larry clicks on the door and we're in an impressive gallery site. Paintings and exhibitions of well-known artists are advertised. 'Nice, eh?' Then there is a picture of a man with blond hair and glasses and he is listed as the gallery owner.

'Who's the guy?' I peer at the screen. A little closer. Then I turn back to Larry. 'You?'

'Me in an earlier incarnation,' he says. 'But that's what I'll be like. I'll change the picture once my hair is dyed. This one is just to give you an idea.'

Disguises? Fake websites? This is not what I expected. It all sounds a little illegal. 'Isn't this illegal?'

'Am I not entitled to dye my hair?' Larry asks puzzled, big grey innocent eyes all hurt and sad looking. 'Can I not boast about myself online? Tell a few lies. I'm sure people do it all the time in chat rooms?'

'This is a website that says you're a gallery owner!'

'Am I not allowed have my dreams?' More hurt looks.

'No,' I stand up abruptly, knocking over my wine glass, which thankfully is empty. Rubbing my hands over my face, I mutter, feeling a mix of agitation and confusion, 'I can't do this. I can't.' I look down at Larry, 'Thanks for the idea but I think I'd rather confess that the painting was a big fake.'

'Would you?' Larry nods, seemingly unperturbed. He stands up too and shrugs. 'Well, OK so. If you'd rather do that, go ahead.'

'You don't mind?' He's not offended, that's good.

'Why would I mind? It's your choice. And if things don't work out, I'll visit you in prison.'

I think he's joking.

'Don't eat the shepherd's pie, though,' he continues. 'It's rank.' He touches me briefly on the shoulder and winks. 'Be seeing you so.'

I watch with a mixture of despair and relief as he pulls open the balcony doors.

'Thanks anyway,' I call weakly.

'No problem.'

As he disappears, I'm reminded of the time in school when the popular girl offered me a cigarette. The idea was that I should take it and then I'd be cool too. But I refused and she and her mates walked off scoffing to themselves and instead of feeling all virtuous at my decision, I felt like a big loser. A big chicken. That's how I feel now. And, as I hear him sliding open his own patio window, I realise that I'm kidding myself, I can't confess. It was the reason I asked for his help in the first place. And if I tried to get the painting back, how would I do it? On my own? I flirt with the idea of writing an anonymous note to the person who has the painting warning them that it's a fake. But no. This collector, whoever he or she is, needs to feel as happy after I've got the painting as before. And Larry is right, the only way to do it is to buy it back at a good price. Though the 'good price' bit is a tad worrying. But maybe I can cross that bridge when I get to it.

Damn it, I think, pacing to and fro, from white wall to white wall and back again, I've no choice but to go along with his plan. But is it legit? I suppose he's right, there is nothing technically illegal in pretending to be someone you're not. And there is nothing illegal in buying a painting. I mean, if I go to buy a washing machine they don't ask my name so why should it matter if I fake who I am to get this painting back. And maybe I'm insulting Larry by thinking that he's going to do something illegal. Why would he do that? He wouldn't want to end up in jail again, especially for a person he hardly knows. Maybe I'll give it a chance. Maybe I'll do it. For now. See how it goes. And so, without thinking any more about it, I march out of my apartment, across the landing and rap on Larry's door.

He opens up and manages to look surprised to see me. 'Well, hello there. Want to borrow a cup of sugar?'

'You're right,' I say, ignoring him. 'It's not illegal. I think we should give it a go.'

He winks at me, a downright sexy wink. How can he do that? One minute he's all innocent, the next, I can hardly think straight. 'Give what a go? I'm not used to being propositioned on my doorstep. You're very forward.'

'Ha, ha.'

I stare impassively at him.

'Oh,' he says, eyes widening, voice loud, 'Oh, I know you! You're the faker girl!'

'Will you shut up?' A flutter of anxiety. He is obviously not taking this seriously. 'Larry, this isn't a joke. This is my life.' The incessant beat of music from the flat below grows louder and drowns out the last of my sentence.

Larry looks a little contrite. 'Sorry. Come on in.' He pulls his door wider and I slip in.

We stand in the centre of his apartment and face each other.

'So, you're up for it, yeah?'

'I have no choice.'

'You do have a choice.' He pauses. 'But it'll be great, you'll see. We'll need money though. Have you got much besides the eleven million?'

'Nope.'

'Can you get a loan?'

'Why do we need money?'

'Travel. Clothes. Other stuff. You're rich, remember?'

I feel physically ill. I can't answer. Instead I nod. Robert might be good for a few bob, he certainly owes me.

There is a silence.

'If we do this, you'll also have to have about ten grand in ready cash with you. If you can't get it together, take it out of the bank account with the millions in it. Then we can split it, I'll carry four and you take six on board.'

'Ten grand?' I hadn't wanted to touch that money at all.

He nods. I don't know if Robert will lend me that much. Though, he might.

Larry crosses to me. 'You sure you're OK with this?' For the first time, he actually sounds as if he cares how I feel about it all. He bends down and looks into my face. 'You don't have to. It's the only way I can think of helping you.'

'I know,' I mutter. 'And I'm grateful.' Then, biting my lip and taking a deep breath, I ask the question that I hope won't offend him, 'Why though? Why are you helping me? You hardly know me. It's a risk for you.'

Larry smiles a little. I can't quite make it out. It's a sad sort of smile. Wistful. It pulls me right in and I wish I hadn't asked. 'I'm helping you because, quite frankly, Eve, I've nothing else to do. I'm unemployable. I'm bored. I got the brush-off at my audition. And I'm helping you because I believe we've a fighting chance of getting your painting back but you have to trust me.' He pins me with his gaze and asks so quietly I can hardly hear above the party music, 'Do you trust me?'

And despite all I know about him, or maybe because he had the honesty to tell me, I nod, 'Yes, of course.'

'Cool.' He sounds delighted. 'I like that.'

I have no option but to smile back at him. The best I can hope for is that the private buyer is a woman. He might be able to charm her to give it to him for nothing.

Some hope.

11

The city is bustling as I take my life in my hands and leg it across College Green, earning a blast of a horn from a grumpy driver. The gates of Trinity face me and as I step inside its grounds, the sounds of the city recede and are replaced by the chatter of students and the far-off sound of a band playing somewhere. I inhale deeply and make my way to Robert's rooms which are up at the very top floor of the college. I've been there before, but never with the horrible sense of trepidation that I feel now. He had told me delightedly when I rang that he had an hour's window that afternoon and even though I was meant to meet Olivia and the gang for lunch, I knew the sooner I talked to him the better. There is a sign on Robert's door saying 'Do Not Disturb'.

I knock loudly.

'If that is Evie, come in. If it's anyone else, can you not read for God's sake?' Robert calls from inside.

His cross voice makes me smile. He obviously uses it on his students as I've never heard him talk like that in my life. I open the door and peer around. 'It's Eve.'

'Well, come in.' His smile is broad. 'Would you like a drink?'

He pulls a bottle of whiskey from his drawer.

'No thanks.'

I glance around. His room has been painted since I was last here. The once fawn-coloured walls are now a delicate shade of yellow. Frilly yellow curtains have been added to the windows.

'Denise's influence,' Robert says, not sounding too happy about it. 'She thought it was a dreadful dreary office when she came here and she bought paint and made me do it up.'

'It's nice.' Though it's not Robert, I think. On the desk, there is a picture of Denise in her button-up blouse and brown skirt, smiling at the camera. Her hair cascades across her shoulders and contrasts boldly with her prim image. She even looks like she's pouting. 'And you even have pictures of her here too,' I tease gently, slipping into our old friendly banter. 'Lovely.'

He smiles. 'Isn't she?' He shakes the whiskey bottle. 'Sure I can't tempt you?'

'I'm driving.'

'Will *I* need it?'

'You might.'

'Oh.'

'In fact you might need a very large one.'

'I love large whiskeys usually.' A small smile. Then replacing the bottle in the drawer, he adds, 'But not today.' A pause. 'Look Eve,' he begins, 'you've no idea how sorry I am. Sometimes, we make the wrong choices for the right reasons. Can you forgive me?'

'Of course I forgive you.' That's a ridiculous question. I mightn't be able to forget but I have no problem with forgiveness. Despite what has happened, Robert was the fun guy of my childhood. A family friend who became a father figure. As we took long walks through Dublin city, he told me the history of every place, making it come alive and breathe for me. We'd visited the Hill of Tara and he'd regaled me with tales about the Celts and Druids and the beginnings of religion. The room he occupies now is peopled by the ghosts of those who had it before him. Robert weaves a compelling tale, he is probably the most entertaining lecturer. He lives and breathes the past, revels in the dust and grime of centuries gone by and that is the part that I can't get to grips with. The part I will always have trouble forgetting, the part that disturbs me the most – he messed about with the history that he professes to love so much. He changed the history of a family in France. He changed Van Gogh's history. Again, the feeling of being at sea in my judgement is pretty scary.

'Thank you,' he says softly. 'That means a lot. So, how've you been?' He sounds a little nervous. 'Your mother said you'd called in to her.'

'Does she tell you everything?'

'You know she does.' A glimmer of a smile which I return.

'Look—'

'I need—'

He gestures for me to go first. I plunge in. 'I need two things from you, Robert.'

'Anything.'

'I need a loan and I need information.'

There is a silence. Outside the door, feet pound and people joke with each other. The sound of someone singing rises up from below and I can hear them through the open window.

Robert leans across the table, frowning, 'Information?'

'Uh-huh. I need to know who bought the painting.'

Robert freezes, his body still hunched towards me, before he pulls back slowly, his eyes taking on a look of fear. 'Why?'

'Because,' I say, with a lot more confidence than I feel, 'I'm getting it back.'

'Damn it! Are you mad?' He bends towards me again. 'And how on earth are you going to do that? It's madness.'

I don't reply, just stare him out of it, before his shoulders slump and he asks more quietly, 'How are you going to do it?'

'That doesn't matter—'

'Of course it does, you can't just go in there and demand it!'

The door pops open. A young kid, obviously a first year, pokes his head in. 'Hello, Dr Lynch, I—'

'Can you not read?!' thunders Robert, standing up.

The door slams closed.

'There is no need to yell,' I say, feeling sorry for the poor kid.

'So, what are you going to do?' Robert ignores me and starts pacing up and down behind his desk, his hands to the back of his head. 'Good God, Eve, you can't just go and ask for it back.'

'I know that,' I say, determined to keep the upper hand by remaining composed, 'I have a plan, don't worry.'

'Don't worry!' He swivels on his heel and glares at me. 'Don't worry she says! Ha!' He rolls his eyes. 'Of course I'll worry. I'm sorry, Eve, there is no way I'm helping you.'

'You owe me, Robert.' Oh please don't cry, I tell myself. Please don't cry. I really don't know what to do if he won't help.

'What would your mother say? Huh? She'd kill me for helping you with this.'

'I am twenty-eight, I am not a kid. My mother has no control over what I do. Now, I can get this information from you if I have to, Robert. I can get a court order. I can call into the gallery and look up the archives, but you can make it easier.' I shrug, 'But,' I add, 'if you don't, I will take action.' I'm not sure if I could do what I've just threatened, but I'm impressed at how convincing I sound.

Robert crosses towards me. 'You wouldn't.'

I suddenly feel a little vulnerable because I'm still sitting whilst Robert towers over me. 'I would actually.'

'Fine,' he says sounding pissed off. 'And what are you going to do then?'

'I need money. I need money to carry out this plan I have.' I don't mention Larry, as both Robert and my mother would have a breakdown. 'I need as much as you can give me. I promise I'll pay it back. And I also need – if I haven't enough money to cover the mortgage on my place – for you to pay it for me. I might be gone away for a bit, depends on where the painting is.' It's the first time I've ever asked him for money and it feels all wrong. I've always liked to be independent. 'I will pay you back, I promise,' I repeat.

'Eve, you know I'd give you money for anything. You know I would. But please, rethink. Use this.' He taps the side of his head. 'The painting is OK. You're overreacting.'

I don't bother to refute it. 'Will you lend me the money or not, Robert?'

'This plan of yours, what is it?'

'I can't say.'

He looks at me hopelessly, but in that look I know that he'll do whatever it is I ask of him. I've always been able to wrap him around my finger. Still, he tries once more, 'I'll go and confess, right now.

How about that?' He even makes a move to get his jacket.

'I'll still be implicated,' I say, halting him. 'You know that. And anyway,' I stand up and cross toward him, 'I don't want you to go to jail. You're far too much fun.'

To my surprise, his eyes fill up with tears and he blinks a little rapidly and seems to have difficulty finding his voice. 'I love you, Evie.' He catches my arms and looks straight at me. 'You have to be careful. Promise me you'll be careful.'

'I promise.'

'I always wanted a child and you were it. You,' he chucks me under the chin. 'And I will go to jail for you. I will tell the police everything.'

'All I want from you Robert is some money and information about who bought the painting.'

His eyes bore into mine. I hold his gaze before he bows his head in defeat. 'OK,' he sounds resigned. 'His name was Derek Anderson and he owned several shops. I'll get back to you with full details tomorrow, how's that?'

'That's great. Thanks, Robert, I'm grateful.'

'He was an arrogant bastard, we met him when he came to view the painting. Loads of security.'

If he's trying to put me off, he's succeeding. For a start, I'd been hoping for a woman.

'Do you need help with this plan of yours? I can take leave.'

'You'll be recognised,' I smile affectionately at him. 'Anyone who meets you can only remember you.'

'I made a pretty good Frenchman.' The memory makes him sad, I think. 'Poor John was terrified, but I knew it'd work. All that acting stood me in good stead.' His gaze rests on my face. 'I wish it hadn't now.'

'You and me both.'

'Excuse me, sir – oops, sorry!' Another student who is sent scurrying by a stride across the room from Robert.

'I make a pretty good terrifying lecturer too,' Robert jokes feebly.

'And you make a damn fine stand-in dad,' I tell him.

His enfolds me in a bear hug.

I'm glad we're friends again.

12

Larry is fantastic on Google. He can pinpoint exact information in a few searches. I'd be trawling around for days looking for what I want. We're sitting at his kitchen table, which is a sad-looking thing. Four mismatched chairs and a table that looks like an abused housewife. Two hefty mugs of coffee sit in front of us, along with a packet of plain biscuits. Larry, to my horror and ashamed fascination, has hacked into someone else's broadband, which is a bit much I think, only I don't say it.

'Chill,' Larry smiles over the top of his laptop at me, as if having read my mind. 'I'm only using it for a search. It's not going to cost this person anything extra. Now, let's see.' His fingers fly across the keys. 'Derek Anderson,' he says as he types. Then, 'Shops.'

'How did you get their password?'

'Oh, there's loads on this guy.' He's ignoring me.

He peers at the screen and scans the entries quickly. His eyes are flicking left to right, reading whatever has popped up on his screen. Another tap of a key. Another entry and he reads something else. I figure I'm better off not hearing how to hack internet lines anyway. I study him, his fabulous-looking face, his golden voice, his likeability, and wonder if he is who he seems to be. Well, yes, he seems like a con man now. Hacking into computers, creating fake websites. Once again, a sense of unease fingers its way into my mind and then he looks up at me, his eyes sparkling, and my disquiet vanishes like a wisp of smoke in the wind.

'Bingo!' He beckons me to sit beside him and I hop up to slide into the free chair. There's a page onscreen that seems to be a biography of Derek Anderson. I read a lot more slowly than Larry and he waits patiently, chin in the crook of his palm, eyes observing me intently as I study the article. Derek Anderson was born in Chicago in an impoverished neighbourhood. His dad left when he was five and his mother struggled to bring up Derek and his five siblings. Despite this, he did well in school and got a job at fourteen, stacking shelves in a supermarket to help out his mother. He gave all his money to her so she could buy them clothes and shoes. There was nothing worse than being taunted over your clothes in school, he said. By the time he was fifteen, he had left school to work full-time in the supermarket. At eighteen, he had been promoted to manager. He left at twenty, having turned that shop around with his money-saving ideas. He got a loan and opened his first 'Shop Smart' shop in Chicago at twenty-one. By the time he was thirty, he owned a string of shops that stretched from one end of the US to the other. The ethos of his business was value for money. Inexpensive goods and clothes piled high and sold cheaply. Now, in his mid-forties, he owns property all over the world, an impressive art collection and ten high-end cars. He'd built a huge house for his mother and siblings and he himself lives like a king. He is a hard businessman and doesn't suffer fools lightly. The head office of his corporation is in Chicago, though he lives in Florida. He was quoted as saying that it's only in books that hard childhoods are romanticised. 'It was hell, I hated it. I have spent my life getting away from it and I never want to go back.'

'Fair play,' I say, finishing up. I feel awful that he was conned.

'You should never put so much information about yourself online,' Larry says, smiling. 'Never ever ever.'

I wonder what he'd think of my Facebook, Twitter and MySpace pages. I'm not as bad as I once was, but I still update my profile all the time and have loads of online friends.

'There's not much there,' I say. 'The man is in his forties and his biography is only a page long.'

'It's enough,' Larry grins. 'Enough to know how to approach him anyway.'

His fingers tap in another search. He's looking up the number of the Shop Smart head office in Chicago. Then, to my horror, with finger to his lips, he dials the number into his new mobile which he informed me he bought especially for his new persona as a gallery owner.

'Larry don't—'

'Hello,' he says, standing up as his call is answered. I blink, in semi-shock. It's as if he's morphed into another person. Suddenly, he's standing up straighter, no longer the casual fun Larry that I know. Instead, even in his combats and yellow T-shirt, he looks every inch the businessman. His voice has taken on a mellifluous tone and he sounds smooth and assured and very different. 'I'd like to speak privately with Derek Anderson please.'

A pause as the person at the other end says something.

'Yes, I do realise that he's a very busy man. So am I, as it happens, and this call is not made lightly or on the spur of the moment. My name is Michael Shanagher and I'm an art dealer. I represent a number of wealthy clients, one of whom, for a number of years, has been trying to trace a painting that your director acquired some years ago. In fact, this client of mine was quite miffed when Mr Anderson outbid her for it.' He laughs here, a rich deep sound. 'She's used to getting her own way,' he adds smoothly. 'Anyway, she has appointed me to negotiate a price for the painting if Mr Anderson is agreeable. Would you pass on this message? I'm based at the moment in Ireland but can fly over at a moment's notice. She would be most grateful. Yes, I can give you my number.' He rattles off his number. 'Thank you so much. When can I expect to hear back? OK, thanks.'

Larry clips the phone closed and nods.

'I thought we were going to mail other galleries so it wouldn't look so obvious?'

'I have done. They've sent me jpegs of what they might be able to get for you, but I've asked them if they know where we can get our hands on *Man with Swollen Face*. Your story is that you want it to complete a portrait collection and that, ten years ago, this man outbid you for it. Nice for his ego. He sounds like a man with a lot of ego.' He turns back to the screen and pulls up an image of Derek Anderson. The man is small, with a narrow face and a huge bald dome of a head. His eyes are a brilliant intelligent blue, but his smile is unsure or maybe he just doesn't like having his photo taken.

'A guy like that,' Larry taps the screen, 'who is small and poor, they grow up with a chip on their shoulder. Robert said he was arrogant. He's someone that doesn't feel all that important inside. Appeal to his vanity, his ego and he is yours. Lock, stock and one Van Gogh.' He laughs at the rhyme.

'How do you know that?' I can't laugh.

Larry shrugs. 'It's easy.'

'Not to me, it isn't.'

'Well, I dunno. I just know these things about people. The stuff they say, what they don't say, how they walk, it all tells a story.' Not for the first time, he touches the tattooed fish on his wrist. He's quiet for a second, his dark hair shining in the sunlight, and then he looks up at me. 'It's what I was good at,' he says, and I wonder if I imagine that he sounds a little ashamed. 'Reading people.'

The kitchen suddenly becomes a little claustrophobic. It's obvious that I'm useless at reading people, I've got it wrong my whole life. I want to ask what he reads when he sees me, but I can't. I'm not sure that I'd like what he might say. 'That's quite a gift.'

'It can be.' He drops his wrist. 'So, next thing. Have you got money?'

'Robert transferred some cash into my bank account.'

'And the ten grand?'

'Robert.'

Larry looks impressed. 'The most generous man is a guilty man,' he says.

'He'd have given it anyway,' I defend Robert. Because he would have.

'I've some money too,' Larry says. 'We both need to invest in some decent clothes. No accessories,' he says then. 'I, eh, I have quite a few things that'll pass as the genuine article.' A quick grin.

'And, no, it's not illegal and, no, they're not stolen and, yes, I've had them since my bad old days.'

His words reassure me. 'What did you use them for?'

His face shuts down. 'You don't want to know. Lots of things. So, anyway, a trip to the US might be in order. Have you got a passport?'

'Yep.' I look at him. 'You?' I pause. 'Do they let,' I don't know how to say criminals tactfully so I just say, 'ex-criminals into the US.'

'No.' He sits down then looks up at me; his great grey eyes are wary. 'Now, don't freak, but my brother lets me use his passport now and again.'

'What?'

'His name is Declan and I look like him. It's no big deal.'

'Yes it is!' I take a step back so I can look at him properly. 'It *is* a big deal. I can't be involved in using fake passports. You can't be involved in using fake passports.'

'It's a genuine passport. It's just a fake name. For me.'

'No. If you're caught you'll go to jail.'

'I won't be caught. Trust me. I've done it before. He's my little brother, he'll come and live here and it'll look like I'm still here. Anyway,' he stands up, changing the subject so abruptly my head spins, 'let's hope the painting is in Europe or somewhere instead. I'd better go, I'm meeting a mate in the pub tonight.'

'No, hang on.' I stand in front of him. 'I appreciate you helping me Larry, but I draw the line at using your brother's passport. It's illegal. I said I wasn't doing anything illegal.'

'You are very sexy when you're worried,' he gives a crooked grin and I blush like a kid.

'Yeah, well, in that case, I'll be very sexy by the time all this is over so.'

'Good.' Another grin. Then he sighs comically, 'Can I state the blindingly obvious? You will book your seat on the plane. I will book mine. We will not travel together, so you will be doing nothing illegal. You can't stop me coming, Eve.'

'I can report you.'

'You could. But you won't. Now, I have to go out, so?' He looks expectantly at me.

And he's right. Of course I wouldn't report him. I say nothing, feeling foolish as I move out of his way.

'I'll let you know when we get the call back from Derek Anderson's people,' he says.

When, not if, I think. This guy is cock sure of himself. 'OK. Thanks.'

He closes his door and I head across to my place. Damn it, I think. If he can go out, then so can I.

13

'I can't go out, hon,' Olivia tells me when I ring her. 'I must have the same cold you had. I'm in bed. Eric is minding me.' She sounds hoarse.

'Nice one,' I smile, wondering who'd mind me if I was sick. Robert and my mother, no doubt. How sad is that?

'Hmm,' Olivia's voice dips. 'He's being a little too attentive. I'm beginning to feel he might be more into commitment than he lets on.'

'No! How awful. A man that wants to commit. Oh, my God, I couldn't think of anything worse. Oh, God, how—'

'You can take your sarcasm and feck off,' Olivia manages a laugh before starting to cough. 'Anyway, you're better off staying away or you'll catch it.'

'I don't mind. I'll call over if you like, give Eric a break.' Even as I say it, I know I shouldn't. Calling her was a bad idea. I'll only start blurting out my problems.

But she must sense the desperation in my voice because she pauses for a second and asks, 'Are you OK, hon?'

And I swallow and throw caution to the wind. 'Can I call over? And if I tell you something, can you promise on your life that you won't tell anyone else?'

She doesn't sound surprised, which surprises me. 'Come right over.'

*

Ten minutes later, I'm outside Olivia's tiny little cottage. Her dad bought it for her because there was a small shed for kilns in the garden at the back. Olivia pays him from her earnings. Even though I live in a built-up area, a ten-minute drive towards the mountains takes me to countryside. That's the beauty of living in Dublin – city, country, mountains and the sea all to hand. Olivia's cottage is just a little way off the road, up a small pot-holed driveway. She's at the door as I pull up and I immediately feel guilty for burdening her with my problems because she looks awful, her eyes are streaming and her face is pale and blotchy. If Eric has seen her like this and not done a runner, he must be really into her.

'Come in,' Olivia sniffles as she opens the door into her narrow little hallway and leads me into the kitchen. 'I got Eric to put the kettle on before I booted him out. Now, as I'm the sick one, you can do the honours.'

I make us both a cup of tea as she watches from her position at the table. When I have placed hers in front of her and she has blown her nose all over it, she looks up at me with watery eyes and says, 'Well?'

'I don't think you're going to believe this,' I begin cautiously, wrapping my hands about the mug because I feel cold all of a sudden.

'Try me,' she says and her grin, full of bravado, makes me suddenly glad I've come.

'I don't believe it,' Olivia is gasping like a fish on a bank as she gawks at me. 'Your dad and Robbie?'

She blows her nose and wipes it vigorously with a tissue. 'Your dad and Robbie!' she repeats, pocketing her hankie in her dressing gown.

I nod miserably.

'And Larry, your neighbour, is going to help you?'

I nod again. I haven't told her about Larry's past. It doesn't seem fair to him. So that part of my story has bewildered her totally.

'But what makes him such an authority? I mean, I could say I'd help you but I wouldn't have a clue what I'm doing.'

'Well, he does know. He has a plan.'

'Which is?'

'I'd rather not say.' The fact is that if I voice it out loud, I'll probably chicken out. Or Olivia will start pointing out all the flaws and terrify me. But even more than that, if I get caught, I don't want there to be a chance that Olivia could be implicated by knowing about it.

'Oh, God,' she puts a hand to her mouth, 'Eve, are you sure about this?'

'No.' I swallow hard, wishing I was drinking whiskey instead of tea. 'But I know I need that painting back.'

Olivia sits back in her chair and studies me. 'Could you not just leave it and hope for the best?' Her voice is so muffled, it takes me a second to figure out what she has just said.

'If someone used one of your cups and pretended it was by a big-time artist, wouldn't you want to get it back?'

'Hey, I resent that,' she smiles lightly, 'I *am* a big-time artist.'

I smile too before sinking back into misery.

There is silence for a few moments. I know Olivia is watching me, but I can't meet her gaze. I'm glad I've told her, it's good to share it with someone but I just wish she'd told me that I was doing the right thing.

'I'm so sorry, Eve' Olivia says, breaking the silence. 'It's, it's—'

'Unbelievable,' I finish for her. 'I know.'

'If there is anything I can do ...'

'There isn't,' I say. 'Just don't tell anyone. Larry will kill me.'

'God, I hope he isn't some sort of psycho killer,' Olivia suddenly gasps, causing her to cough again. When she stops, she says, 'Have you thought about the possibility that maybe he's out to steal your money or—'

'I haven't exactly got many options,' I say. Then add, 'But he's a nice guy.'

'Hmm,' Olivia folds her arms and studies me. 'In other circumstances, I could see the advantages of spending time with him.'

'Trust you.' But her comment has the desired effect and we laugh a little.

Then after a bit, she says, 'I'm glad you told me, I knew there was something wrong the past few times we met up and I kept trying to ask you but you were so busy chatting David up—'

'I wasn't so much chatting him up as avoiding you,' I admit.

'Poor David, he'll be devastated.' We both smile a little again, then she says, 'I did notice that you seemed preoccupied, though I thought you were just worried about Della Sweeney or something.'

The worry over Della's painting seems like another life. 'I wish.'

'I'll say it again Eve, if there's anything—' She starts to cough, big hacking sounds. Oh boy, she's really sick.

'You should be in bed,' I tell her, standing up. 'Go on, and I'll bring you in a hot whiskey.'

She must be bad because she doesn't object, instead she hobbles into her bedroom and as I'm making the hot whiskey, she falls asleep.

I'm afraid to leave her, so I sit in her kitchen and start to drink it myself, feeling like a Saturday-night loser. I flick on the TV, trying to pretend I'm having a good time with some brainless reality show. Larry will kill me, I think, as he'd said the fewer people who know, the better – but I know Olivia won't tell anyone. She's right, too; since my life fell apart, I've tried to avoid all one-on-ones with her because I just didn't know if I could carry off the deception as she knows me too well. It was easier in the group, because I could ignore her and focus on David focusing on me. And by focusing, I mean that he buys me loads of drinks which is pretty darn cool, though if my dad could see how much drink I've been imbibing in the past few weeks, he wouldn't be pleased.

I shake my head, but now that I've thought of him, memories keep resurfacing no matter how much I try to stop them. Bitter-sweet now and tainted with reality, they parade in front of me as I get slowly sloshed. The two of us painting in silence together in the shed out the back garden. He was tall and sandy haired, lean and fit from running five miles each morning. Thin from the stress of running a gallery that made very little money. He taught me how to blend and mix colours and he admired my early attempts to fake Van Gogh. And that's what we called it – fake. I remember him cajoling me, giving me hints about how to improve, the two of us studying the brushwork of all the Old Masters. I basked in his praise. I remember him and Mam coming to my first exhibition. It was in the local library and I'd done some great copying work. Nothing was original. In fact, the only semi-original thing I'd ever done was the Van Gogh that had been sold. I remember Robert, leaning in close to my canvases as he inspected them and then his voice, tinged with admiration as he too told me I was wonderful. The way he and Dad were so close, like brothers. I remember Robert slipping me twenties as I got older and tapping his nose as if it was our secret. I'd give the money to my mother because I knew she needed it and I think that was what Robert wanted all along anyway. And then, eight years ago, Dad told us he was sick. He died three years later. It was so hard on the three of us, me, Mam and Robert. I've been painting ever since.

I wonder what is wrong with me that I can't do an original painting for Della Sweeney. She's rung me wondering what progress I've made and I know she's going to blow me off soon and ask for her cash back. It depresses me more than it should. What is lacking in me that I have no need to be original? I didn't mind two weeks ago, so why do I mind so much now? And I do mind. I actually do. I've never seen myself as a cheap piggy-backing forger before I suppose. I want to be nobler than that, damn it.

I pour some more whiskey, neat this time, and close my eyes and wonder where all this will lead. Maybe it'll be an adventure. I've never been to America. Or anywhere worth talking about in Europe. The only place I've ever been to is Spain when I was in transition year in school. My parents didn't have a lot of money for holidays and when Dad got sick, we couldn't have gone anywhere even if we wanted to. My mind hops to the motor neurone disease that killed my dad but, before it did that, it brutally stripped him of everything he was, so that finally, when dignity at last dissolved, all that was left, at least to the onlooker, was a shivering shell in a wheelchair.

More drink – and I remember Robert and me shaving him and dressing him and attempting to have a conversation with him, as my mother cried and cried. She'd read to him and chat to him, but she'd never do any of the hard stuff and that had annoyed me at the time. But that's the way she is. I love her but she's useless in a crisis.

I remember showing Dad my paintings and I remember how his face would light up, his smile twisted and painful looking. That was when I knew that, despite everything, my dad was still in there. That my paintings made him happy.

I loved him. I still love him. And I know with certainty that part of me is rescuing this painting for him too. So that he'll never be exposed as a crook, but will always be remembered as the man I know he really wanted to be. One bad action does not a bad man make.

I feel that if I hold this in my head, I'll go through with this mad scheme of Larry's.

14

Two days later, when I've half-heartedly begun a new *Sunflowers* for a customer in Germany, Larry startles me by pounding on the patio door. Stepping inside, he holds his phone and says, 'We're in.'

'In?' I stare stupidly at him, my paintbrush in mid-air. 'In where?'

'The woman I was talking to the other day in Shop Smart, she rang me back.' He clamours over some canvases. 'According to her, Derek Anderson will be in Florida next month to launch an exhibition of his private art collection in the Florida Gallery of Art. As far as she knows, a couple of the pieces are for sale. She can book us tickets.'

'No.' I can't believe it. It's too easy. 'No way.'

'It's all true.' A huge smile this time.

'And my portrait? Will he sell it? Will it be there?'

'I'm not sure, I didn't ask.' He eyeballs me. 'Anyway, we're booked in for the opening night of the exhibition. I paid three hundred dollars for the privilege. It's for charity.'

I open my mouth to protest, but nothing comes out. This is what I wanted after all. Instead, I say, voice trembling, 'OK. I'll pay you back.'

'It's fine. You can pay for the hire car, that'll cost a fair amount. We need a really fancy car, top of the range. Book your flights, Aer Lingus for the twenty-third of June. There's one direct flight so be on it. We're going for two weeks, which should wrap it up. We can change the dates if we have to. Buy some good expensive clothes and we'll book into a place when we get there.'

'Fine.' It's like I'm being pelted with bullets. Each word hits me, making me flinch.

'Are you OK? You've gone pale.'

I shake my head and wave his concern off. Putting down my paintbrush, I take some time wiping my hands on a rag that hangs beside the canvas, deliberately not looking at him so he won't see the panic in my face. 'I'm just being stupid. I can't believe this is actually happening. It's all a bit mad.'

I want to sit down. Instead, I lean against the wall.

'Yeah, isn't it?' Even though Larry is agreeing with me, the fact that it's all a bit mad doesn't seem to bother him; in fact, I'd bet money that's he's loving it. He moves a few blank canvases out of the way and comes to stand in front of me, invading my space a little. I feel I can't breathe. 'Look, Eve,' he gazes into my eyes, his are almost hypnotising, 'you'll be great, I know it. All you have to do is pretend to be a bigger pain in the arse than you are already.'

'Ha, ha.'

'Just be Evelyn Coleman, that's the name I told them. You're a big-time art collector on behalf of' – he pauses and then adds delicately – 'Della Sweeney.'

At first, I think I've misheard. There is a beat of silence then, 'What?'

'Della Sweeney,' he repeats patiently.

'Della Sweeney?' My voice rises upwards in a sort of semi-hysterical way.

'Yeah,' he nods.

'You can't drag someone else into this. You can't drag her into it.'

'Well I can't plant stories about Evelyn Coleman, who doesn't exist, all over the internet can I? It'd take ages. But Della Sweeney is there and you've met her and been in her house so ...' he gives a nonchalant shrug, 'it makes sense, eh?'

I shake my head. 'No, no that wouldn't be fair. She's been very good to me. We haven't agreed on that.'

'The most believable tales are the ones where you mix a little fact with fiction,' he says patiently. 'And besides, who is going to believe that you were outbid for a painting ten years ago? You look too young.' He studies me, his head to the side. 'I have a hairpiece that will make you look older but using Della will allow us to be more credible.'

'No,' I shake my head.

'I promise, we won't mention her name unless someone asks us directly. Chances are she won't even know she's in on it.'

'I don't care. Oh, God.' I push past him and start to pace around my tiny studio, which is cheerful in the morning light. Outside, down below, life is going on as normal. I wish I could throw myself into the throng and disappear like sugar in a cup of hot tea.

Larry watches me, saying nothing, chewing a little on his lower lip but otherwise not showing any sign of discomfort.

Finally, I stop my pacing and stare at him.

He raises his eyebrows hopefully.

'I'm going to have to return her cheque. I can't take her money and do this to her.'

He laughs loudly at my capitulation and I'm forced into smiling too, though I really don't want to.

'But I'm uncomfortable with it.'

'Well, buy a cushion.'

'Fuck off.'

'Ha!'

God, he seems to have the ability to make me smile, even when I feel I can't. 'So, the way you see it is that I'm working for Della Sweeney and you are working for me.'

'Yes.'

'And we're going to buy my painting back.'

'Yes, and you let me do the talking and say nothing. I'm good at this, OK?'

'OK. And you promise Della Sweeney won't find out.' I can't help it. She believed in me, it seems so unfair to treat her like this.

Larry gives a shrug that I interpret as a 'yes' before he says, 'And when you have to talk, don't give any real information about yourself. That's important. And like I already said, I've a great hairpiece you can wear over there and when we get back,' he pauses and for the first time, I detect some shiftiness in his manner, 'when we get back, get a haircut.'

'Get a haircut?' I finger my long brown locks. It had taken years to grow. 'But short hair doesn't suit me.'

'It'll grow again.'

'Yeah, it'll take until I'm about fifty and don't want it.'

'Eve, you've got to listen to me. If I say get a haircut, get - a - bloody - haircut.'

Everything is changing in my life and my hairstyle is probably the only thing I have control over. I just can't get it cut. 'Don't talk to me like that,' I say instead.

'If you keep moaning, I will talk to you like that. Now, you either do what I say or it's off. Get a haircut when you come back.'

'I'm not moaning.' And I don't think I am. But there is no way I'm cutting my hair. To my dismay, Larry rolls his eyes and stomps towards the patio door. 'Where are you going?'

'We agreed,' he says and his tone brokers no argument, 'that I am in charge. If you want this to go your way, you do as I say.'

We eyeball each other. He makes to turn away again and the words are out of my mouth before I'm even aware I'm about to say them. 'Sorry, sorry. I will get a haircut. I will listen to you.'

He turns back towards me. I offer him a tiny apologetic grin. It always worked on Robert and my dad. It seems to work on him too. 'One smile doesn't make it OK,' he says gruffly.

'How about two?' I give him a bigger one. Of course, I have no intention of listening to him. If I wear a wig when I'm away, I won't need to change my hairstyle.

'For the way you go on, fifty thousand wouldn't work.'

'I'd only give fifty thousand to very special guys.' It suddenly dawns on me that I'm flirting with him. How stupid is that? For all his charm and his handsomeness, we're still working together and he's asking me to use Della Sweeney's name in vain. Plus, he has a lot of money for someone who doesn't work. That thought hits me suddenly. 'Where did you get three hundred dollars?'

He flinches, my abrupt tone startling him slightly. 'That is none of your business,' he says, matching my abruptness. 'You do your bit, I'll do mine.' And then without saying any more, he exits through my patio. 'June twenty-third,' he calls back as he begins to slide the door closed. 'Direct Aer Lingus flight.'

'Larry?' I call out suddenly.

He pauses, looks at me.

I wait a second before uttering a soft 'Thank you.'

'You're very welcome.' A nod, a grin and then he's gone.

Half an hour later, I've booked my flight to Florida and our car. No going back now.

15

Two days to go. List in hand, I recheck my packing. OK, fancy clothes? Check. Underwear? Check. Shoes? Check. Make-up? Check. Hairdryer, shampoo, conditioner? Check. Normal casual clothes? Check. Cleansers? Check. Moisturiser? Damn. Gone. I jot down a note to buy it later. Sun cream? Check. Passport? Check. Travel documents? Check. Dollars? Check.

The word 'dollars' has a funny effect on me. I have to sit down on the bed, the list of things to bring clutched in a hand that's suddenly sweaty as the reality of my situation hits home. My stomach rolls, making me feel sick. It's not as if I haven't thought about things, but socialising and keeping busy kept it at a distance. Now it's on top of me, like the unwelcome drunken uncle who has been hiding in the closet suddenly jumping out and ruining the party. My tummy heaves again, and I'm forced to run to the bathroom, where I dry retch into the toilet.

Oh, God, I have to get it together. I can't be like this in Florida. It'll be worse then, when I'm answering to a different name and pretending to be someone I'm not. I close my eyes and take a deep breath, slowing blowing it out through my mouth. And again. And again. Little by little, the sickness abates and my heart rate slows. I pull a towel off the hook and wipe my face with it.

'Hello?' Larry calls from the balcony. 'Anyone home?'

How can he sound so cheery? I stand up and walk to my studio shakily. It looks really tidy because I've packed a lot of stuff up.

'Can I come in?' Larry calls through the glass.

'Why can't you knock on my front door like everyone else?' I ask, sliding open the balcony door.

'Ouch, someone is in a bad mood.'

'I'm not in a bad mood. I just had an attack of nerves. I'll be fine.' He even looks cheery, though his clothes are a bit on the scruffy side. Old combats and trainers. A moth-eaten ragged blue sweatshirt.

'That is why I'm here,' Larry says easily. 'D'you fancy a spot of fly fishing?'

The comment is so unexpected that I laugh. 'What?'

'Fly fishing?' he smiles. 'It'll calm you down. Always works for me.'

'What do you mean it always works for you? How many times have you done something like this?'

'I mean that fishing is calming,' he says. 'You *are* in a bad mood.'

I turn away from him, not able for his casual air. 'I don't think killing fish would calm me down.'

'It's catch and release,' he says, following, only to end up standing in front of me so that I'm forced to look at him. 'You know, you catch a fish and you set it free.'

'I think I know what that means, thanks.' I sound almost tearful. I wish I could get out of this mess so easily.

'So, you want to come?' He sounds sympathetic. 'I'm leaving in thirty minutes. I can throw some spare waders in the boot if you want.'

I suppose it'll at least take my mind off things. And being out in the fresh air might tire me out, so that I'll sleep tonight. 'OK so.'

'Great,' Larry smiles and all of a sudden I'm reassured. We will be OK. 'See you at my car in thirty minutes. Wear old clothes.'

And he's gone. Back out my patio door.

Thirty minutes later, dressed in a grubby jumper, old jeans and trainers, with my hair tied back in a sloppy ponytail, I help Larry to load his equipment into the car. His rods are in smaller pieces which we put in first and then he hefts up a large bag containing all sorts of things that rattle. Slamming the boot closed, he crosses over to the passenger side of the car and, in a gentlemanly gesture, opens the door for me. 'OK, sit yourself down.'

'Thanks.' I sit into what is a very smelly vehicle that reeks of fishing expeditions gone by.

He doesn't seem to notice or else he feels no need to apologise for the pong. He straps on his seatbelt and we're off.

'Where are we going?'

'Kilkenny.' He says it as if it's just down the road.

'But that's miles away.'

He snorts back a laugh. 'It's just down the road, only takes about an hour twenty.'

I smile at his attitude. 'Eighty minutes drive is not just down the road.'

'That's because you have no life, Eve,' he teases, his great eyes crinkling up at the corners.

'I do so have a life.'

'Well, then live it, for God's sake. Kilkenny,' he says as he eases out into the traffic, 'is great for salmon fishing. I have caught more fish on the Nore than anywhere else in Ireland. It suits me, that river.'

'Have you been fishing long?'

He nods, a small smile curling his lips. 'My old man bought me my first rod when I was six. We fished every weekend, spending hours just sitting by the side of a river, waiting for a bite. My brother would come too, but he hadn't the same interest.'

It reminds me of how my dad and I would spend hours painting together. 'Is he still alive, your dad?'

He indicates and we're turning onto the N7. The traffic is very light.

'Why?'

'Why?' I half-laugh. 'I don't know. It's just a question.'

'Oh, right.' He says it casually but his meaning is clear. He does not want to talk about it.

'Sorry. I wasn't being nosy.'

He shrugs. 'Yeah, I know.' He sighs, then adds unexpectedly, 'He, eh, well' – a cough – 'he left. It was a long time ago.'

'Oh, I'm sorry.' There is a catch in my voice. I reach out and gently touch his shirt sleeve.

'So was I,' he says in a terrible attempt at humour. When I don't laugh, he continues, 'I was only about ten. It was a shock. It was all so weird.'

'Yeah, I bet it was. Did you just wake up one morning and he was . . . gone?'

'Yep.'

'Poor you.'

'Hey, he taught me how to fish and I'm grateful for that.'

I rub his arm again. 'Good. And I'm sorry for asking.'

'No, it's OK. Happens every day to someone I guess.'

He's not such a good actor now, I think, because from the way he clenches the steering wheel to stop the shake in his hand as he changes gear, I think his dad leaving is a long way from being OK with him.

I know how he feels.

It takes just over an hour and a quarter to reach the river. Larry doesn't go all the way to Kilkenny, instead he turns off the main road and the car bounces along country roads for about ten miles until we come to Thomastown, a picturesque little village on the shores of the river Nore. Larry parks and I help him unload the gear.

It is a beautiful late spring day and a gentle breeze whips the stray hair from my ponytail about my face. The air smells sweet and clean and even though Thomastown is actually slightly bigger than my idea of a village, it is fairly quiet at this time of day. A few cars trundle by and a mother pushing a toddler in a state-of-the-art buggy stares at us, or rather she stares at Larry. He seems oblivious as he hefts his fishing bag over his shoulder and slams his boot closed. Pressing his key, the car clicks, locking the doors. 'Now come on, assistant fisher girl,' he says, striding ahead of me so that I have to trot a little to keep up.

'Where are we going?'

'Upriver of the bridge,' he says pointing to the gorgeous bridge, one of those beautiful ones with four arches that span the river.

'The best place for salmon is about half a mile from the viaduct. There's a sort of pond there.'

It's a long time since I've walked anywhere and half a mile sounds quite a lot of walking, but we cover it in about ten minutes. We're in a valley and walls of trees rise up on either side of us. It's breathtaking. The only sounds are the water gushing, our feet squelching on the marshy ground and the breeze. It's as if we're the only people left alive in the world.

'Midweek is good,' Larry says, stopping on the edge of the bank. There is not much space, so I stand a foot or two behind him, a little afraid that I'll fall in. I hold on to a sturdy-looking shrub and plant my feet firmly in the loose muddy earth. Larry seems quite at ease, unpacking everything, fitting the rod together, hanging what looks like a yellow fly on the end of his line. 'There are fewer people around because they're all working. Being unemployed has its advantages.' He grins at me. Then, laying his rod down carefully, he rummages about in his bag and pulls out two pairs of horrible-looking waterproof trousers with braces. 'Put those on.'

I stare in dismay at them. 'Why?'

'Well, most people like to keep dry when they wade into the river.'

'Most people like to stay dry by sitting on a bank.'

'Oh, you disappoint me, Eve, you really do.' Larry pulls the horrible trousers on and even though he looks ridiculous, he's still a fab specimen. 'Well, you sit there and watch if you like, but you'll have better fun with me. I even got you a fishing licence for the day and everything.'

Oh, to hell with it. I grab the waders and pull them up. Needless to say, they're enormous and I look like a clown. Larry guffaws at me and winks. 'Looking good there, Evie.'

I flinch when he calls me that. It's what Robert always says, and I feel such a longing for normality that my heart actually aches.

Larry, rod in hand, strides into the river, though in a gentle way, so as not to disturb the fish I suppose. I gingerly follow him, holding on for dear life to the bank until I'm so far out that I have to use all my strength just to stay upright in the water. It is freezing and I gasp. Larry keeps going, it looks like he's making for the deepest part of the river and the depth grows alarmingly.

'Hey, I can't keep up with you.'

He turns around. 'You'll be fine. This is as deep as it gets.' He holds his arms out, the water is halfway up his thighs.'

'You're taller than me.'

He offers me a hand. 'Come on, I'll help you in. Go carefully.'

I grasp his hand and he catches mine in his firm grip. Heat suffices my face and my body. His touch is like a rush of static electricity, shocking me. Lust is a terrible thing. Larry gently pulls me towards him and I step over the uneven surface of the river, my own feet slipping and sliding in the waders.

'Now,' he says, letting me go, 'that wasn't so hard, was it?'

My hand feels cold and empty without his. Oh, to be pressed to that body in the same firm way . . . but, no, I shove that thought firmly aside. Larry is the bar of chocolate at the bottom of the shopping basket. Bad for me, deeply unsatisfying but longed for all the same. The water is up to my waist and it pushes and shoves all around me. I sway alarmingly.

'Go with the flow,' Larry advises me, his voice amused. 'No point in fighting it.'

And he's right. The minute I stop battling, the water doesn't seem as threatening – in fact, I can stay upright more easily.

'Now,' Larry dangles his fishing rod in the water, 'I'm just going to test the fly, see if I can see it a few feet down.'

He submerges the fly in the water and it glimmers. Larry grins. 'The water is still so cold,' he says, 'so I figure we need something bright to wake up the salmon. Something to get their interest.'

'What can you do to get my interest in this freezing water?'

Larry laughs.

'Now, watch me,' he says, as he lines up his rod. 'The cast is all important. First you have to figure out which way the river is running, the depth of the fish and the type of cast you might use. I'm going to spey cast. Now. See how my line is straight?'

I nod.

Larry then goes into a lesson on casting. I don't really

understand it, what I do notice however is his grace. The line arcs out into the air in front of him and he bends forward to accommodate it, then pulls back. The movement is so stylish that I have to admire it.

'Now,' Larry whispers, 'stay still, keep quiet. Let the rod do the talking.'

And so we stand, shoulder to shoulder in the river, perfectly still. The only sound is the gurgling rushing of the water and the rustle of leaves from the heavily foliaged trees. Somewhere in the distance cars pass on the road, but, right here, right now, it's as if someone has turned the noise switch in my head to mute. I watch as Larry works the line, moving with it, reeling it in, trying to tempt the drowsy salmon from their dull day. When it comes in empty, we move a little farther downstream. 'You have to keep moving,' Larry says, 'someone else will want to fish that part later.'

I follow him to his new spot and he casts off again. Smooth and easy and silent.

It's almost hypnotic, the casting, the waiting, the slow reeling in, the glint of the yellow fly underneath the dancing sparkle of the water.

And again he casts off.

And again.

He asks me if I'd like to try.

'Yeah, OK.'

He hands me the rod, very carefully. Then he stands behind me and catches my hands in his. 'Place your hands here,' he says, and I'm aware of his breath on my ear as he talks. He puts my hands on the rod. 'One low and the other a little high,' he says. 'Now bring the rod vertical and point to where you're attempting to cast to, like so,' he begins as he pulls me towards him, my back to his front. I reckon if he were ever trying to seduce a woman, this would be the place to do it, only she'd have to wade into freezing water and wear waders. He swings my hands back and the line rushes out across the water. 'Hey, not bad. Now start fishing.'

I do what I saw him do, reeling in slowly. My heart is hammering and I'm not sure if it's from his proximity or from the fact that I would love to catch a fish. It's kind of exciting, the anticipation. But my rod comes in empty.

Larry lets me cast a few more times, the last time on my own. Then he takes over. About two casts later, just as I'm beginning to feel hungry, there is a sudden tautness on the line. Larry grins at me, 'I think we've got one.'

'Really?' I can't hide the excitement. I have never seen a fish caught before and the fact that this one will live makes me feel better about the thrill I'm experiencing at seeing the line begin to pull as the poor fish battles for its life. Larry goes with the line before beginning to reel it in, totally in control and, again, his grace surprises me – as well as his strength as the rod itself begins to bend.

'He's a fighter,' Larry whispers, eyes shining. Soon, I see a large silver fish, flapping violently about at the other end of the line. 'Get the net,' Larry says, his eyes focused on his catch, and I pull the net from his pocket. 'Now dip it into the water, we don't want him to be too shocked.'

I dip the net in and, as the fish draws closer, I scoop it under him and there he is, large and shining and pretty annoyed judging by the way he's flapping about.

'What a beauty,' Larry grins. 'Hey big fella, I'm going to measure you up, then you can go.' He takes a tape out and measures the fish from top to tail and around his girth. 'It's about 13 pounds,' he declares proudly.

'Is that big?'

'One of the biggest I've ever caught.' He bends over the fish and very gently, almost tenderly, takes the bait from its mouth. Then he tells me to dip the net deeper into the water and the salmon swims off, looking no worse for its ordeal.

'That was great,' I say enthusiastically.

'Isn't it?' He glances at his watch suddenly and then asks, 'You hungry?'

'A bit.'

'Yeah, we've been here for ages. Come on, I know a nice pub, we'll grab a bite to eat.'

'My treat,' I say, adding, 'It's been a great day, thanks Larry.'

'Good,' he pauses, then continues, 'and it'll all be fine, you'll see.' He indicates that I should lead the way out of the river and I do, striding with confidence across to the bank where we find Larry's fishing bag and divest ourselves of the horrible waders. Larry packs everything away and we put all the equipment into the boot of his car before we walk across the square to a cute little pub that advertises 'All day dinners'.

My eyes take a second to adjust to the darkness inside the pub, but Larry has obviously been there before because he shouts out a greeting to the barman and asks for the Guinness Stew. 'You?' he turns to me.

'I'll have the same.'

We find comfortable seats right at the back, against a brick wall. Various fishing implements hang from the ceiling along with nets and buoys. The whole place reminds me of something from fifty years ago, and it's the better for it.

The barman, a guy in his fifties with huge forearms and a massive stomach, arrives pretty quickly with two enormous plates of stew. He sits opposite us and smiles, showing startling white, even teeth. 'Catch anything, Lar?' he asks pleasantly.

'Salmon, I reckon it was about thirteen pounds.'

'It was huge,' I contribute.

The barman turns to me. 'I'm Geoff. This guy here,' he indicates Larry, 'has been coming into this pub for the past year or so. He always catches something – I dunno whether to believe him half the time.'

Larry laughs good-naturedly. 'Well, I've a witness today,' he smiles.

'Where'd you catch it?'

'Up beyond the viaduct in the pool there.'

'Hi, Larry.' A girl's voice. I glance up. A woman, about the same age as me, only taller and darker sits in too. She's pretty in a very obvious way, bee-stung lips, big breasts, huge eyes, well padded without being overweight, nice skin. I'd imagine men would find her sexy. She glances at me and nods a 'hello'.

'Hi.' I am busy eating the stew, which is delicious.

'This is Geoff's daughter, Lena,' Larry says.

'Oh, right,' I smile. 'You do look alike all right.'

I think it's the wrong thing to say. Lena is not impressed. Her eyes narrow and she glares at me. 'Aye,' Geoff chortles, 'she has the Doyle arms all right.'

'Dad!' Lena hisses.

'It's a joke,' her dad winks at Larry.

'Are you entering the fly-casting competition next week?' Lena turns her huge eyes on Larry and leans across the table giving him an ample view of her cleavage. 'I am.'

'Well, I'll cheer you on in spirit,' Larry answers. He seems totally at ease, leaning back against the seat, his legs crossed at the ankles. 'I won't be around, though. I have to go away on business.'

'I thought you weren't working? Sure, Dad offered you a job here, and all.'

'Family business,' Larry clarifies.

'Oh,' she seems embarrassed now. 'Nothing wrong, I hope?'

'Stew is gorgeous,' I pipe up.

'Lena made it,' the man beams at his daughter. 'She's a chef.'

Lena blushes prettily. 'Larry always orders it when he comes, don't you?'

'I do.' Larry lifts a spoonful up and eats it. 'Best thing about Thomastown.'

Lena laughs. 'He's a charmer,' she turns to me, as she stands up, giving Larry a great view of her backside as she wriggles out of the confined space. 'Watch him.'

I think she's doing enough watching for the both of us.

'Right, well, I suppose we'll leave you to it,' Geoff stands up too, his knees cracking with the effort. He groans and laughs a little at the noise. 'Nice to meet you,' he says to me.

'Yeah, you too,' I say.

We watch him leave. When he's out of earshot, I nudge Larry. 'You've got an admirer there,' I tease.

'What? Geoff?' He feigns bewilderment. 'I don't think so.'

'The gorgeous Lena. It's not only her stew she's offering on a plate.'

Larry snorts out a laugh and starts to choke. I hastily hand him a glass of water and he takes a gulp, still laughing. 'Jaysus, don't say things like that when I'm eating. Christ.' He takes another gulp of water and looks at me with his laughing grey eyes, 'You really think so?'

'Eh, yeah.'

He nods. 'Cool.'

I don't know what 'cool' means, but I take it he's pleased.

We eat up the rest of the stew in companionable silence, then after bidding our hosts goodbye we leave. It's a shock to see that it's still sunny outside, though the sun has begun to dip and paint the sky a mix of gold and reds.

We barely talk for the first few miles, both of us tired from a day in the open air. Larry navigates the country roads and then, as he indicates to join the main road home, he asks me if I mind if he puts the radio on.

'No, go ahead.' I wish he wouldn't as I feel so calm and nicely tired, but it's his car so I don't object. He presses a button and Lyric FM's dulcet tunes spill out from the battered radio.

'My favourite station,' I grin, surprised.

'Me too,' he says.

And it's the perfect end to what has been an unexpectedly perfect day.

16

The day before I leave, I call into Della Sweeney to return her deposit. She is not impressed. She leads me into her enormous, stone-floored kitchen which is dominated by a large wooden table and a cream Aga. We stand facing each other across the expanse of table. Della doesn't even ask me to sit down; instead, folding her arms, she asks incredulously, 'You're giving me my money back?'

'Eh, yes.' I can feel my heart beginning to pound. She reminds me of a cross teacher I had in primary school.

'Are you saying that you're turning down my offer?' Her brow wrinkles and, head to one side, she studies me as if I'm a particularly nasty insect. 'Are you?'

'No,' I answer, intimidated by her cross face. 'I'd really love to take you up on it, but I just don't think I can.' I pull a crumpled cheque out of my jeans and, flattening it out, hold it towards her. She makes no move to take it from me so I step gingerly towards the table and place it there. Why on earth has she such a big table, I wonder, when it's just her. Nodding towards the cheque, I add, 'I, well, I just feel I can't do anything original.' It's true, if not the whole truth.

Della clicks her tongue. 'I find that hard to believe.'

Her tone implies that only an imbecile wouldn't be original. 'Well,' I bristle as my glance flicks to a crucifix she has hanging on her wall. 'You believe in God, so it shouldn't be too big a stretch.'

'You are a very cheeky person,' Della sounds appalled, though there is a ghost of a smile on her face. 'I can safely say, Eve, that I have never been turned down before.'

I bet she's never been used in an art-buying scam before either. 'Well, I'm sorry, but I paint fakes.' I wince as I say it. Then sounding a little tearful, I add, 'I just don't do deep and meaningful.'

'Why?'

I blink. 'Sorry?'

'Why don't you do deep and meaningful? Or shallow? Even something shallow would say a little about who you are. Why do you paint copies? You're brilliant technically, you know.'

I feel a flash of pride in her comment before I'm forced to damp it down. 'It's just not me.' It comes out sounding quite blunt. 'Anyway, I have to go. Sorry if I messed you about.' I turn to leave.

'Eve?'

I pause and turn back to face her. 'Yes?'

She picks the cheque up and holds it towards me. 'One day, perhaps you will decide to paint an original. Take this as a deposit on your first painting. No matter what it is, I'll buy it.'

Is she kidding me? 'I couldn't do that.' Oh, God, I really couldn't.

'Of course you can.' She comes towards me. 'Take it, spend it how you will, but remember, I'm your first buyer.' Then she pauses, just at the edge of the table, and inhales deeply, her face suddenly white.

'Della?' I take a tentative step towards her.

She waves my concern away. 'I'm fine. It's just a little dizzy spell, give me a second.'

I stand uselessly by but note with relief the colour flooding back into her face. 'Age,' she explains, sounding embarrassed. 'Now, this cheque. Take it.'

Her generosity makes me feel like a total heel. What would she say if she knew what Larry and I were going to do? But, then again, she never will know. He's promised me. 'Oh I—'

'I was wrong to pressure you,' she interrupts, 'I just thought you needed a push.' A pause before she continues thoughtfully, 'But you really just need to, I don't know . . .' her voice trails off. 'Take the cheque. I'll see it as a high-risk investment.'

I swallow back a sudden lump in my throat. Her gesture touches me deeply. This was not meant to happen. Larry had advised me to cut loose. He might be a bit mad when I tell him I hadn't the heart or the will to refuse her. But I don't have to tell him, do I? 'That's so nice,' I say softly.

'It is,' she retorts. 'I don't normally do this but you have a certain spark about you that I think will translate well when you start to paint for real. Take it.'

Three thousand will help a lot, I think as I reach for the cheque. And there's no pressure to paint. And even though I feel more like a fraud than ever, her belief in me is touching. 'Thanks.'

'Now go. I'm going out in an hour and I've to get ready. There's a Ben Nicholson coming up for auction in London this week. I'm flying over to see it.'

'OK. Well, good luck.'

'And to you too.'

With that, I am dismissed.

I walk out into the dour-looking day, kicking myself for not being able to refuse her and yet consoled by her belief in me. Maybe when I come back from Florida, I'll need some sort of an ambition because, right now, I just can't see myself going back to the copies. It's become impossible to walk in Van Gogh's shoes these past few weeks, especially when I feel that I've cheated the poor man. I'm sure he's turning in his grave at the thought that I had the cheek to emulate him. I fear, however, that the gap between fakes and originals will be a bit too big for me to bridge and that, on my return, I might fall down in the cracks and never be seen again. Better not to think about it.

Hopping into my car, I drive across town to meet my mother and Robert for a farewell lunch. I've told them both that I'm going on a residency to Paris to try to get inspiration. Which I think they both know to be untrue, though neither of them will say it. Later on, I'm meeting Olivia and everyone for a quick drink.

I have an urge to connect with them all before leaving, just in case I end up in a Florida jail and don't see them for years and years. Larry laughed when I told him, but when I suggested to him that maybe he should do it, he got a bit cross and told me not to be so melodramatic. It's hard to know how I feel about Larry now. He seems to have shed his nice-neighbour-next-door skin and morphed into a man who is at ease with lying and setting up fake identities and websites.

The first time I met him, I thought I was seeing a glimpse of heaven. An Adonis in faded denim, achingly handsome, asking to borrow a screwdriver. I didn't have a screwdriver so I lent him a knife. An hour later, he returned my knife along with the present of a screwdriver and I invited him in for a coffee. Who wouldn't have? As I made us a cuppa, hardly able to believe my luck at having such a view across the hall, he admired my paintings. And so it grew. Him having coffee, me drooling. Him attending the Party People's parties, me drooling. It was pure lust and it felt great. There was something about him that stopped me from wanting him properly though.

After about four months of surface chit-chat, he blurted out that he'd been in jail. I don't remember how the subject came up, but the hesitant, ashamed way he confessed won me over. His inability to look me in the eye melted my heart. A poor broken man, how much sexier could he get? When I asked him what he'd done, he'd brushed it aside with 'not murder or GBH or possession of a firearm or anything violent like that'.

I took it that he'd wanted it to remain private and didn't ask again. Once he was OK to me, I figured I should mind my own business. But now, well, he's not as broken as he first appeared. In fact, the only thing that's broken is my head. It's melted from confusion. The Larry that I thought I knew is not the one that is organising this scheme. His keenness for the plan scares me a little. I do know I need him. I do know that I'll never get the painting back without him and I'm grateful to him for bothering, but I'm uneasy with his unbridled enthusiasm for it all.

I locate a parking space across from the restaurant where I'm meeting my mother and vow not to think of Larry any more. The funny thing is that when I'm with him, the doubts vanish – a smile, a word, a reassuring gesture is all it takes. And I have to trust him, that's the deal. That's what he insisted on.

And so I will.

Kind of.

Meeting my mother and Robbie for dinner proved to be a lot more stressful than I'd anticipated. Though reluctant to say it outright, it was very clear that neither of them believed that I was going to an artist's retreat in Paris for a couple of weeks. But because Robert had taken it upon himself to invite Denise to the gathering, my mother couldn't delve too deeply into what I might be doing in Paris. When Denise asked me what I was planning, I lied and told her that I was going to paint original paintings because I was trying to get away from the whole Van Gogh thing, to which she uttered the worst sentence she ever could have, 'Oh, Eve, you shouldn't give up painting the fakes, they look so real.'

My mother and Robert both stiffened up like the bristles on a hedgehog and my mother had to leave the table, only to return with a tissue pressed to her eyes.

All in all, a great success.

So, as I squeeze in beside Olivia and our friends for my farewell drink, I'm feeling just a teeny bit rattled. I know I'm going to have to lie to them again and I really don't like it. But at least Olivia knows so she can help me out. The usual six people are here. Olivia, who looks gorgeous, her red hair piled high, little tendrils of it sneaking down to caress her face; Eric, looking way too young to be with her; Laura, June and David, who looks better than ever and who makes a point of moving up for me and letting me squeeze in beside him. Then without having to ask, in the manner of a professional magician, he produces a neat whiskey and places it, with a flourish, in front of me. 'Got it in advance,' he smiles, showing a dimple in his left cheek.

He looks pretty damn good, I have to admit, a gorgeous blue and white shirt over dark denims. His face has the chiselled look of a *Thunderbirds* character, but in a good way. And the fact that he always remembers my favourite drink is a big plus in his favour.

'Thank you,' I smile at him, picking up the glass and letting the amber drink slide down my throat slowly, burning its way into my stomach. God, how I love it. 'I needed that,' I say with so much conviction that he looks a little startled. 'Not in an alcoholic way,' I clarify with a laugh.

He smiles too and despite Olivia telling me that he's shy, his smile has a wickedness about it that promises a lot of fun. He angles himself towards me. He's the biggest guy at the table, probably the biggest guy in the pub. Larry, with his toned runner's physique, is only half his size. David's throat looks so kissable. 'So,' his eyes linger on my face in quite a delicious way, 'you're going away to paint for two weeks.'

'Yep.' Aware that he is watching me, I try to avoid slugging back my whiskey, opting instead to sip it delicately, which isn't half as nice. I hope he won't ask me anything else about my trip, I really don't want to lie any more.

'I'm so glad you're taking the Della Sweeney commission so seriously,' Olivia says loudly, sensing my discomfort. 'It could be a whole new career for you if she likes your stuff.'

I smile, trying desperately to think of a rejoinder. My mind is blank. A bit like my canvases.

'Talking about a whole new career,' June pipes up, 'I got a job.'

Everyone turns to congratulate her. I'm relieved the spotlight is off me.

'It's nothing brilliant,' June confesses. 'It's in a sandwich bar.'

'Making the sandwiches?' David asks.

'No,' June grins, 'I have to rollerblade around the city with a haversack of sandwich orders.'

'On, like, skates?' Eric asks, wide-eyed.

June nods. 'Yeah, wearing a cheerleader's costume.'

No one quite knows what to say to that.

'It'll keep you fit,' David says eventually.

'I didn't know you could rollerblade,' Laura sounds impressed.

'Well, I can't actually,' June makes a face. 'I just rip off the skates and run like mad.'

I laugh so hard I forget why I'm here for just the tiniest second. A little sliver of my old life and it feels good.

'Can I get you another drink?' David asks some time later, when the lights in the place have dimmed and the music has stopped and the end of the night seems to be calling. I notice, somewhat blearily, that his body is closer to mine than it was, that his leg is touching the top of my thigh, that his face, as he offers me another drink, is inches from mine.

I pause for a second, wondering if he will say anything else. He's so close that his warm breath fans my face. His blue twinkly eyes meet mine, then, surprisingly, a slow flush spreads across his cheeks.

'Are you sure that it's just a drink you're offering me?' I tease.

He blinks, startled, and draws back slightly. I wonder if I have ruined my chances. But then he gives the slowest, softest, sexiest grin I have ever seen. 'Am I that obvious?' he asks, wincing.

'No,' I shake my head, feeling a bit mean for embarrassing him, and wanting him to go on smiling that smile, 'it was just a joke.'

'Oh,' he pauses, seems to take a deep breath and then says in a sort of a rush, 'because, I have to say,' he moves in closer again, lowering his voice so that the others won't hear, though out of the corner of my eye I can see Olivia nudging Eric, 'I think that, you're one of the most, well, nicest girls I've ever met.'

The sincerity of the compliment wins me over completely. 'Aw, thanks.'

Another smile, his dimple flashing in and out. 'And, you know, I don't want you to go falling for some Frenchman—'

'I won't,' I can't help my big grin now. He's actually going to ask me out.

'You might.'

Seeing as I'm going to Florida, that would be hard, but I just ask, 'And what if I do? What if some hunky Parisian caught my eye?'

'I'd be kinda kicking myself that I was too chicken to ask you out before this.'

'You would?'

'Uh-huh. So, eh, would you be interested in, you know, going out with me sometime?'

I can't help my delighted smile. Don't want to, in fact. 'I think I might, yeah.'

'Sometime soon?'

'Sometime very soon.'

David grins. 'Great, brilliant. That's great, Eve.' A pause. 'So, eh, maybe I should take your number?'

'That would probably help you contact me all right,' I laugh.

'Hurray!' Olivia cheers. 'He's actually done it, Eric. David has done it!'

David flushes and looks up. 'Were you listening?' he asks indignantly.

'Only a little,' Olivia grins, giving me a smug I-told-you-so look.

'Go get your own life and stop ear-wigging on mine,' I joke to her.

'Well said, Eve,' David laughs and whips out a pretty fancy iPhone and rapidly punches in the number I call out.

'I'll probably be out of contact for a couple of weeks,' I warn him hastily, not wanting him to ring when I'm buying back a forged painting. 'So, when I get back, call me and we'll meet up.'

'I can't wait,' he says with such honestly in his voice that I like him even more. Then he leans across and places a soft kiss on my cheek.

My insides fizzle.

17

We don't travel together or arrange to meet in the airport the following morning. Larry thinks it'll be better that way. He says if he's caught using his brother's passport and I'm with him then I'll be in trouble too. That's very noble, I think, but I feel guilty that he's taking the risk for me. And while he has said that he needs the excitement, I'm not quite sure it's the kind of excitement he should be aiming for. Nevertheless, I agree to his terms.

Still, not being with him, I worry in case he oversleeps or doesn't turn up at all and I find myself in a strange country, having hired a monster car, not at all sure what to do. There's also the small matter of him having four thousand of my dollars in his possession. Yes, I trust him, but it still niggles, how easily he could just disappear with it. Am I mad?

I enter the airport terminal, find my check-in area and join the queue. It's quite a long one. I can't see Larry in front and, as I move nearer the top and other people join the queue, I can't see him behind me either. He has told me not to ring him, so I can't even call his mobile to see if he's on his way.

Five minutes later, and still no sign. There are five people in the queue in front of me and if I check in, there's no going back. I glance behind. Nothing.

Up at the top, a blond man is talking to the check-in lady. She's laughing at something he's said and the man's bags are tagged and they trundle off to wherever bags go. Four more people in front of me. The blond man turns and I catch a glimpse of profile.

My God.

I do a double take. It's him. Larry. He's had his hair cropped and dyed. I watch in fascination as he pockets his passport and boarding card and, holding a small carry-on bag, heads towards the boarding gates.

The relief is instant as my legs almost buckle. He's here. He was actually here before me. And I didn't see him scanning the queue for me. All I want now is to check in and grab a cup of strong tea.

Many hours later, we start our descent into Orlando airport. Then the pilot announces that because of bad weather conditions, he can't land just yet.

'Bad weather conditions?' I yelp without meaning to. 'What does that mean?'

The American beside me points out my window, saying, 'Storm. Happens most days here. It'll be gone in an hour.'

I had noticed the rain but it's only now that the lightning seems to join in. In the flashes, I see all the other aircraft circling about like electronic vultures in the sky. In and out and in and out. My stomach muscles clench. What if a strong gust of wind blew us off course? What if our wing tip touched another plane's wing tip? What if lightning strikes us?

I close my eyes. I can't afford to panic over every little thing. I have to pretend to be calm if nothing else and this will be good practice.

'Nervous, huh?' the American asks.

'Not at all. I'm just anxious to get off the plane, stretch the legs.'

'O-kay,' he says in a tone that lets me know he doesn't believe me. He pulls a little bottle of whiskey from his pocket. 'You feel you want some, you just ask.'

'I might have a sip,' I say.

He hands me the bottle and, without thinking about it, I lift it to my lips and take a glug. And then another. He looks at me in amusement. 'You sure are a calm one,' he grins.

I smile back, nice hot whiskey burning its way down my gullet.

He closes the bottle and tucks it back into his jacket.

Endless minutes later, the pilot announces that we're going to land and I start praying to God in my head.

And he's listening, because we land safely.

I spot Larry in the queue in front of me at passport control. He's chatting to a couple who look as if they are on their honeymoon, the way they touch each other and smile into each other's eyes and laugh at what the other has to say. Larry is smiling along with them and seems to be advising them about where to go as he has a map in his hand and is jabbing at various points on it. They nod vigorously and look gratefully at him. Then someone else behind joins in the discussion and soon a whole host of people, as far as I can make out from my vantage point, are asking Larry for advice on what to see. I hadn't known he was here before, he'd never said.

Some queues seem to move more quickly than others and the trick is spotting the fastest one. One or two people are asked to accompany staff to a holding room where their passports are checked out. I watch anxiously as Larry gets to the top. He's chosen a female but she is resistant to his charms. She doesn't even raise a smile at him and he stands obediently in front of her as she checks him out, before waving him on.

I get through no problem and follow everyone else. We collect our bags, catch a shuttle to the other side of the airport and again I wait in line to pick up my monster car. It's about midnight back home, yet it's only seven in the evening here. I don't feel tired at all. My head is buzzing. Despite the fact that I'm here to buy back my painting, I'm a little excited too because I've never been to America before; what with Dad being so sick for years, I just never went anywhere really.

A year after he died, Mam sold up and we both moved out and, because I bought at the height of the property boom, I never had any spare money for travel. I am going to enjoy this, I decide suddenly. Yep, it'll be stressful but there is bound to be some good I can take away with me. The girl in front of me peels open a

Hershey bar. Oh, how American. Another little buzz of excitement.

The car queue moves very slowly. Once again I wonder where Larry is, but I know he'll find me. I didn't even spot him on the flight, he was so good at concealing himself.

Finally, I'm at the Hertz desk and I hand in my passport and driver's licence and am given the keys to the car with instructions on how to find it. The girl might as well be talking in Greek for all I follow. I have to ask her to repeat it and it's then I realise that I am tired. I pick up my bags and the keys and turn to go, when from nowhere, Larry pops up.

'Can I help you with those?' he asks.

'Oh, thanks.' Immediate relief.

Larry has donned a cap. He keeps his head dipped. It's so he won't be recognised later on camera, I think immediately.

Together we head out of the airport into the day.

And it's as if I've just walked into a concrete wall of heat. A very heavy, very humid, wall of heat. The kind you find in swimming pools, only a million times worse. 'Oh, God,' I turn to Larry. 'This is incredible.'

'I'd take off the coat if I were you,' Larry grins, 'or you'll collapse.'

I do as he suggests and, following behind Larry, who seems totally familiar with the place, we soon end up beside a massive car. I don't even know what make it is, but I feel with a sinking heart that all my holiday money will be used up in feeding it petrol.

'I am liking your style,' Larry says in a faux-American accent as he walks around the car.

'Well, I hope I'm going to be liking your driving,' I say back, tossing him the keys, which he deftly catches, 'because there is no way I'm going near that hulk of a thing.'

He catches the keys and unlocks the doors. I hop into the passenger seat. Larry takes a second to worship the interior before firing the engine. 'It's an automatic,' he says, 'I love those.' The car starts with a purr and as smooth as melted chocolate. Larry drives it out of the space and into the day. 'See if you can find the air con,' he says. 'It'll cool us down.'

I fiddle about with a few buttons but to no avail. This car looks like NASA control.

'Little hint,' Larry glances at me in amusement, 'it probably is a button marked "AC".'

I press the button and the temperature lights up. I press an arrow to adjust it. It's pretty impressive. Well, I suppose after my fifteen-year-old banger, anything would be.

'Nice,' Larry bathes his face in the coolness now coming from the heater. 'So, were you OK on the plane?'

'Yep. Where were you sitting? I couldn't see you.'

'In business class. They upgraded me.'

'No way!'

'Uh-huh.' He smiles at my incredulous face.

'How'd you manage that?'

'Mostly with a smile.'

I don't know whether to believe him. 'You didn't pay?'

'Now that would be defeating the purpose,' he snorts, his eyes on the road. We're still navigating the enormous airport.

'So, you just, what, smiled at her? What did you say?'

'Nothing. I asked were there any business seats free, she said yes, told me which ones and I declined them all. And then, when I got on the plane I just sat in business class.'

'You can't do that!'

He looks at me in amusement. I think he's laughing at my naivety. 'You can if you hold up the plane and they're anxious to get going. I just sat down and acted like I belonged there.'

'But they must have checked your boarding card.'

He shrugs. 'They were on a timetable.'

'I don't get it.'

A pause. He bites his lip, not really smiling now. 'Nah, you wouldn't,' is all he says.

I leave it at that. I cannot believe while I was stuck with plastic spoons and forks he was living it up in business class.

I look out the car window. It feels weird to be driving on the other side of the road. The day has grown brighter now, the storm having passed. The sky is turning dark quite rapidly though and the sun has all but set, though the car tells us that the humidity outside is hitting seventy-five per cent. We're on a freeway now and, to my absolute delight, it's everything I imagined America to be. Big wide roads with palm trees down the centre and lining the sides, big cars and trucks, flashing neon signs advertising motels and places to eat. There aren't many footpaths and only the odd pedestrian light. It'd take at least a week to walk across the roads because they're so enormous. Everywhere I see diners and clothes stores. I spot a Denny's and an Applebees and vow to eat there once we settle in.

Larry seems to know where he is going. He drives confidently, not too fast but not hesitating either.

'Where are we going?' I ask.

'I checked online and thought we might get a villa about twenty minutes out.'

'Oh look, Disney World!' I shriek, making him swerve, as I point to a sign hanging over the freeway. 'Look!'

'I checked online and thought we might get a villa about twenty minutes away,' Larry repeats.

'Oops, sorry,' I'm barely listening. Disney World. I've always wanted to go there.

'We probably won't have time for Disney World,' Larry says like a cross parent. 'We're here on a mission, remember?'

A mission. I sigh like a bold child, watching the signs for Disney World disappear like a mirage in the desert. But he's right of course. 'A villa?' I ask, attempting to sound interested, my heart flip-flopping in panic as the reason for us being here crashes back in.

'Uh-huh. The keys are at a check-in box in a hotel and we pick them up with directions to the villa. Keep an eye out.' He gives me the name of the hotel.

'Is this expensive?' I think of my small stash of cash.

'Nah, cheaper than a motel. It gives us privacy too. Now keep a look out.'

About ten minutes later we've spotted the hotel, located the keys and are on our way to the villa.

It's dark now but there are plenty of lights on the road and from diners.

'Hungry?' Larry asks.

'A bit. Why?'

'It's just you've eyed up every restaurant we've passed with a sort of ravenous look on your face. D'you want to stop in and grab a bite?'

'Can we go to an Applebees?'

His answer is a loud laugh.

We eat in companionable silence and I sense that Larry is as tired as I am. He probably just wants to get where we are going and then crash out. 'So where is this villa?' I ask as the waitress delivers our bill.

'Not far now. I think you'll like it, it has a pool.'

'A pool?' I wince. 'But I didn't bring any swimwear.'

'So much the better,' Larry grins. He picks up the bill and announces that dinner is on him. I follow him to the till and he manages to confuse the poor cashier by asking for change and paying at the same time. She begins to get flustered and Larry calms her down so that, by the time we leave, she has promised to keep us an extra big slice of pie for our next visit.

We hop into the car and, fifteen minutes later, just as we're turning into the driveway of what seems to be a gated housing estate which I am admiring and getting a little excited about staying in, it strikes me what Larry has done. 'You short-changed that waitress,' I gasp out. 'You asked her for change and then you confused her, so she gave you back more than she should have.'

'Really?' Larry frowns. He seems to have a think about it himself before shaking his head. 'Nah.'

'Yes,' I nod. 'See what you did was—' I don't get a chance to finish because Larry pulls the car to a stop outside a fairly big-looking villa. Then he hops out and calls, 'Come on in, Eve, let's see what sort of a place we have here.' He lopes up the short driveway and unlocks the front door.

I follow him. 'What you did was you asked for— Oh, my God. Oh, wow, Larry, it's great.'

The villa is gorgeous. Two storeys, detached, with a small front garden. As I step inside, the blast of the air conditioning hits me like the deliciousness of a cool glass of water in the heat. There's a fairly decent open-plan kitchen and living room. In the living room, which is decorated in terracotta and a mellow yellow, there is a huge television and a massive comfortable-looking sofa with copious cushions. Patio doors from the kitchen open out onto a kidney-shaped pool, which is glimmering under pool lights. There is a mesh-like structure built all around the pool so that it's protected from all sorts of horrible insects. Off the living room, down a corridor is a laundry room with the biggest washing machine I have ever seen. There are three bedrooms, all fairly big, one on the ground floor and two upstairs. Two of them are en-suite and the en-suites are bigger than my kitchen at home. In fact, the whole place is bigger than Larry's and my apartments combined.

I love it.

'Nice eh?' Larry says as, after our tour, he stands appreciatively in the middle of the living room.

'Great. It's great.' I plonk down onto the sofa and sink right into it. Oh, I love sofas. And cushions.

And then the oddness of the situation takes me by surprise. Here I am in the middle of Florida with a guy I hardly know, sharing a villa. I start to laugh a little. Larry looks at me for a second before asking why I'm laughing.

'I don't quite know,' I chortle. 'This' – I gesture around – 'is so bizarre and yet, it makes sense. D'you know what I mean?'

'Not a clue,' Larry says, making me laugh more.

Then, to my alarm, he whips off his T-shirt.

Six-pack heaven. I gulp back my laughter, my eyes transfixed.

'Last one to the pool makes breakfast in the morning,' he grins, making a dash for the door.

Two seconds later, he has plunged into the pool in his jeans.

I decide to be the one to make breakfast, but then he jumps out, sopping wet, squelchy feet making puddles in the kitchen and across the tiled living room floor. He grabs my hand and drags me in, kicking and screaming. We spend the next glorious worry-free half hour splashing about like two kids.

18

It takes a couple of seconds the next morning for me to remember where I am. I opted for the downstairs bedroom purely because I did not want us running into each other half-dressed. Besides trying to stop my eyes from popping out of my head, I figured that while he might look good with his top off, I wasn't so sure that I would.

The heat wakes me. The sun is pouring through the light blinds, making the room hot and bright. I turn over in bed, sticky with sweat and suddenly, because I'm looking at a fully furnished room, I realise I'm somewhere strange. And then I remember. Sitting up abruptly, I glance at the small alarm clock I've brought with me. Ten o'clock. From the kitchen, I hear a kettle boiling and Larry humming a pop tune as he potters about. Sliding quietly out of bed, I grab a quick shower before pulling on a pair of shorts and a T-shirt. It feels so good to wear summer clothes. My hair is still wet as I join Larry in the kitchen for breakfast.

'Coffee in the pot,' he calls as he slides open the patio door and takes a seat at the poolside patio table.

I pour myself a cup and join him. There is no food in the presses, only coffee and tea.

'We have to do a shop,' I say.

He nods.

The air is hot and heavy, lying like a thick blanket around our shoulders. I'm glad of the mesh structure around the pool as, outside, a small lizard-like creature is climbing up and down, looking for a way in.

'Did you sleep well?' Larry asks.

'Yeah, I was wrecked. You?'

'Not bad.' He takes a sip of coffee. 'Don't forget to ring home today.'

'I won't.'

He looks about, then lowers his voice, 'We need to talk about tonight,' he half-whispers. 'About what we're going to do.'

His words make me freeze, the cup halfway to my mouth. I take a deep breath, force myself to sip some coffee, then I say with as much confidence as I can, 'I'm Evelyn Coleman, you're Michael Shanagher. I work for Della Sweeney and you are my buyer.'

'That's right,' Larry nods. 'And just so you won't be too easily recognised I took the liberty of bringing a wig for you.'

'A wig?' I gawk at him. 'What sort of a wig?'

'I told you about it already. A wig that goes on your head?'

I'm forced to smile. 'You told me to get my hair cut when I get back, surely that'll do.'

'I don't think it will. Everyone back home knows you with long hair. I'm not saying that the police at home will be looking for you after this, but better safe than sorry. So I got you a blonde wig, longer than your own hair, which should transform you.' He studies me critically. 'It'll add years to you.'

'Oh gee, thanks.'

'And another thing,' he says, 'whatever I say, you go along with, no arguments. I reckon this guy will try to charge us a fortune for the painting. He probably reckons it's gone way up in price.'

'We can't promise what we don't have.' This is the bit that's been worrying me. What if I can't afford the bloody thing? What then?

'Well, in this case, we will promise it and we'll see how it all pans out. It's all about rolling with whatever happens and adapting. We—' he stops abruptly as a couple with a young child make an appearance poolside in the villa next door.

Their little girl, who looks so cute in a frilly pink bathing suit and high pigtails, has a rubber ring around her waist and she gleefully jumps into the water, shrieking with delight.

Her mother and father watch her indulgently.

'She's enjoying that,' I call out and they turn to me, smiling.

'Yes, she is,' the mother says, setting down a bowl of cereal on her patio table. She sounds English. 'You two on holidays then?'

'We are,' Larry nods a goodbye as he gets up and walks back inside.

'Irish, eh?' the man asks, sitting alongside his wife.

I'm clever enough not to tell the truth. 'Yes, we're from Cork. We came to get away from all the rain.'

'Us too. Have you ever been here before?'

'No, first time. I can't wait to see Disney World.'

'Oh, you'll love it,' the woman says as she pulls off her T-shirt to reveal a black bikini top and a deep tan. She hands a tube of sun cream to her husband and he starts to rub it into her back. 'Millie had a great time there, didn't you darling?'

Millie looks up. 'Mickey Mouse,' she shrieks.

They turn and smile at her again.

I think the conversation has run its course and, my coffee finished, I hop onto the sun lounger and close my eyes.

'What are your names, then?' the woman asks. 'I'm Valerie and this is my husband Peter.'

'Well, I'm—' I pause. Should I say Eve? Or Evelyn? Or other names entirely? I open my mouth but nothing comes out. The two look curiously at me.

'Honey, can you help me with this please?' Larry. Thank God.

'Oh that's, eh, himself calling,' I hop up quickly and shrug. 'Men, totally useless.' I scurry inside, glad to get away.

Larry is standing by the cooker, his arms folded and his face like thunder. 'Never ever talk to anyone you don't need to talk to,' he hisses. 'What are you trying to do, eh?'

'It's called being friendly,' I say belligerently.

'Eve,' he crosses towards me, his hands grasp my arms gently as he looks into my face, 'you do realise that we really don't need anyone recognising us. We can't afford to get friendly with too many people.'

'I just said hello to them,' I mutter, knowing though that he is right. 'It'd have looked odd if I hadn't.'

'And what were you going to say our names were?' He quirks his eyebrows, mockingly.

'I dunno, I was going to say you were called Grumpy Bastard, but I don't think that's a real name.'

Despite his frown, his eyes crinkle up slightly.

'So what will I say if they ask again?'

He lets go of my arms and turns away. 'Let's hope they won't but if they do, tell them something you'll remember.'

'Olivia and Eric?'

He stares at me.

'That's the name of my best friend and her boyfriend.'

'Fine. Let's hope we don't see them again. Now, come upstairs with me and we'll try on this wig.'

I follow him to his room. His case is dumped in the middle of the floor and an assortment of T-shirts and shorts spill out. A suit is hanging from the handle of his wardrobe. An unopened laptop is sitting on the dressing table. The photo of the little girl that I saw that day in his apartment is placed on the bedside table facing his bed. Again, I wonder who she is.

Larry coughs and I wrench my gaze away from the photo to see him holding up a long blonde wig which he must have taken from his case. His fingers brush through the strands of hair, straightening them before he holds it out to me. 'OK, try it,' he says.

I bunch my hair up and Larry gently lowers the hairpiece into place. He spends a few minutes adjusting it, before standing back and nodding. 'It might have been made for you,' he says. 'Tonight we'll secure it a lot better, but, for now, have a dekko.' He indicates the full-length mirror on the door and I turn to look, the hair swishing about my shoulders.

Oh, God, if I'd ever thought of going blonde, I never will now. The thing is horrendous. It washes out my skin and I look haggard. 'No one would ever wear their hair this colour on purpose if it made them look as awful as me,' I gasp, dismayed.

'Evelyn Coleman would,' Larry pronounces. 'She's consumed by art and her appearance doesn't bother her that much.'

I gawk at him.

'So she wears clothes that don't particularly do much for her.'

'I have a nice dress all picked out for tonight,' I tell him sternly and then realise that when my hair was its lovely auburn, it was nice. It mightn't be so cool against the blonde hair. In fact, I know it'll look atrocious. 'You'd imagine I'd know about colour if I was into art,' I say then.

'Wouldn't you?' Larry nods. 'Only thing is Evelyn Coleman is blind.'

'What? You're not serious? I'm not going to pretend to be blind.'

'Gotcha,' Larry winks.

'Fecker!' I fire one of his T-shirts at him.

He catches it and laughs. Then, as I turn again to look at myself, I spot make-up on the corner of his dressing table and it's my turn to laugh. 'What is that?' I hold up a concealer and a lipstick and some brushes.

Larry holds his wrist to me. 'Gone.'

It takes me a second to realise that his tattoo has disappeared. 'Wow,' I examine his wrist. 'Good work.'

Then he eyes my ankle bracelet tattoo. 'You'll have to do yours too, but first, a little quiz. Now remember, whatever you do, whatever information you give, remember it. So, you are going to tell me all about yourself and this is the story you stick to no matter what happens. Have you thought about it?'

I nod. He'd told me to write a biography for Evelyn Coleman and it had been quite fun, inventing a persona for myself.

'Off you go,' Larry, unsettlingly enough, lies back against his pillows, arms behind his head, his T-shirt riding up and giving me a glimpse of his flat stomach.

I have to swallow first to compose myself. 'Right, Evelyn Coleman is twenty-eight years of age—'

'She looks older,' Larry remarks, 'and I do not want her being the same age as Eve Cole.'

'How old do I look?'

'At least thirty-five,' Larry says, scrutinising me, 'maybe older.'

'Evelyn Coleman is thirty-four years of age.' I stress the 'four' and he smiles a little. 'She likes art, particularly Van Gogh. Ten years ago, her aunt made a bid for the Van Gogh portrait and lost out to Mr Anderson. Now she's hoping to buy it for Della Sweeney again. It would give Della a portrait by most artists of that era.'

'Really?' Larry asks speculatively, 'What ones has she got?'

I rattle off a list of paintings.

'And the real owners can't be checked out on Google?'

'Nope.' I'm proud of that. 'It only lists the buyers as private.'

'And Derek Anderson wouldn't know anyone with any of these portraits?'

I pause. Shrug.

'No, you and your aunt want it because you love Van Gogh. That's all. Don't complicate it.'

'Fine,' I say with slightly bad grace.

'Go on,' Larry says.

I tell him where Evelyn Coleman went to school, who her first boyfriend was, what her first job entailed and finally how she ended up working for her aunt Della. And how she's long been associated with Shanagher galleries and of how wonderful Michael is at sourcing paintings.

'What paintings has he found for you?'

I name a few obscure paintings and Larry asks a few questions about them, committing them to memory.

'And where did he get them?'

Again I make up plausible stories and, again, Larry repeats them back to me.

I finish and a slow smile spreads across Larry's face.

I find myself smiling back at him and I don't know why. 'What?' I ask.

He begins to clap. 'You beauty.'

'Eh, not with this hair, I'm not,' I pull it off and shake my own hair free. 'So I'll pass, will I?'

'You will, if you don't get nervous.' A pause, 'You won't get nervous, will you?'

That's a laugh. I'll be petrified. 'No,' I lie. And that gives me confidence because I sound convincing.

'You have to act like you belong,' he says earnestly. 'So where are you staying, Evelyn Coleman?'

'I've rented a villa in Hanes City.'

'Nope,' Larry says, 'You have not! Your aunt has booked the Embassy Suites on Lake Street for you. It's an expensive place.'

'But will we not get caught out? They might follow us or anything. They might try to contact us there?'

Larry half-laughs as he hauls himself to a sitting position on the bed. 'They won't. We're buying a painting, not setting up a huge drug deal. It's important they believe we have money. So, here,' he pulls out photographs of the Embassy Suites and tells me to study them. 'We'll go there for tea this evening, before the charity event,' he tells me. 'It'll be fresh in your mind and that way you'll really know what you're talking about.'

I pick up the paintings and say, 'But if we offer to buy the painting, people are going to believe we have money anyway.'

'It always helps to build the illusion,' Larry says. Then, biggest surprise of all, he slips a wedding ring on his finger. 'And, eh, I'm married by the way. I have a little girl who's three and her name is Carly. I dote on her.'

'Oh. Why?'

'Because Derek's grandchild is the exact same age and he dotes on her. Nothing like a bit of bonding.'

That, of everything we've discussed, makes me the most uneasy. 'That's not very nice, pretending to have a child just to fool someone.'

Larry says nothing. How could I ever have thought that he was shy and vulnerable?

'Larry? Did you hear me? I said—'

'I heard you. You can walk away if you like.' His voice is flat. He stands up. 'It's your choice, Eve. I'm not forcing you. Don't blame me for wanting this to succeed.'

And he's right. I *am* trying to blame him. I'm trying to make myself feel better by making out that this is all his doing. But the truth is, I want that painting and I will die to get it back and he knows that. 'Sorry,' I mutter. 'You're right.'

He accepts my apology with a nod of his head before tousling my hair. 'One thing,' he says softly as he pins me with a look from his massive grey eyes, 'don't let this change you. Do it, get the painting and then move on, I like you the way you are.'

But his words make me realise that of course doing this will change me, I know it will, just like selling the painting in the first place must have changed Robert and my dad.

19

At five that evening, two hours before we head to the Embassy Suites for a cuppa, I ring my mother. It's midday back home and I know she'll be anxiously waiting for my call. She picks up on the first ring.

'Hello? Hello? Eve, is that you?'

'Hi, Mam, how's things?'

'Are you all right? I tried ringing you earlier but there was no answer.'

I'd told her not to ring. She sounds really stressed. 'I was working, Mam. I have my phone off. It's that kind of place. Anyway, I told you not to bother, that I would ring you.'

'Well, what did you expect me to do? All that bad weather. How are you?'

'Fantastic,' I answer. 'I'm getting loads of work done and everyone is really nice. I'm even getting a tan.'

There is a silence from her end of the phone. 'A tan?' she finally says. Then adds, 'You don't have to protect me, Eve. I saw it on the news.'

'Sorry?'

'The storms in Paris! They're flooded out. The worst weather in over a hundred years.'

Shit! Typical. 'Well,' I say hesitantly, 'that's true, but it's warm here all the same.'

'You're hardly out in it!' She's hyperventilating now. 'Eve, you have to stay indoors. No one should be out in weather like that.'

'Well, I'm in now,' I splutter. 'I'm fine now. The rain is pretty heavy but we're on a hill here so there's no chance of any damage, don't worry.' Is the retreat on a hill, I wonder? She'd hardly google it, will she? Still, there's nothing I can do about it now.

'You should get the first plane back. I'm not happy about this.'

'Look, I swear I'm fine. Anyway, the planes won't take off in bad weather, will they?'

'Hmm.'

'And I'm getting loads of work done and the other artists are so friendly. You have no need to worry.' I change the subject before I give myself away. 'Now, have you any news there?'

She digests the fact that I seem to be fully alive before answering, 'Well, yes, as it happens.' She gives a little cough and says, 'Liam asked me to the pictures yesterday. And, well, I said yes. And we're going tonight.'

'Who's Liam?'

'Liam!' my mother says again as if it's obvious. 'You met him, that day in my apartment. He's in my book club.'

'The bald guy? Sort of drippy?'

'He's not drippy,' she sounds annoyed. 'He's a very clever man, you'd really like him.'

'He's taking you to the cinema?' That's weird I think. 'Why?'

'Why do you think?' my mother's laugh tinkles like a bell. 'He likes me. He likes my company.'

'Oh.' It comes out sounding surprised, shocked and disapproving all at the same time. God, I hope she doesn't like him.

'Thanks.' And she sounds miffed.

'Well, I hope you enjoy it.' Not, I want to add childishly.

'I'm sure I will. It's a French film, set in Paris,' she laughs gaily, 'so, Eve, I'll be reminded of you when I watch it. And it's about the underbelly of society or something like that. It'll be subtitled.'

She'll hate it, I think cheerily. My mother likes romantic films where the end is predictable and everyone is happy. Underbellies of society will not appeal to her. Or to anyone, I shouldn't think, unless you happen to be called Liam and read pretentious books.

'Well, have a ball,' I say to her. 'Don't worry about me. I'll send you a text tomorrow around the same time and I'll ring you the next day, OK?'

'OK.'

'Love you.'

'And I love you too,' she says with feeling, 'so take care. And I hope you really are—'

'Oh, the weather's affecting the phone. Can't hear you. Bye. Love you.' And I hang up.

Two hours later, I'm in my blonde wig, looking awful, despite the dress and the snazzy shoes. The dress is a nude colour, so crap with fair hair unless I happen to look like Cameron Diaz, which I most definitely do not. It's mid-length and flips out at the end. The only thing in its favour is that it shows off my figure. My shoes are dark brown, high and shiny with a bow that ties around the back instead of a strap. They are killer heels and not in a good way. My feet are crucified in them and I haven't even walked anywhere yet. To top all that, my make-up is doing nothing for me.

Larry is delighted. 'You're not bad looking in real life,' he announces approvingly, 'but, as Evelyn, you're not the best.'

I bristle, but can see the sense in his words. He, however, looks way better than in real life. I've always been a bit of a sucker for a man in a suit and Larry wears his grey two-piece with distinction. His dazzling white shirt and skinny grey tie give the impression that this man is a bit of a dynamo. Even his blond hair, which isn't as nice as his dark hair, doesn't detract from the mesmerising quality of his eyes and face. He's a fine thing altogether.

'Now,' Larry takes a look out the front window, 'we can't let the smug marrieds next door see us.'

'Valerie and Peter,' I correct.

'They'll wonder why you're suddenly blonde.' He seems satisfied that the street is deserted, so he tells me to wait inside until he has the car opened. He dashes out, unlocks the car and then I hurriedly follow him, having first locked up the villa.

I navigate our way to the hotel as Larry drives. It's only when we finally arrive at the imposing entrance bearing the words 'Embassy Suites' on a large white rock at the beginning of an imposing driveway that I finally look up from the map. 'Oh, wow,' I peer like a kid out the window as we near the building. This place is worth a visit.

Larry pulls the car to a stop in front of the entrance and I step out. A valet appears as if by magic and Larry hands him the car keys. Behind us another car pulls up, not as swanky a vehicle as our own, and another valet materialises.

Larry, his palm lightly on the small of my back, propels me quickly inside where I gasp at the pain in my feet and at the sheer size of the luxurious marble foyer. I'm like a kid in Willy Wonka's chocolate factory as I take it all in. We enter a bar and Larry orders us both a coffee.

We sip our drinks in silence, me because I'm trying to remember everything about this place and because I'm trembling inside thinking about what lies ahead. I suspect Larry just likes silence. He never seems to feel the need to keep a conversation going. After about twenty minutes, when we've finished our coffees, Larry stands up, a few dollars change rattling in the palm of his hand. 'I'll pay.'

'No, no, let me.' My voice is loud in the bar and a few people glance in our direction.

Larry flushes at the attention as I mouth a silent 'oops'.

'Let me pay,' I say quietly, though quite firmly, and he shrugs and sits down.

I'm uneasy about Larry paying. Today, I reckon he pulled the same short-changing trick in Walmart by asking the cashier for change as he paid for our groceries. I've been going over the conversation in my head ever since, and though I was never the best at maths, I'm pretty certain he short-changed the girl. I don't want him to do it again. It's not fair.

When I challenged him about it, he looked confused. I hadn't the nerve to suggest that he'd done it deliberately, but I think he did.

I head up to the bar and hand over my money. The barman doesn't glance twice at me, except to utter, 'Have a good evening, ma'am.'

I nod a thanks, signal to Larry and together we walk out the front and the valet brings our car around. I marshal all my nerve and prepare to become Evelyn Coleman.

20

Parking is at a premium outside the gallery, Larry drives around in circles for a while until someone pulls out of a space and he slides our car in. Turning off the engine, we sit for a few seconds in silence before he turns to me and asks on a smile, 'All set, kiddo?'

'All set, boss.'

He nods. 'Right, let's get going. We stick together for the first few minutes, then when we spot the marks—'

'Marks?'

He flushes, 'Our targets,' he clarifies, 'when we spot them, I'll tell you what to do, OK?'

'Yes, I know. I'm not going to blow it, Larry. I'm in now. I need that painting back.' I say it like a boxer preparing to go ten rounds with a young fit Ali.

He nods, reassured. 'OK, Miss Evelyn Coleman, may I escort you to the gallery?'

'You may indeed, Mr Shanagher.'

Larry gets out of the car and, running around to the passenger side, opens the door for me. I climb out, my mind beating to the rhythm of my heart, 'I am Evelyn Coleman, I am Evelyn Coleman.' Larry offers me his arm; I take it and together we cross the road towards the gallery, which is ablaze with lights. A banner proclaiming 'Anderson Exhibition' hangs over the enormous front door. The heat of the night is oppressive and I feel a light sweat coating my face. Larry strides confidently up the wide steps to the entrance as I totter painfully alongside him.

'Tickets?' the man on the door asks importantly.

Larry produces two tickets from his breast pocket. The man glances at them and waves us through. 'Have a good evening,' he calls after us.

'We hope to,' Larry winks at me but I can't smile back.

The foyer is huge and very modern. To my relief, the air-conditioning is working full blast, and it's pleasantly cool. A wide wooden desk dominates the left-hand side while, in front of us, a set of marble stairs sweeps imperiously upwards. A cute little signpost tells us the Anderson Exhibition is somewhere at the top. Behind us, more people enter, talking with loud, cheerful American accents.

'That's the way you should be,' Larry whispers.

'Give me a chance,' I whisper back. I know I'll be fine but I just need to get the message through to my legs, which have begun to shake and which I feel I cannot control. If only I'd worn something longer, something to disguise their trembling and some lower heels to disguise my rapidly evolving limp. Hopefully, though, everyone will be far too busy looking at the paintings to bother staring at my legs, which aren't that great to look at anyway.

We ascend the stairs and can just about detect the murmur of voices. At the top, to the left, a wide white double door stands open and, inside, throngs of well-dressed people are chatting, laughing, drinking wine and eating delicate-looking canapés. We stand outside the room for a second, just taking it all in.

'Lots of money for this charity,' Larry remarks, no doubt multiplying the number of people present by the price of the tickets. He looks down at me, 'OK, Evelyn, let's go have a look.'

We enter the tall-ceilinged, chandeliered room. A man, standing just inside, offers us a glass of champagne from a silver tray. I take one.

'Make it last most of the night,' Larry warns. 'We don't want you on your ear.'

'Spoil sport,' I mutter, taking a sip and hoping that even a glass as small as this will relax me.

Another tray bearing little bite-size vol-au-vents arrives and, delicious as they look, I can't face the idea of eating anything. Larry declines too and it crosses my mind that despite his air of calm, he's bound to be a little nervous, though he probably likes the buzz. We move through the crowd effortlessly; it's as if Larry with his good looks commands attention. People stare at us as we approach before moving aside to let us pass. It's quite eerie actually. A few minutes later, and Larry has manoeuvred us to the top of the room where a little podium and a microphone are positioned.

'We'll see Derek Anderson here for sure,' Larry bends down to whisper in my ear. 'And more importantly, he'll see us.'

I nod and drink some more champagne.

Behind the podium is another set of double doors, around which hangs a huge pink ribbon. Behind the doors, I realise, is the exhibition. I find it hard to imagine that my painting is in there somewhere, posing as something it's not.

A bit like me, actually! The comparison causes me to titter.

Larry looks questioningly at me and I wave him away.

'Excited, huh?' A big, red-faced man in an ill-fitting suit pokes his face between us, totally invading our space. Larry and I take a step back.

'Yes, we're very excited,' Larry says smoothly, any trace of his Dublin accent gone.

'You're not from the US,' the man says, sounding delighted for some reason.

'No,' Larry smiles, 'we're Irish. We travelled over especially for this.'

'Especially for this?' The man nods, impressed. 'Wow, all the way from Ireland.' He nods again. 'Ireland,' he says. Then adds, 'D'you folks know Derek? Is that why you're here?'

'No we don't know him, not yet,' Larry answers. 'Do you?'

'Hell, yes,' the man says loudly. 'Everybody knows Derek. He's one of the biggest employers in the country. You shop in Shop Smart?'

'We had a look today,' Larry lies. 'Fantastic concept.'

'It is, it is.' The man takes a slurp of his champagne and wipes his mouth lustily with the back of his hand. 'It sure is.'

'So, tell me,' Larry asks. 'Is Derek here yet?'

'Oh, yeah,' the man says, scanning the room. 'I saw him earlier. You'll see him in a bit. He'll be making a speech soon.' He turns around in a circle. 'There he is!' He jabs a pudgy finger in the general direction of the door we came in. 'See him in the blue suit, small guy with the,' he lowers his voice, 'bald head.' He looks about shiftily, 'He don't like being told he's bald.'

'I would imagine he doesn't have to be told,' Larry says, and our new American friend wheezes with suppressed laughter.

'I'm Tyler Williams,' Tyler holds out his hand. 'I'm here with my wife. She loves art. And you are?'

'I'm Michael Shanagher,' Larry shakes the man's hand. 'And this is my,' he looks at me quizzically, 'it seems strange saying employer?' he jokes.

'Well I am,' I say, in a voice that isn't mine, as I hold out my hand to Tyler. 'I'm his employer and I have no problem saying it.' Where have these words come from? And my tinkly laugh? 'I'm Evelyn Coleman and I'm very pleased to meet you.'

Tyler shakes my hand vigorously; his palm is coated in sweat. 'And how are you his employer?' he chuckles, casting a sideways glance at Larry. 'See, I can say it too.'

Larry laughs good-naturedly. 'I own an art gallery back home in Dublin,' he says. 'And Evelyn and her aunt are my two best customers. They've been after a Van Gogh for a while now and we heard there was one they particularly liked on show here, so we came over.'

Tyler looks impressed. 'You hoping to buy?' he asks.

Larry shrugs. 'Maybe, if the price is right. I hope he's hoping to sell.'

'Well, I guess that would depend on if the price is right!' Tyler wheezes with laughter again.

A woman, maybe around fifty, slightly plump and with a friendly face, sporting dyed blonde hair that suits her, crosses towards us and places her hand firmly in Tyler's large one. She smiles graciously at us before turning to Tyler. 'Honey,' she says, 'Madison Smyth is here. Come say hello.'

'This is my wife,' Tyler announces, wrapping his arm about her shoulder. 'Ain't she a peach?'

Tyler's wife rolls her eyes as if to say, 'Isn't my man the most impossible flirt?' Then she extends a hand saying, 'Hi, I'm Mary. Has this funny man been making a nuisance of himself?'

'On the contrary,' Larry smiles that big grey-eyed smile at her, 'he's been very helpful.'

'This is Michael,' Tyler introduces us, 'and this is Evelyn. They're Irish.'

'Irish?' Mary says. 'My great-grandmother was from Ireland.'

'Yeah, you have an Irish look about you,' Larry pronounces. 'You're very good-looking.'

Mary laughs and blushes and flaps her hand at him. 'And you've the charm,' she says.

'But he's right,' Tyler squeezes his wife's shoulder, 'you're the best-looking woman in this room tonight.'

It's lovely the way she blushes as he says this. I find myself feeling all mushy inside. I glance at Larry who is watching them speculatively, his head to one side, and then as they turn again to him, he grins at them.

'Well I—' Mary is about to say something else when a man brushes past us and walks straight to the microphone on a small podium near us.

'Welcome,' he says and everyone claps.

'That's the curator of the gallery right there,' Tyler whispers to us. 'He's a great pal of Derek's.'

The curator then gives a speech about how happy the gallery is to be showcasing Mr-Derek-Shop-Smart's wonderful collection. 'It's the first time that some of these paintings and sculptures have been seen in public since they were bought,' the curator goes on. 'And you are the privileged few, not only to see this but also' – he pauses for effect and shouts – 'to have raised over seventy-five thousand dollars for charity!'

There's piercing feedback on the mike and everyone covers their ears.

The curator flushes and attempts to turn the microphone off, but finally the noise abates and he apologises and repeats his sentence and everyone claps, though some people are looking a little shell-shocked.

'This exhibition will continue for two weeks before it travels to Chicago. So I will now,' the curator says, sounding very flustered, 'call upon Mr Derek Anderson to say a few words.'

Amidst cheering, Derek waddles up the room; the internet photo is flattering, the reality is not. He's a fat little man with a wide smile on his jowly face. He takes a position in front of the microphone and waits patiently as the noise dies down.

'Welcome, everyone,' he says.

More cheering.

Derek laughs and continues over the commotion, 'I know some of you have come a long way to be here tonight.' He lists the states that people have travelled from and in the crowd people cheer at the mention of their home place.

'Ireland,' Tyler shouts loudly, pointing to me and Larry. 'That's where these two have come from.'

Heads turn to look at us and we smile around at everyone. A polite smattering of applause.

'Really?' Derek smiles. 'Well, that's fantastic folks. You're most welcome.' He then goes on to talk about various paintings in the exhibition and tell stories on how he acquired them.

Oh, God, I pray, don't let him talk about the Van Gogh. Don't let him talk about the Van Gogh.

'And then, of course, there is the wonderful story of the Van Gogh portrait,' he says and I sway slightly.

Larry catches my arm as the sorry tale is imparted to the room.

'And,' Derek eyeballs us, 'the guy who sold me the painting was from Ireland. Three cheers for Ireland!'

And, mortifyingly, the whole room cheers and looks benignly at Larry and me.

Derek moves on. He talks for about twenty minutes, just until the crowd is getting a little restless. And then he says, 'I have a surprise for you guys!'

Everyone looks up.

'I would like to call on,' he pauses for dramatic effect, 'Julian Oxley to officially open this exhibition.'

Julian Oxley! That hadn't been mentioned on the invite. I gasp as do all the other women and some – obviously gay – men in the room. Julian Oxley, TV star and hunk extraordinaire. Mary almost faints with excitement as Tyler looks at her in amusement.

Julian appears at the back of the room and trots up, waving at everyone.

'Who the hell is he?' Larry asks, bewildered.

'An actor,' I gasp. I'm not normally a girl for celebrity, but Julian is in a whole different league. He's an ultra celeb – gorgeous, apparently very nice to his fans, single, a bit of a bad lad but in a nice way, according to some article I'd read. And to my amazement, he's better looking in real life than he is on the telly. Blond and tanned with white straight teeth and dazzlingly blue eyes, he is charmingly shy as he smiles around the room. I wish I didn't look as awful because then he might bestow me with a grin just as he's doing to the twenty-something girl on my right.

'This is truly an honour,' Julian says softly, his voice commanding more attention than if he'd raised it. 'I'm humbled to be asked to do this.'

'Oohh,' the blonde girl says in a high, squeaky voice, making the people around her titter.

'I met Derek a few years ago at an art exhibition, before I became known, and we've been in contact ever since. He encouraged me to follow my dream,' Julian's voice cracks with emotion, 'to achieve my potential, to be the person I knew I could be, inside.' Julian taps his heart passionately and my crush on him withers like a leaf in autumn. 'Go, Derek!'

Beside me, Larry suppresses a laugh while I ache in embarrassment, but the rest of them are lapping it up. Julian leans forward, hands half in, half out of his trousers, his loose tie swinging a little. There is a collective intake of breath from every female present. 'Scissors please?' he says and he makes it sound quite sexy.

'Does he need a scissors to extricate the bullshit?' Larry whispers as I elbow him in the ribs.

A girl, red faced and thrilled, bustles up and hands him a pair of scissors.

'Thanks, darling' Julian says, winking at her.

She stands, frozen, looking at him in awe. A rabbit being slaughtered on the altar of charm.

Cameras start to flash furiously as Julian makes his way towards the door with the ribbon. The crowd press against us. Larry grabs me out of the way. 'Damn,' he exclaims softly, 'I wasn't expecting that. Stay out of any photos.'

I nod.

Julian stands beside the door, posing for the photographers, scissors held aloft. Turning slightly so that his face can still be seen, he says loudly, 'I now declare this exhibition open!' He cuts the ribbon, which floats to the floor, and two men, dressed in identical uniforms of blue and white, make a big production of pushing the doors inwards to reveal the exhibition room.

A loud cheer goes up and we all make our way inside. We lose sight of Tyler and Mary in the crowd, but I'm glad because the minute I set foot in the room, I spot it. Derek Anderson may have many fine paintings and sculptures taking up space in five interconnecting rooms of this gallery, but I can spot my little portrait from afar. It's across the room from me but I recognise its blue and yellow hues, though from this distance, to anyone else it's a bit of a blur.

'Over there,' I whisper to Larry, nodding in the general direction.

Larry spots it too and together we make our way across. No one is near it, not yet. People have gravitated to their own personal favourite artist or are just going along, taking in everything in an orderly manner. The Van Gogh, or rather the Eve Cole, is not one of the first pieces on display. It's as if the painting is calling to me, drawing me towards it. I feel compelled to look at it even though I don't want to, much like staring at natural disasters on the telly.

Soon, both of us are in front of the painting. It's more vibrant than I remember, culled from the amalgamation of two other paintings Van Gogh did while he was in hospital. The colours are as beautiful as when I laid them on the canvas, though I can immediately spot where Robert and my dad aged it. There are cracks in the oil, paint flaking slightly; it's quite a good job actually.

'Nice,' Larry comments. 'I can see why you'd want it Evelyn.'

But in that moment, I'm not Evelyn. I couldn't be Evelyn if my life depended on it. I'm Eve, the teenager, laboriously working on a painting I'm so proud of. A Van Gogh original fake. I'd loved painting this; I study the swirl of lines, the brush strokes. I'd been a mix of me and Van Gogh when I'd done it. The style of the artist and yet the soul of a girl wanting desperately to impress her dad. I can't believe no one noticed. This is so obviously a fake it might as well have a sign hung around it.

'Fabulous, isn't it?' The voice from behind makes me jump, guiltily. My feet scream out a protest.

'Yes. We love it,' Larry smiles easily, 'That's why we're here.'

To my horror, I look up from my aching joints and come face to bald head with Derek Anderson. He looks up and smiles in a curious way at the two of us, his dome-like head shining under the lights. 'I believe you've come all the way from Ireland to see this?' He quirks his eyebrows questioningly.

Larry nods. 'I left a message with your head office? Evelyn Coleman here is very interested in acquiring it on behalf of her aunt.'

Derek nods, watery blue eyes swivelling in my direction. 'So I believe.'

'It was the one that got away,' I explain, hoping my story won't sound too nervous or too rehearsed. 'We, eh, wanted it and had put an offer in for it initially.'

'I was never informed of that,' Derek says, turning once again to the painting.

'At the time, we couldn't hope to match the price you paid so maybe there was no point,' I answer, my voice shaking as I mentally curse myself. 'But now, well . . . ' I let the sentence hang, barely trusting myself to go on.

Derek looks keenly at me and nods. 'Well, I can tell from your voice you really want it,' he smiles.

I manage a smile back. He has no idea.

'I'll have it valued and let you know. After the exhibition, I'll be sending a few pieces to auction. The Van Gogh was one of them, but if you can put in an offer for it, we'll see. Enjoy. I'll be in touch.' He looks at Larry. 'My lawyers have your number?'

'Yes, I believe they do,' Larry nods. 'We're in the country for the next two weeks, so it would be good to be able to finish the deal by then. It'd be nice to bring the painting back with us if we can.'

I stand shell-shocked beside him thinking of how easy it had been.

'We'll see,' Derek nods and smiles.

'Thanks,' I say, unable to stop the relieved smile breaking out over my face. 'Oh, this'll mean so much to me— eh, my aunt.'

Derek gives a smile. 'Who is your aunt?' he enquires politely. 'Would I know her?'

I am horror-struck. I open my mouth to answer but I can't bring myself to drag Della into it. Meanwhile Derek is gazing expectantly at me.

'Della Sweeney,' Larry says swiftly. Then he attempts to deflect his answer by saying something truly stupid: 'The painting looks so fresh, you'd think it was only done yesterday.'

I gasp involuntarily. What the hell is he playing at? It was bad enough saying Della's name but now he's drawing attention to the newness of the painting. But to my relief, Derek's concentration is diverted from my 'aunt' as, after a tiny beat of silence, he nods.

'Indeed,' he says. Then he adds, 'I find it wonderful to think Van Gogh actually touched that canvas and left something for us all to appreciate.'

'Like all the paintings here,' Larry says.

'Yes.'

The two men eyeball each other. Larry eventually smiles and Derek smiles back.

'Oh, Derek, come here, come here,' a shout from a few feet away.

We turn to see an overdressed woman, silver and diamonds dripping from every conceivable part of her, including her hair, hurrying towards us. 'Derek, you just have to meet this man, he's eager to have a word with you, come on.' She takes Derek by the arm, nods to us and pulls him away.

He smiles a semi-apology and leaves with her.

Neither Larry nor I say anything for a bit, both of us frozen in front of the painting. I'm caught between collapsing with relief and cheering. But I can do neither so I have to concentrate on remaining calm, which is hard. It was nothing. So simple. I could have done it myself. All this trickery, and for what? He was selling it anyway.

I risk a look at my companion. He's barely smiling.

'Larry?' I venture.

'Shush!' He shoots me a warning look.

'Michael,' I correct myself. Then, my voice jumping up an octave with suppressed excitement, I squeal, 'He's going to sell us the painting.'

He bites his lip and nods, a tiny frown line between his eyebrows. He's not as happy as I thought he would be. 'Isn't it great?' I coax.

'Um, oh yeah, fantastic,' he says. Then he adds, 'Right, let's go have a look at all the other things here. We are art collectors after all.' He moves away from the painting and I follow him.

I can barely concentrate as we move about the room, though I know conversation is expected of me, if even to maintain the illusion of who I am. But I figure that it's all a little pointless. We're going to get the painting and that's what we came for. However, it doesn't take long before I'm captivated by the sculptures and the photographs that Derek Anderson has collected. Some of them are from people I'd never heard of, Americans I presume. Larry wanders away from me after a little while, but I find I don't mind so much. I'm in my natural element, he's the fish out of water. I'm not sure how much time has gone by, but eventually I look up and scan the room. I can't see him anywhere. I mosey around, looking into various nooks, and still no sign of him. Maybe he's gone outside for air and now that I'm finished looking around, I decide that we can probably leave.

I've just made it as far as the top of the stairs when I bump into Tyler and Mary again. They're with some other people but they beckon me to join them. I don't feel I have a choice.

'This is Evelyn from Ireland,' Tyler says. 'She's an art collector.' He peers at me, 'Isn't that right?'

'Well, my aunt is really,' I explain in my Evelyn voice, 'I just try to locate what she wants and Michael helps me.' I give what I hope is a cheeky smile, 'And it was great that what she'd like to buy now is located in Florida, a perfect excuse for a holiday.'

They laugh in appreciation as Tyler introduces them to me. The tallest woman with a mane of luxurious hair and a midnight-blue dress is Derek Anderson's wife, Simone. I have to physically restrain myself from running away when I find out who she is, but she seems gloriously uninterested in my false persona and more interested in finding out about Ireland. 'I've never been there,' she says in what I imagine is an upper-class American accent. 'Derek has, just once to buy a painting.'

'That's the one that Evelyn and Michael are hoping to buy,' Tyler chimes in.

'Really?' Simone drawls. 'How nice. Anyway, Derek said the weather over there was perfectly unpredictable and so I had no desire to visit.'

'Well, it is unpredictable, but on a good day it's a lovely country for scenery,' I try to do my best for the Irish tourist board, while simultaneously wondering how on earth I can escape. The longer I'm here, the higher the chance that I'll make a mistake. And I can't afford to do that now. 'Anyway,' I nod to them all, 'it was so lovely to meet you but I really have to go. Has anyone seen L— eh, Michael about?'

'Oh, yeah,' Tyler says, 'we were talking to him and then he got a phone call so he went out.'

'OK, thanks.'

'You over for long, honey?' Mary asks.

'Two weeks, we hope to get the painting,' I say that for Simone's benefit, 'and see some of the sights.'

It's the wrong thing to say as there follows a long conversation which then turns into a laughing argument about what I should see before I go back home. Then, when they've agreed to disagree, Mary insists on giving me her phone number just in case I'd like to ask her advice on things while we're here and that we're welcome to visit her and Tyler any time at all. Just call in advance. It really would be lovely to see us and what sort of art did Michael have in his gallery because she'd like me know that she has quite an impressive collection herself and we really must see it. We really *must*.

I take her number and finally escape down the stairs. They're all so friendly, not at all the big brash Americans that are portrayed in some of the films I've seen. I can't see Larry in the foyer, he must be outside. I nod to the guy manning the front door as I push it open. Once again, I'm surprised by the blast of heat that hits me, but not as surprised as I am to see Larry chatting to a tall guy across the street.

Maybe it's someone he met at the gallery? I strain my eyes but in the dwindling light, I can't make out if I've seen him before. The man is tall, dark, his whole body angled towards Larry as if he's listening intently. Larry is shaking his head and gesturing and the guy shrugs. Then Larry pats him on the back and the man seems to laugh before walking away.

Larry turns back towards the gallery and our eyes lock. I wonder if I imagine the look of surprise on his face. I think maybe I do because he crosses back towards me with an easy grin. 'You finished in there?' He nods towards the gallery.

'Who was that man you were talking to?' I ask.

Larry shrugs. 'Just a guy I met inside. He was asking about my gallery.' He cracks a conspiratorial smile. 'Turns out he's wondering if I'd be interested in some of his paintings. I had to turn him down.'

I think of the way Larry shook his head and patted him consolingly on the back. That makes sense. 'Oh, right. I hope he wasn't too disappointed.'

'Nah, he was just chancing his arm. So, you OK to leave?'

'Yes.' I follow him down the steps and into the car. As Larry reverses the car out, I turn to look behind and am pretty sure that the guy who I'd seen with Larry is watching us as we leave. He is half hidden in the darkness, but his face is illuminated by light from a window above him. 'That guy is staring after us,' I tell Larry.

Larry glances in the rear view mirror. 'What guy?'

'That guy—' I point, but he's gone. Melted back into the night. Maybe it's my imagination.

'So,' Larry says, grinning across at me. 'Halfway there, eh? Now, we just have to wait and see what he wants for it. And—'

'And whatever he wants, we agree to,' I nod. 'Totally.'

'Actually,' Larry says slowly, his eyes still on the road, 'we'll see about that. It might seem more realistic if we negotiate.'

'But you said—'

'Eve, you did good tonight. But now, it's my gig. I'm the buyer, remember. Just chill.'

'If you negotiate and he says no, then he might withdraw the painting altogether. Or someone else might want it and offer more. Larry, we need to get it.'

'I know that,' Larry flashes me a grin, and then in a perfect take of Julian Oxley, he says, 'I just want you to get your painting, to be the contented person I know you are inside.'

I laugh out loud and he flicks on some classical music and, as we drive back through the hot, dark night, past palm trees and neon lights, I think that this is one of those few perfect moments, a moment in which I'm relaxed and laughing and that, in some weird way, I know I can cope with whatever comes along. Well, that is unless someone does offer more for the painting than us. 'What if someone offers more?' I can't help asking, spoiling the moment a bit.

'Trust me,' Larry says, staring straight ahead, 'no one will offer more than us.'

'How do you know that?'

'Instinct,' he says. I open my mouth to say something else, but he turns up the volume on the radio.

'And do you think they'll remember Della's name?' I yell over the din.

'Dunno.' He ups the volume even more.

I let it go. For the moment.

21

Click clack. Click clack. Click clack.

I wake slowly, layers of unconsciousness peeling away so that I blink in the bright light of morning. What has woken me? Something did. I stretch underneath the covers knowing that I can't go back to sleep, not now.

Click clack.

There it is again.

I sit up and look around. I wonder if it's Larry in the kitchen or something but the house appears to be quiet. Larry has obviously slept in this morning. A few seconds later, the noise comes again, but when I swivel my head to look around, it disappears. I'll get up and investigate. My feet hit the floor and it's then I spot it. It freezes mid-scuttle. I freeze. Both of us still as stones, staring at each other. It's the most massive cockroach and it appears to be glaring at me. For a second, we both assess the situation, then wham, he runs, his black armoured body clacking along with all the speed I lack. His sudden lunge scares me and I scream while simultaneously making a pathetic attempt to kill him. He disappears into a hole between the wall and floor. I kick the wall in frustration, forgetting I am in my bare feet. 'Owwww!'

Feet pound down the stairs and Larry skids to a stop just inside my bedroom door. 'What? What?' he says, his voice croaky with sleep, his hair tousled. He's breathless. 'What's wrong?'

I'm acutely aware that I'm in my tiny little pyjamas, small shorts and a vest top and that he is semi-naked himself. I flush. 'Sorry. Cockroach.' I point in the general direction of his escape.

'A cockroach?' Larry exhales in relief and leans up against the door frame as he rubs his hand over his unshaven face. 'A cockroach,' he repeats.

'It was massive,' I defend myself, a smile creeping up the edge of my lips. 'I'm sorry if I gave you a fright. Look, there he is!' I jab towards where the cockroach has poked his disgusting head out to have a peek around, and then I run quickly in the other direction. Larry immediately picks up one of my sandals and flings it across the room. He's a good shot but the fecking cockroach is the Usain Bolt of the cockroach world. He disappears and this time we don't know where he's got to.

'I have to get out of here,' I gingerly step across the floor, picking up a pair of shorts and a T-shirt. 'I'm having a shower and I am not going near this room today.'

'That'll teach him,' Larry jeers gently.

'Oh shut up and put the kettle on,' I make a face at him.

Ten minutes later, we're eating breakfast beside the pool again. It's like a little piece of heaven. Today, though, because of our shopping spree yesterday, we're consuming large amounts of toast and massive bowls of cereal. Two large mugs of coffee and a silver coffee pot are also on the table.

Larry is sitting in the shade, a cute denim hat on his head. He suits hats. A pair of quite cool reflective sunglasses complete his nonchalant image. He already seems to have picked up a tan, which makes me slightly envious. I'm in a light pink T-shirt and a tiny little summer skirt, determined to get as much colour as I can before I leave. Then I remember that it's meant to be raining in Paris, and I wince.

'What's the problem?' Larry asks, noticing, so I tell him about Paris and he laughs so much he almost chokes on his toast. 'Well,' he grins, 'we'll just have to find out about the weather for you over there, won't we?'

'That would help,' I drain my coffee and pick up the sun cream. One day of sunbathing can't hurt and, after all, I'm bound to get a little bit of colour in Paris at this time of year. A few hours in the heat are all I'll need and, anyway, I love the feel of the sun on my skin. I squeeze out some cream and begin rubbing it into my legs and on my arms and lathering it on my face. I wish I had a pair of togs but even if I did, I'm not sure I'd have the nerve to wear them in front of Larry.

'So,' I say, 'when do you think Derek's lawyers will ring us with a price?'

'When they know what price they want,' Larry says, biting into some toast and appearing unconcerned.

'And when will that be?'

Larry presses his fingers to his temples and begins a chant, pretending, I think, that he's psychic.

'I'm serious,' I say.

He's about to reply when 'Hello!' from the woman next door stops us dead.

'Feck's sake,' Larry mutters under his breath.

I wave a 'hi' at them, then lie back with my eyes closed on the sun lounger. I hear Larry as he moves around picking up the cups and plates, obviously heading inside to avoid them.

'Do you mind if I say something?' Valerie asks.

My eyes pop open and Larry freezes mid-step with the dishes. The little girl next door, complete with rubber ring, hops into the pool with a splash. Her dad laughs.

'Say what?' Larry says pleasantly, though I know from his rigid back he's on edge.

'It's just,' Valerie sounds nervous, 'well, it's not advisable to leave the kitchen door open when you have breakfast. I hope you don't think I'm being terribly nosy but an open door attracts cockroaches.'

'Oh God, oh God. Close the door Larry,' I yelp, hopping up.

The pair next door laugh at my reaction, but Larry merely stomps inside, closing the door after him. And I realise that I've called him Larry. Shit. He'll kill me. 'Thanks for that tip,' I call out breezily.

They're hardly listening, just looking in astonishment at the way Larry has reacted to their help.

'I, eh, hope we haven't—' Valerie starts to say, then can't continue. Instead, she gestures lamely at the kitchen door.

'No,' I shake my head, bright red, and not from sunburn, 'he's, eh, even more afraid of insects than I am. And he's shy. Terribly shy.' Then I close my eyes so she won't see I'm lying. There is no way I'm going inside to face Larry's wrath. If I have to stay here and burn to a crisp, I will. If I have to stay here all night, I will.

'OK,' Valerie calls and, after a bit, I open my eyes a teeny way. I watch the three of them next door and they seem so happy together. They're like an advertisement for a twenty-first-century version of *The Waltons*. The little girl splashing about in the pool before mammy makes the perfect dive to join her picture-perfect daughter. Then he joins them, not a stray hair on his body. I wonder if he waxes. I watch them splash about as the sun moves higher into the sky, its heat massaging my body and relaxing my mind. The term 'sun-worshipper' was coined for me. Slowly, lazily, my eyelids close. It's as if all the stress of the past few weeks is dissolving. Slipping away like water down a drain. Easing—

Splosh!

I jerk abruptly upright, spluttering and gasping, drenched to the skin. 'Oooooh! Oh! Oh!' For a second, I'm so shocked that I can't figure out what has just happened. Then Larry laughs and I glance up, through the strands of my dripping hair, to see him standing in front of me, cracking up, a saucepan dangling from his hand.

'That'll teach you,' he grins.

The couple next door have left. I must have fallen asleep.

'You could have drowned me!' I splutter indignantly, drops of freezing-cold water trickling down my back and making me shiver.

'No such luck,' Larry remarks, still grinning as I hop up from the soaked sun lounger and make a vain attempt to pull the wet clothes away from my body. 'Might be better for me if I had.'

'I don't know what you mean,' I grouch. Damn, my T-shirt is so soaked it's skin-tight.

'I know what you were up to,' Larry sits down on my lounger, ignoring the fact that it's sodden. He looks full of himself. 'You'd have stayed here all day rather than listen to me lecture you, wouldn't you?'

I flick my eyes away from his face. 'The damage was done so there was no point in a lecture.'

'Yes, there is that,' he concedes, as he looks up at me, pinning me with his gaze. Then he says, his voice low but intense, 'Eve, you have to take this seriously. We can't afford it to go wrong.'

I sit in beside him. 'For what to go wrong? We are going to get the painting. He's selling it anyway. You didn't have to be a gallery owner to get it.'

'So, you would have liked to tell him that you were the daughter of the guy that he bought it from originally, would you?'

I squirm and don't answer. He has me there.

'D'you think he might have got a bit suspicious?'

I stare straight ahead.

'Nah, he wouldn't have, would he?' Larry pokes me in the arm, mocking me, 'He'd have thought—'

'OK, enough.' I hold up my hand and he laughs. I turn to face him. 'I'm sorry about calling you Larry. I am. I just got a fright. One cockroach is bad enough.'

'Try seven,' Larry winces. 'I've counted seven so far, unless the one you saw this morning is Houdini.'

'Seven,' I wince in disbelief. 'Oh, God, I can't go back in there.'

'We'll have to get something to kill them off. What is their rate of breeding, d'you think?'

'Go!' I push him off the lounger. 'Go on, go. Get everything you can find for them.'

'Oh, I'm going and you're just going to sit here, yeah?'

'Lie here,' I correct him, grinning. 'In the sun. Go on, go.'

He salutes me, then bending down he whispers, 'I'm Larry, you're Olivia, just in case it happens again. We're a couple on holiday, from—'

'Cork. I told them Cork.'

'In a middle-class Dublin accent, wonderful.' He rolls his eyes but he's smiling.

'I'm from Dublin originally,' I quip, 'that's why.'

He shakes his head in what I suppose is a gesture of hopelessness at my amateur conning abilities, then he leaves.

He arrives back some time later, no doubt having confused yet another shop assistant – which is another reason I wasn't keen on going with him – with a glass jar and some Vaseline along with a large tin of boric acid.

'The boric acid will kill them,' he informs me, coming to join me beside the pool. My skin is tanning nicely, I think. 'But a guy behind me in the queue in Walmart said that if I put some water and coffee grounds in a jar and have some little sticks leading up to it, that the cockroaches will climb in and not be able to get out. Some Vaseline inside will make it more difficult for them. He also said that they mainly come out at night, when it's really quiet.'

I flinch, envisioning an army of roaches marching through the villa at night. I'm not normally squeamish around insects but they are truly horrible creatures and the fact that they can move so fast and are virtually indestructible is freaking me out a little. 'Make it so,' I say firmly à la Captain Picard, and Larry smiles a little.

At that moment, his mobile phone begins to ring. He fishes it out of his denim shorts and, placing a finger to his lips for me to be quiet, he says 'Hello? Michael speaking.'

The person at the other end says something to him. Larry does a lot of uh-huhing and OK-ing. Then he says, 'I'll put it to my client we'll get back to you in a couple of days.' He thanks the person at the other end before hanging up.

He stares at the phone for a few seconds as if pondering something, so that I'm finally forced to ask, 'Who was that?'

'That,' he eyeballs me, tapping his phone against the palm of his hand, 'was Derek Anderson's solicitor, the man who we will be dealing with when we're buying the painting. They've put a price of sixteen million on it.'

'Sixteen million.' I gasp.

Larry nods.

'But we don't have that amount of money!'

'Chill,' he sounds unconcerned, 'we'll bargain him down, that's the way these things work.'

'If he had the painting valued, he knows how much it is worth.'

'Yeah,' a faint grin lifts Larry's mouth, 'and he'll try and get as much out of us as he can. We'll get him down. Just wait.'

He sounds so confident, but I'm still not sure. 'But if we pay less and someone else wants to pay more—'

'There was no queue to look at the painting last night, Eve. It'll be cool.' He sounds like he wants me to shut up, so I do. For the moment. 'In the meantime,' he continues, 'we'll let them stew for a couple of days.'

'Why?' I just want it over with.

'I just want to find out a couple of things first. It's not going to affect the sale, don't worry, but it might, just might put us in a stronger position if anything goes wrong.'

'Nothing will go wrong, you said it yourself.' I'm sweating a little now and it's not from the sun. I swing my legs to the ground. 'Are you God or something?'

He looks faintly surprised, 'What?'

'You know, the loaves and the fishes, make sixteen million from eleven. Can you do that?'

Larry laughs. 'Nope.' He taps my nose, 'You'll just have to wait and see.'

The kitchen door to the house beside us opens up and Millie, cute in a blue swimsuit with a frill, dances out. I reckon she has more swimsuits than Imelda Marcos had shoes. She stops dead at the sight of us, then shyly gives us a wave.

I give one back and she giggles delightedly.

'Isn't she gorgeous?' I whisper to Larry.

He blinks and doesn't answer but his profile catches me by surprise. He looks so devastatingly sad. His eyes are fixed on the little girl next door with her golden curls and cherub plump body.

'Larry?' I ask. 'Are you OK?'

'Huh, me, yeah, cool.' He stands up and points to the bug bait. 'I'll get cracking on this.'

'Hello,' Millie pipes up. 'Are you the odd man?'

Larry blinks. 'What?'

'My mammy said you seem rather odd.' Her voice is clear as a bell, piping up.

I start to chuckle.

'I am very odd,' Larry has a hint of fun in his voice. 'And you can tell your mammy that I said that.'

'OK.' Millie dances back into the house and Larry turns to me with an anguished look on his face. 'See, look how you made me look in front of the neighbours.'

'You did it to yourself, you anti-social man,' I chortle. 'Now, if you come out again, will you bring my sketchpad? I'm getting bored just sitting here relaxing and taking it easy.'

'So come help me lay bug traps.'

'Just get my sketchpad.'

I spend the next couple of hours sketching the pool and the things I can see from the sun lounger. Drawing has always managed to take my mind off my problems, and it succeeds once again. I try drawing the same things from different angles in different light. Finally, around four, Larry comes out carrying a glass of orange for both of us and he lies down on another lounger, his hat over his face, and I sketch him. It's a long time since I've done a body, but his is so divine that it's a pleasure. And it's a good excuse if he catches me looking at him. Finally, he sits up, and the light catches the gleam of his hair, one bare shoulder and a slant of his face. 'Hold it,' I call. 'Hold that pose.'

'Like this?' he says, glass half up to his lips.

'Like that, just for a couple of minutes.'

'But I'm thirsty.'

'Pleeease?'

'Go on.'

And I draw the muscles on his arms, his fine fingers, his strong jaw, his stubble, his tight blond hair, his almond-shaped grey eyes. My pencil skips across that page in a frenzy of delight. He's lovely to draw, interesting and strong. I'd say he takes a mean photo.

'Let's have a look,' Larry asks when he senses that I'm finishing up.

I flush. 'Well, it's only a sketch, I'd have to fill it in if I was doing it properly.'

'So?' he crosses over and has a look. He bends over my shoulder as I hold the pad out to him. Taking it, he cocks his head to one side and a smile curls his lips. 'Is that how you see me?' he asks, sounding pleased.

'Yeah,' I nod. 'Why?'

'I look good,' he hands it back and struts to his own side of the pool. He gulps down the rest of his orange.

'You look all right,' I clarify in a mock snotty voice. 'Don't go getting above yourself now.'

He laughs and lies back down, hat back over his face.

I take one long look at him, fold up my pad and lie down too. Maybe the cockroaches will be dead by the time the afternoon is over.

22

Only one cockroach has fallen for the coffee grounds. And it was the one in my bedroom, which gives me a certain amount of relief. Larry had drawn the curtains all over the villa to darken it to see if they'd come out. Only one had been stupid enough. Larry takes the jar out of my room and empties it into the trash.

'Well, at least you'll sleep tonight,' he says cheerily.

I don't contradict him, but wish he hadn't told me about cockroaches being nocturnal creatures. There are at least six others roaming around and what's to stop them paying me a visit? Larry says his goodnights and I hear him padding up the stairs to bed. He seems to find my uneasiness quite amusing. Oh, if only I'd slept in the room next to his so that he could be close by.

I listen as he prepares for bed and then I hear him switching off his light. I wait a few seconds, just to be sure that he's not coming back down, then I tip-toe across the floor and very quietly flick my light back on. I don't want him knowing what a wuss I am.

Suddenly, my mobile rings, making me jump. Scrambling back towards the bed, I flick it open. It's Robert.

'Hey,' I say, breathlessly, my heart hammering.

'How's things in Paris?' His tone is slightly mocking, especially when he says 'Paris'. 'Your mother thinks you'll be drowned. She told me to ring you to make sure you're not just telling her a load of rubbish to ease her mind. Well?' he demands.

'I am fine.' I can't quite bring myself to lie to Robert, I don't think there'd be much point anyway. He has his suspicions.

'I called by your apartment this afternoon, just to keep an eye on it.'

'Oh, yeah?' I'd given him the key and told him to check on it only if the alarm went off. 'Thanks, but you don't have to do that.'

'That Larry person seems to have disappeared, a man that looked a little like him came out of his flat when I was there.'

'Really?' I try to sound as if I'm teasing him. 'Disappeared? How do you know the guy you saw wasn't just a visitor? Larry has friends you know.'

'Well, according to the man that came out of his flat, Larry has taken a holiday.' Robert's words are loaded. 'And at the same time as you! Imagine?' Now, he sounds as if he's teasing me, only his voice has an edge to it.

'Imagine,' I say. Then add, keeping up my jocular tone, 'It's probably because he couldn't face being in the apartment block without me so he took off too.'

'You're a clever girl, Eve, don't do this,' Robert warns, sounding stern.

'Do what?'

'The man is a con artist.'

His words stun me. As far as I know, I'd never told either him or my mother what Larry had been in prison for.

'Oh, yeah,' I scoff, 'how do you know that?'

'I googled his name. That's if it is his real name.'

I'm speechless, not able to answer. I'd never thought of googling Larry. I wouldn't have imagined that details like that would be put up on the net.

'Do you know how con artists operate? Do you?'

'Well if I did, I'd be a con artist myself. Anyway, what has Larry's past to do with me?'

'Nothing, I hope,' Robert says and then, without waiting for me to answer and his voice steely with determination, he continues. 'They find out what you want and they promise to give it to you. They do it by making you trust them, by being what you want them to be, by charming people. If they were legitimate operators, we'd probably have world peace, but they use their charms, their looks, whatever they can, for their own ends. Larry is a bona fide con man.'

'So what if he is?' I flash right back at him. 'You're a con man yourself.'

There is a silence. I feel a little guilty but, honestly, talk about the pot calling the kettle black.

'I only did it once,' Robert seems to be finding it hard to talk, 'and that was for your dad, my best friend. Do not dare put me in the same category as your new best friend!'

He's furious. 'Robert, I'm sorry. But—'

'You ask your friend, when you see him, about the garage scam. You ask him.' Then he hangs up.

I stare at my phone, not able to believe that Robert is cross with me. That man has never once raised his voice to me in all the years I've known him. How could I have called him a con artist? Frantically, I dial him back. His phone goes to voicemail. There is only one thing for it, to tell him the truth. 'Robert,' I begin, slowly, 'I'm sorry. I really am.' I pause, wondering what to say next, how to phrase things so he won't be offended again. 'You're a good man,' I say with conviction, 'but, you know what? Larry is too. I really believe he is.' What else? Oh yes, 'Tell my mother not to worry, I'm going to be fine. And you're right, I'm not in P—'

The phone bleeps to signal that I've run out of time for my message. I stare at it, heart beating, hardly able to believe that I was going to tell Robert where I was. Saved by the bell. Larry would have freaked completely.

I heave a sigh, blink back a few tears at the row, because I hate rowing with people, and lie back against my pillows. Then I sit back up, redial Robert, who is still not answering, and ask him to please, please ring me back.

Then I close my eyes and try to get some sleep.

It's no use, four hours later and I'm still awake. I don't know if it's because of the row with Robert, the cockroaches or the fact that it's too bright in the room with the light on, but I can't get to sleep. Two things are out of my control, but I can turn the light off and maybe that will help. My legs shaking with exhaustion, I hop out of bed and pause. Was that a noise? I wait and hear it again, it's faint but there is no doubt about it. Larry is moving about upstairs. What's he doing up at, I glance at my phone, three thirty in the morning? I wonder whether to call up to him or to leave it. But I can hear him talking, so he must be on the phone. I listen again; yep, I can definitely hear his voice. Robert's words flash back to me. What if Larry is conning me? What if he's going to run away with all my millions? Well, not my millions but Derek Anderson's millions. My heart starts to hammer again. I owe it to myself to find out. If he catches me, I'll pretend I'm sleep walking. Or something.

Feeling a bit sick with the tension, I very gently ease the bedroom door open. It's a testament to the condition of the villa that I can move the door without as much as a squeak. Once outside my bedroom, I listen hard. There he is again, talking. And I can now hear him plugging something into a socket. What's he doing? I tip-toe across the hallway to the end of the stairs.

Click clack. Click clack.

A cockroach scuttles in front of me and I almost yelp. Instead I jump out of the way, holding in a gasp.

Then another one runs on by.

Oh, holy God, how many of the creatures are in the place?

I don't have time to think about it because next thing I hear a light 'ping'. He's obviously plugged in his computer and booted it up.

I gingerly test the first step of the stairs. Silence.

Then another. No creaks. Nothing.

Larry is still murmuring into the phone. What is he doing? I feel a bit guilty for spying on him. My gut tells me he's a decent guy, but maybe, as Robert says, it's an illusion. Maybe I should just barge in and ask him. That would certainly be the most honest thing, but the fact that he's on the phone in the middle of the night means he's not being honest with me, is he?

It's blindingly obvious that it's someone he doesn't want me to know about, which is damn suspicious.

He is honest, the softie in me says. He's a good guy.
Then why is he making sneaky late night phone calls?
I owe it to myself to find out.
Decision made, I very quietly ascend the remaining stairs and within ten seconds I'm standing on the landing; Larry's door is straight in front of me. It's closed but there is a sliver of light peeking out from underneath it, so he obviously has the light on. What do I do now? It's hard to hear anything, the low murmuring only slightly louder than it was downstairs and I only heard that because part of Larry's room is directly above mine.
I tip-toe over to the door.
He's on the phone. He sounds cross. Really cross. 'Damn it,' I can hear, 'you owe me that much.'
Whoever he's talking to says something.
'I swear if I don't get a picture at least, you'll see how bad I can be.'
I freeze at his words. He doesn't sound like the easy guy I know at all. Or even the confident con man he morphed into. He sounds like a thug. What picture is he on about? Mine?
'I am not threatening you, this is a promise. You can't fuck around with me like this. I've done nothing wrong. If I don't get something from you lot, I will turn up there whether you like it or not. Hey, don't hang up on me – don't—'
There is silence in the room. He seems to be cursing under his breath. Then I hear the bed squeak. He must have sat down on it.
Click clack.
Oh, another one. The biggest yet goes strutting by. I swallow back a scream.
Then I hear footsteps coming towards the door. Oh, God, if he opens it, I'll be discovered, in fact I'll probably fall into his room, my ear is pressed so hard up against the door. I freeze. There is nowhere to go without making a racket. But to my relief he doesn't come out. He's started tapping away on his computer now. I stay there for another few endless minutes, listening to him. Then, because I believe that I'm not going to learn any more I decide to go back to bed. I straighten up and my back gives this enormous crack.

Damn. I freeze midway, like a cartoon character, holding my breath.

The tapping stops. I picture him, also frozen, also holding his breath. 'Hello?' he calls cautiously. Is there a hint of unease in his voice?

'Eh, hello,' I call back. 'Larry? You're awake. Can I come in?' What the hell am I going to say? What am I going to say?

There is a bit of a scramble from his room, but I push the door open anyway. 'Oh,' I feign surprise, 'you're up.' My gaze flicks toward his computer.

He nods. 'Uh-huh. Couldn't sleep.' Then indicating his computer, he adds, 'I had some stuff to check from home. My brother just e-mailed me to say how the apartment is and stuff.' He shifts from one bare foot to the other, 'So, can you not sleep either?'

'No. There are roaches everywhere. I've seen piles of them.'

'The boric acid will do the trick.' He shrugs. 'Well, seeing as it's four in the morning and we're both awake, d'you fancy some wine or something to conk us out? We can crack open one of the bottles we bought.'

I want to ask him about his phone call, but I'm afraid to. Better just to keep on his good side and see what happens. All I want is my painting back. And oblivion in a bottle of wine sounds good. 'Open up,' I say.

We go downstairs, meeting a few more roaches on our way, and Larry pulls a bottle of white from the fridge. I note happily that another roach has found its way into a glass jar and has given up trying to climb out. Hopefully a few more of his mates will have joined him before the morning. Larry pulls a couple of glasses from the press and pours us both a drink.

He sits in beside me on the sofa. His eyes are tired, not sparkling the way they normally do, and he has black circles underneath them. 'You look wrecked,' I observe.

'Oh, I'll live,' he offers me a glum smile, then clinks his glass off mine. 'Cheers.'

'Yeah, cheers.'

We drink in silence for a bit. 'So how come you couldn't sleep?' I ask him.

He shrugs. 'Dunno.' He stares into his glass. Ponders for a second and says 'Dunno' again. Then he turns to me. 'You?'

I shift uncomfortably. 'The cockroaches for one thing and, for another,' I pause, 'I had a bit of a row with Robert.'

'Oh.' He relaxes back against the sofa and stares straight ahead. 'D'you want to say what it was about?'

'He knows you're with me,' I answer. 'Or he at least suspects it.'

Larry gawks at me, 'You didn't tell him?'

'No, but,' again I hesitate but in the end decide to go for it, 'he also knows you're a con man.'

Larry doesn't seem all that surprised. He sounds resigned. 'Yeah?'

'He told me to ask you about a garage con, or something. He said he read it on the internet.'

Larry closes his eyes, rubbing one hand across his face and cradling his glass of wine with the other. When he eventually opens them again, he sighs deeply and swallows a lot of the wine in one gulp. 'Your stand-in father or whatever he is should learn to mind his own business.'

'He worries about me.'

The words hang in the air for a second until Larry begins to speak. 'The garage con was what got me put in jail. It was, looking back, inventive but stupid.' He allows himself a tiny smile.

'What did you do?'

Again, he rubs a hand over his face. Without looking at me, he asks, 'Ever hear of the guy who sold the Eiffel Tower?'

'No.'

'Aw, doesn't matter, it just gave me the idea for the garage scheme.'

'What did you do?' I'm half-scared to find out, but I have to know.

'Well, I contacted a number of garage dealers and asked them to a meeting in a hotel room I'd booked. When they came, I informed them that I had flown in from the US and that I was a representative of the industrial components division of Ford or something like that, I can't quite remember. Anyway, I sounded like a pen pusher. I told the dealers, in confidence, that we had recently discovered a problem with the brakes in one of the car models. In two weeks, we were going to recall all the cars for repair and we were going to use four specially selected garages for these repairs. I asked them to tender for the jobs.'

'And?' I can't see how that would have made him money.

'They had to tender within two days. It was a big rush, I told them. Anyway, I picked out two guys from the bunch who looked to be struggling and I let them know that surviving on my salary was tough. I could always use a little help,' I said.

'And?'

Larry looks at me in disbelief before a smile breaks out, transforming his previously tired face. 'I'd never con you, would I?' he half chortles. 'Subtlety is obviously not your strong point.'

Maybe it's the late hour or the wine, but I haven't a clue what he's laughing about.

'Well, *they* understood my meaning. By telling them I could use some help, I let them know I'd be open to being bribed. Which they did. Very nicely, thank you very much.'

'Oh, Larry.' I know he was a con man, but I'm still shocked.

'It was their own greed,' he mutters, then shrugs. 'Anyway, I was long gone by the time the con was discovered. My mistake was trying it twice more. I got caught the third time.'

'And you made loads of money?'

'A bit.'

I digest the story. I find it hard to believe that the man I'm sitting beside could do that to people, but he doesn't even sound that remorseful.

'I needed the money at the time,' he adds.

'Did you have to give it back?'

'Yep, but it was gone or,' he adds a tad mischievously, 'it couldn't be found.'

'You stole money.'

'No, they gave it to me. Willingly.' But he sounds as if he only half believes it himself. He polishes off his wine and pours himself another glass and then he tops up mine. 'So that's the garage scheme, Eve. No one got hurt or killed. Greed always gets people in the end.'

'And how did you pick out the guys to con when you had six at the meeting?'

Larry laughs. 'That was the easy bit. They looked and acted desperate. You can always tell.' He pauses and frowns, 'Or maybe I can always tell, I dunno.'

I wonder if he thinks I'm desperate but I don't ask, not quite trusting him to tell me the truth anyway. But, then again, anyone he's conned before never knew he was a con man, but he's told me up front so maybe he is on the level with me. Maybe . . .

'So,' Larry says, 'you can tell Robert you know all about the garage scheme.'

'I will not, he'll know you're with me for definite then.' I swirl my glass around and take a sip. The wine is delicious and seems to taste even better at this time of the morning. I turn to face Larry, who's watching me with a speculative look. 'When are you going to ring that solicitor back?'

'The day after tomorrow.'

'Why not tomorrow?' I sound a little panicked. I'm certain if we play too hard to get, the painting will be gone.

'Well, I'm sure your aunt will have to see if she can raise the funds, that could take a couple of days,' Larry says reasonably. 'And when I ring, I'll say that she can only raise fourteen million.'

'But we don't even have that!' Oh, God, this is like déjà-vu.

'Then when we're certain that they've accepted, which they will of course,' Larry ignores my comment, 'we ask to examine the provenance and pay a deposit—'

'You won't have to pay a deposit. And we don't have—'

Larry winks. 'Trust me.'

And it's only two words but I wish so much I could embrace them completely.

23

I wake up on the sofa the next morning, a duvet over me and a cushion for a pillow. I must have fallen asleep after we'd drunk the wine. I try to remember what we last talked about, but it's a bit of a blank. I'm sure it'll come back to me. I lie there for a second and savour the silence and the warmth and the light. Despite the fact that getting the painting back is stressing me out, moments like this are so relaxing. The sofa is surprisingly comfortable and, as my gaze drifts lazily around the room, I'm heartened to see that two cockroaches are now trapped in the glass jar.

Larry must have covered me with the duvet from my room before he headed to bed and the thought of him doing so makes me blush. Trying not to dwell on it, I stretch, extending my arms over my head and yawning widely. Oh, it feels great. The sun is high and I wonder what the time is. I throw off the duvet and, hopping from the sofa, pad over to the kitchen, flick on the kettle and have a quick shower while it's boiling.

When I finish up, there's still no sign of Larry, but I spy a note on the table.

Hi Sleepy Head, gone fishing, won't be back until after tea. I've taken the car. Enjoy the day. Tomorrow the work begins. L

And then I remember that, just before I'd gone to sleep last night, he'd told me he'd booked a day's fishing. Well, the fact that he's gone out means I can go shopping and buy a pair of togs and have a swim. A sneaky little part of my head says that I can also have a scout around Larry's room and see if he's on the level with me. But I dismiss it. That'd be just plain horrible. Then I think about it again. Is he being devious too, though? Would it be a terrible invasion of his privacy? Would it be justified? Do I have a right to know if he's planning to dupe me? I can't help liking him but isn't that the whole point. Would I be here with him if I didn't like him? Would he be able to con me if I didn't like him?

I decide to give it more consideration after I've had my breakfast. The thought of sneaking uninvited into someone's room does not sit well with me. I grill two pieces of toast and pour a glass of orange. Then I carry my breakfast outside, closing the door firmly behind me. It's late enough because the neighbours are not about, they've obviously eaten and headed off. This is great. I'm on my own, at liberty to do what I like, in a nice sunny, albeit very humid, place.

I stay outside longer than necessary to eat my breakfast. Once finished, I know I have to decide whether or not to go into Larry's room. But after an hour, having consumed an enormous pot of coffee, aside from caffeine overload, there is not a lot else I've achieved. Damn it, I'll tidy up, I think, before making up my mind. Five minutes later, I'm standing in the centre of my room, having deposited my cup and plate in the dishwasher and put the duvet back on the bed.

Job done. The place is as clean as a hermit's cell.

My eye falls on my mobile and I wonder if Robert has been in touch. I flip it open, my hands shaking and ... nothing. There are two missed calls from Olivia though. It's one o'clock here which would make it, I calculate quickly, about eight in the morning over there, so on the spur of the moment I decide to ring her and ask her advice on what to do about Larry's room. Obviously, I'm not going to tell her the whole story.

My call is answered almost immediately. 'Hey, you,' Olivia's cheerful voice make me feel homesick suddenly. 'How's things?' She dips her voice. 'All going well?'

We'd agreed that we'd sort of talk in code, just in case Larry or Eric were about.

'Going as well as can be expected. How is the Dublin potter?'

'I'm fantastic.' Then her voice dips, 'Have you seen it yet?'

'Yep. And we're about to buy it back.'

There is a pause. 'I'm scared for you, Eve.'

'Don't be. It'll be fine. It's been easier than I hoped.' I speak with bravado. I don't tell her that we're five million short. 'How's David?' I attempt to change the subject.

She embraces it, more for my sake than hers. 'Well, I'm so glad you agreed to go out with him, he's fancied you for ages.'

I laugh. Thinking of him makes me long to get home.

'And talking of new romances,' Olivia goes on, 'I ran into your mother during the week. And she was with this man!' Olivia makes it sound as if my mother was spotted picking her nose on TV. 'Has she got a boyfriend?'

'She's got a friend,' I state, my voice getting defensive. 'He's certainly no boy.'

'OK, has she got a partner?' Olivia chortles at the word.

'Moving on,' I find I'm grinning though I so don't want to. The idea of my mother and a man is, well, revolting actually. 'Can I ask you something, Ol?'

'Yes, David is a nice guy.'

'No, it's not about him. I want your advice. It's about Larry.'

'Larry? Don't tell me you fancy him too. Though, stuck in a strange country with him would be any girl's idea of—'

'He's helping me, Olivia, nothing more. It's just, well . . . ' Oh God, I feel bad saying it out loud. 'I don't know if I can trust him.'

'Oh,' she is horrified. 'What makes you think that?'

'Nothing in particular,' I hedge. Again, I don't tell her about Larry's record. I just can't do it to Larry, much as I am wary of him. Plus, Olivia would probably catch the next plane over or something. 'I mean, he's grand so far, but well, if you were me would you search his room, you know, just to satisfy yourself as to his trustworthiness?'

'I think you should get the hell out of there,' she gasps. 'I told you it was weird that he offered to help you in the first place. He's not a normal run-of-the-mill man in my opinion. He could be a killer.'

'He's not going to kill me, would you cop on,' I almost laugh, but don't. 'But I'm afraid he might do a runner with the painting or the money or—'

'Is he there now?'

'He's gone fishing.'

'Go up now and check him out.' Her voice brokers no argument. 'Now!' she says. 'And ring me back when you're finished.'

'OK.'

And like some ominous sign from the gods, the sky outside blacks over. And a large boom of thunder shakes the house. The usual midday storm.

'Was that thunder?' Olivia asks.

'Uh-huh. Happens most days, though we've been lucky so far.'

'Well, if Larry is gone fishing, you'd want to hurry up to his room because no one would fish in the middle of a storm.'

She has a point, calling out a goodbye, and with promises to call her, I hang up.

Outside, sheet lightning lights up the sky like a cinema screen. I jump. I hate storms.

Crash.

Is it my imagination or does the house tremble?

Feeling awful about it, but determined to uncover something to either put me on guard or ease my mind, I run quickly up the stairs, taking them two at a time. I hesitate briefly outside Larry's room, before taking a deep breath and pushing down the handle of his door. Stepping inside, I see that his room is much as I had seen it the day I tried on the wig. His bed is unmade, the duvet thrown to the floor in a crumpled heap. The photo of the mystery girl sits as it had before on the bedside table. I pick it up to have a closer look. The girl in it is really very cute and her smile makes me smile. Who is this little dote? I look at the back of the frame and see that it can be unclipped. Biting my lip, I wonder if I should. But I don't wonder for too long; I know nothing about this man except that he has a brother and that his dad left. I feel I'm owed more. I've put my future in his hands. Feck it, my fingers tremble as I push up the little latch and gently pull the frame apart. The back of the photo lies exposed and across the top edge someone has written, 'Libby. France'. The writing looks female, full of swirls and loops. A teeny love heart has been coloured in over the 'i' in Libby. And that's it. Nothing else. I don't know what I'd been expecting.

I replace the back of the frame, which thankfully closes without any trouble, and put the picture back in place. Straightening up, I scan the rest of the room. His suitcase is on the floor, clothes randomly scattered about. I cross over and kneel down in front of the case. I have to be careful here. Very gently, I sift through his T-shirts and shorts. Nothing. His underwear and socks are in a separate compartment and I glance in there, not willing to poke about too much. Nothing. A few zips reveal empty compartments. His passport is in one of them and I pull it out. Flicking to the photo page, I study Larry's brother. At first glance, he does look like his younger brother, but on closer inspection, I can see that the shape of his eyes is slightly different. Larry's eyes are wider, more innocent looking. Larry's face has a more chiselled look about it whilst his brother's is softer and rounder. I wonder what this guy, Declan, makes of Larry using his passport to travel around. It's a hell of a risk.

Crash!

Once more the thunder echoes around the house and rain teems against the windows. I can't see Larry fishing in this weather and I wonder how far away he is. I'm sure I'll hear him coming in. Where to next? Frantically, my eyes scour the room and fall briefly on his computer. Then flick away and then come back to rest on it. I'll probably never get into it. It's probably password protected. Still, I cross over, press what I suppose is the 'on' button and to my stunned amazement, the screen flicks to life. The home page. What? Did he go on it this morning and forget to turn it off? No, I think suddenly, it was last night. He had it on and I disturbed him. He must have forgotten to log off and then the screen went blank and he must have assumed it was off.

I can hardly believe it. Once again, doubts assail me but I ignore them as best I can. His screen saver is nothing more than a picture of a fish jumping up a dam. A long silver fish that I assume must be a salmon. The man is obsessed with angling. Finger shaking, I press his e-mail icon. The mail server pops up and in horror I watch a message pop into his inbox. Oh God, will he know that I've been on if that message is not highlighted when he gets back? Very quickly, I mover the pointer to an old message below. It's from Declan, which, judging by the message, I can only assume is his brother.

All fine bruv. Nosy neighbours asking questions. Take care. See you soon. Behave :)

I re-read. The message is dated yesterday. *Behave?* Does that mean that he's actually thinking of not behaving? I swallow hard, feeling uneasy. *Behave?* What am I getting myself into?

I go to the next message. It's from a guy called Niall. All it says is:

Will check.

It looks like Larry has replied to that one, so I go into his sent box. He's written:

Feel certain, so don't let up.

The next message, also from Niall reads:

OK.

I scan down that one and Larry's message appears underneath. He's written:

Contact Declan. Has details.

And that was in response to '*cossies*', whatever that is.

Whoever these guys are, they know the real meaning of brevity. I can't make head nor tail of any of it. There are no more mails. They're obviously the most recent ones. In fact, they only came in yesterday so it's a fair bet he was planning on deleting them last night when I interrupted him. I re-read, afraid to go to the latest message in case Larry cops that I have read it. None of the correspondence appears sinister except the one where his brother is warning him to behave himself, but even that is accompanied by a smiley, so maybe it's a kind of joke? I run a distracted hand through my hair, read again and then log out.

My eye runs through the rest of his computer files. I go into his music. It's filled with rock and pop. Rock and pop? That's strange. In fact, of all the stuff I've found so far, that makes me the most uneasy. He told me he liked classical music. I flick down through the album list again. There is not one classical piece in his files. And then, like a bucket of cold water on a hot day, I shiver as I remember him saying that he was going to pretend to have a child to bond with Derek Johnson, that having something in common tends to make people trust each other. I feel chilled right through my bones. Of course, Larry would have known that I liked classical because the walls in our apartments are paper thin and he'd have heard me playing it. Is he only pretending to like it? Looking at the computer the answer seems obvious. I have to sit on the bed to try to absorb that. My mind rattles off all the things I can do to see if he's a fake. I'll ask him questions on his favourite composer, his favourite instrumental, the sort of music he doesn't like. But I'll do it in a subtle way. I vaguely become aware that the rain has eased a little but that the thunder is still booming. The sky looks a little lighter now. I have to hurry. On the computer, the only files I haven't gone into are his photographs. I'm so annoyed at what I perceive as his deception that I access them without feeling any guilt. If this man thinks he can make a fool of me he'll be in for a surprise.

There are only four pictures. Once again, the little girl who I now know as Libby features. This time, she's being held by a woman sitting on a tartan rug in what seems to be a park. The sun is shining on Libby's curly dark hair. The woman in the picture is very attractive, with long hair to her waist. It lies in sexy disarray across her shoulders and she's wearing a tight, low-cut T-shirt, three-quarter length jeans and a very inviting smile. She is laughing at whoever is behind the camera. Or so it appears.

The next picture is of a very tiny baby. Small, wrapped in a pink blanket with a little button nose. Tiny curled-up fists are poking out the top of the blanket. 'Libby' the picture is called. Now I feel bad. Libby must be Larry's little girl. But where is she? Maybe she's his niece. But how many men carry around pictures of their nieces on their computer? I look at the child again, wondering if I might see a likeness to Larry, but it's hard to tell, she's so bundled up.

The next picture is—'

'What the fuck do you think you're doing?'

I jump so hard that I actually feel my ankle twist, the pain shoots up my leg bringing tears to my eyes. But it isn't half as horrifying as the look on Larry's face.

'Well?' He stands in the doorway, hands on his hips, legs apart, dripping water all over the carpet, his face as dark as the thunder clouds overhead. He takes a step into the room and I take a nervous step backwards. 'Are you looking at my fucking photos?' he shouts.

I flinch at his language. 'I, eh, wanted to eh, check my e-mail,' I babble, my face flaming red, 'to see, you know, if Robert contacted me and I thought I'd try your computer and—'

His eyes narrow. 'And you went into my pictures instead of the internet?' He takes another step towards me.

I swallow hard. Go even redder.

'Well?' he bellows.

I have never seen anyone so mad in my life.

'Yes,' I say, 'I did.' My voice comes out stronger than I'd intended and I can see that he's momentarily taken aback. 'You keep telling me to trust you,' I say, 'and yet, you're a con man. It's bloody hard.'

'So you went through my private stuff?'

'I, well, I suppose I did, yes.' He is going to kill me, I think. He really is. And I don't know that I would blame him. If he did it to me, I'd high tail it out of there.

'And what did you find?' His lip curls up in disgust, 'Anything interesting?'

'Look,' I say. 'I'm sorry. I am. But I am here with you and right now you're holding all the cards. I don't like that.'

Larry laughs humourlessly, 'Yeah, that's the first honest thing you've said, d'you know that, Eve?'

'What?'

'It's not just me you don't trust, is it? Fact is, you don't let too many people in, do you? Oh you laugh and joke with them, but they don't know you. Ever since your dad died, you've wanted a stress-free life. You need the control.'

'Pardon?'

'You love having your easy life, painting easy pictures, not being on show for everyone to see. You love it when things are predictable. I'll just bet that when your dad was dying you decided never to get that used up again, eh?'

I am stunned that he'd bring my dad into it. 'Don't you bring my dad into this!' My voice wobbles.

'I'll just bet that you spent all your time taking care of your dad and minding your mother and that when you came out the other end, you felt all used up.'

'You just stop!' I blink hard. 'You stop!'

'So you decide to do what was easiest, paint fakes and stay happy in your own little world and—'

'Do you have a child you don't see?' I shout out before he can say anymore. 'Is that who Libby is?'

It's as if I've hit him. He opens his mouth, then closes it, then opens it again. 'You get the fuck out of here,' he says in a quietly furious voice. 'You get out and you never ever go near my stuff again.'

'Aren't you going to answer my question?' I say brazenly and somewhat cruelly. But how dare he bring my dad up! How dare he use him like that. And if he can do it, then so can I!

'No, I am not,' he glares at me, though I feel that his anger is underpinned with a barely suppressed sorrow. 'Just because the truth hurts, just because you're way too chicken shit scared to be yourself and to trust anyone, don't think you can hurt me because I tell it how it is.'

Each word he utters is a punch in my gut. Not that it's true – I mean, I have loads of people I trust – but it does hurt. I let Larry in, didn't I? And he's twisting everything I've told him. I blink back some furious tears and, pulling back my hand, I hit him, right across the face. The thwack echoes in the room and drops into the stunned silence as Larry stares at me and I stare at my hand, which looks pretty red.

Finally, Larry rubs his jaw and turns from me without saying anything.

'I—I,' I attempt an apology, but realise I wouldn't mean it.

I leave the room.

It's only when I'm outside and I've slammed the front door that the tears come.

24

I plod for ages on my sore ankle in the humid heat. Nobody walks anywhere in Orlando and now I understand why. It's too hot, too humid, there are very few paths. But on the upside, there are no people about to witness my tears. I walk and walk and walk, shoulders heaving, scrubbing my face with balled-up fists. What had started out as a promising day has turned into a disaster. How can Larry and I ever come back from this? In fact, the thoughts of returning and facing him make my stomach roll. How can we get back on track? Now that I know what he thinks of me, I am too embarrassed and angry to face him. And to think I actually liked him. I know searching through his room was wrong, but I had to do it. And, in fact, if I hadn't, I'd never have found out that he'd lied about the classical music, so how many more lies has he told me? I can't believe I hit him though. Imagine me doing that! I've never hit anyone in my life. I wish we could go back to the simple friendship we had in the beginning – there was no pressure, no complications, just cups of tea and—

All of a sudden, I feel faint. My head swoons in and out and my legs feel rubbery. It occurs to me that I've been walking for ages. The path I'm on stretches far behind me and in front, it's all but disappeared and I have to cross the road to find the continuation. My T-shirt and shorts are wet with sweat and my hair, which I haven't tied up, is plastered to my face. I push it back behind my ears but get no relief. The air is heavy despite the recent storm. Across the road, there is a shopping mall, so I think maybe I'll head in there and avail of the air conditioning before attempting to walk back. If only I had a bottle of water, but I didn't bring any money with me so no point in wishing for that. Maybe they'll have toilets in the mall and I can drink from the taps. And splash my face. The thoughts of it make me feel faint again.

I stand patiently, legs trembling, waiting for the lights to change. Oh, God, I really do feel awful. I sway a little and grab onto the traffic lights. Then just as I'm giving up hope of the green man ever flashing, a car skids to a stop beside me and the passenger door pops open.

'Get in. You'll get dehydrated.'

I blink and turn my head slowly. Like a man in the desert, I'm not sure if Larry is a mirage or not. I think not though because if he was a mirage, I'd have him smiling kindly at me; instead, he still looks mad.

'Get in,' he says again crossly.

I climb into the car meekly and no sooner have I shut the door than he pulls back out abruptly, earning a horn blast from the person behind and almost throwing me onto the floor.

'Thanks,' I mutter as I hastily snap my seatbelt closed.

He says nothing, his mouth set in a grim line. Instead, he drives faster than he should, but I haven't the nerve to tell him to slow down, I'm so glad to see him. My eye flits to the dashboard clock and I calculate that I've been walking for close on two hours. No wonder I feel rotten. I notice that I've got sunburn on my arms and down the front of my legs. Even now, in the cool of the air-conditioned car, I can feel the heat pulsating from my limbs. I lie back in the seat and close my eyes.

'There's water in the back,' Larry growls.

I turn around and spy a blessed bottle, cold to my touch. I screw the top off and polish off three-quarters of it in thirsty gulps.

Larry says nothing.

'Thanks for coming to get me,' I say.

His response is to accelerate. I figure it's better to stay quiet or he'll get us both killed.

Fifteen minutes later, he pulls up in front of the villa. He hops out of the car and slams the door. Valerie, Peter and Millie have just arrived back too and they offer him hesitant smiles. I don't know if Larry reciprocates, but they look a little miffed at his unwillingness to talk. I undo my seatbelt and gingerly open the car door. To compensate for Larry, I call out a cheery 'hello'. Meanwhile Larry has opened the villa and stomped inside. They nod to me and I know they're wondering what on earth the story is with us. I continue to smile a little crazily as I walk past them and into the house, shutting the door behind me.

Larry is sitting on the sofa, the remote for the TV in his hand and he ignores me as I stand in front of him. We stay like this for a while, neither of us looking directly at the other. A ridiculous home movie programme is on. I begin to feel a little stupid standing there and wish I knew what I could say to make him talk to me. I am grateful that he came after me, but I've already thanked him for that. I think I'll have a cold shower and maybe by the time I've freshened up, he'll have calmed down.

Fifteen minutes later, he doesn't look any more approachable. He still refuses to acknowledge me as I come back into the room, towelling my hair dry.

'D'you want a cuppa?' I ask.

'No.' His gaze is still fixed on the telly. He has kicked off his sandals and planted his feet on top of the coffee table.

I put the kettle on and after pulling out some ham, cheese and tomatoes from the fridge I busy myself making a sandwich. When I'm finished, I place the sandwich on a plate, pour milk into my tea and blurt out, 'You're right. I do like to be in control of things.'

The confession shocks me as much as it does him. For the first time since the row, he fixes his grey eyes on me. 'I know I'm right,' he says evenly, 'I'm *always* right.'

Now I feel as if I have to defend myself. 'There's nothing wrong with wanting to be in control,' I say, leaning on the counter that separates the living area from the kitchen.

He shrugs.

'And it's hard for me now, because I have never done anything like this before.'

His lip curls up in a slightly mocking way that I don't like. 'You're such a good girl.'

'I try to be.' Oh, God, I sound so self-righteous.

He rolls his eyes. 'D'you know what, Eve?' he smirks, pointing the remote at the television to turn it off. 'When I met you first, I thought you were cool. I really did.' He stands up. 'Now, you're just annoying.'

I watch, taken aback, not able to retaliate, as he turns away and makes for the stairs. He's almost halfway up when I shout after him, my voice wobbling, 'And you are just, just—' I can't think of what he is. 'Yes,' I shout instead, 'I looked in your bloody precious room! And guess what? I looked in your suitcase—'

'You what?' he whirls around, voice quiet, eyes narrowed.

'And, oh, my God,' I feign horror. 'I checked out your photos!' I pause. 'So hang me.'

He says nothing.

'I. Am. Sorry.' I enunciate every word, 'OK? I'm sorry. I am not saying it again. But you can't blame me. If I was a criminal wouldn't you be wary of me?'

'I am bloody wary of you anyway, you're a mental case.'

'I am sorry for asking about the little girl in the pictures. I know it's none of my business but you hurt my feelings.'

His expression softens a little once I mention Libby. 'And you hit me,' he says, as if I needed reminding.

'I know. I'm sorry. That was . . . well, it was . . . it wasn't as if I'd planned to. It just happened.' I sniff. 'You dragged my dad into it and he was such a good man and you . . . well, you have no idea how awful it was when he died.' My voice cracks. I suddenly don't feel hungry enough for a sandwich. I turn away slightly and try to wipe a tear that has somehow slid out.

Larry says nothing. He doesn't move from his position at the stairs. I take my tea and sit down at the kitchen table and try to get myself under control. In the silence that follows, I wrap my hands about the mug and sip my tea. But I can't help the silent tears that leak out. It hurts to think badly of my dad, it hurts to think of him, full stop. To talk about him, well, that's even more painful, though I try to, just to keep his memory alive. To let others know that he lived. I'm not very good at it, though. I don't like the feelings, the tightness, the way my heart squeezes up because he's gone, the remembrance of the powerlessness of being unable to help him. I squeeze my mug tighter and try to focus on the warmth coming through.

After what seems ages, Larry slides in beside me and says softly, 'Well, I'm sorry for doing that. I didn't know it'd upset you so much.'

I look up into his grey eyes, which are now less annoyed-looking, though not exactly as repentant as I'd like. I blink hard and swallow. 'You did know it would upset me. You know everything, you just said so.'

'Touché.' He chews his lower lip and says after a pause, 'But I am sorry.'

I accept his apology with a shrug, 'Motor neurone disease, that's how he died,' my voice barely creeps above a whisper, 'It took a few years and, in that time, he lost everything.'

'Oh, now, Eve—'

I don't care if he's going to listen or not. Now that I've put it out there, I have to go on, to tell him. 'He lost all control. In the end he couldn't do anything for himself, he had no dignity and he couldn't paint or talk or anything. I was his legs, his ears, his eyes. My mother cried all the time. Robert helped, but now I know why he kept a low profile, but it was me who kept the show on the road.'

'Eve—'

'Three years of submerging yourself in caring for someone makes you a bit of a control freak. Three years of having no control makes you a bit of a control freak. Makes you want the easiest life you can imagine with no complications ever again. And I'm sorry if you think I'm annoying, I'd rather call it self-preservation.' I sniff loudly and a big tear drops into my tea.

'You're not annoying,' Larry says as he touches me briefly on the arm. 'I only said that to hurt your feelings.'

'Yeah? Well, you succeeded.'

'You hurt mine by going through my stuff,' he says simply.

I look at him, scrub away a tear, 'I did?'

He nods. 'I thought you trusted me. No one trusts me when they find out I've been in jail. I thought you were different, it made me, well' – his eyes flit away, then come back to rest on my face, as he admits reluctantly – 'it made me happy.'

'I'm sorry.'

More silence. Only a nicer silence than before. It's as if we're both mulling over what has been said.

'It is hard to let people in when you think they'll only complicate your life for you,' I admit reluctantly.

'I know,' Larry says, as if he really does know.

A beat of quiet. Larry breaks it.

'Can we start over?' He offers me his hand.

I take it. His fingers curl about mine in a firm, warm grip. I think I'd like to hold his hand forever. 'Absolutely,' I say.

His smile lights up the room.

It's only afterwards, when I think about it, that I realise that he found out all about me and I found out nothing about him.

But so what? If I get the painting back, there'll be time enough for that.

I text Olivia later on: *All good. Don't ring me. Too risky now. I'll catch up when I get back.*

I think about it for a second before pressing 'send'. It's better this way. If Larry finds out I told her after he'd warned me not to, he won't like it and I really don't want to hurt him anymore. Or make him cross.

25

The next morning, to our surprise, Derek Anderson's solicitor phones us before Larry has a chance to phone him. I listen with mounting concern as Larry nods and 'uh-huhs' and thanks him very much before hanging up the phone.

'What?' my stomach churns as I look at him, though he's grinning.

'All set. We are going to a party tomorrow night in Derek's house.'

'What?' I gawk at him. 'A party? A fecking party?'

'He's arranging for us to view the painting privately and to discuss the price.'

'We don't need to go to a party to do that!'

'If this was a real deal, we'd accept his invitation.'

'It *is* a real deal.'

'Yes, exactly.' He takes the sun cream from me and begins to plaster it on his face.

'We won't last a whole night pretending.'

Larry quirks his eyebrows. 'Eve, you disappoint me. Look, these people want us to buy their painting. They must do, or they wouldn't have pre-empted our call. And the more they want it, the less they'll notice a few inconsistencies. Hopefully, there won't be any, but if there are, they'll rationalise it away. It's the reason they bought that painting in the first place. They wanted to believe it was a Van Gogh. All they needed was someone to tell them.' He chucks me under the chin in a patronising gesture, 'Believe me.'

'Hmm.' I pull away and lie down on the sun lounger, closing my eyes and feeling the instant heat of the sun over my body. 'I will believe you on condition that you go and get me an orange.'

He chuckles and I hear him heading into the kitchen and closing the door carefully behind him. I'll tackle him when he comes back out. Four more cockroaches have bitten the bullet since yesterday, but there are more wandering around. Next door the sliding door opens and, within a couple of seconds, I realise that whoever has opened it hasn't closed it after them, which is unusual. I pop open a lazy eye and see Millie on her own standing beside the pool. She's staring over at me as if unsure whether to say hello. Then she goes for it. 'Hello,' she calls.

'Hi Millie,' I smile, sitting up, 'don't you look lovely? I like your shorts.'

She sticks out her tummy and places her hands on her hips, supposedly to give me a better view. 'My mum bought them for the holiday,' she chirrups. 'They're pink. I like pink. Pink is my favourite colour. What's your favourite colour?'

'Blue.'

'Blue's for a boy,' she giggles. Then she points to her top. 'This is my swim suit. See, I have it on and have the shorts over it.'

'Cool.'

Then she pulls down her shorts to show me the rest of her togs.

'Cool.'

'I can swim now. My daddy said I'm the best swimmer. Shall I show you?'

'Oh, I dunno—'

And with that she jumps into the pool.

I wait for her to start swimming as her head bobs up, but instead, she goes back under, her little arms flailing. Is she playing? 'Millie?' I stand up. 'Millie!'

She seems to be struggling. Her head bobs up again and this time, I know she's not playing. 'Millie!' I scream and make a dash to our mesh pool doorway. Pulling hard, I yank it open, yelling for Larry because I know I'll not be able to get the neighbour's door open. They probably have it locked from the inside.

'Larry! Larry!' I yell, in between yelling for Millie's parents. I push on their door, but it's as I feared. I start to kick it. Larry appears at my side and, pushing me roughly out of the way, he aims a ferocious kick at the gate. It makes a dent.

'Millie, kick your legs,' I shout in but she's too panicked to hear me and I don't know if it's my imagination, but her struggles seems to be getting weaker.

Larry kicks again and the hinge tears away from the side of the meshing, but we still can't gain access.

'Valerie! Peter!' I shriek.

Then just as I hear footsteps inside the house, Larry's third kick breaks the gate and he charges to the poolside and jumps in. He grabs Millie, who to my alarm has gone limp, and pulls her to the edge of the pool. Valerie and Peter have arrived and Valerie is shrieking, hands to her face.

'She just jumped in,' I say tearfully,

Larry lays Millie tenderly on the ground and begins doing gentle CPR on her.

Nothing. His eyes meet mine. He looks panicked. He tries again.

'Millie! Millie!' Valerie kneels down beside her daughter. 'Millie, please. Breathe, Millie.'

Time seems suspended as Larry continues to work on Millie. It's as if the only noises in the world are of Valerie softly crying and begging her daughter to breathe. Peter stands shell-shocked beside me. Larry breathes into Millie's mouth once more and, suddenly, the little girl's body jerks and water spills from her mouth. She begins to cough and sob.

Larry sinks to the ground, suddenly exhausted.

Valerie almost folds over in relief as she scoops Millie into her arms, both of them crying. Peter crosses over and embraces them, all three are kneeling on the ground.

I take a second, before crossing to Larry and wrapping my arms about him. His face is chalk white and he looks dazed.

'Thank you so much,' Valerie sobs, looking over at us. 'Oh, God, you saved her life.'

'We thought she was watching television,' Peter says. 'We were cleaning the front garden and she didn't want to help.'

'I hate the pool, Mummy,' Mille sobs loudly. 'I hate it.'

'You should have had your ring,' Valerie says, kissing her face. 'You silly billy. You gave us all a fright.'

'I hate it!' Mille shrieks.

'Nothing wrong with her voice then,' Larry smiles weakly as he rises shakily to his feet, running his hand through his wet hair. 'You're lucky Ev— Olivia was in the back and saw her.'

'We can't thank you enough,' Valerie sniffs. 'Thank you.'

I nod, hardly able to talk in case I cry. My legs are trembling.

'No problem,' Larry says in my stead, catching my hand in his, 'Come on, Olivia, let's leave these people to it.'

I follow Larry through the broken gate and back into our own backyard. I'm nauseous with the shock of it but I'm sure he feels worse.

'You OK?' I ask.

'A bit shaken,' he admits. 'D'you fancy a stiff one?'

'If by that you mean a drink, then, yes,' I joke, trying to make him smile.

It works. 'Eve Cole, you're a bad-minded girl.' A wink. 'But I like you.' And he wraps an arm about me and pulls me in close and I wrap my arm about him because somehow, I sense he needs it.

Two hours later, I still haven't been able to go back outside. I just can't reconcile the idea of sunbathing when ten feet away a little girl almost drowned in front of me. I'll probably be better tomorrow – or will I with a flipping party looming? Now, however, I just want to get as far away from the villa as I can. Take my mind off everything.

'We could go to Disney World,' Larry suggests, 'All those scary rollercoasters will take our minds off what didn't happen.'

And he's right, Millie didn't drown. It could have been a lot worse. 'OK,' I smile, a little banner of excitement fluttering in my stomach, 'Let's go to Disney World. The real one with Mickey Mouse and Cinderella and everything.'

Larry grins and we spend a little time packing a rucksack with a couple of rain jackets and bottles of water. Then we strap on money belts and head out of the house and into the car.

Before we leave, I say, 'Let's not talk about anything to do with the painting or Millie. Let's just make today about us.'

'About us,' Larry nods, 'sounds good.' And he gives me a lovely smile. A really lovely smile.

Disney World has its own road network, with various routes to the different parks. Larry picks 'Magic Kingdom' because that's where Mickey Mouse is and we drive up a road that eventually leads into a massive car park. A short train ride drops us outside the entrance to the park and once we pay for our tickets, we hurry inside. The place is heaving with people of all nationalities. Straight in front of us, at the top of a road that would pass for a good quality motorway, is the iconic Cinderella Castle. The park spreads out from there in four or five different directions. The sight of the castle is overwhelming. Since I was a child, I've been waiting to be here and now that I'm here, I feel like a child. I know I look totally goofy – how apt – as I stand gawping at the castle as the crowd ebbs and flows around me. 'It's huge,' I breathe.

'It's a fair few acres,' Larry agrees, referring to the park as he studies his map, 'so I think we should get cracking.'

And we do. I drag him up the boulevard towards the castle. On the way, we pass a statue of Walt and Mickey and I wish we had a camera. But Larry has insisted, no cameras. How would it be, he said sternly, if I had pictures of Florida on my camera when I was meant to be in Paris? I told him it could be Disneyland in Paris but he didn't buy it.

We examine the castle for a bit until I notice Larry looking bored. 'What's wrong with you?'

'Can we get more hard core?' he asks. He sounds a little manic, as if he needs the distraction.

'How?'

He glances at his map and pronounces that we definitely need to go to Splash Mountain. It's a flume ride with a drop of about fifty feet or so. He doesn't need to ask me twice, I'm a speed and plummet junkie and the two of us soon find ourselves in a queue for a seat in the front of the boat ride. We reach the top of the queue after half an hour and, feeling excited but a little apprehensive, I sit into the little boat.

In the beginning, the ride isn't exactly exciting, as the boat bobs gently along to chirpy music, but there are cute little things to look at along the way. There are a couple of false alarms too, when we think that a big drop is coming but it doesn't. After one of them, Larry laughs loudly and turns to me and whatever he is about to say dies on his lips as he catches my eye. I suddenly find myself equally tongue-tied and we both hastily turn away from one another. What was that about?

The boat continues to bob along, sometimes in darkness, building up the expectation and the nerves and then, out of nowhere, straight in front of us, is the enormous climb to the top. The boat in front of us begins to ascend and our little boat follows. Little animated puppets start issuing warnings. 'I'll show you,' they shriek manically and my heart picks up pace, half in fear, half in anticipation.

Our boat chugs along, the climb seemingly endless. The boat in front of us disappears from view amid lots of shrieking.

There is no backing out now.

'OK,' Larry says, eyes twinkling, 'I'll bet you won't hold your hands up in the air as we go down.'

'I bet I will,' I answer back. 'You just watch.'

Chug. Chug. Chug.

And then we're at the top, only we can't see anything because our boat is suspended over the drop. And fifty feet looks a lot more when you're at the top. Far below, people wander by, chatting, laughing, eating ice-cream, oblivious to my mounting terror. Our boat judders and points downwards and I scream, and grab on to a laughing Larry before remembering what he said. To hell with it, I shove my hands up in the air and yell at the top of my voice as the boat zips downwards at incredible speed.

The exhilaration when we reach the bottom, unscathed.

'Wow!' I cheer and Larry whoops.

And then it's on to Space Mountain and Thunder Mountain, before the child in me reasserts itself and I pull Larry along to visit Mickey Mouse's house and then Minnie's.

'They're a very Catholic couple,' Larry observes wryly, making a few people behind us laugh.

The day speeds by until the sun has dipped and night creeps in. By ten o'clock, it's dark and people have begun to gather around the castle for the parade and fireworks.

And what a show it is. It's like every best parade I've ever been to multiplied by a million. Lights and music and spectacle with each display better than the one that went before it. I stand beside Larry and feel bizarrely at peace as characters from my favourite films and cartoons dance on by, shaking hands with the kids and looking just as magical in reality as they do on the screen. Glancing sideways, I see that Larry appears to be equally charmed. On this hot night, standing beside him and watching this is all I want to be doing.

'It's brilliant,' I whisper, at a loss to describe how I feel. 'Really great.'

Larry smiles, and it's a little sad, I think. 'It makes you feel like you're a kid again, doesn't it?'

I nod in agreement. It makes you feel like a kid in that you suddenly believe that the world is a good and safe place and that you'll always be lucky. Without thinking, I reach out and grab Larry's arm. If he minds, he doesn't say so. Instead, he smiles down at me and, in that moment, I think I fall for him just a little.

And the night is spoiled, because that is most certainly not part of the plan.

26

The next evening, just as I'm selecting an outfit to wear to the dinner in Derek Anderson's house, my mother rings. Why is she calling me? I ring her every second day and text her every other. That's the arrangement. Cautiously, I press the phone to my ear, 'Hi, Mam.'

'Eve, what did you say to Robert?'

'I'm fine, thanks and how are you?'

'I'm waiting.' She is not amused.

With a sigh, I answer, 'I called him a con man, but,' I add quickly before she can interrupt, 'I've apologised to him on his voicemail and he hasn't called me back. He seems to think that I've gone off with Larry.'

'Yes, he told me that,' my mother says dismissively, 'but, honestly, does he think you're a complete idiot? I told him it was ridiculous. Imagine going away with that man?' she snorts at the very idea of it, 'Sure, you'd want to have a knife about you full-time. So, you have definitely contacted him and apologised.'

'Yes I have, though really, Mam, it's not your business.'

'Of course it's my business; he's like a wet tea towel at a party. No good for anything. And, apparently,' she lowers her voice, 'he's had a bit of a bust up with Denise.'

'Pardon?' Should I wear the white top or the blue? I try to think which one I paid more for. And what do rich people wear to a casual dinner?

'She thinks that there is something Robert is not telling her and, of course, he told her that she was being ridiculous and they had a row.'

'But it's not ridiculous. He's not telling her he pulled an art scam worth ten million and that I am being forced to—'

'Well, he's hardly going to tell her that!' my mother scoffs as if it's obvious. 'How could he tell her that!'

'Well, he probably will have to if he wants her back.'

'I told him to make something up to tell her.'

'You'd never make a relationship counsellor.' I shake my head. 'That is such a bad idea, Mam. I think—'

'Eve!'

'Who was that?' My mother barks. 'Was that a man?'

'Just another resident,' I say loudly so Larry can hear. Then add 'Mam' so he knows who I'm talking to.

'There is no need to shout,' my mother reprimands. 'Anyway, Robert is a bit miserable at the moment, so ring him again and maybe he'll talk to you.'

'I will.' Poor Robert. He really liked Dee too. The blue top, I think.

'And thanks for asking how Liam is,' my mother says almost accusingly. 'You don't like him, do you?'

'I never got a chance to ask,' I defend myself as I pull the top over my head whilst trying to keep the phone balanced between my shoulder and ear. Not an easy job. And no, I want to add, even though I hardly know Liam, I don't like him.

'So, are you going to ask how he is?'

She's like a kid. 'How is Liam?'

'You could sound as if you actually care.'

I say nothing and wait for her to continue, which she does after a small beat. 'He is fine, thank you very much. He recommended another book for the book club this week. *Secrets to the Ying and the Yang of the Soul*. It's set in Libya.'

'Oh, right.' I grin a little and ask, 'Have you noticed a drop off in your book club numbers lately?'

'I have actually,' my mother sounds amazed that I would know something like that, before she cops on to my sarcasm. 'Oh, ha, ha. Very funny. It's a good book, I'll have you know. Very complex.'

'It sounds it.' Where is the woman who loved a good romance gone?

'And the weather over there has begun to be lovely, I believe.'

'Mmm,' I am non-committal. I haven't checked the Parisian weather in the past day or two. 'Anyway, Mam, I have to go. Dinner is on now and it'll be gone by the time I get down.'

'OK, you enjoy it. See you in a week, I'm missing you.'

'Me too,' I smile as I hang up.

I finish pulling on my top and team it with a pair of white trousers. Unfortunately, they are cheap white trousers but I figure that no one tonight will be wearing Penneys jeans so I'll be safe in that respect. Oh, God, I feel sick.

Larry is dressed in a light pair of beige jeans and a cream and beige shirt. I know for a fact that both of them were bought in Dunnes Stores because Robert has the same shirt and Eric has the trousers. But Larry, despite the cheap clothes, manages to look classy.

'OK, Eve, here is your hair.' He holds out the wig and helps me to adjust it. From being semi-attractive, I now look like someone desperately trying to hold on to my youth and rapidly losing grip. 'Amazing how it transforms you,' Larry says in admiration. 'OK, let's go.'

He peers out the window to make sure no one is around but we're out of luck, because Valerie is striding up the front pathway.

'Shit,' Larry says under his breath. 'Eve, you're gonna have to hide.' I duck down behind the kitchen counter as Larry opens the door just before Valerie knocks.

Valerie seems to stumble and she gives a nervous laugh. 'Goodness me, I wasn't expecting you to open the door just then, I almost fell through it.'

'Um, sorry.'

There is a silence.

'Yes?' Larry asks then. 'Can we help you?'

'Oh, well, yes. Well, I mean no. I, eh, well, Peter and I were wondering if we could take you out to dinner as a way of saying thank you for what you did yesterday. Obviously, we know we can't repay you but—'

'Just me?' Larry asks teasingly.

'Oh no, Olivia as well. Of course.' Poor Valerie misses the humour. I think she's a little scared of Larry.

'That was a joke,' Larry explains.

'Oh.' Valerie attempts an unsuccessful laugh.

'Anyway,' Larry says a little abruptly, 'no need for dinner. It was a pleasure.'

'A pleasure?' Valerie sounds startled.

'Well, not a pleasure,' Larry backtracks rapidly and I have to stifle a giggle, 'obviously it wasn't a pleasure, I mean, it was no bother, there is no need to thank us. We only did what anyone would do.'

'Still, we want to thank you. Please let us thank you.'

Larry sighs quite rudely, I think, but he must nod, because Valerie's next words are, 'I'll give you a choice of dates and you can let us know what suits, is that OK?'

'That's great,' Larry says and I must know him well because he doesn't sound as if he thinks it is. 'Looking forward to it.'

'Tell Olivia I said hello.'

'Will do.' Larry closes the door and says, 'Valerie says hello.'

I pop my head up from my hiding place, laughing at him. 'She's a nice woman,' I say. 'Dinner with them will probably be a lot more fun than dinner tonight.' I open the fridge. A tiny bit of wine is left in the bottle. 'Dutch courage,' I say to Larry as I drain it. Oh, that feels nice.

'Dinner with them is unnecessary.' Larry shakes his head at me and, waiting at the window until he is sure that Valerie has gone back inside, he throws me a rain jacket. 'Put that over your head going out,' he orders.

I decide not to point out the obvious, that I'll look ridiculous with a rain jacket on my head in the blazing sun. Valerie and

Peter don't strike me as the sort of people who'd peep out of windows so, chances are, they won't see me. I pull the hood up and with Larry behind me, to block me from view, I sit into the car. He runs around his side and hops in, flicking on the sat nav and inputting Derek Anderson's home address.

'Now,' Larry says as we get underway, 'remember what we're doing tonight.'

'I have nightmares about it,' I say to him. I lean back against the seat and close my eyes, letting the air-conditioned air flow over my face.

Massive is too small a word to describe the building that squats at the end of the long scenic driveway lined with tall palm trees. The porch of the house is about the same square footage as my apartment. The door is the size of my back wall. There are more front windows glittering in the sunlight than in the whole of my and Larry's apartment block. OK, that's an exaggeration, but there are a lot of windows. The only thing I reckon that fits into these salubrious surroundings is our hire car. It's sleek, expensive and blends beautifully with everything. Larry and I pull up to the front entrance of the house where a valet, dressed in a black suit and white shirt, relieves us of our keys and indicates for us to go on in.

Larry nods his thanks and, taking my arm, lightly escorts me into the large hallway which is dominated by the most beautiful chandelier. Its light scatters across the marble tiles and stark white walls upon which are hung the most fabulous tapestries I have ever encountered. Ignoring everyone, I cross towards a lilac and dusty pink one and stand in awe before it. Oh, to have so much money you can purchase a thing as lovely as that. I sense Larry at my elbow. 'Isn't it gorgeous?'

'Isn't it indeed.'

It's our host, who seems to have a habit of creeping up on us when we're standing in front of his artwork.

'Where did you get this?' I ask, forgetting my nerves for a moment in my appreciation of the tapestry, 'I love it.' I'm relieved to note that Derek is dressed as casually as we are in three-quarter length white canvas trousers, exposing incredibly hairy legs and an open-necked polo shirt, again showing off copious chest hair. It's as if he's grown hair all over his body to make up for the lack of it on his head.

'Russia. The girl is talented, isn't she?'

'Yes, you must give Michael her contact details, he might like to display her, eh Michael?'

Larry nods. 'It's a little different to what I'd normally buy, but, yes, I'd be interested.'

Gosh, we sound so plausible. I feel a little more confident.

Derek Anderson smiles. 'I will, though she's not cheap.' He takes my hand in his and shakes it vigorously. 'Welcome to my home.' I try my best not to wipe my damp hand on my trousers when he lets it go. I'm not sure if it's my sweaty palms or his. He turns to Larry and shakes his hand too. 'So glad you two could make it. We'll leave business until later, OK?' Without waiting for us to answer, he says loudly, 'Everybody, everybody,' and the conversation goes from full blown to a dull murmur. 'Everybody, I'd like you all to make these two feel at home. They've come all the way from Ireland.'

'Ireland?' someone hisses. 'Where is that?'

'I think it's in Europe,' someone else says.

'We're beside England,' I say and, immediately, everyone nods, which is a bit insulting.

'Come on and I'll get you a drink,' Derek says. 'What are you having?'

We follow him into a lavish reception room where many more people are sipping cocktails. A barman in full uniform is dispensing drinks. 'You just ask him for what you want and he'll get it for you,' Derek says jovially. He lowers his voice, 'And I may have a surprise for you two later as well.'

'Oh,' Larry says. 'And what might that be?'

Derek tips his nose and chuckles. 'Later.' Then he sweeps away from us, leaving us alone.

'Asshole,' Larry whispers.

'A surprise,' I gulp out. 'What the hell could it be?'

'I dunno.' Larry chews his bottom lip.

All I can think of is a jail cell, or the police. Oh, God, I feel sick again.

'Hey!' The barman greets us. 'What can I get you guys?'

'Orange and . . . ' Larry looks at me. 'Evelyn?'

'Whatever is in that woman's glass,' I point to a tall woman who's drinking something purple. It looks toxic and alcoholic.

'Coming right up.' The barman whizzes around like an open-ended balloon as he mixes and shakes and stirs and pours and crushes ice. A few minutes later, a tall glass of freshly squeezed orange stands in front of Larry and a purple concoction is placed in front of me.

'Whoa,' I'm like a kid. I take a cautious sip through the straw as the barman, head sideways, watches me with an amused smile. The drink is delicious. 'Wow, what's it called?'

'If I told you, I'd have to kill you.'

'Seriously,' I say, 'what is it? I have to know what I'm drinking.'

'That's the name,' the barman's eyes twinkle. 'I invented it. It won me bartender of the year last year. If you were to buy this in a bar, it'd cost you fifty dollars.'

About a dollar worth of the drink spurts out of my mouth. 'Oh, sorry.' I mop my mouth with my hand. 'Fifty dollars?' I say in disbelief.

'Uh-huh. Enjoy.' He laughs and walks off to serve someone else.

'Fifty dollars,' I hiss to Larry. 'Can you believe it?'

'Eh, yeah,' Larry hisses back. 'We are in billionaire territory here.'

Of course we are, I realise. And in fact, I'm supposed to be rich too. But really, fifty dollars for what is only a drink, albeit a lovely purple sweet drink. I could buy a nice pair of sandals for that or a couple of T-shirts. I take another long sip and follow Larry from the room, though not through the door we entered. This exit leads outside onto a patio area, which is akin to an acre field. A pool lies to the left and straight in front of us is a space set with long tables, heaving under plates and bowls of the most delicious-looking salads and chunky fries. Some brave souls are swimming in the pool and mucking about. People with gorgeous figures and toned bodies, of course. Not the flabby ones like me who will probably spend the evening sitting in chairs and scoffing everything in sight. I wish I could run, but it's too hot. And I wouldn't anyway, because I need this painting.

'Well, hello. How are you?' It's Tyler and Mary. Tyler is wearing wide, patterned Bermuda shorts and a blue stripy shirt that reminds me of a circus tent. He's sweating copiously and he mops his head with a handkerchief. Mary looks lovely in a white, empire line summer dress that somehow suits her, though I get the feeling it was designed with a twenty year old in mind.

'Hi Tyler, Mary,' I nod to them. I'm feeling a little hot too. I think the wig is making me sweat. I take a gulp of my drink, bypassing the straw to try and cool down.

'Lovely to see you all again,' Tyler says. 'I believe you went and bought the painting.'

'Not yet, but it's in the pipeline,' Larry answers.

'Come and get some food,' Mary says, 'come and sit with us.' She leads the way to the buffet.

We stand in line as our plates are heaped with the most fabulous fare. Mary keeps us amused by scolding Tyler every time he reaches for anything remotely fattening. In the end, his plate looks quite dismal with some chicken, tomato, cucumber and a lot of lettuce leaves. She calls out 'a-a-a' when Tyler reaches for some dressing and he glares at her. I'm beginning to feel that sitting with them will not be a lot of fun.

But as Larry has reminded me, this is not fun, it's business. I take another long sip of my drink.

Two hours later, I am smashed. I've had three purple cocktails, knowing that I will never again have the chance to imbibe one hundred and fifty dollars worth of drink in an evening. But whatever is in them has my head spinning and my stomach churning. I think my anxiety has fuelled my alcohol consumption, but I really didn't intend to feel so . . . so . . . sprawling. It happened all of a sudden. One minute I was on my third cocktail, then I was on my ear. I am vaguely aware, through a benign sort of haze, that Larry is looking increasingly alarmed, but as he raises his eyes and scowls at me, I think how utterly cute he looks and smile back at him, but it's an uncoordinated smile that wobbles a bit. I wish I could sleep.

'I think we should go find Derek,' Larry says in a low, cross voice, 'before you fall asleep.'

'Oh, Michael, don't be cross with her,' Mary flaps a hand at him. 'She's here to have a good time. And she's your boss.'

'Hurray!' I call loudly and collapse in a heap of laughter.

Tyler mutters something about practising what you preach.

'Pardon?' Mary says.

'Well, I was out to have a good time tonight and what was I allowed to have? Sparkling water and a few lettuce leaves.'

Larry stands up as they begin to bicker. He pulls on my arm. 'Come on, party girl, let's find Derek.'

'Derek, Derek, Derek,' I sing and then don't know why. I clamp my hand over my mouth and start to laugh again. I throw my fake hair back from my face and say, 'Oh, this hair is making me hot.'

'Up!' Larry wraps an arm around me, helps me to stand and I lean into him. Bidding goodbye to our dinner companions, he leads me across the patio and back into the house. Derek Anderson is standing there with a man and they seem to be having words about something. Recovering quickly, he turns to us and says, 'Hello you two, I was just about to come find you.'

'My hair is too hot,' I say but my voice rises up for some reason and sounds really loud.

Derek Anderson gives a tight smile. The man he's with coughs loudly.

'I've the painting upstairs if you'd like to see it again and we can discuss the price.' Then he smiles, 'And there's a surprise there too.'

'I hate surprises,' I say.

'You'll like this one,' Derek says as he begins to lead the way. 'Come on.'

'Great,' Larry tightens his grip on me and I think he's a bit cross. I seem to bring out the grump in him. But he looks gorgeous any old way, so who cares?

Derek looks back curiously, then beckons us up a massive stairway. The steps are the width of my apartment. At the top, the stairs break in two and sweep away in opposite directions. Derek leads us to the right. Larry props me up and glares at me every time Derek isn't looking. I know I have to behave. Behave Eve, I tell myself sternly. And I so want to, but my legs and arms and head won't listen.

We reach the top of the stairs, walk along the landing and Derek finally stops, pausing outside a white door. 'In here,' he says, his voice dipping, 'is a thing you folks might be interested in. If you take it now, we can do a deal for the two paintings. If you don't, I'll be selling it at auction next year.' He pushes open the door and I know instantly that we're in a temperature-controlled room where very precious painting are kept. A few pieces hang on the walls and Derek leads us to ... I can hardly believe it. Another Van Gogh portrait. This time it's a painting of another of the patients.

Oh, my God. My own one is hanging beside it, but it looks so fake to me I want to laugh out loud and tear it down. I inhale deeply. Whenever I see a genuine Van Gogh, I'm awestruck. It's like meeting my favourite movie star and getting completely tongue-tied, though at the moment, my tongue feels as if someone has knotted it up anyway. 'How wonderful,' I say, though I'm not sure if it comes out like that. I approach the painting with caution, Larry hovering behind me like an anxious parent. I think he's afraid I'll fall into the painting and break it.

Derek Anderson watches me, smiling. 'I'm afraid I've gone off Van Gogh a little. I'm more interested in collecting new artists now.'

'You don't go off Van Gogh,' I splutter, a little crossly, 'he's not like some sort of cheap plonk.' I turn back to the canvas and sigh contentedly. The line, the light, the brush strokes, the balance, the colours, the . . .

'So what's the deal?' Larry asks. 'You would like to sell us this too.' Is it my imagination or do his eyes look suddenly wolf-like? He's dead sexy.

'For thirty-two million euro, you can have both,' Derek looks at us. 'I'll give y'all a day to think about it. If you're not interested, that's fine, but you did say Ms Sweeney likes the portraits, Evelyn.' He turns to me.

'Yes, I did,' I agree, nodding. I almost tumble over. Larry deftly catches me by the arms and squeezes hard. 'Ow!'

He doesn't bat an eyelid. 'Thanks, Derek,' he says. 'We'll talk to Della and see if she's interested. My feeling is that she won't have the money. However, she might decide to buy that one instead of the other one.'

'No she won't!' I almost shriek. 'She loves the other one. That's the one she wants.'

Both men flinch. Unfortunately, I'm sober enough to know that I've embarrassed myself. I feel my face reddening.

'This Van Gogh is not for sale as a single item at this time,' Derek says.

'May I ask why?' Larry asks smoothly.

'Well, frankly, I prefer this painting to *Man with Swollen Face*,' Derek half-smiles. 'So I'm more anxious to sell that first, as you can understand.'

I'm insulted that he prefers the genuine painting to my fake one. Then think that maybe it's not surprising and start to laugh to myself.

'Is she OK?' Derek asks. Do I catch a hint of concern in his voice?

'She will be,' Larry answers heartily. 'So how much for *Man with Swollen Face*?'

'I've had it valued at sixteen million,' Derek answers. 'I think you were already told this?'

'Sixteen?' Larry shrugs. 'Twelve and I could say "yes" right now.'

'Twelve?' I gawk at him. We don't even have twelve million.

Both men seem to be ignoring me.

Time seems to go on and on.

Finally Derek says, 'Fourteen.'

'Done,' Larry shoves out his hand, which Derek shakes. Then he says, 'I can give you a deposit of five thousand dollars now just to secure the painting until the rest of the money comes through, if that's OK?'

Derek waves this away. 'Not necessary.'

'I'm afraid it is for me,' Larry says smoothly. 'You see, I offered for a painting before and thought the deal was done and was then usurped at the last minute. Unless I can pay a deposit and get a receipt from you, then the deal is off.'

Derek looks surprised, but I'm thrilled. Now no one can out-pay us. 'Well, if you insist. And you have the money now, you say?' He looks amused.

'In the boot of the car.'

'You Irish,' Derek snorts. 'OK, bring it in.'

I hadn't known Larry had taken half of the money with us.

Larry nods and he steers me out of the room and back down the stairs. 'Thanks, Derek, back in a second,' he calls back.

As we exit through the front door, the wall of heat almost flattens me, but thankfully the valet somehow remembers us and our car is driven to meet us before we descend to the end of the steps. 'Now *that* is service,' I tell the young man who hops out of the driver's seat and hands the keys to Larry.

'Thank you, ma'am,' he says.

'No, thank you very much.' I make an attempt to sit into the passenger seat but the doorframe is lower than I remember and with a crack, my head wallops off it.

Larry says nothing as I struggle to adjust myself. When I'm comfortably in, I find it hard to get the seatbelt into its slot. 'Damn thing is broken,' I mutter as it, once again, fails to make contact.

'Damn woman is drunk,' Larry says back as he leans across and buckles me in. 'Now, stay there and don't move. I'll be back in a minute.'

I watch in a haze as he hops back out and takes the case full of money from the boot. He arrives back fifteen minutes later with a slip of paper in his hand. 'Receipt,' he says to me and kisses it. His eyes are glittering. He hands the receipt to me, 'Kiss that darling, that is our passport.'

I kiss it too and then he takes it from me and slips it into his pocket. Now no one can take this from us. I sigh contentedly. 'You wonderful man,' I mutter.

Larry says nothing, just fires the engine and roars down the driveway. The stress suddenly leaves me or gets to me, I'm not sure which. I lean back and close my eyes. Inside my head, things tip sideways. I have to open my eyes again and very quickly too. 'I feel weird,' I mutter.

'Well, what a bloody surprise,' Larry answers coolly.

'Who rattled your cage?' I ask.

'You did,' he snaps, his gaze straight ahead. 'Honestly, Eve, you're plastered. Who knows what you might have said.'

'Hmm,' I sigh. 'I could have said that you are one sexy man. One wonderful man who got me my painting. A man that everything about him screams sleep with me, I'll give you a good time.' I pause. 'But I didn't.'

'Jesus,' Larry snorts, 'stop!' A faint smile plays about his mouth.

'I could have said—'

'Eve, stop. You're not so drunk that you'll be able to forget it in the morning.'

'I love you in your running gear,' I say dreamily. 'Back home, I'd watch you running out of the apartment block in your teeny shorts with your lovely long legs. You don't wear shorts like that here,' I add mournfully.

'Well, thanks for the admiration.' He flicks a glance over at me and I smile brightly. 'Now,' he goes on sternly, 'I just want you to know that I am really annoyed over this. You can't get bloody drunk, Eve.'

'There was rocket fuel in those cocktails,' I say thickly. 'And I drank mostly through a straw. Come on. Gimmie a break. I thought they were mild. And I was nervous.'

'I'm still annoyed.'

'But, thankfully, it doesn't make you any less gorgeous.'

'Oh, Christ,' he rolls his eyes and shakes his head. 'Bed for you to sleep it off.'

'Yum. Yum.' And then my stomach sort of heaves. 'Oh, stop the car. Stop the car. Oh, please.'

Larry yanks the steering wheel, pulls across a lane and just on time, I fling open the door and vomit onto the verge. 'Sorry, oh, I am sorry.' I pull off my wig and the blessed coolness of it. Then, I get sick again.

This, no doubt, is the most humiliating moment of my life.

No, scrap that. The most humiliating moment of my life is when Larry asks, 'Are you finished now?'

Oh, I'm so finished, he wouldn't believe. Wasted, I think, is the word.

'Yeah,' I say weakly.

'Come on,' his voice is softer now, 'in you get, party girl. Close your eyes, we'll be home in thirty minutes or so.'

I haven't the energy to answer. I can't even look at him. I just close my eyes and, despite the swirling in my head, somewhere in those thirty minutes, oblivion hits.

27

The next morning, sunlight hurts. Opening and closing my eyes hurts. Moving hurts. Thinking about getting up horrifies me, so I opt to stay in bed.

In bed?

How did I get to bed?

I glance down and see that I'm still fully clothed, which is a relief. Larry must have carried me in and covered me up, which was so nice. Well, it was practical too. I mean, he was hardly going to leave me in the car on my own all night, was he? I roll onto my side and to my embarrassment see he has placed a bucket near the bed. Oh, God.

Images of the evening flicker by. I think I carried it off OK. I didn't get drunk until we were nearly leaving. Then in the car. Oh, Jesus. I told Larry he was sexy. I told him I liked his running gear. I can't breathe at the memory. I'm crucified to the bed, rigid with mortification. How could I have said that? How could I? Well, the fact that I was plastered made it a lot easier. Hopefully he won't refer to it. That way we can both forget about it and minimise the horrendous humiliation I'm feeling.

'Hello, you're awake then?'

I jump, wondering if he knows I've just been thinking about him. Then blush guiltily.

'Hello!'

His voice sounds too loud in my jarring head.

'Hmm,' is about all I can manage. There is a terrible taste in my mouth.

'Would you like this super sexy guy to get you a cuppa?'

Bastard. I go even redder. 'About that—' I croak out. 'I was drunk. I had my gargle glasses on.'

He makes an anguished face. 'No? And here was me thinking you meant it. Do you enjoy toying with my emotions?'

I'd enjoy toying with something all right, I think crudely, but immediately banish the thought. I must still be a bit intoxicated. 'Sorry about last night. Those cocktails were powerful. And as for the cuppa, I'd prefer tea, thanks.'

He grins.

'And some water. And a couple of Disprin.'

'Coming right up.' He winks and leaves the room.

He *is* damn sexy though.

A couple of hours later, I've recovered enough to drink another cup of tea. Larry is waiting in the kitchen for me, laptop on, as I shamble in.

'Hi,' I croak out. 'You did good last night.'

'Yeah, I've been on to Derek's solicitor this morning and told him Della will be able to get the money transferred into his bank account four days before we leave. We can pick the painting up on the day it's happening.'

My stomach lurches. I'm not sure if it's from all the alcohol or the realisation that we just agreed to buy something we can't afford. 'But the fourteen million,' I say as I slide wearily into a chair, 'what about—'

'It'll be cool, he'll eventually accept what we have.'

'No,' I shake my head and it pounds, 'I don't think so.'

'Eve, trust me,' Larry says, pushing my phone across the table to me. 'Why don't you go and ring your godfather? Ask him for the bank details for the transfer.'

'He has to talk to me first.'

'He will. You're such a nice girl.'

'Shut up.' Damn it, how can he be so cool about everything! He begins tapping away on his laptop. I study him for a second but decide that he must know what he's doing. I mean, the deposit thing was genius, I'd never have thought of it. And the way I feel now, I haven't the energy to argue. Still, we have four days to talk about it. So, right now, there is nothing I can do except dial Robert.

My finger trembles as it punches in the numbers and the ringing of the phone on the other end hurts my ears. As per usual, Robert doesn't answer. Honestly, he's really taken my comment too much to heart. As each little ringtone passes, I feel a growing guilt for my remarks. I must really have hurt him. Finally his phone goes to voicemail. 'Robert,' I say, 'sorry yet again if I hurt you. You know you've been the most important man in my life since Dad died. Please ring me back.' I pause. 'And for the record, Larry says that you're not a con man because you only did a scam once and real con men do it over and over.' Then I hang up. From across the room, Larry smirks at me over his laptop. He seems to be e-mailing people, what about, I have no idea nor does he tell me and after snooping about in his things, I don't feel I have a right to ask. 'He'll know you're with me now,' he says.

'D'you know what? I don't care. We'll be out of here soon anyway.'

Larry returns to his computer and just as he does so, my phone rings. It's Robert.

'Hello, Robert.'

'You *are* with him,' he half-shouts at me. 'I was right.'

'You were right,' I say. 'What are you going to do about it?'

A pause. 'Where are you?'

'Paris.'

'You are no more in Paris than I am.'

'Madrid.'

'Are you?'

'Nope.'

'Eve, this isn't a joke. You are with a known felon. I will turn myself in, just come home.'

'We've got the painting.' It's not a lie, more a shrewd prediction based on knowledge.

A very long pause this time. 'No way.'

'Yes and we've met Derek Anderson and he's very nice.'

'He's an asshole,' both he and Larry say together.

'Is that him?' Robert pounces. 'Is that Larry I hear?'

'Yep. He says you're not a con man.'

'Put him on.'

'He wants to talk to you,' I hold the phone towards Larry, who shakes his head. 'He's busy,' I tell Robert.

'I'm sure he is,' Robert snorts. Then he says, 'Well, you tell him from me that if he harms a hair on your head, if he so much as cons you out of one single cent, if he gets you into trouble, I will hunt him down and kill him.'

The idea of awkward, placid, lanky Robert hunting anyone down makes me splutter with laughter. He wouldn't stand a chance with Bambi.

'I don't know why you're laughing,' Robert says grumpily. 'If your mother knew—'

'Well she doesn't. Liam is keeping her from thinking about me too much at the moment.'

'Yes, she does seem quite taken with him,' Robert admits. 'I'd never have put them together.'

'Me neither,' I agree, 'hopefully she'll see through him. She's gone all pretentious on me.'

'I know,' Robert says glumly. Then adds, 'Don't try and change the subject.'

'And I was sorry to hear about Dee.' I try it again.

The silence this time is loaded. 'Thanks,' is all he says.

'She thinks there's something you're not telling her?'

'Yes. And, of course, there is. So your mother said to—'

'I know what she said, Robert. Don't listen to her, she hasn't a clue. If I were you, I'd tell her the truth.'

'The truth? Oh no, I couldn't. She'd despise me.'

'She won't. She might think you're the stupidest man ever, that you never should have done it and that you've made me into a nervous wreck.'

'And I'd rather she left me than think those things of me, Eve,' Robert says quietly. 'I can't forgive myself for doing it to you.'

'I was half-joking,' I say, regretting my remarks. 'Just go to her,' I urge, 'talk to her. She's mad about you.'

He says nothing, though there's an audible gulp.

'And if she throws you out, go back. And keep going back. You were made for each other. Talk to her,' I say firmly again.

'When did you get so grown up?' he mutters.

'When I grew up,' I answer smartly. 'Now it's your turn.'

'Cheeky girl,' he sounds amazed, but I think he's smiling.

'Robert,' I say softly and with feeling, 'can I just say that you are a legend. You are so important to me and I don't want you in jail, I want you to be happy.' It's so much easier to say this emotional stuff over a telephone line.

'And I feel the same about you, Evie,' he says.

'Go after Dee. She's good for you.'

'Steer clear of Larry, he's bad for you.'

We're at an impasse. 'Love you, old timer,' I say instead.

'Love you too. When are you back?'

'This day next week. You'll have to e-mail me the bank details for the transfer of money. Can you get them?'

'I can. Don't let Larry see them, though.'

'OK.' I don't know if that'll be possible, but I agree anyway.

'Travel safe.'

'I will.'

We both hang up and I glance up to see Larry grinning widely. 'OK,' he says to me, 'next Tuesday we get that painting back.'

I feel suddenly ill and I'm not sure if it's last night's drink or nerves about what is going to happen next.

28

Larry had wanted to keep a low profile in the last couple of days before we get the painting, but there is no escaping Valerie and Peter and their determination to thank Larry for saving their daughter. So, while Millie is at home with a babysitter, Sunday night sees the four of us sitting in an upmarket Floridian restaurant. Larry is antsy in case any of the arty crowd frequent it, it'd be just our luck to be spotted by Tyler and Mary or someone who recognises us from our dealings with Derek Anderson. Though it's highly unlikely they'd recognise me, but Larry, with his white-blond hair and stunning looks, would stand out like a beacon. We order our starters and then, after the waiter leaves, Valerie asks, 'Is this your first time in Florida?'

'Yes,' I say.

'No,' Larry says.

'Oh,' Peter and Valerie say.

'Larry has been here before but I haven't,' I explain unnecessarily.

They both focus on Larry.

'I was here a few years ago,' Larry takes a sip of his wine. 'I, eh, came with a friend, but it's much better being here with Olivia.' He smiles at me. I smile back, thrilled, until I realise that, of course, he's lying. Valerie and Peter think we're a couple so we're acting like one. It's quite nice actually. I've almost forgotten what it's like to have a boyfriend. I take full advantage of the opportunity and rub his arm affectionately.

Valerie takes note of my arm rubbing and rubs her husband's arm whilst asking, 'Have you been married long?'

'No,' I say.

'Yes,' Larry says.

'Oh,' Valerie and Peter say again.

I wince. 'A year isn't long, is it?' I attempt a laugh.

'It's a lifetime when it's with you,' Larry jokes back.

Valerie and Peter don't know whether to join in the laughter or to look, as they do now, acutely uncomfortable. I want to kick myself. Larry and I agreed we'd been going out for twelve months but we never went into the nitty-gritty of things. I'm an amateur, but Larry is meant to be the professional, you think he would have decided whether a year was a long time together or not. Still, he's preoccupied with getting the painting back, so I can forgive him.

He's taken to referring to it as the 'operation'. Whenever I ask how he's going to make eleven million into fourteen, he says that that's not an issue and not to be worrying. But of course I'm bloody worrying. To be so near and yet so damn far. He keeps telling me to relax but it's hard.

'—meet?' Valerie, chin in hand, is looking at me. I notice that Peter has wrapped an arm about her shoulder.

'Huh? Pardon?'

'Valerie would like to know how we met,' Larry's eyes are twinkling. 'I think you should tell her.' Now his arm snakes its way about my shoulder.

'Really? You're better at that than I am.' We hadn't discussed that aside from the fact that we met at a club. I thought Larry would have something ready and now he's landing me in it, which is not like him. I think he's testing me. My heart 'whumps' in alarm.

'Not at all,' Larry shakes his head. 'You tell the story so well.'

He's laughing now because he knows I'm panicked. My eyes narrow as the nasty part of me comes out to play. 'You sure?'

'Oh, yes,' Larry swirls his wine about in his glass. 'Wait until you hear this, you'll laugh.'

Oh, so now he's challenging me to make up a funny story. Fecker. I kick him under the table and he winks at me.

'It was like this,' I begin only to be interrupted by the waiter as he lays our food in front of us.

When he leaves, Valerie nods, 'Go on. I love a good story.'

'Well,' I abandon the club story and decide to give Larry a good old-fashioned fright, 'Larry moved into the apartment beside mine about eighteen months ago.'

Beside me, Larry stiffens. This is a little too close to the truth for him. 'And because of that we went to the same club,' Larry says, eyeballing me.

'But we were neighbours first,' I say back sweetly.

'Neighbours!' Valerie smiles, 'how lovely.'

'How convenient,' Peter chuckles dryly, and we laugh.

'See, told you it was a funny story,' Larry nods. 'Now—'

'And because our apartment block is huge and full, there are always people coming and going,' I interrupt, 'I never got much chance to get to know people, and so I never really spoke to Larry. Then,' I lower my voice dramatically, 'one night, I heard an enormous yell from next door.'

'No!' Valerie and Peter say together.

'No,' Larry mutters in my ear.

'Oh, yes,' I nod. 'A yell that sounded as if someone was in trouble. Or scared or something. And, then, there it was again. And I realised that it was coming from Larry's apartment.'

'Were you being burgled?' Valerie asks Larry.

He shrugs, his eyes narrowing a little.

'So,' I say, 'I hopped out of bed and grabbed a big spanner, a really heavy one.'

'There was a spanner beside your bed?' Peter asks.

'Yep. Security. So, now, I inch open my door a little and hear the sound still coming from Larry's. Next thing he races into the hall in his boxers.'

'No!' Valerie and Peter again.

'Yep. Turns out he was overrun with mice and he was petrified.'

Peter and Valerie laugh delightedly.

'Poor little boy was all scared,' I tweak Larry's cheek. His smile is decidedly forced. 'Screaming like a girl. So, he had to sleep on my sofa while I laid traps for the mice. I caught about fourteen of them. It took you how long to go back into your place, Lar?'

'Why don't you tell us?' Larry says evenly, though I think behind his glower, he's amused.

'Oh, ages,' I roll my eyes. 'Honestly, I will never forget the look of naked terror on your face for as long as I live. He was on top of the sofa with a saucepan in his hand at one stage.'

Valerie chortles. 'No way!'

'Doesn't she tell it well?' Larry stands quite hard on my foot under the table.

'I'm surprised you let her tell it, mate,' Peter shakes his head as he digs into his crab starter. 'I'd be paying her not to.'

'She's not the sort of girl you can bribe,' Larry's eyes twinkle at me. 'She's as honest as the day is long.'

'I am too,' I say smartly.

His gaze holds mine and I can't take my eyes off him. Then he smiles slowly at me and a rebel flutter of longing uncurls itself inside my stomach. This is all wrong. I try hard to think of David and it sort of works. Larry breaks my gaze by turning to our hosts and asking cheerily, 'So, tell the two of us all about yourselves.'

They don't need to be asked twice. Amid much smiling and touching and loving gazes, they tell Larry and me their own story. I am aware as the night goes on that I'm looking wistfully at them and envying them their relationship. I've never had anything even approaching that. Never really let myself, I think, in a flash of uncomfortable insight. I glance at Larry at one stage and he's studying them with the same wistfulness I feel myself. Again, I wonder what Larry's real story is.

Valerie and Peter drive us back and invite us in for a night cap. We both refuse, pleading tiredness. Larry wraps an arm about me and walks us up the drive. 'Gotta keep it real,' he whispers into my ear.

Unlocking the front door, we bid Valerie and Peter goodnight.

As Larry closes the door, I kick off my sandals and plonk down on the sofa. 'They're a nice couple,' I remark.

Larry says nothing. He pulls a beer from the fridge and looks questioningly at me.

I hold out my hand and he crosses over and hands me one, then he sits in beside me and tips his can off mine.

'They seem so much in love, don't they?'

'Hmm,' Larry flicks on the television and plants his feet on the coffee table. Even though the sofa is wide, he is still sitting up against me, the length of his arm brushing off mine.

I take a sip of my beer and angle my body towards him, folding my legs under me. 'At least they don't think you're a big weirdo now.'

Larry flicks a glance at me. 'Yeah they do. A guy who's scared of mice?' He pokes me in the arm. 'Where did you come up with that?'

I laugh. 'Serves you right, big smart arse, getting me to tell the story of how we met.'

He grins a little too. 'It was a little test.'

'Did I pass?'

'Uh-huh. I would have told a nicer tale though.'

'Yeah? Like what?'

'Oh,' he puts his can down on the table and faces me. 'I dunno,' he pretends to think deeply, 'I spot a cracking looking girl walking by my apartment every day and despite being fresh out of jail, I pluck up every bit of courage I have to talk to her.'

'This, eh, sounds like what actually happened,' I say, confused. Though I'd never have thought he needed courage to talk to anyone.

'I ask her if she has any screwdrivers despite the fact that I have one in my place.' His voice grows husky.

'You did?' My heart is pounding. Is he leaning closer to me than before? I can feel his breath, smell his deodorant, see the flecks of black in his grey eyes, his lips look so kissable and—

'She doesn't have one as it happens, but what she does have,' he definitely moves closer, 'is a sheer black negligee and a garter and a silk— ow!'

I hit him hard in the chest. 'That is so not what happened,' I laugh, disappointed though that he's been leading me on. I take a sip of my can. 'I was very helpful, I lent you a knife.'

'A knife, darling girl, is not a screwdriver. It does not work.'

'It does for me.'

'No, tight running gear works for you,' he grins cheekily.

'Can we not refer to that again?' I say a little crossly. 'I was drunk.'

'Well, then, you should get drunk more often,' he says, and I'm not sure if it's a joke. 'It was nice to hear.'

'Huh,' I wave my hand dismissively and lager slops everywhere, 'at least I'm honest. I know nothing about what you like, nothing.'

'I like you.'

The simple statement floors me. I open my mouth to give a smart retort and then notice that Larry's expression hovers between defiance and embarrassment.

'Yeah?' I raise my eyes, determined not to get sucked in, yet feeling that I have to reciprocate in some way. 'Good. I like you too.'

His cockiness resurfaces, 'Well, I know that, you especially like—'

'Shut up!'

A smile.

The man is irresistible and available and in front of me. He makes me laugh and he's not a pushover and while every instinct screams at me not to get involved, it's not enough. David's gorgeous body and downright decency are not enough. Even as I touch Larry's arm and move in beside him, Robert's warnings, followed quickly by my mother's, crash into my mind. But, honestly, what is the point in being attracted to someone, having them there and not taking a chance? Yes, it might end badly but at least I'll have tried. Looking at my father wasting away, I'd made a vow that life was not going to stop me living, if that makes any sense. And, yeah, I played it safe and painted replicas, but I liked doing that. And at the time, it certainly felt as if I was taking control of my life and not bowing to the expectations of my mother or anyone else, though I'm not so sure now. But this, this is different. I know I'm playing with fire, but, damn it, I haven't ever done that. All this goes through my head as my hand reaches up higher still and touches Larry's cheek.

He looks at me, quizzically at first, then with what I hope is desire. His hand covers my hand and he presses his cheek against my palm. My heartbeat goes off the Richter scale. I can feel his eyelashes with the tip of my finger and the tiny pulse underneath his skin. And then, something in his eyes changes and he says, 'Eve, what are you doing?'

'Touching your face.'

'Why?' His breath sounds a little ragged.

'I want to.'

To my surprise, he takes my hand down and holds it between his own. He seems to compose himself, before he says firmly, 'I can't let you. You don't know me and I do have some scruples, you know.'

'But there's mayonnaise on your face.' I have no idea where that comes from, only a desperate sense of self-preservation kicks in. Otherwise I'll curl up and die.

'Oh, right. Oh, for a moment there I thought—'

'—that I was seducing you? What a laugh! As if!' I snort loudly. 'No way! God, the thought of it! No way.' Even I know it sounds false. 'No way!' I add anyway. My face is probably so red I'll combust in a second.

'All right, thanks.' He rubs his own face. 'Gone?'

'Yep.' Big cheery tone.

He stands up then, and I notice a bulge in his jeans. At least I turned him on.

'I'm heading to bed. See you in the morning.'

'OK. Bye now.' I watch him leave and want to kick myself. Still, I console myself that at least I tried, but it's a crap consolation.

Hours later, I'm lying awake, unable to sleep. And it's not because of the deal, which has caused my insomnia up to now, it's because I'm mortified. I keep going over and over what I did and wincing at my too hearty response to his rejection. How could I have phrased it differently? How will I behave tomorrow? It was one thing being drunk and spilling my guts, but being sober and trying to seduce him and getting turned down is in another league completely. It's like an anonymous affair compared to a Bill and Monica one.

'Hey?'

It's Larry. He's in a pair of boxers and stands just inside my door.

I lift myself up on an elbow. 'Hi.' I go all red. And a little flustered. I'm a sucker for Bart Simpson boxers.

'I can't get you out of my head,' he says, sounding annoyed with himself. 'And I'm sorry if I embarrassed you earlier.'

'I'm fine,' I say.

He crosses towards me, and with every step my poor heart hammers a little harder. 'I might have more mayonnaise on my face, d'you want to check?'

I splutter out a laugh. 'Oh, God, that's an awful line. How long did it take you to come up with that?' I'm going to have a heart attack, I'm convinced of it. He has fabulous skin.

'Hours.' And I think he's telling the truth. He pauses in front of me. 'Eve, I am seriously attracted to you. It's why I'm here in Florida with you in the first place. I've tried to keep it professional, but I can't.' A pause. 'And it scares me.'

Is this going to be my lucky night? My jackpot night. My euromillions night.

'I might as well just come out with it,' he says and all I can think of is, please do, and hurry up. I can't wait to see it. 'You turn me on something rotten.' There is a tiny smile on his face, though his eyes are wary. 'And I don't know if that's a good thing.'

Well I do. I push the covers off and stand up, his bare chest inches from mine. I'm wearing my teddy-bear print pyjamas. I skim my hands lightly across his tanned torso and he barely suppresses a groan. 'That'll do for me,' I say. 'Though it's not nearly as exciting as the running shorts.'

He laughs gently and tips my chin up and kisses me so exquisitely, I gasp. Then his hand finds its way into my hair and he pulls me in close and I find that I can't get near enough to him.

As my teddy-bear pyjamas go flying, I think that it's a perfect end to the evening.

29

We spend all of Monday in bed. Forget about drawing as a way to escape things, sex is way better. I haven't thought of the painting once. Well, maybe just once. Oh, I can't get enough of him, his arms around me, his nose nuzzling into me, his soft kisses, his hungry kisses, his smile, his teeth, his eyes. The way he looks at me, talks to me. The rumble of his laugh. I could go on forever. If he feels even a fraction of what I feel, it's a powerful thing. I lie in the crook of his arm and tell him stories about myself. About Olivia and Eric. About my schooldays. I say nothing about David, there is nothing to tell anyway. But the horrible moral person who lives in my head says there was a promise, an expectation on David's part. I push that away. It's like asking a sales assistant to reserve a pair of jeans for you and then finding a nicer pair in another shop and not going back.

No it's not, the moral person says nastily. You can't compare a nice man to a second-best pair of jeans.

Larry's finger tracing its way across my cheek banishes my dilemma. And I talk about other stuff. And he says the right things and laughs in the right places. Then I realise, yet again, that he hasn't said one word about himself. I turn into him, my palm flat on his chest, loving the feel of his skin under my fingertips. 'So, Mr McLoughlin, what about you? Just the one brother? Any sisters?'

'No sisters and, yep, just the one brother. Declan. Four years younger than me.' He catches my hand and lightly kisses my palm, pinning me with his gaze.

'And your mother?'

'Just the one.

'Stop,' I smile, 'I'm serious. I want to know all about you.'

His eyes flick away from my face and I become aware of a tension about him.

'Why don't you like to talk about yourself?' I ask.

There is a few seconds before he says quietly, 'Maybe because I've spent so much time conning other people into believing I'm someone that I'm not, that I don't quite know who I am. Don't quite want to be who I am.'

For some reason, that makes me really sad. 'So, who are you?' I ask carefully.

He shrugs before a slow grin works its way over his face, 'I think I'm a man who finds you incredibly sexy.' He attempts to kiss me but I push him off.

'No, Larry, that's not good enough.'

'OK, incredibly intelligent and sexy.'

I don't even smile.

He holds my gaze for a second before turning away. There is a silence. I break it. 'OK, I'll be honest with you,' I say, wondering if it is completely wise. 'I have never felt about anyone else the way I feel about you. It's lust, pure and simple.'

He laughs a little, but I haven't finished. 'I feel, Larry, that I could love you if you let me in but otherwise it's no good. In fact, feeling this way about you is weird for me because, bizarrely, I've never felt this way about any guy before, and I still think you might con me tomorrow and I feel bad thinking that because when I'm with you, you make me believe everything you say.' I heave a sigh of pure relief. 'There.'

At least I've got his attention. He's staring at me again and he looks a little hurt. He lifts himself up on his elbow and looks down on me. 'I won't con you tomorrow,' he says passionately. 'No matter what, you have to believe that. Do you believe that?'

And looking at him, with his solemn face, of course I believe it. But I'm not going to make it easy for him. 'So how will you do it?'

'Quite easily.' He pauses. Then says, 'OK, look, ask me some questions about myself and I promise to answer them as well as I can.' He reaches up and touches my face. 'I'm not used to this stuff. But,' he gives me a bleak smile, 'you might not like what you hear so . . . ' his voice trails off and he flushes a little.

I wonder if it's worth it. I really fancy this guy, but I don't know how I'll feel if he tells me something awful about himself. And in that case, how will we continue to be together for the next few days? Was sleeping with him a gigantic mistake? Eh, no, I think. It was knee-tremblingly fabulous. Does my lust go deeper? It might be a good idea to find out before I go back and disappoint David. I decide to ask something simple to start off with. 'Your tattoo of the fish. Why?'

He flinches a little and subconsciously he rubs the tattoo on his wrist, the way he did once before when I asked him. 'Well,' he begins hesitantly, 'I got it when I came out of prison. It's a salmon.'

I nod encouragingly. I already know this. 'So why a salmon?'

He swallows hard and I can't decide if he's ashamed or embarrassed when he admits, 'Well, when salmon are born they leave their birthplace and then later, against all the odds, they make the trek home.'

I get the feeling I'm supposed to understand but I don't. 'So?'

'That's what I wanted to do when I left prison,' he says softly, 'make the trek back to where I was before I started this kind of life.'

'Oh,' a stab of remorse hits me. 'Did I spoil it for you?'

'Nah,' he shakes his head and the look in his eyes makes my heart flip over like a pancake on a pan. 'I'm a sucker for a damsel in distress. Especially cute ones with little button noses.' He tries to smile but it's half-hearted. 'Anyway, this is a good thing we're doing.'

'It is,' I say adamantly, 'we're giving money back and taking a faulty painting off the market.'

'Exactly.'

He leans down and kisses my forehead. I close my eyes and I wish we could just stay here forever. But, of course, me being me, I have to ask, 'And the little girl in the pictures on your computer?'

His soft kisses on my forehead come to an abrupt halt and he pulls away from me. 'My daughter,' he says tersely, as if he's whipping off a very painful plaster and it has to be done quickly. 'She's, she's . . . well, she's my daughter.'

'And?'

He looks quizzically at me, though there is fear in his eyes. 'And what?'

'Where is she now? Is she with her mother?'

He turns away. 'Yeah, yeah, she's with her mother.'

Something in his voice doesn't quite add up, though my gut feeling is that he's telling the truth. 'And do you ever see her?' I touch his arm but he pulls away.

'No.' The pain in his eyes hurts me. 'Can we not do this? It's, well, I can't talk about her.'

'Will she not let you see her? You have rights you know.'

'Yeah, I know.'

'You need to go to a solicitor and tell them—'

'Eve. Stop. It's fine.' His tone is abrupt. To my surprise he hops out of bed and says, 'I'm starving. What do you fancy? Pizza? Burgers? What? I'll take the car and find a takeaway.'

'That's it? That's all you'll tell me?' I'm gutted. 'It's not much. I need more.'

'I'll settle for lust for now,' he cracks a grin. Then he sits back down beside me and a shiver runs through my body. 'I need time,' he says after a bit and he sounds sincere. 'I'm good at scamming, lying, cheating. Not so good on the caring, sharing stuff.'

'How reassuring,' I answer dryly, bitterly disappointed.

He doesn't reply, just stares me out. And I know that it's more than lust for me and that I will give him time. I've let him in, the first guy in so long, and I need to know it was worth it. 'Surprise me,' I say. Then at his puzzled look, I add, 'with dinner.'

'OK.' He looks relived as he heads out of the room. 'I'll grab a shower and go then.'

'You can grab me if you like,' I smile.

His laugh can be heard all the way upstairs.

He takes ages to get back. In fact, I'm beginning to worry when he eventually returns with some Indian food.

'Where the hell were you?' I ask. 'God, I was getting worried.'

'Finding an Indian is no easy task, and I fancied a spicy dinner.'

'In this heat?' I smile at him as he starts to dig in. Then I sit in beside him and he wraps an arm about me and it seems like the most natural thing in the world.

I think, and it's a bit scary, that I have just fallen in love.

30

Tuesday morning I am a puddle of nerves. This is it. D-Day. According to Larry, we should have the painting back by the afternoon. I've given him the bank codes for the money, but I don't know how we will buy the painting as no extra cash has miraculously appeared and Larry hasn't made one phone call to bargain Derek down. He still won't tell me what he has planned and I have visions of him overpowering Derek Anderson and his solicitor, grabbing the painting and making me run for it. I couldn't possibly run in my high heels. I can barely walk in the stupid things, but they're a necessary evil in Evelyn's case.

At eleven, we're ready to go. Larry, dressed in a fabulous light-grey suit with a grey shirt, is gorgeous. In fact, just looking at him turns me on. I, however, look awful as usual. The green suit I'm wearing makes me look not unlike Kermit the Frog. I reckon that Della Sweeney would go mad if she thought for one minute that a troll like me was representing her interests in the US. Poor Della. Every time we use her name, I cringe with guilt. If there is any way at all I can be original, she will benefit. I swear.

'Hey,' Larry grins at me, 'you ready?'

I smile bravely, my stomach churning. 'No choice, have I?'

'Nope.' Larry stands back and surveys me. 'You look great. OK, next door have gone out, so we're ready to roll.' He ushers me to the door, bleeps the car open with his keys and I make a dash for it. He follows, after first depositing the last five thousand of cash in the boot. It's in a few cases for some reason. Is that part of the plan?

'Let's go.' He's just about to fire the engine when his mobile bleeps. 'Gimmie a sec.' He pulls the phone from his inside pocket, reads the text and sends one back. 'Just my brother wondering if I'm OK,' he says.

'He should have sent it tonight, you'll know for sure then.' I try to make light of it, but my voice trembles.

Larry looks anxiously at me. 'Deep breaths, Eve. It'll be cool to sound excited at the gallery, don't for God's sake sound as if you're going to collapse.'

'Yeah, I'll be fine. Let's go.' The sooner it's over, the better, I think.

The traffic is heavy and we're a little late but, as luck would have it, there is a parking space right opposite the gallery. 'There, over there,' I jab my finger in its direction but Larry drives on by. 'There was a space there,' I say.

'Not big enough,' Larry pronounces, before finding what looks to me like a smaller space and pulling in. We're a block away from the gallery now.

'I will not be able to walk all the way over in these shoes,' I moan, knowing that I'm being petty but, hey, I found a perfectly good space and he drove by it. Larry laughs, uncaring. I do believe he's enjoying this. 'You're loving this, aren't you?' I say as I unclip my seatbelt and adjust my hair in the mirror. I look terrible.

'Beats sitting in my apartment all right,' he says as he hops out. He seems to scan the area before beginning the walk across the road. I clip clip alongside him, my heels wobbling dangerously. There should be lessons on how to walk in stilettos. I feel like a newborn colt trying out his over-sized legs. Larry walks beside me solicitously until we're at the base of the gallery steps, then as I cautiously put one high heel in front of the other, Larry strides confidently up to the door and over to the reception desk. I pause just before I enter the cool foyer and turn to look back to the street. This is it, no man's land. When I go into this building, there will be no turning back. I will be finally committing myself to the 'operation'. Right now, there is still time to back out. I could call it off, here and now. I stare across the wide concourse, to the road and the blue sky beyond. I look at the people strolling up and down on the sidewalks, at the dogs trotting obediently beside their owners, at women in short shorts and shorter tops, rollerblading their way up International Drive. Kids eating oversize ice-creams and babies being wheeled in buggies. There's a man across the road and he's staring at me. I squint a bit but, sensing my gaze, he turns away quickly and walks off. There is something about the way he scurries along that makes me uneasy. My heart skips a beat and I turn back towards the gallery and see Larry flirting shamelessly with the woman on reception.

'Lar— Michael,' I call, 'can you come over here a minute.'

'Yes, boss,' Larry strides towards me. 'What the hell are you playing at?' he hisses. 'Don't call me Larry.'

'Someone is watching us,' I say, and my voice is frayed with panic. 'I saw a man staring at me. I really don't have a good feeling about this.'

'Who?' Larry squints into the glare of the sun. 'I can't see anyone.'

'Well, he's gone now. It was a man in a sort of blue uniform.' I gasp as a thought hits me. 'It could have been a policeman. Oh, God.'

'Calm down,' Larry casts a glance at the receptionist, who is watching us. Turning back to me, he says, 'What reason would a policeman have to follow us? Eh? I mean look,' he indicates the street, 'How many people are wearing blue?'

And he's right. Loads of people are.

'It could just have been a random passer-by,' Larry says reasonably.

'Yeah, you're right.' I'm letting nerves get the better of me. But the uneasiness still persists, even as I follow Larry towards the desk. It was the way the man looked at me, as if he knew. I don't think Larry would understand if I tried to explain it though.

The receptionist looks questioningly at us. 'Y'all OK?'

'She's not feeling too well,' Larry explains. 'Because of the heat.'

I give what I hope is a wan smile.

'Aw, hon, that's too bad,' the girl says sympathetically. 'You don't want to be wearing that green suit all day, y'hear?'

'I hear,' I smile.

'Now, you go on up to the fourth floor. The director and Mr Anderson are up there.'

'That is fantastic, thank you,' Larry says. 'Come on, Evelyn, you'll feel a lot better when you see the painting.'

'Yes. Yes I will.' And my voice sounds normal and strong and even a tad excited. It belies the churning inside.

We ascend in the lift, a plush affair with mirrors and carpet. Larry stays in character; I suppose he's afraid there'll be a camera or something in the lift. Both of us look downwards so no camera will capture our faces. We don't exchange a word.

The lift pings as we reach the fourth floor then Larry stands aside to let me out. I walk as confidently as my heels will allow towards a door at the end of the corridor that says 'private viewing, do not enter'. Larry hurries along at my side, every inch the deferent employee.

Knocking, we're told to enter and I see that there are three men present. Derek Anderson, the director of the gallery and the man that was at Derek's house the night we saw the two paintings.

'Hello, gentlemen,' I say and I like the imperious tone in my voice.

'May I make the introductions?' Derek says, coming out from behind a large mahogany desk, and without waiting for anyone to agree, he immediately starts introducing us all. It turns out that the man we haven't met before is the solicitor. His name is Kurt Brandonberry, which sounds more like a sports star than a solicitor. Once we all know who everyone is, the director unlocks a small door at the back of the office and pushes it aside. Entering the small viewing room, which is climatically controlled, we see the painting hanging on the far wall.

Larry and I immediately make our way towards it.

'Looks great,' Larry says. 'You happy with that, Evelyn?'

'Yes.' I turn towards the men. 'And the provenance? Can I study it?'

'Indeed, if you'd like to come back outside,' Kurt ushers us out and, without closing the door, as Larry is still peering at the painting, he opens his briefcase and extracts a brown file. 'It's all here. Amazing, really, that it's all so perfectly chronicled. Now,' he spreads the papers on the desk and I sit in front of them, Larry coming to lean over my shoulder. I can feel his breath on my neck. In normal circumstances, that would turn me on something rotten, but this is far from normal. I take up the pages and marvel at Robert's ingenuity. A letter, the page aged, probably with tea or something more sophisticated, written in French. I haven't a clue what it says but Derek has helpfully included a translation for me to read. Then a photocopy from the French archives with records of this fictitious family. And photographs. And letters from the family to the imagined individual in my painting. They christened him Jean Claude, which is a bit of a stereotypical French name, I think.

'Amazing,' Larry breathes in awe. And it's not an act, he really is impressed.

'Indeed,' I say, carefully laying the papers to the side as I read them.

'And the painting was found in an attic by the great-grandson of this person?' Larry asks.

'Yes, and in perfect condition too,' Kurt answers. 'Obviously, it wasn't framed.'

'Obviously,' Larry agrees and again turns back to the letters. His phone bleeps and he looks apologetically at the men. 'Sorry, business. I'll just get it.'

'No problem,' Derek Anderson says. He's been staring out the window. He sounds a little nervous too, for some reason.

Larry attends to the text, while I sit, trying to compose myself. This is forgery on a grand scale. I know the details of it had been explained to me by Robert, but just being presented with the work involved almost takes my breath away. I place the final piece of correspondence back in the folder and look up to find all three men staring at me. 'Well, this all seems to be in order,' I smile, my heart jack-knifing in trepidation.

'Great,' Derek says, slapping his palms together. 'Now, shall we discuss the transfer of money?'

'All I have to do is ring the bank,' Larry says, holding his phone aloft. 'Now, if you'll bear with me, here is the receipt for the first five thousand we paid as a deposit.' He lays the receipt on the table beside the provenance. 'Now, I'll just call the bank to release the funds.'

He starts to dial and my mouth goes suddenly dry. How is he going to do it? Where will the money come from?

Just then, someone knocks on the door.

'We're not to be disturbed,' the director, who hasn't said a word so far, calls out crossly.

'Police, sir, please open up!'

The police? My heart gives a huge lurch and I have to hold on to the table so I don't fall out of my seat. Larry glances at me and he, too, looks a little freaked. His finger pauses mid-dial.

'The police?' the director says startled. He moves towards the door just as Larry makes a move to stop him. But it's too late, the door is opened and three burly officers burst in. I gasp as Larry attempts to make a run for it but unless he plans on jumping out the window, he hasn't a hope. Two of the officers grab him immediately, throw him to the ground and cuff him. I can't move at all. I'm frozen to the seat.

'Let me go! What is all this?' Larry struggles on the ground.

'Yes, what is this about?' Derek asks, looking alarmed.

'Let me go!'

I think I'm going to be sick.

'You have the right to remain silent. Anything you say can and will be used against you in a court of law. You have the right to speak to an attorney and to have an attorney present during any questioning. If you cannot afford a lawyer, one will be provided for you at government expense.'

'Hey!' Larry protests again.

'Sir,' the tallest of the policemen says to Larry with perfect calm, 'you will be quiet or I will be forced to restrain you.'

Larry glances up at me. I feel like I'm in a dream, as if this can't be happening. But I'd been uneasy, I should have trusted my gut . . .

'What is going on?' Derek Anderson asks again. His lawyer is gawping open-mouthed at the three officers while the director of the gallery is peering at me.

I can't meet their eyes. All I can do is stare in horror at Larry as he's hauled roughly to his feet.

'This man is in the United States illegally,' the officer states. 'He's been using a false passport and is posing as an art collector. We've been following him since he arrived.'

'Posing?' Derek says.

'And you, ma'am,' the second officer says through a thick bushy beard, 'are under arrest too for aiding and abetting a criminal.'

I give a low moan. 'But we weren't doing—'

'Shut up,' Larry barks at me.

'No,' I say, standing up with some difficulty, one hand holding on to the table so I won't collapse with fear. 'Let me tell them. You see officer—'

'You'll have all the time in the world to explain at the station, ma'am.' Then to my horror, he turns me roughly around and I'm cuffed as well. And he tells me that I have the right to remain silent too.

The three men are open-mouthed now. It would make a great photograph, I think unexpectedly. 'Can someone please tell me what is going on?' Derek Anderson demands in the manner of someone who is used to his questions being answered promptly. 'These people were going to buy one of my paintings.'

'We have reason to believe that Mr McLoughlin was purchasing a painting with stolen money,' the officer says.

'No that's—' Again I try to explain but the officer holding my hands gives me a very rough shake and I stop abruptly. Visions of being in jail are nothing to visions of being in jail in the US. How will anyone ever visit me? I look at Larry and feel desperately guilty. If it wasn't for me he wouldn't be in this mess.

'It's my fault, not his,' I gasp out.

'Shut it!' Larry snaps, and there is something in his eyes that makes me do as he says. It dawns on me that we've never concocted a story to tell the police in case we were caught.

'They were about to buy my Van Gogh in there,' Derek Anderson splutters, jabbing in the direction of the small viewing room. 'Stolen money?'

'Take them away,' the tallest officer commands, and the way he says 'them' is full of such disdain that I cringe. He turns to the tallest officer, 'Dan, go check the painting out.'

Dan strides into the viewing room as Larry and I are frog-marched out of the office.

'I'll take the blame for it,' I tell Larry tearfully as we're pushed towards the lift. Behind us, Derek Anderson's raised voice can be heard berating someone. The man sounds distraught and I feel sorry for him. 'I'll say it was all my fault.'

'Aw, would you?' Larry looks gratefully at me. 'Thanks.'

'Shut up!' Another push from the officer.

I am a bit taken aback at the way Larry has accepted my offer. I mean it but I didn't think he'd actually let me take all the blame. I didn't mess anything up. He should have known they were on to us. Didn't I say there was a policeman watching us today? If he had only listened—

And then it dawns on me how far we actually got. We'd been in touching distance of the painting. Another day or so and we'd have been safe and whatever plan Larry was working on would have succeeded.

Behind me, Derek Anderson is yelling loudly for some reason. Yelling and cursing. I'm glad I'm not the one he's taking his bad temper out on. I don't have time to think about it though because we are manhandled into the lift and when it pings open we're pushed roughly across the foyer as the receptionist gasps. Larry keeps his head low and so do I. He struggles a little and, watching him, I do too, though I have never felt so sickened in all my life. This is even worse than hearing about the painting in the first place.

We're hauled out into the street where a crowd seems to have gathered and then we're shoved roughly into the back of an unmarked van. The policeman hops in beside us and there's a small wait as the back doors are slammed closed. Minutes later the other two emerge from the building and I can see through the small grille in the van that Derek Anderson and the solicitor have followed them out. They look quite subdued, maybe they're in shock.

I give a low moan as the two policemen hop into the front of the van and put it in gear before swerving away from the sidewalk, blue light screaming.

Larry and I spin onto the floor.

I knock my head.

'Jesus Christ,' Larry picks himself up. 'You OK, Eve?'

I nod miserably.

Then Larry calls to the two officers in front, rather bravely, I think, 'Can you not slow down? You've bruised me enough as it is.'

'Just keeping it real,' the cop in the back with us says.

The exchange confuses me. I'm further confused when the policeman unlocks Larry's cuffs and then indicates me to turn around so that he can do mine. 'What— why?'

There's a second's pause and then one of the policemen in the front says incredulously, 'You didn't tell her? Larry, that's terrible.' And they all start laughing for some reason. I look from one to the other in total confusion.

Larry grins at me. 'Only way it could be done,' he says, 'I'm sorry, Eve, I couldn't tell you because your reaction had to be real.'

'What?' Next thing my handcuffs are unlocked and fall to the floor of the van.

'She's not the brightest, is she?' the bearded officer laughs from the front.

Larry smiles in response. 'Eve,' he says, 'meet my associates.' He indicates the beardy one, 'That's Clive, who I think you met before.'

Shell-shocked, still not fully comprehending, I stare in amazement at Clive; well, I can only see the back of his neck. 'Clive?' I say and he nods. 'You look different with the beard.'

'You look different with the wig,' he says.

'And John and Paul.'

The two others nod to me.

Like an electric jolt through water, it suddenly occurs to me that I'm not under arrest. That I am not going to prison for the rest of my life and I have to sit down. I feel sick.

'You OK?' Larry asks.

'Just, just so horribly glad.' I half-laugh, half-cry. Then I wonder why. What's it been for? 'What was the point of that?'

'Clive,' Larry says, winking at me, 'can you show Eve the point of that?'

'With pleasure,' Clive reaches down and tosses a special looking briefcase into the back of the van. 'Open it,' Larry grins.

'Derek Anderson's own,' John pipes up. 'He insisted on putting the painting into it himself.'

'The painting is in there?' I can hardly believe it. I run my hands over the case and Larry, bending down, clips it open for me.

And there it is, perfectly placed so it won't crease, perfectly temperature controlled so it won't decay.

'Oh, my God.' I pull a little back, overawed, and stare at the three of them. 'How did—'

'Easy.' Larry closes the case again and takes it, placing it carefully beside his feet. The van hurtles along, rattling and screaming, and yet Larry looks perfectly at home. 'Once I'd placed the deposit on the painting and had got a receipt, it was all evidence. And this painting has to be logged as evidence because Mr Anderson was selling us a painting he knew to be fraudulent.'

'What?'

Larry grins. 'He knew it was a fake, Eve. I could tell from the very first time I met him and I said that it looked as if it had only been painted yesterday.'

'No way!' I'm appalled that Derek would sell us a fake, then realise the hypocrisy of that and feel like giggling.

'He denied it, you know,' Clive says from the front. 'When we put it to him, he said he didn't know it was a fake but, after a bit of a shouting match, he agreed that we could impound it so it could be tested. I told him to stay in the area in case we needed him, that this Van Gogh was likely to be one of a hoard of fake paintings that had come onto the market about ten years ago. He acted all surprised.'

'He's acting all right,' Larry is adamant.

'And why did you get us arrested?' I ask, rubbing my wrist where the cuffs had bit into them.

'The best way to get us out of there. He's not expecting to hear from us now.'

'We've a maximum of three days' grace to get out of the country before he realises the painting is gone,' Clive says, turning back to the road.

'What would you have done if he hadn't known the painting was a fake?' I ask.

'Same thing,' Larry answers. 'Whether he knew it was a fake or not, he'd still have had to hand it over.'

'Why didn't you just do that instead of this whole charade with me and you?' I am utterly confused.

'I told you, because it's all evidence.'

I've no idea what he means but I'm sure it'll become clear to me as the days unfold. I'm so relieved not to be facing years in jail that I can't think straight.

'So,' Larry says, making my heart flip again, 'we have now officially stolen the painting and the five grand left over – Eve, I hope you agree that can be distributed to my loyal henchmen. They have to pay their expenses and they didn't come cheap.'

I am in no position to disagree so I nod without actually saying 'yes'. I am now paying criminals. Christ.

'Didn't come cheap,' Clive scoffs from the front. 'My arse. We only did it for you.'

Larry looks pleased all of a sudden before he turns to me. 'OK. What happens next is that one of the lads has taken our hire car and he'll bring it back to the villa tonight. I'm going to drop you off at the villa, Eve, and you can stay there until your flight back. You're better off keeping to the same flight, that way no one gets suspicious if you don't turn up at the airport on the day.'

'OK.' I am dazed. I wish I could get my brain to go faster, but it's desperately playing catch up. My mother once threw a surprise party for my birthday whilst pretending that we were going for a quiet dinner together. All that night, as I looked at the faces of my friends, I still couldn't get my head around the fact that I was at my own party. I feel a bit like that now, though not as happy. 'And you?'

'The less you know the better.' He taps his nose.

'So, so you're leaving me?' I hate the needy sound in my voice, but I've just been involved in a crime and I'd like someone to be with me. And I feel a little angry too. How dare he put me through that. How dare he tell me the less I know the better. How dare he pretend that he was going to let me take all the blame.

'For now.'

'But what about the painting and the money?'

'It's cool. Trust me. Now,' he reaches up and pulls the wig off my head and then tenderly removes my glasses. 'Much better,' he pronounces. Holding out a pair of my shorts and a T-shirt, he says, 'Put those on, we're going to drop you at the top of the road to the estate.' I take them from him, not even bothering to ask when he took them from my room. Then he digs into the pocket of his suit and hands me the key of the villa. 'Take that and safe home.'

It dawns on me that this is the last time I'll see him until he decides otherwise. I want to hug him but his body language isn't particularly encouraging. Instead, I change into my shorts and T-shirt as the men politely look away, and then, as the van pulls up at the entrance to the estate, I hold out my hand and he shakes it. 'Take care,' I say.

'Bye, Eve.'

'Thanks, guys,' I add.

They all wish me luck.

Then I hop out and walk on without looking back. I barely register that he now has my money, the painting and the details to the eleven million sitting in the bank account.

I suppose I really have to just trust him.

31

The next couple of days crawl by, a bit like the cockroaches as they march in and out of the kitchen. I catch a few of them but can't help feeling desperately sorry for whoever hires this villa after us.

I'm a bit paranoid about going outside, even into the pool area. Each time I hear feet approaching the house, I think it really is the police coming to arrest me. I'm tempted to pack up and move somewhere else, but since no one knows I'm here, it'd be stupid. And besides, it might look odd if I did. I've spent some time sketching, though there is only so much I can draw from the limited view of the back window and I'm way too nervous to go farther afield. So far, there has been nothing in the media about the theft of a painting, though I suspect when the 'police' don't get in contact with Derek Anderson, the shit will hit the fan.

I wonder where Larry is now. When I got back that day, I let myself in and the thought occurred to me that Larry hadn't packed, that he had no clothes. How would he get his belongings home? Or his laptop? Was he expecting me to do it? I'd run up to his room, remembering the last time I'd been there, and pushed open the door. It was empty. The bed was perfectly made, the curtains pulled, the bathroom shining. He'd obviously packed and put his case in the car along with the money when I hadn't been around. The room looked as if he had never been there.

There was no message for me. No instructions about what to do. I'd sat down on his bed and the doubts had assailed me. What if I never saw him again? What if he's taken my painting and is even now selling it on? But then I think of the guy who'd held me in his arms and kissed me and confided in me and, suddenly, I don't believe that he would cheat me.

On Tuesday night, late, someone had driven the car back to the villa and left the key on the front seat, which was a bit risky, but then maybe not. For the first time it occurred to me how much planning had gone into this ... operation. Larry had packed his clothes, put them in the boot and then given the key to someone without me being aware of it. They'd also hired costumes and the word 'cossies' from the e-mail I'd found on his computer makes sense suddenly. I wonder when his friends had flown in to Florida or if they'd been on the same flight. I remember the guy he'd talked to the first night of the gallery opening, the one he'd said was a potential artist. Yeah, I think wryly, a potential con artist.

On Friday, the night before I leave, I take the last bottle of wine from the press and pour myself a substantial glass before settling down in front of the television. I've drunk quite a lot of wine the past few nights, I find it stops me worrying about my painting and Larry and driving the monstrosity of a car back to the airport.

It's nine o'clock and the news has just started. I'm about to flick channels but a big picture of a beaming Larry fills the forty-inch flat-screen.

'Oh shit!' I splutter on my wine, droplets fall over my blue top and create a hell of a stain. My finger remains frozen over the remote control and I know that even though I don't want to watch this, I will. It's sort of like being at a boy band concert.

Has Larry been arrested?

'Have you seen this man!' the anchor man, whose name appears as Chuck Ryan, bellows.

Intro music.

'And we lead tonight with an audacious robbery of a Van Gogh painting by an experienced team of con artists,' Chuck says excitedly. He starts recounting an accurate version of the story and then some very grimy footage of Larry and me is aired. Blessedly, I don't think anyone would recognise me, but Larry is a little more conspicuous. 'While we have no details of the female involved, we can be sure that she is no relation of Miss Della Sweeney, a prominent art collector. Miss Sweeney denied knowing anything about it. The details on the supposed art dealer slash gallery owner calling himself Michael Shanagher are as follows. Brad?'

Poor Della. Shame knows no boundaries with me now. I swallow hard and hope she's OK.

Next thing, Brad appears holding an enormous microphone. He's dressed in a stripy suit and looks more like a gangster than Larry ever could. Brad looks thrilled to be part of the story. 'Michael Shanagher' he hollers, 'is believed to be a consummate con man. While no name has yet been released, it is believed that this man was released from jail in Ireland in the past eighteen months. He specialises in business scams. Police have said the man widely suspected of this con is an enigma. There is not much background information on him, but it seems the boy has been in trouble from a young age, preferring to hang out with petty criminals rather than attending school. After the death of his father in tragic circumstances, his mother struggled to support him and his younger brother. His first scam involved defrauding restaurants out of small amounts of money. He made over four hundred dollars before the scam was discovered. Tragically, his mother was unable to look after the boys and they were put into care until this man was eighteen, when he took responsibility for his younger brother. Two months later, the boy is reported to have pulled his first serious con when he scammed two thousand books from various book publishers by pretending that his original purchase was faulty. He was later found selling his books from a car boot. A year later, he reportedly scammed two thousand pounds from the bookies in a race meet. He quickly progressed to other major business scams.'

He outlines some other scams Larry has pulled but all I can focus on is that Larry's dad died in tragic circumstances. Larry hadn't said that, he'd told me his dad had left them. Had he killed himself? Or has the news got it wrong? I think of my own dad and of how I'd been prepared for his death. It hadn't made the grief any easier, but at least I'd understood. What must Larry and his brother have gone through? And then losing their mother, albeit in a different way?

'And what makes a guy into a con man, Brad?' the anchor man asks cheerfully.

'Well, Chuck, I've a doctor of psychology here.' The camera pans to a very serious-looking woman, hair in a bun and wearing a dark suit and a sombre expression. 'Dr Gena Ryan,' Brad says, 'can you tell us what makes a con man?'

Gena blinks slowly, coughs slightly and licks her lips. She begins to speak in a measured, posh sort of a voice, 'Well, Brad,' she smiles widely at Brad, 'as you can appreciate, analysing con men is difficult because you simply cannot trust a word they say.'

I swallow. Great. I take a drink of wine.

Brad laughs heartily.

'They discover at a very early age how to manipulate people,' Gena carries on 'They're also masters of body language and they can read people very well. In fact, they'd make great politicians. One of them once told me that he could go into a room and pick out the most vulnerable person in it in an instant. Con men specialise in finding out what you want, promising it to you and then ripping you off. What is unusual here is that there seems to have been a well-organised gang involved led by this individual. Most con men operate alone or with just one other person. I can only conclude that this man operates out of necessity. It is interesting to note that his first serious con was done only after his father's death.'

'Well, thanks for that, Dr Ryan. Back to you Chuck.'

The camera goes back to the studio. Chuck looks intently at me, or so it seems, 'Still on the story, we talked to a few people who had had contact with the couple during their stay here. Many of you will recognise Tyler Smith and his wife Mary.'

Tyler and Mary appear. Tyler has his arm reassuringly about Mary's shoulders as if Larry had personally attacked her. 'Hello folks,' Chuck says, 'can you tell us how you met the couple?'

'At a public display of Derek Anderson's artwork,' Tyler says gravely. He's loving his moment in the spotlight, I think.

'I thought they were the loveliest people. I really did.' Mary's lower lip trembles.

'They were, for sure,' Tyler says. 'He was as smooth as icing on a cake, said all the right, sweet things. You know the type.'

'I do. I do.' A split screen shows Chuck nodding so vigorously I think his head will fall off.

'And she was nice too, though she wasn't exactly a pretty woman,' Mary adds.

'No, that's for sure,' Tyler agrees. 'She looked like she swallowed a porcupine. Very tense. Very edgy. Bit of an alcohol problem.'

I drink some more wine. Refill my glass, unable to tear my eyes away.

'And she had a bit of a thing for him,' Mary says. 'And he for her too,' her voice dips disapprovingly, 'despite the wedding band on his finger.'

'No he didn't!' Tyler splutters.

'I know what I saw,' Mary says sharply, cutting him off. Then she nods sagely, 'I know what I saw.'

'Well thanks folks and hello Derek Anderson!'

'Hello, Chuck.' Derek looks furious.

'The last time you were on this programme was when you opened your fifty-fifth store. Did you ever think the next time you'd be on was because of something like this?' Chuck asks.

'No, I hardly thought so,' Derek answers dryly.

'So can you tell us what happened? How did you cotton on to the fact that these two were in fact thieves?'

And Derek tells his side of the story, saying that they managed to persuade him that his painting was needed as evidence. He conveniently leaves out the word 'forged'. 'And you know me,' he says humbly, 'I'm always happy to help the police. I thought it was unusual certainly, but if we can't trust the police, we're in a terrible country.'

'Indeed,' Chuck nods sympathetically. 'So, why would the couple have wanted that particular painting? You did offer them another one too, did you not?'

Derek shrugs, 'Who's to say why they picked it. A Van Gogh is always desirable, though I have to say, it wasn't my favourite.'

Huh, I think. You still paid millions for it.

'And at any time were you suspicious?'

There is a pause and Derek shakes his head. 'Honestly, no. I liked them. He in particular was quite likeable. Told me all about his kid, his wife. They took us all in.'

I squirm, feeling bad. Then remember that he was trying to dupe us too. 'Asshole,' I hiss.

Again a picture of Larry flashes up on the screen followed by the grainy one of the two of us. 'Though they might be long gone by now,' Chuck intones, 'if you do happen to see this couple, ring the number below.'

And the number scrolls along the bottom of the screen as Chuck calls it out.

I wonder if I should ring Larry, but he's told me not to contact him. Anyway, I'm sure he's ditched his phone by now.

The news moves on to other things as I get slowly sloshed and fall into an uneasy sleep.

32

The next morning, I have the hangover from hell. It's even worse than the one I had after Derek Anderson's dinner. And then I remember Derek Anderson and the news of the previous night and my stomach heaves. I lie very still until it settles back down again. I'm so glad I've already packed so that I can stay here until the banging in my head abates, which happens around three o'clock, the same time as my phone rings.

It's Robert. 'Hi, Robert,' I mutter weakly.

'I'll keep it cryptic,' he says shortly. 'We've seen the news.'

'What?' I sit up, my head jars and the world swims slightly out of focus.

'Oh, yes, it's all over the papers here. Could he have been any more identifiable?'

'He dyed his hair. And anyway, he's only a suspect.'

'Is he there?'

'No, he's gone. I'm on my own.' Ouch! Ouch! Ouch! Ouch!

'I'll kill him.'

'He hasn't left me,' I protest as strongly as I can through the pain. 'We're just making our separate ways back. It's better for me this way.'

Robert pauses. 'And have you got what you went for?'

I wince, knowing he's going to blow. 'He has that. But,' I raise my voice over his snorts, 'I trust him. I'll get it back and destroy it or maybe he will.'

'I hope so,' Robert says and he sounds worried now. A pause. 'Well, you get yourself safe home. What time is your flight getting in?'

'Early tomorrow morning. Seven Irish time.'

'I'll meet you there.'

'You don't have to do—'

But he's hung up. I lie back down and close my eyes and push the worry away as best I can.

It takes four attempts to back the car out of the driveway. I pull it to a halt, hardly able to stop my hands slithering off the steering wheel, they're coated in sweat. There is no way I'll manage to get this car safely to the airport. That was part of the plan Larry never envisioned, me being a crap driver of an automatic. I lay my aching head onto the steering wheel and groan.

A tap on the window startles me. I jump and the action makes my head swim. I think that maybe I'm still too full of alcohol to drive anyway. I turn towards the window and see Peter's friendly face beaming in at me. 'Hello!' he says. 'Are you in a bit of trouble?'

That would be a slight understatement, I think wryly. I press a button and the window rolls down. 'Larry had to go back early,' I explain. 'Business. And I got stuck bringing this monster back. I can't get the hang of driving it.'

Peter's eyes gleam. 'I'd love to drive it for you,' he says. 'May I?'

'But how'll you get back from the airport then?'

'Oh, don't worry about that, I can get Valerie to pick me up or catch a cab. It'll be worth it. This is a beauty.' He eyes the car like a lion coveting a particularly nice deer.

'Well, that'd be great, if you're sure.'

'I'll just tell Val. Wait there a second.' He bounds off to his villa as excited as a kid at a birthday party only to re-emerge with Valerie and Millie in tow. I'm pretty sure Larry would have preferred me to sneak away quietly, I think, half in amusement. I grin as Valerie smiles at at me.

'So you're off then?' she says, enfolding me in a hug. 'Well, it was nice meeting you and we'll be forever grateful to you and Larry.'

'He saved me from the pool,' Millie adds.

'He did,' Valerie nods. She holds out a slip of paper, folded over. 'This is our address, we'd love you both to keep in touch.'

I take it, feeling sad that I'll probably never use it. They were nice people and in different circumstances ...

'Open it, make sure you can read it,' Valerie urges and there is something in the way she says it that gives me pause.

Unfolding the slip of paper, I see a neatly printed address and phone number. Underneath, Valerie has written:

> ***Our house is isolated, you can stay there and no one would ever know. If you needed a place to say you were, we owe you.***

Slowly I raise my eyes to hers. She meets my gaze with a small smile.

'It's not like you think,' I say softly. 'We're not,' I shrug, 'thieves.'

'I don't think anything,' Valerie says. 'He saved Millie's life. He's a hero.'

'Thanks.' So she won't see my eyes water, I stoop down to Millie and, fumbling about in my pocket, pull out a fifty cent. I fumble about again and find a dollar. The third attempt is a little more successful. 'Buy some sweets,' I say, handing her a ten-dollar bill, 'or something nice to remember us by.'

'Oh, wow!' Millie waves the money about joyfully. 'Wow! Is this a hundred pounds?'

I laugh. Valerie hugs me again, whispering that she means everything she's written, and I move across to the passenger seat as Peter starts the engine. Just as I've slammed the door closed, the car roars into life and we're off.

Peter drives like a maniac. Too late I find out that in his youth he'd been a boy racer, that he has a passion for all sorts of cars, that his aim in life is to drive everything just once. He's driven a bin truck, a bus, a five-ton lorry, he tells me proudly, a motorbike, a Harley, which is a motorbike but sort of a really special one, a Porsche, a Lamborghini and about a hundred others. 'But this,' he says, as the car roars up the freeway, 'is fantastic.'

I smile weakly and clutch my seat as the world outside whips by.

Eventually, after what seems ages, which is ironic considering our speed, we arrive at the airport. Peter tells me to go on and check in and that he'll drop the keys back to the car hire company. He hastily hugs me goodbye, tells me earnestly to 'take care', injecting a wealth of meaning into his words, then, picking up my bags, I go to check in. My heart is hammering as I hand over my passport wondering if I'll be recognised. But it all seems to be in order. The woman on the desk hands it back to me along with my boarding pass and before long, I'm sipping coffee in duty free.

I can't help looking out for Larry, though I know, instinctively, that he is not going to be there. Whatever way he is getting home, it's not going to be on an Aer Lingus flight from Orlando. I scan the departures hall for anyone connected with his 'gang' but I saw them all so briefly, I doubt I'd even recognise them.

A man sits alongside me at the counter. He lays his chocolate muffin and massive coffee down before unfolding his paper. 'Art Theft' is the headline and Larry's picture makes the front page. I gasp and the man looks curiously at me. 'You OK?'

'Grand.'

He doesn't seem to understand what 'grand' means, but my smile must reassure him because he resumes perusing his paper. I suddenly get an inkling of how a celebrity must feel when their marriage has broken up. I'm afraid to look up in case someone spots me, afraid to be noticed, afraid to even move. Oh God, Eve, I tell myself sternly, pull yourself together. It's done now, so you just have to get on with it. Larry has told me to trust him and I will. I will trust a man who lied about his childhood whilst he lay in bed naked with me. Stop! I close my eyes and breathe deeply.

'You sure you're OK, hon?' the man asks warily, his eyes imploring me to say yes.

'Nervous flyer,' I answer.

'Oh,' his lips curl into a relieved smile, 'well, then I have just the thing for you.' He pulls from his pocket a grubby-looking packet of small white pills. 'Take one of these and you will float home. If the plane goes down, you won't even notice.'

'Eh, what are they?'

'I don't know,' he says cheerfully, 'my doctor told me to take them. Have one!'

Not wanting to appear rude, I pop a pill out of its foil. Of course I have no intention of taking it.

'When is your flight?' The man leans his elbows on his newspaper and studies me intently, blessedly covering up the piece about Larry.

'In about an hour.'

'Oh, then you want to take that now, here.' He solicitously fills me up a glass of water from the jug on the counter. 'Off you go.'

I have no option. I place the pill on my tongue, determined to hold it under my tongue as I drink the water but I miss it. Down goes the pill.

'Now, you have a pleasant flight,' the man beams.

'Thanks.'

He turns back to his paper and I return to my coffee.

By the time my flight is called, I am completely chilled. In fact, I find it hard to walk. I stagger a lot as I make my way towards the plane. I take ages fumbling for my passport and hold lots of people up and they grumble behind me, but do I care? Nope.

I eventually plonk down into my seat and think that if I was Larry, I'd have managed to wangle a first-class place. But I just have to make the best of being squashed up beside two kids who are bickering. I feel like telling them to stop, that I've got a headache, but then I conk out.

I wake up as the flight circles for landing. A beautiful day has begun, the sun a white disc in a clear blue sky, and I really wish that guy on the other side of the world had been able to tell me the name of those tablets. They were brilliant.

'Mammy, the drunk girl just woke up,' the little girl beside me shrieks and is immediately told to shush.

I wonder who the drunk girl was. I wonder if she caused much trouble. Then, as the two kids stare curiously in my direction, I realise it's me. 'I wasn't drunk,' I try to say brightly. 'I was drugged.'

This comment is met with a horrified gasp. Mammy, who is sitting behind with two other children, glares at me.

'As in taking a tablet for the plane journey?' I rush to explain. 'I'm a nervous flyer.'

'Well, you made the rest of us nervous flyers,' Mammy says. 'Tossing and turning the way you were.'

'I don't actually remember that,' I say crossly, 'I was asleep at the time.' Then I turn away from her.

She mutters something under her breath.

Oh, God, I am so thirsty. My mouth and eyes are like the Sahara. The minute we land, I'm going to grab a bottle of water. At least my headache has lifted and, as the plane taxis in, I think that Florida and Larry seem so far away.

Robert is waiting for me in arrivals. Dressed in blue corduroy trousers and a blue jumper, he looks every inch the respectable professor of history and not someone responsible for me going halfway around the world in search of a fake painting. He doesn't seem to know whether to hug me or berate me, but I make up his mind for him as I enfold him in a hug. He holds me tight for a few minutes, then hisses, 'You'll have to tell me what on earth is happening.'

And I realise that I haven't a clue what is happening, other than that I am home and safe. And that I have missed him and my mother so much. 'Oh, Robert,' I kiss his cheek and wrap an arm around his waist, 'I have missed you. How are you?' He looks thin and a bit shattered.

The grim line of his mouth softens slightly at my words. 'I've missed you too,' he says gently. 'And as for how I am, well, I'm all the better for seeing you safe and sound.' He wraps a companionable arm about my shoulder and pulls me to him. 'You've no idea how worried I was.'

'How worried *you* were? Hello? I was pretty worried too.'

He allows himself a smile. 'So, where is he?'

I shrug. 'I don't know. Lying low, I suppose. They know who he is.'

'They're speculating,' Robert answers. 'They've no proof. If he was innocent, he'd come out and say so. His silence is making things worse.'

His words cause a fizzle of apprehension to unravel inside me, but I damp it down. 'Larry knows what he's doing,' I defend him. 'And Derek Anderson will soon realise that we stole nothing. Larry is going to transfer all the money into Derek's account.'

'The money won't cover what Derek was looking for for the painting. Anyway, won't he wonder why you are giving him the money?'

I don't want to think about it for the moment. My head hurts to think about it.

Robert seems to sense my mood, because he gives me one final brief hug before lifting up my case and ordering me to follow him.

'She knows,' Robert says as we pull up in front of my mother's apartment. I groan. I hadn't wanted to see my mother and had begged Robert to bring me back to my place, pleading jet lag, but Robert had announced that he was more scared of my mother than he was of me and so, here we are, about to call in on her. My mother is obviously looking out for us because as we come up to the door she buzzes us in straightaway.

'Hi, Paddy,' Robert greets the doorman.

'Hello,' Paddy nods to both of us. 'Welcome home, Eve.'

I brace myself for an onslaught of questions from him and my mind runs through a list of fake smartass compliments but, instead, he goes back to reading his newspaper.

I can't help glancing back at him as Robert and I make our way to the lift. That is so not like the Paddy I know and detest. 'What's happened to Paddy?' I ask as we hop into the elevator and the doors ping closed.

'Oh, of course, you wouldn't know,' Robert says. 'His wife died about two weeks ago. D'you remember that awful doorman was in charge for a bit, it was like doing an interview for the Gestapo every time you visited? He was relieving Paddy.'

I hadn't even known Paddy was married. 'Oh, poor Paddy.'

'He said his job here was a life saver, it kept him going when she was really bad. He was devoted to her apparently.' Robert sighs deeply, 'Still, the fact that he felt like that makes him a lucky man.'

I say no more, feeling a little ashamed that I'd been so dismissive of Paddy, thinking him a dirty old man when, in fact, remembering our exchanges, his comments had been quite harmless and had never crossed the line of bad taste. I suppose everyone needs a diversion from their troubles and his was probably having a laugh at me.

The lift opens to reveal my mother standing in her doorway, peering up and down her hallway like a spectator at a particularly manic tennis tournament. 'In, in,' she whispers urgently, gesturing wildly to us, as if we wouldn't know how to get into her apartment. Once inside, she slams the door and stands with her back to it. Eyes wide, she demands, 'Eve – what have you done?'

'And it's great to see you too, Mother.'

'I thought you were in Paris.'

'I know. Any chance of a glass of water?' I make my way towards the kitchen, determined to keep it light.

She follows at my shoulder. 'And you were in Florida!'

'Mam,' I say as I grab a glass from the press, 'the people on the ground floor might have missed that so why don't you shout it out again.' Turning on the tap I fill the glass with water and drink it in thirsty gulps. There is silence from behind and, turning around to face them, all the fight suddenly goes out of me. Robert has his hand on her arm and they look so concerned and angry and upset that I feel awful for what I've done to them. I slowly place my glass on the counter top.

'OK,' I say softly, 'I'm sorry for lying to you both. But I had to get that painting back and Larry knew how to do it.'

'But you stole it,' my mother says, the fight gone from her too. She reaches out and touches my hand, 'You are both fugitives from the law, Eve.'

And dramatic as that may sound, she's actually right. The truth of her words hits me like the slap of a wet cloth to my face. 'I know,' I can't help the agitation in my voice, 'but Derek Anderson wanted fourteen million for it and we didn't have that. Larry never told me that he was going to steal it and, anyway, we're transferring the money into Derek's account.'

'The money is gone,' my mother says. 'I got a statement today.'

'Well, good,' I say, 'Derek Anderson will get it soon then.'

They both look at me as if they don't believe it. 'He will. Larry said he'd take care of it.' I need to believe that or I will go to pieces.

A silence. 'And what if he doesn't?' Robert asks the hard question. 'What if this Larry chap has taken off with it?'

'I really don't think Larry would do that to me.' And I don't. I mean, I believe he'd do it or might have in the past, but he'd never do it to me.

My mother groans dramatically, making Robert and I jump. 'You've fallen for him, haven't you?' she almost wails, her face pale, her hand to her mouth. Without waiting for me to confirm or deny it, she goes on bitterly, 'That was his plan all along. To make you fall for him. I've read about men like him.'

'No I—'

'Eve, I know you. I know when you've fallen for someone. I've watched you turning guys away and worried because you lived in your own little bubble and then, when you do find a man, it has to be him.' My mother shakes her head, upset. Her voice rises, 'I really thought you had more sense.' She turns to Robert, 'Is it my fault? Is it?'

'Oh Iris, not at all. It's—'

Her voice rises again in growing hysteria. 'What have I done to rear a girl that falls for the surface and ignores the, the horribleness underneath!'

'He's great,' I snap. 'He is.'

'Well, don't come crying to me when he lets you down.'

'And why would I come crying to you?' I say, my own temper flaring. 'What good would you be?'

'Pardon?'

'Aw now ladies—' Robert tries to calm us down.

'Pardon?' I mimic her, shoving my face into hers. 'Pardon? How could I pardon the fact that when Dad was sick, I did everything while you wailed and moaned about how terrible it all was? Eh? Or, or that when we found out about this painting you wanted to bury your head in the sand, yet again? I had to do this, the same way I've had to fight all my life. I could never depend on you. I never wanted a boyfriend because I didn't want to be depending on someone who might let me down.'

'Oh, I can see why you chose a con man then,' my mother retaliates sarcastically. 'He'd never let you down.'

'Not in the same way you did,' I shout back, almost crying, buried feelings rising to the surface.

'That is enough!' Robert shouts over me.

'Well then don't let her tell me that I can't come crying to her. As if I bloody would!'

I storm out of the apartment, slamming the door, and bump into Liam in the hallway. He looks startled to see me.

'Back already,' he says.

I push past him, tears stinging my eyes. Dashing a hand over my face I run down the hallway and down the stairs, across the foyer, startling Paddy who jumps up and asks me if I'm OK, and because his wife has died, I can't just run off, so I stop and nod and scrub my face and tell him I'm fine and that I'm sorry for his loss.

'Oh. Right. Well, thank you.' He swallows and nods and turns away because I think that my mentioning it has upset him.

And I leave.

I realise once I'm in the open air that I can't go anywhere. I have no money to get a taxi and Robert has the keys to my apartment but I can't stand beside his car until he comes out, so I decide that I'll walk home and he can pass me by on the road.

Ten minutes later, he pulls up beside me. I'm exhausted, even though I slept on the plane.

'Get in,' he orders crossly and I'm reminded of Larry in Florida. I pull open the passenger door and sit in beside him. 'Your mother is very upset,' he remarks.

'*I'm* very upset,' I say back.

And that is the end of the conversation until we get to my place. When he parks the car, I climb out, he pulls my luggage from the boot and hands me my keys. 'She was so upset, she even gave Liam his marching orders,' Robert half-smiles at me.

'Every cloud has a silver lining.' I don't smile back. I take the keys and nod thanks. 'He will do the right thing,' I say. 'I know he will.' And I know I sound scared in case he doesn't.

'I don't care about the money,' Robert looks sadly at me, 'but if he breaks your heart, then I get mad.'

And that is what I'm most afraid of too.

33

The next few days are so hectic that it sort of takes my mind off the fact that Larry still eludes me. I ring my mother to check in, but she's quite frosty with me before playing the hurt card so I hang up. Then she rings me and I am frosty with her so she hangs up. And then I guess we both go through a bit of a stalemate because neither of us contacts the other.

Robert calls in and he brings me some biscuits and wine and as he's unpacking them into my cupboards, he asks me what I'm going to do now and I tell him I don't know. I can't paint Van Gogh anymore. Then he says that there is a good movie on and would I like to go with him. He says Dee had wanted to see it, and, no, before I ask, he hasn't talked to Dee, but he's sure the film is a chick flick and, big saddo that I am, I agree to accompany him and it's a sad film and I don't cry. Then on the way home, we spot a sofa on a skip and it's the same colour as Larry's and I suddenly want it. So we take it off the skip and carry it back to the flat where we have nowhere to put it so we leave it in the kitchen. Robert needs a drink afterwards.

Olivia rings and I tell her that I'm fine and that I'll call her soon. We don't talk about the painting or Larry, though I know she wants to. I can't though, not yet. Not until he walks in the door with the painting under his arm.

And when night falls and I'm alone and it becomes clear to me that another day has come and gone with no word from Larry, my heart seems to ache and I think I'm going to have a heart attack, so I drink some red wine which is good for the heart and I conk out on the rescued sofa which smells rotten in the heat of my flat.

And as the days pass and my sofa gets smellier, I don't cry because something in me has to believe that Larry will get in contact. I have to believe that what we shared was real. Yes, he didn't tell me the whole truth about his parents, but talking about them would have been very painful for him, I'm sure. The papers are keen to stress that there is still no proof linking Larry to the crime, that according to records, he'd never have been allowed into the US due to his criminal record. The only reason that they suspect the ruse was carried out by him is because of his similarity to the Michael Shanagher as described by Derek Anderson. His brother, Declan, is in the news, saying that Larry was the best brother and son that anyone could have had. He brought him up, that, yes, he scammed, but he always spent his money on the family. His mother died peacefully because she knew they'd both be OK and that was because of Larry. Declan's physical resemblance to Larry hurts me and I flick off the TV and turn on the radio. Della is on the radio, sounding pained and terse, and guilt gnaws at my heart.

Olivia rings again and I tell her that I'll call her. 'Are you OK, hon?' she asks and it is the only time I come close to crying, but if I do, it means that I doubt Larry. So I say that I'm fine, that it's better if she leaves me alone for a while. If I talk to her, I think I'll fall apart.

'Will I call over? I'll bring takeaway.'

'No. Honestly, Olivia, it's better if you leave it.'

I can't have her call when Larry might arrive.

But the days turn into a week and the news slips to the back pages and I find myself filling in the sketches of him that I did in Florida. I sit on the sofa, legs tucked under me, ignoring the stench and add depth to his fine eyes, a quirk to his smile. Then I mix it all up and on a canvas I paint the spirit of him as I saw it. It's my way of being close to him, sad bloody case that I am. My smart arseness seems to have temporarily shut down. My fear of being caught lessens with each passing day, the buzz of the bell announcing a visitor no longer makes me think that I'm going to be arrested. Not that there are many visitors, just Robert. I don't jump when my mobile rings. Instead, I look longingly towards the patio door and wait for his knock.

It never comes.

Then, on day eight, I get a call from a number I don't recognise. My heart pings and seems to stop and then stutters back into a rhythm. Is it him? I slowly pick up the phone, a silent prayer flipping over and over in my head. 'Hello?'

'Eve, hey!' The voice is cheery, but it's not Larry's.

'Who is this?' Maybe it's one of his friends.

'David. D'you remember? You said I could ring you when you got back from Paris. Well, I left it a week so you wouldn't feel crowded.'

David. I'd completely forgotten about him. Disappointment washes through me. 'Oh, hi.'

'Gee, I've been told to piss off in a friendlier way that that,' he remarks wryly.

I smile. 'Sorry,' I apologise. 'I'm having a bad day. It's, eh, nice to hear from you.'

David digests this. I suppose it's not the enthusiastic response he was hoping for but he obviously decides that it'll do. 'Well, would you like to make your bad day into a good night?' he asks. 'Like I don't want to appear too keen, but I am free tonight if you like.'

I think about it. What if Larry calls when I'm out? But he won't, a part of me says. He won't call. The knowledge of this floods right through me, nearly knocks me over with its force. Larry is not going to call into me. Wherever he is, he is not on his way over to my apartment.

'Eve?' David startles me.

'Yes,' I say suddenly. 'Great.' I could do with a night out. It'll take my mind off Larry for a start. And I like David. He's good and reliable and all the things I should be looking for in a boyfriend. 'OK,' I agree, 'And without wanting to appear too desperate, I'm free at short notice too.'

'Pick you up at eight,' David says, 'and I know where you live because Olivia told me.'

'Now that appears too keen,' I joke and he laughs.

*

At eight, I buzz David up and take a final look at myself. I've got quite a nice tan so I opted for a short skirt and a T-shirt. It's dressy yet casual as I've no idea where we are going. Now where the hell did I put my sandals? David rings and I tell him to come in. 'Ignore the fact that I've no real furniture here,' I smile as he enters, 'I've no money either.' I disappear into my bedroom in search of the elusive footwear. I eventually find them flung in the back of my wardrobe. I have no idea how they got there. Slipping them on, I go back into my studio and find David staring at my large *Spirit of Larry* portrait.

'This is really good,' he says, turning to me. 'I don't know much about art, but that's amazing.'

'Thanks.' I come to stand alongside David. 'It's the first original painting I've ever done, can you believe that?' I'm thinking of giving it to Della, if I ever get up the courage to call over to her.

'It was worth waiting for,' David looks appreciatively at me. 'Bit like you.'

It sounds all wrong, it should be Larry saying that to me, I think as tears spark. I turn away hastily and manage to blink them back before giving David what I hope is the semblance of a flattered smile. He's a presentable-looking man, not as enigmatic as Larry, definitely more open, more easygoing than Larry, tall, though not as tall as Larry, broader than Larry, with a fantastic body, though he's not half as handsome as Larry. And his hair isn't— I banish the thoughts, cross with myself. 'So,' I try to sound enthusiastic, though already I know this night is a mistake, 'where are we going?'

'Out,' he answers with a wink.

He takes me for dinner to a lovely casual restaurant where we discover that we like the same foods and the same music.

Larry had only pretended to like classical to 'bond' with me, I think resentfully as I down my second glass of wine in a hasty gulp. 'I once knew a guy who only pre-ten-ded to like the same music as me,' I say and the words come out with a little difficulty. 'Imagine that.'

David laughs and pours me a refill. 'Why'd he do that?'

'I think,' I pause for a sip, 'that he thought I'd like him better.'

'And did you?'

'Yep.'

He laughs again. 'There you go so.'

A pause. Then as bitter as a freshly cut lemon, I say, 'I really liked him.'

'I see.' David's smile isn't so bright now. His eyes flicker with uncertainty.

'He told me lies about himself too,' my voice rises as I think how awful that was. 'Lies about his family.'

'Well, I won't. I've got four brothers—'

'He only had one. Just one.'

'Did he? Well, I have four, I'm the eldest.'

'So was he, the, the fecker.'

There is a pause. David says nothing, just spoons some spaghetti expertly onto a fork and into his mouth. I look at my food. The idea of eating it, of actually twisting it onto a fork, seems too hard to do now that I've almost had three glasses of wine. I sigh, pick up my fork and say, 'I'm an only child.'

'You must have been spoiled rotten.'

I shrug. Everyone always says that when I tell them. Well, everyone except Larry. I stare morosely into my wine. This was a bad idea. My head is too full of Larry. That man has trampled all over my life. Over my heart. For the first time, I felt something for someone and – I glance up. David is watching me carefully. I glance furtively about. Are other people watching me too?

'I was spoiled rotten as well,' David gallantly attempts to get the conversation back on track. 'Cause I was the first grandchild on both sides.'

Another pause as I give an obligatory smile. I really do not want this pasta now. I couldn't eat.

David leans across his half-eaten meal, sending my thoughts scattering. 'So,' he says, 'do I stand a chance against this guy or what?'

I jerk and my fork falls from my hand and clatters onto the plate with a pinging sound that echoes through the restaurant.

'Sorry,' I say to the room in general. When I eventually meet David's gaze again, he's still looking at me as if he expects an answer to his question.

'Well?' he coaxes.

I flush. 'AmIzatbad?'

'Huh?'

Oh God, I am drunk. I open my mouth and enunciate carefully, 'Am. I. That. Bad?'

'Worse.' He sits back and sips his water. Then folds his arms and says, 'Olivia told me you were a free agent, you're obviously not.'

Oh, I can see Olivia's hand in this. She probably encouraged him to ring me when I wouldn't talk to her. 'I am,' I state in the regal manner of the drunk. 'I'm a bitter, twisted free agent.' I try to make it sound like a joke. Only it doesn't. It sounds bitter and twisted. And slurred.

David nods, looking a little defeated, 'Eve,' he says, softly but with conviction, 'I'm not looking for bitter and twisted, I liked what I saw the first night I met you.'

Only thing is, I'm no longer that person. When he met me, the only thing I'd ever had burned was every dinner I'd ever tried to cook, but now, well, I've had my fingers burned and believe me, it hurts like hell. My fingers and my toes and my heart. Mostly my heart. I'd guarded it so jealously, never wanting to be hurt or wanting to lose something I loved and all Larry had to do was wear his flipping tight running shorts and flash me a grin and get me to rob a painting.

'Do you have tight running shorts?' I ask sadly.

'What?' David looks startled.

'Didn't think so,' and my eyes tear over and I excuse myself to go to the bathroom.

The dinner, which had got off to a promising start, grinds to a slow and horrible end. We both decline dessert and coffee and, as David pays the bill, I just wish I could evaporate and somehow transport myself back to my apartment. David escorts me back to his car.

'I'm sorry,' I say as I get in. 'I never should have agreed to go out.'

David looks at me and says, 'You never should have agreed to go out with me, but you should go out.' Then, without another word he drives me home.

As he pulls up in front of my flat, I turn to him, trying yet again to apologise. It's hard when my head is all muddled with wine and no food. 'David,' I slur, 'you're a nice guy, a very nice guy—'

'I do my best.'

'It's me. I just—'

'Naw, it's the guy in the picture,' David interrupts. 'The one you painted. Stupid bastard whoever he is.'

I'm stunned, almost sober, that he interpreted my work so well. It was pretty abstract. 'Yeah well . . . '

'You get over him and I might still be around so give me a call, eh?'

I nod, knowing I don't deserve him to be so nice. If a guy had treated me like that, I'd have been highly insulted. 'Thanks.'

'Go on now.' He manages a smile, the smile that made me fancy him in the first place, straight teeth and a flashing dimple. A smile that held just a hint of sinfulness. Why has it all changed? I stumble out of his car, not wanting him to witness my watery eyes and wobbling lower lip. But once inside, with my door safely closed, I slide down onto my bean bag and the tears, which I'd been so determined not to shed all week, tumble out. It's as if I've been used up and abandoned by him, like a crisp bag or an old shoe that doesn't fit anymore. I've become someone I despise. A puddle of broken-hearted self-pity and I hate girls like me. But why won't he contact me? Where the hell is he? Was I a fool? The pain is a physical ache, like grief. Only unlike grief, I wasn't expecting it. Love snuck up on me and sideswiped me with sexy smiles and funny jokes and long days by a pool. And now that it's gone, I feel that I've gone too.

And finally, in desperation, I stand up, take down a canvas and start to paint.

34

I think I go a little mad over the next few days. I get up, paint, fall asleep, get up, paint, fall asleep, get up, paint.

It's as if I'm a machine and someone has pressed the go button and I just go without thinking, operate without knowing exactly what I'm doing. And the pictures emerge. Pictures of grief and loss and love. They grow from greys and blues and reds. They swirl and tumble and cry out and crash and make noise in my head and I'm like a person possessed. If I paint hard enough, I'll get the feelings out. I can exorcise them and then I'll be still inside again. Flashes of Van Gogh come to me and of how he painted in swirls and bright lights, his madness making his paintings glow. And while I'm no Van Gogh, I am bloody mad. Furious. And hurt. And sad. And finally, on the third or fourth day, my stomach rumbles and I realise quite suddenly that I can't remember the last time I ate. That's a bit shocking. I pause, paintbrush dripping indigo blue onto my floor. I also realise that somewhere in the last day or so, the phone had rung and I'd ignored it because I felt that if I stopped, I could never start again. If I stopped, I'd have to think. But now, my arm feels heavy and tired. My legs are weak. I can feel a huge spot on my face.

And the paintings are all over the place. A little scared, I glance around at my very crowded studio filled with ominous-looking canvases. Piled against the wall, shoulder to shoulder, they stand and reflect back at me the anguish of the last while.

It's a pity they're crap.

And kind of scary. I wouldn't like to be in a locked room with them.

But I am. It makes me smile a little, though I don't really feel better. Well, maybe a little calmer, but certainly not happier. Though, I think suddenly, these paintings are original. Wow. Loads and loads of original work. And I didn't have to think deeply about them at all. Not at all. The paint drips onto my leg and I can feel it tickling as it trickles down. And then, as the paint dribbles into my sock, making my toes squirm, I realise in a moment of absolute clarity, like the way the sky looks on a bright blue day, that in order to do something original, I had to feel. I had to feel very deeply, crap and all as they are. And that, I realise, is something that I haven't done in a very long time. Losing Dad and supporting a hysterical mother had claimed all my energies. It had sapped me so that I never wanted to be like that again. I'd run those horrible five years on autopilot and never switched back to manual. And even after Dad died, I hadn't mourned him the way I was mourning Larry now. No, I'd moved out of home and covered myself in the comfort blanket of churning out paintings where the only thing I'd have to engage with was a man who'd been dead a long time, but a man who when alive had felt things too deeply. There's a certain irony in that.

A very sad irony.

Looking at the paintings as they look back at me, I realise that I haven't only painted my anger at Larry; these paintings are about my dad too. They're everything I'd held in. I'd wrapped my arms around myself so that I wouldn't go whizzing off into pieces, soldiered on whilst cracking jokes. And then Larry had come along, in his tight running shorts, and taken my arms down and wrapped his around me instead. And that was all I'd needed to let him in.

And it hurts again, but instead of painting it away, I let it wash over me. I cry so hard I think I will shatter.

And after a while, the tears stop and my stomach rumbles and I know I have to get food.

And maybe then I'll paint properly.

*

Not all the paintings are rubbish, I discover as I look through them later, with a view to scraping the canvases clean. One or two are worth saving. One or two are surprisingly good, I think in a slowly dawning amazement. I did something worthwhile in those mad couple of days. I place the two I like the best against the wall and take a step back and study them. What makes them work, I wonder? Well, the colours suit the mood perfectly and the paint strokes complement that. I can't even remember how I mixed those colours, which is a bummer.

I look at them for a bit and come to a decision. While my life is a mess, there is something I can do to alleviate things. I can take these two paintings over to Della Sweeney and settle my account with her. Giving her a painting of Larry seems wrong somehow. And even though she only wants one, the second can be a silent apology for what she'll never know I did. Plus, I doubt anything I do will ever sell for the amount of cash she's promised me.

And now, that decision made, I pick up my mobile and brace myself to hear the messages I've missed in the past few days.

Eleven missed calls, my mobile tells me.

Oh dear. I dial my message minder.

'You have six new messages.' Well that's not so bad.

The first message is from my mother wondering why I'm not answering my phone and telling me to call her so we can talk. The second is her telling me if I want to be like that well fine. The third is from Olivia wondering how the date with David went as he won't tell them. The fourth is from Robert wondering how I'm doing and the fifth is Olivia again, sounding worried. Oh, God, I've been horrible to my best friend. The sixth is a hang up.

I scroll through all the numbers of the past few days of missed calls to see who the hang up might be, but two of the numbers are 'withheld' so it could be any one of a number of people. Including Larry.

But I'm not going to dwell on Larry any more. Not if I can help it anyway. Until he gets in contact, there is really nothing I can do, which is scary as I'm not used to not knowing what is happening in my own life. Which is why I'm going to take a couple of photos of my canvases and call in on Della Sweeney to see if she'd be interested in them. I suppose I could e-mail her but I'd be on tenterhooks waiting for a response and I also want to see her. Like a criminal – OK, I am a criminal – returning to the scene of the crime, I want to see if she'll mention the matter of the Van Gogh. I want to reassure myself that she is OK and not too traumatised about it. Then I'm also going to ring my mother and Robert and Olivia. And I'm going to see if there is any sign of Larry's brother in Larry's apartment. As far as I can remember, Robert said he'd met him.

Feeling better, I shower, take my photos, print them out but bring the camera anyway as my printer isn't massively fantastic. Then I shove everything into my canvas bag and for the first time in days, I leave my apartment.

35

It's a dingy day outside when everything looks just a little bit sadder than usual. Thin spits of rain splatter down and the sky is a uniform block of dark grey. I root out a multicoloured cap from my bag and am preparing to make a dash for my car when from somewhere a raspy voice hisses, 'Eve! Pssst! Eve!'

The voice is so furtive, that despite my best intentions, I will it to be Larry. I stop abruptly. Whoever it is is to the right of me and as I've just come out of my apartment, I turn in the direction of the car park. There's a battered grey car parked in a visitors spot and a man I know I should recognise is leaning half out of the window.

'Eve!' He hops out of the car and slams his door closed so hard that the poor vehicle trembles. He looks familiar but it still takes me a second to recognise him. I always find it hard to identify people who appear in my life out of context. This man belongs down the hall from my mother.

'Liam?' I gawk at him in open surprise. His literary air of suave sophistication has been replaced by a man in dire need of a shave and a hair brush. 'What – what are you doing here?'

'Looking for you,' he answers, patting down his errant mop of remaining hair and adjusting his suit so that it hangs straight. 'I drove up yesterday evening and slept in the car so I'd catch you whenever you went out today.'

Isn't he lucky he hadn't come two days ago, I think wryly. 'You slept in your car?' He doesn't seem like the type.

'Yes,' Liam nods, and then adds, 'And I don't mind telling you, your apartment block is very noisy. One apartment in particular. They partied all night.'

It's a testament to my mini breakdown that I hadn't even heard it.

'And they're very rude,' Liam goes on, his voice acquiring a slight whine of self-pity. 'They kept coming up to me and calling me a—,' he pauses, obviously rethinking the wisdom of telling me what they called him, 'well, maybe you don't want to know. You'd probably prefer to know why I'm here.'

'Is it something to do with my mother?' I gasp suddenly, the thought only dawning on me. 'Is she OK?' Oh, I'd never forgive myself if—

'Oh, no, no,' Liam answers hastily, 'she's fine. Sorry now, I didn't mean to shock you.'

The relief makes me weak.

'Sorry now,' Liam apologises again and I wave him away.

'So what's wrong?' I ask. I mean it has to do with my mother or he wouldn't be here. Liam and I are hardly close.

'Well, you know we had a short relationship,' Liam says.

Ugh. But I nod.

'Well, she refuses to see me anymore. She won't say why but I think I know why and I think she knows I know why, and that's why she doesn't want to see me because she's too embarrassed to admit why.'

I blink, wondering if I'd just heard that. 'Pardon?'

Liam looks about furtively. 'Can we go somewhere? Maybe I could buy you a coffee or a cake or a sandwich or crisps or a muffin or whatever you'd like.'

'Oi! Eve, is that your old man?' one of the Party People shouts out through his window. 'He was outside all night, we thought he was a perve.'

'See,' Liam says in horror. 'That is what I had to put up with!'

'This man is a friend of my mother's,' I yell back.

'Not any more,' Liam mumbles.

'Oh right, and where were you last night?' Party Person yells. 'We thought you'd pop in.'

'I was tired.'

'Aw, sure next time, eh?' And Party Person slams his window closed.

'They're OK really,' I say to Liam. I feel a little sorry for him, he looks so dejected. I wonder how he knew where I lived. My mother probably. 'Why didn't you buzz up last night?' I ask.

'I wasn't sure which flat was yours.'

'There are only three that are occupied.'

'I know but,' Liam shakes his head, 'I really didn't want to engage those people in conversation. The number of people who went in and out of that flat last night made my mind boggle. They could have set up their own country by midnight.'

I smile a little. 'Come on, let me buy you the coffee, you look like you could do with it.'

Liam gallantly offers to carry my canvas bag and I lead him to the coffee shop across the road.

Once inside, Liam excuses himself to use the bathroom as I get two large cappuccinos and two chocolate muffins. When he arrives back at the table, he appears to have washed his face because part of his hair is damp where water must have splashed on it. He slides into the chair opposite me and takes a grateful sip of coffee. 'Thank you,' he says.

'So,' I lean across the table, 'what do you want? I have to warn you, my mother and I are at loggerheads at the moment.'

It's as if I've just told him that I've banished all his favourite books in the world; his eyes droop, as does his mouth. 'Oh dear,' he says. 'Well, maybe you should sort out your differences with her first. That's definitely more important.' After a brief pause, he says nervously, 'I hope I haven't come between you, that would be terrible. I wouldn't want that.'

I wish it had been him, I think. 'No, it's not you, though I have to admit, I never would have put you both together.'

He pauses in the middle of a bite of chocolate muffin. 'Why?' Bits of the muffin spray in my direction and I do a tactful dodge.

'Well, I think, to be honest, that she's not into all your books and films. My mother likes good old-fashioned romantic films and books about girls going on holiday and pictures of hens.'

To my surprise, Liam smiles slightly. 'Well, when I found her quoting my Amazon review of *The Tide of Time and Treason* back to me at our book club, I realised that she was googling reviews of the books and not reading them at all. It came as a bit of a shock to me, I can tell you, but I admired her ingenuity.'

I try not to laugh. 'No way!'

Liam nods. 'And I said it to her after the book club and she denied it, and now she won't talk to me at all. The day you came back from Paris she slammed the door in my face. I had only called in to welcome you back because I know she was very worried about all those storms in Paris.'

Oh, I think, that was nice of him.

'And I rather think,' Liam goes on, 'that none of your mother's friends liked my book suggestions because they hardly come any more.' He takes another bite of the muffin and chews for an age before saying, 'And I feel I've driven them away. So, I had an idea how to fix things but I wanted to see what you'd think, you know her best after all.'

'Go on.' I'm not sure if I want him to fix things. I'm not sure if I want a replacement man in my mother's life. But, then again, he seems all right and he cares for my mother and that's good. And I have a sudden lump in my throat at the thought of it.

'Well, I had this idea of ringing all your mother's friends and telling them that the book club choice for a week's time was some book that they might enjoy. Maybe you could suggest one. And that we could all turn up with the book read as a surprise to your mother.' He sighs. 'All I wanted was a bit of company, Eve, and I don't care what we read. And the bonus was that I met your mother.'

I have to gulp really hard to get my coffee to go down. His little speech has moved me something ridiculous. How nice that my mother has inspired this in him, even if she was a big faker. I wonder, though, will he like my mother for who she is rather than what he thought her to be?

'And it wasn't your mother's brain I liked,' Liam gets in hastily.

'You liked her body?' I can't resist the tease.

'Oh, no, no!' Again the muffin crumbs spray like a hose that someone has lost grip of, 'that's not what I meant!' He looks horrified. 'I meant I liked her conversation, her wit, her taste, her sense of humour. She's very funny, you know.' He sits back, his face red, 'You remind me of her.'

I can't think of a worse compliment. But, then again, my mother does have a good sense of humour and she is witty, it's just that somewhere along the line, I've lost sight of that. A picture surfaces of her surrounded by her friends at my twenty-first, making them laugh at some anecdote she was telling. I remember being so proud of her when I was young because she was the prettiest mammy at our school cake sale. Maybe I've let her become too dependent on me, controlling her the way I've controlled everything else. Maybe it's a habit we've both slipped into.

'So?' Liam asks as he wipes his mouth with a napkin, 'what do you think of my idea? Will she like it?'

I know she'll love it. Any romantic gesture will win her over. 'She'll love that, Liam. She really will,' I answer, my voice suspiciously wobbly. 'And I'll have a think of a book you can do and text you it. Give me your mobile number.'

He calls his out and I key it into my phone.

'Well, thank you very much,' Liam beams at me, looking relieved, 'you're a lovely girl, just like your mother said.'

'Well, I hope she thinks that when I eventually call in to her,' I half-joke.

'Oh, she will.' Liam stands up. 'Now, if you don't mind, I'd better get going. I rang in sick to work this morning and I'm a bit scared of being caught. Bye now.'

'Bye Liam.' I watch him leave and think how lucky my mother is to have him go the extra mile for her like that. And how lucky she is that she cares for someone who cares for her back.

I drain my coffee and, picking up my bag, I head back onto the street to go to Della's.

Time to start making things right.

36

Della is in. Her big car is parked in her cobble-locked driveway and, as I near the house, I can see her in her drawing room admiring her artwork. I don't blame her; if I had a le Brocquy on my wall, I'd probably never stop looking at it either. But it's sad too – there she is, in her big house, all alone with only her paintings for company. All her money and she's probably worse off than I am. No, scratch that. I'm definitely worse off, being poor and a bloody fool.

I take a deep breath and finally pluck up the courage to ring her doorbell. I wonder what she'll make of my paintings, maybe she'll hate them, which would be a bit devastating as I really feel that this is my best work to date. OK, my only real work to date. She looks a little startled to hear the bell ring and in a moment I hear her clitter clatter up the hallway. She opens the door and in the bright white sunlight, she appears a little pale.

'Hi, Della,' I smile.

'Oh, Eve,' the door opens wider and to my surprise, a smile breaks out across her face. 'How are you? You've a lovely colour, were you away?'

'Paris,' I can't meet her gaze. 'I, eh, decided to paint over there.'

'Oh,' Della beckons me toward her massive kitchen and bids me sit down. 'That's exciting. You can tell me all over a coffee, one moment.'

I'm about to tell her that I don't want a coffee, that I'm in a hurry, but something in the enthusiastic way she pulls mugs from the press stops me. She wants me to have a coffee with her, I realise. She wants the chat, the company. 'That'll be lovely,' I say instead.

Five minutes later, she has managed to coax a truly crap cup of coffee from a state-of-the-art coffee machine. I sip it and watch as she puts some biscuits on a plate before sitting opposite me. 'So,' she says, smiling, 'tell me what you did.'

'Well,' I open my canvas bag, which is full of the usual clutter, my sketch pens and pencils, sketchpad, receipts from fast-food takeaways, my tatty purse, a pair of socks and a lot of other stuff. I pull out a few things in the search for my camera. Locating it, I flick it on and say, 'Well, I did these two paintings over there and I was wondering if you'd like them. You're welcome to both of them.'

'Not at all,' Della waves the suggestion away. 'I asked for one and one I will take,' she pauses, 'provided I like it of course.'

I hand her my camera, which is now displaying the first painting. That's my favourite one.

'Oh,' Della says and I can't tell if it's an impressed 'oh' or a slightly shocked one. She studies it for a bit before flicking to the next painting and utters another 'oh'. Then she is silent.

I fumble with the toggle on my bag and can't look at her. This is another reason why I never did anything original, I think, because it's not just my paintings being judged, but me too. And I so don't want to be found wanting, to be vulnerable to what someone thinks of me. And, yet, there is nothing I can do to control that either. I am what I am. So I raise my eyes and look up at Della. 'Well?' I ask and it comes out sounding almost defiant.

She puts the camera down slowly and sits opposite me. 'I'd need to see them in reality,' she says slowly.

'Oh. Well, that'll be a little while. I have to varnish them and—'

She holds up her hand, 'I haven't finished.'

'Oh, sorry.' Disappointment that she's not dancing around the room saying how wonderful they are pricks at my ego, so I add, 'It's just when you stopped talking I assumed that you had.'

She pauses and studies me. 'You are impudent,' she finally pronounces. 'Do you respect anyone?'

I shrug and mumble, 'Sorry.'

'Anyway, what I was going to say before you barged on was that I'd need to see them in reality so I could choose which one I liked the best. They're both,' she pauses, then says slowly, 'very very good, Eve.'

'Yeah, well . . . ' I can't help a tiny smile. Then add, 'You can have them both, I already said that.'

'Then I would be getting a bargain.'

'Isn't that what you always try to do?'

'Yes.'

'Then take them both. I'll do some more.'

Della smiles. 'We'll see. So, tell me, what inspired you to suddenly turn out such,' she takes the camera again, 'such interesting studies. I presume something happened?'

Jeez, everyone's a mind reader, I think. 'I guess they're just, you know, feelings and stuff.'

'Cheeky and eloquent,' she teases. 'Well, congratulations, feelings and stuff are exactly what I expected you could do.'

I smile, a little shyly, I think. 'Thank you.' Then I fiddle with the toggle on my bag some more.

'And what else do you plan to paint?' Della asks and before I'm aware of it, she has my sketchpad in her hand. 'May I have a look?'

'Oh, there's nothing in there,' I say hastily, attempting to extract it from her. 'They're just—'

Too late. She is flipping over the pages.

'I'd rather you didn't.' Again I attempt to take it.

'This is very good,' she says.

It's Larry's arm and neck and curve of his face. I stay frozen as she flips the page again. Now she is at the portrait of Larry, the one I sketched in Florida. I feel my stomach turn as a sort of blind panic grips me. Force of habit means I always bring my sketchpad with me and I'd forgotten to take it out of my bag this time. Larry stares up at Della from the pages. For a second, Della stares intently at the image. And it's a goodie too. One of my most accurate drawings. I captured his nonchalance, his air of bravado, his cheekiness. 'That's a guy who posed for me,' I attempt to lie. 'I don't know who he is, he's just a guy I met while I—' I stop because I'm blabbering unconvincingly.

Della shakes her head, as if in a dream. 'That looks very much like the man the police are looking for,' she whispers.

'What man?' I try to sound innocent, but my voice raises a little, sounding ever so slightly hysterical.

'The man that stole the Van Gogh painting two weeks ago. The police showed me pictures of him. He was clean shaven but even with the stubble as in this,' she jabs at my picture, 'this is the man.' She looks at me. Peers even closer, then her hand flies to her mouth. 'And the woman, she had, she had—' she's almost choking on her words.

'Della, sit down. Oh, please!' I go to touch her but she fends me off. I think she's scared of me and I feel terrible. 'Della, please, you don't understand.'

'You must know him,' she is hyperventilating. 'You must. Who is he? Where is he? I haven't slept, I have hardly eaten. How could some man I don't know pretend to know me? Have you any idea what that's like?'

Oh, God. This is terrible. The poor woman. What have we done? 'No, but I'm sure it'll be OK. In fact, I know it'll be OK.'

Her breathing is ragged.

'Della,' I say desperately, 'It was never about you.' Too late, I realise that I've probably said too much. My mouth snaps closed. 'I feel it,' I add feebly.

'You know!' she rasps and she looks panicked and wild. 'Was it you? Did you do this? I know you love Van Gogh.'

'No!' I cry back. I wonder if I should slap her to bring her back to her senses, but that might be assault. 'No, the painting was a—'

And then, like a rag doll, she crumples to the floor, hitting her head off the table on the way down.

'Jesus!' I stand, hands to my mouth in shock. She is still, her head lolling to one side, a bruise already appearing on the side of her forehead. Then from somewhere, some instinct kicks in. Some long forgotten episode of *Grey's Anatomy* surfaces and I rush to take a pulse whilst at the same time upending my bag and scattering its contents in an effort to find my mobile phone.

I can feel a pulse and she's still breathing, so I haven't killed her. Sobbing, hardly able to see through my tears, I press in the emergency number and wait what seems like an eternity until the phone is answered. I am barely coherent as I blubber out to the woman at the other end what has just happened. In a calm voice, she tells me to slow down and I realise that unless I do, Della Sweeney might die and this woman has been nothing but good to me. At this moment, I despise myself and Larry for what we did. OK, this wasn't meant to happen but one way or the other the police would have interviewed Della and the poor woman has suffered because of it.

I will confess, I swear, if only she lives. I do exactly what the girl on the other end of the phone tells me to do whilst at the same time bargaining with any God who will listen that if Della pulls through, I will confess. I won't care if I go to jail, I won't care if my career is ruined before it gets going, once this woman does not die because of what I did.

The ambulance arrives five minutes later, though it seems much longer and I stand numbly by as the ambulance men expertly do their job. One of them asks me if I'd like to travel in the back with Della.

'No, thanks, I'll follow in my car.' What would happen if Della woke up en route to the hospital and found me staring down at her? It'd kill her for certain. And, yet, I have to go to the hospital and make sure she is OK.

'Will you be able to drive, love?' the ambulance man asks.

I nod.

'OK,' he pats me on the shoulder. 'You did great. It's not your fault.' Then he tells me the name of the hospital they're taking Della to and I watch them drive away.

It's only as I climb back into my car that I realise my legs are shaking. I can't even put the key into the ignition because my hands are trembling so much. I take a few deep breaths, trying to calm myself but I can't. I'll have to call someone to drive me. And there is only one person I want to see right now.

37

My mother arrives in her car and finds me sitting in mine, hands on the steering wheel, unable to even move. I'm sure I must look a state with my red puffy eyes and pale face. I feel somehow that if I stay still and don't stir, that everything else will remain as it is and that Della will hang on to life. How could I have been so stupid as to bring my sketchpad? But, then again, if she's been worrying about who this mysterious couple were who linked themselves to her, maybe it's good because I'll be able to explain it to her. My mother sits in beside me and doesn't say anything for a bit, just rubs my back a little.

I still stay, unmoving, barely blinking.

'Eve,' my mother says softly, 'what's happened?' And she doesn't sound hysterical or cross.

'I'm in such trouble, Mammy,' I sniff, and I haven't called her 'mammy' in such a long time.

'Well,' my mother says softly, after a pause, 'I will be here. You know that.' And her arm comes around my shoulder and suddenly I'm crying and crying. And after the past few days, I'm surprised that I have any tears left. But I think I'm crying for the stress of Florida too and the stress of fighting with her. And I blubber out my story just like a little kid who doesn't know where to start or end, but just has to get all the information out at once.

I have no idea if my mother even understands my rambling tale, perhaps she doesn't because she's still calm by the end of it. 'Well, first things first,' she says, and she's making a huge effort to sound matter of fact, and I love her for it. 'We'll go to the hospital and see how this Della person is. Let's just take it from there. 'Here,' she hands me a handkerchief, then tells me to get out and sit in the passenger side as she walks around to the driver's side.

It would have been better if my mother had driven her car to the hospital as mine is a little temperamental and requires a certain skill in its handling. It's pretty old and the power steering is not great. It'd be a marvellous car for building up biceps. My mother struggles with it like a fisherman with a big fish. And the image of a fisherman upsets me and I have to bite back tears.

'Oh, Eve, how do you drive this thing?' my mother wails in despair. 'It's got a mind of its own.'

'I'm just used to it.'

Eventually, we reach the hospital and my mother dumps the car across two parking spaces. Neither of us care. She gets out and heaves a sigh of relief, before crossing over and giving me a hug. Oh, it's so nice to have her arms around me, not in a help-me-I'm-drowning scenario, but in a strong way. 'Now, let's see how this lady is,' she says firmly. She takes my chin in her hand and forces me to meet her gaze. 'All that matters is that she is OK, Eve. We can sort out everything else.'

And she's right. We can sort it out. And if I have to go to jail to sort it out, I will.

The hospital, surprisingly, isn't too busy. There are a few people waiting on hard plastic chairs. My mother and I make our way to the reception desk. 'Della Sweeney,' I gulp out anxiously. 'She was brought in. She collapsed.'

The receptionist looks at the computer. 'Della Sweeney,' she says, repeating the name as she scrolls the screen.

'Only came in a while ago,' I say breathlessly. 'In an ambulance.'

'Yes,' the woman finds it. 'She's undergoing tests as far as I know.' She glances at us. 'Are you family?'

'No.'

'Yes.'

My mother glares at me but I say, 'This woman isn't, but I am. I'm her niece.' Then I realise how that must sound. I mean that's why the woman is in here in the first place. Then I think that I need to know how she's doing, so it's justified.

'OK,' the receptionist says, 'well if you'll both take a seat in the family waiting room, that's the first room on the left, we'll update you.'

I walk as confidently as I can to the waiting room as my mother scurries behind me hissing, 'Do you want to make this worse on yourself, Eve? You can't pretend to be a member of her family. What if her real family turn up?'

'She has no family,' I say.

My mother sighs and follows me in.

Hospitals, as far as I can see, are black holes for conversation. Maybe it's because things are so stressed, so unnatural, that day-to-day talk becomes even more mundane. My mother and I sit in silence for the most part. She's talked about the weather, I've talked about my painting, we've danced a bit around Della and Florida, both of us reluctant to re-examine it because the possibility that someone else will enter the room is too real. We can argue it out later.

And then I remember, though it seems like a hundred years ago, in someone else's life. 'Liam called in to see me this morning,' I say.

If I had announced that I had a bomb and was going to let it off, my mother couldn't have reacted with as much shock. 'What?'

'He called in and I have to say, he was nice.'

My mother is silent, digesting this. She spends a while examining her fingernails. 'Yes,' she eventually concedes, 'he's quite a nice man. What did he call in to you for?'

'He misses you. He wants to know how to get back with you.'

She doesn't smile, merely scrutinises her fingernails more intensely. 'Yes, well,' she swallows hard, 'I miss him too, but,' she pauses and adds a little sadly, 'it's better this way.'

'Why? If you both miss each other?' And I can't believe I'm saying this but life is short.

'He was too . . . ' she wrinkles up her brow, frowning as she tries to think of a way of expressing what Liam was. 'He knew too much. My brain was addled trying to read all the books that he did.'

'Rumour has it that you didn't read them though,' I give her a sly dig.

'Pardon?' She flushes deep red and splutters weakly, 'I did.' Her eyes narrow, 'Did he tell you that?'

'Yes, and he said he admired your cleverness at plagiarising reviews from Amazon.'

'Oh!' her eyes widen and her face flushes a deeper red. Her hand flies to her mouth, 'Oh, my God.'

I manage a little laugh, though it's not a laughing kind of day. 'Tell me,' I ask, 'how'd you manage when he took you to the film that time when I was in . . . ' My voice trails off and now it's my turn to flush, 'away?'

My mother's indignant look fades. 'Well,' she admits, striving to make her deception sound normal, 'I read about the film online, only I couldn't make head nor tail of the review because the stupid thing was that complicated. So, on the night, I just forgot my glasses and wasn't able to read the subtitles. Liam spent the night explaining it to me.'

'You big faker,' I tease gently.

She shrugs a little. 'His wife had been some kind of a professor apparently. I felt that I had to compete or he'd find me boring.'

'You were going to compete forever?' I ask. 'Like, say he'd never found out, what would you have done?'

She doesn't reply.

'You're perfect the way you are, Mam,' I say to her with feeling. 'Honestly, he likes you for you.'

Still she says nothing and, to my surprise, a tear falls down her face and plops onto her hand. She tries to blink it away before I spot it, but it's too late.

'Mam,' I catch her hand, alarmed, 'what's wrong? Eh?'

She shakes her head and says a little tearfully, 'Don't mind me.'

'But you're crying, of course I mind.' I dip my head so that I'm looking up into her face. 'Tell me, please.'

A second or two passes before she says softly, 'You saying that.' She eventually turns her eyes to me, big blue pools of upset, with tears shimmering at the edges. 'You telling me I'm perfect the way I am.'

'But you are.'

She shakes her head slightly and sniffs out, 'I wasn't perfect when John was dying.'

I stiffen. Please don't go there, I want to say, but I can't get the words out.

'I know I wasn't,' she goes on. 'It was just—' her voice breaks and now I think I might cry. Those days are not something we revisit.

'Just what?' I say and my voice sounds as if it's coming from far away.

'Just that, well, I couldn't bear to see the big strong man that I married being reduced to what he became.' More tears, and I pull her hankie from my pocket and give it back to her. She dabs at her face.

'It was so hard, Eve. And I didn't want to be doing things for him that he used to do for himself, I didn't want him feeling beholden to me. Dependent on me. It just wasn't right. I don't think he would have liked it. He revelled in helping me and I always let him.'

And she's right. Dad had done everything for her and I think I'd seen it as a weakness on her part, but maybe she had let him do things because it made him happy. When he'd been ill, she had read to him and told him stories and made him laugh. She'd fed his mind and spirit while I, and later on Robert, had dealt with his physical needs. And maybe in her way, she'd done just as much for him as I had. Only I had never acknowledged that before. Or seen it from that angle before.

'But it wasn't fair on you and a child shouldn't have had to do all that.' My mother places her free hand over mine so that she's clasping my hand in both of hers. 'I'm sorry, Eve. I never realised it until the other evening when you said it.'

I try to tell her that it's OK but the words won't come out because they get stuck in the lump in my throat.

'But you can depend on me, Eve, you can,' she says fervently, 'You don't have to take the place of your dad. I will always be your mother and I'll always be here. I thought you knew that, but maybe you don't.'

And I still can't answer because the lump in my throat has suddenly got bigger, but I reach over and hug her hard.

And she hugs me back.

And it feels so good just to let go.

38

Robert, who my mother must have rung, arrives in the hospital a few hours later bearing takeaway cappuccinos and some nice sandwiches. I can't eat much, but my mother and he tuck in with a forced relish. It's as if they're trying to signal to me that everything is normal and not to worry.

'So, this eh, lady,' Robert says to me, 'how does she fit into this?'

Head hanging in shame, I recount how Larry and I had used her to lend us an air of credibility. 'And because I'd met her and been in her house, it seemed easy.'

Robert nods. 'And still no word from Larry?'

I shake my head.

'And the money and the painting are both gone,' he sighs. He takes another bite of his sandwich and munches on it for a bit. 'Face it, he's never coming back Eve, I think we were all conned.'

'I have to trust him,' I say but the conviction I had had before has seriously waned. 'He has to keep a low profile for a bit.'

'He has to keep a low profile forever,' Robert says. 'The police know it's him though they can't say it and with this woman in hospital, she's going to wake up and start singing like a canary. It won't take long before they put it all together.'

'I don't care. I hope she does wake up and start blabbing. I don't care, I just don't want her to be dead.'

'Hush!' My mother lays a hand on mine.

'If that Larry fella was in front of me, I'd strangle him,' Robert says viciously, startling us. 'How dare he use you like that, Eve!'

'I wanted to be used. I just wanted the painting back and, for a while, I had it. This close.' I place my thumb and index finger a hair's breadth apart. 'Oh God, this is such a nightmare.'

'Hello?' A middle-aged man in a white coat pokes his head into the room. 'Della Sweeney?'

'Yes!' I jump up out of the chair. 'Is she OK?'

My mother hops up behind me and lays a hand on my shoulder. Robert remains sitting, his hands clasped tightly, staring at the floor.

The doctor nods and I give a sob of pure relief. 'Now, don't get me wrong,' he adds gravely, 'she is quite an ill woman. You are probably aware that she has had blood pressure problems for some years. We'll probably keep her in for a number of days to run tests and monitor her. But, for now, she's comfortable.'

'Thank you,' I grasp his hand and shake it vigorously. 'Oh, I don't know what I would have done if she'd died. Oh, thanks.'

The doctorssmiles widely. 'Would you like to see her for a few minutes?'

'Eh, no, no, not yet.'

He blinks in surprise, taken aback at my very firm refusal. 'Oh, right.'

'She's a bit over-wrought,' my mother explains smoothly. 'We're afraid she could upset Della.'

'Oh, I doubt—'

'Thank you again,' my mother says and she ushers me out of the waiting room as quickly as possible.

It's only then that I notice Robert has already left.

I spend the night at my mother's apartment. It's nice for her to fuss over me. She pulls out the spare duvet and covers it with a lovely flowery cover, then finds some big fat pillows and makes me up a bed. And the bed is far more comfortable than the hard one in my apartment and far bigger, and despite the horrible day I've had, I feel as comfortable as a cat in front of a fire.

Tomorrow, though, I will go down to the local police station and confess everything. The thought doesn't frighten me as much as I had expected it to. Sometimes, facing a fear lessens it. Still, it's easy to feel this way when I'm feeling all cosy in a nice bed, in a place where I'm loved.

39

It's the heat that wakes me. I shift uneasily about in the bed and eventually throw off the heavy duvet cover. Duvet cover? Where am I? My own bed has a thin miserable excuse of a duvet, not a big weighty one, like I've just discarded. My half-opened eye focuses on a cream wall with a tasteful but boring picture. For one tiny second, I wonder if I've died and gone to heaven where everything is clean and white and warm. My own place is normally freezing as my bedroom faces north and a vicious wind howls against my apartment most nights, or so it seems. And then, a wave of memory hits me and my heart plummets. I close my eyes and think that I might as well savour what could be my last morning of freedom.

I wonder what the law does to imposters and thieves. I haven't informed my mother that I'm going to the police station as she'd try to dissuade me. But a bargain with God is a bargain. Della is alive and I am more than grateful for that. I feel that I should be punished for what we did.

I sit up, unable to relax. There is a white and blue striped towel, folded carefully, on the white wicker chair in the corner of the room. My mother must have left it out for me. Hopping out of bed, I grab it and pad into the en suite shower.

Washed and wearing some clothes that I'd picked up from my place before coming here last night, I go into the kitchen and grab a bowl of cereal and some coffee.

'Is that you, Eve?' my mother calls from her room.

'Yes, d'you want a cuppa?'

'Oh, that'd be lovely.'

I smile, make her a coffee and bring it into her bedroom.

My mother takes in my appearance as I hand her the mug, her eyes scanning me top to bottom. I know I look unusual, dressed as I am in a good skirt that I never wear because I'm saving it for an interview or some other important date in my life, and a white blouse, which I also never wear for the same reason.

'You look nice,' she says.

She means I look normal, conservative. 'Thanks.' The idea being, obviously, to appear like a respectful citizen who, for some reason, briefly went off the rails. In fact, that is what I am. Looking back, Florida seems like a sort of madness, as if it happened to someone else.

'Are you going somewhere?' My mother eyes me over the rim of her coffee mug as she takes a cautious sip. Then she winces, 'Oh, that's hot.'

I'd forgotten that she likes it with loads of milk, but the heat of the beverage distracts her from her previous question so I take the opportunity to leave her room and finish my own breakfast. As I enter the kitchen my mother's mobile starts to ring. 'Your phone, Mam!'

'It's in my coat,' she calls, 'the one I had on yesterday. Answer it, will you?' She hates to miss a call.

Her coat is thrown across the chair and I make a mad dash for it, but it's too late. The phone stops ringing just as I wrestle it from her inside pocket. 'Missed it!'

'Any idea who it was?'

Just then, the phone starts up again. I flip it open. 'Hello?'

'Who is *that*?' The woman at the other end asks timorously. The voice is familiar.

'Who is that?' I counter.

'You don't sound like Iris,' the person at the other end remarks, sounding even more timid, if that's possible.

Despite the fact that she hasn't told me who she is, I say, 'It's not Iris, it's her daughter, Eve.'

'Eve!' My name is said with relief. 'It's me, Dee.'

'Dee? Robert's Dee?' Why on earth would Dee call my mother? As far as I know, Robert hasn't even got back with her, has refused to talk to her at all.

'Well, yes and no. I was but I'm not now.' Her voice quivers and she pauses, breathing heavily, before asking, 'Have you seen the news?' Then before I can answer, she says tearfully, 'Oh dear, poor Robert. Is he depressed? I thought he was you know.'

'What?' The flood of words washes away their meaning because the woman is talking so rapidly and breathlessly. 'The news?'

'Turn on your television, it's probably over now but it'll be on again at eight o'clock. Or listen to the radio, some of them have the news on the half hour.'

'Why?' Once again, dread uncurls like a stretching cat. 'What's happened?'

'I don't know.'

'Pardon?'

'Robert is all over the news. Well, not all over, but in the news. Something about a painting.'

'Oh holy shit!' He's gone and confessed, I think.

'I think he's had a breakdown,' Dee gulps out, sounding horrified. 'I knew there was something wrong with him. That he was worried and depressed. I wanted him to talk to me, but he wouldn't and now look what he's gone and done.'

'He's not depressed, this isn't about you. I—'

'So, why would Robert do that? He can't paint. He's a history buff.'

'Well maybe—'

'He's been so moody lately and he wouldn't—'

'Dee, calm down,' I say gently. 'I'll have a look at the news and I'll call you back.'

'Are you at your mother's?'

'Yes.'

'Would she mind if I came over?'

'Well, I don't think—'

'She knows him better than anyone. If there was something bothering him, she'd know.'

I don't answer and Dee must take it as a 'yes' because she says, 'See you in a little while.'

And she hangs up and, immediately, my phone rings. My mind reeling from Dee's call, I'm on autopilot. My mother has come into the kitchen, wrapped in a white silk dressing gown. She looks enquiringly at me. I hold my hand up to stop her asking any questions as I fish for my phone.

'Hello?'

'What is Robert playing at?' It's Olivia.

I flick on the TV.

'And I'm not taking a fob off again, Eve. What happened in Florida? Why won't you talk to me? Why was the date with David such a disaster? Not that he's told me anything but it obviously was.'

'Hi, Olivia. I'm so sorry, I was going to call you.'

'Good,' she says in her no-nonsense way. 'Jesus, have you been avoiding me?'

'I've been avoiding everyone. Everything is such a mess.' I sit at the table and drop my head into my hand.

'Obviously. I saw the news on TV as I was eating breakfast. Why is Robert confessing to the forgery? I didn't think that was part of the plan.'

'It's not.'

'They're calling it the 'Van Gogh Cock Up'. He's admitted to faking the Van Gogh painting.'

'He has?' I groan.

'What on earth happened? I thought things were going well.'

'They were. Well, they did, only—'

'What's the matter?' my mother asks anxiously. 'Has something happened? Is it Della?'

'Olivia, I'll fill you in, I have my mother here.' I turn to my mother. 'Keep an eye on the telly, Mam.'

Without asking why, my mother sits down and stares fixedly at the television screen.

'I'll be in touch, OK?' I say to Olivia.

'Again?' she sounds hurt. 'Eve, I've rung and I've rung and—'

'I know, Ol, and I appreciate it.'

'If you don't want to give me the lowdown, that's fine. I just wanted to make sure that you were OK.'

I smile a little sadly, 'And I couldn't answer that, Olivia because I don't know.'

There is a pause. 'Oh, Eve.' And her voice tells me that she knows. She knows I fell for Larry.

'I still don't know.'

'Well,' she says firmly, 'one thing you do know is that you can call me anytime, right?'

I swallow hard, and gulp out, 'Thanks.'

'Take care.' She hangs up.

I close my eyes and wonder if things can get any worse.

'Why am I looking at this?' my mother jerks me out of my self-pity. I join her at the TV and say gingerly, 'I, eh, think Robert confessed about the painting. See if you can find any news bulletins.'

To give her credit, my mother doesn't flinch; instead she flicks through the stations until we eventually find a bulletin. To our relief, Robert is not the lead story. He's not even second. Or third. Instead, he's the amusing, slightly bonkers last story.

'And now,' the newsreader says, as a small picture of Robert, dressed in a striped suit and looking every inch the villain, flashes up behind her, 'in a twist to the stolen Van Gogh story, a history professor, Mr Robert Lynch, confessed to police last night that he faked the painting over ten years ago. He told the police that if the con men attempt to sell it on, it's worthless. It is alleged that he said he regretted fooling the art establishment but that he needed the money at the time and it was the only way to get it. The police have not made a formal statement on the matter as yet.' The newsreader smiles at the camera, 'So there you have it, con men who were allegedly conned themselves.' The news moves on to sport.

My mother and I look at each other. 'They seem to be treating it as a joke,' she says.

'They won't when they start to investigate his claims,' I say. 'They'll see that he got a load of money for the painting and—'

I'm interrupted by the doorbell.

'Hello?' My mother presses the intercom.

'Iris,' Dee says as if my mother is the second coming. 'Thank, God. It's me, I'm here.'

'Evidently,' my mother says dryly as she buzzes Dee up. 'Put on the kettle again, Eve, you've no idea how much coffee this woman drinks. I think her whole jittery personality is just down to caffeine overload.'

'Mam!'

And we share a laugh.

Dee is wearing trousers, light beige with a crease down the front and another frilly blouse, with ruffles on the sleeves and the shoulders. Her feet are encased in the sort of soft walking shoes nuns are famous for wearing, but her hair, loose curls tumbling over her shoulders, looks amazing. It's as if the more exuberant part of her personality can only reveal itself through her hair, while the rest remains constricted in sedate clothing.

She tosses her head as she talks, and her words tumble out in nervous gasps. My mother and I let her talk and talk and talk. Neither of us knows quite how to explain it to her. I think it's probably Robert's job.

'I mean, Eve,' Dee says, blinking rapidly and flipping her hair back over her shoulder, 'you are the artist and if anyone is going to forge a painting, you probably could.'

'Well actually—'

'Oh, now,' she says hastily, waving her thin hand around, 'don't get me wrong. I know you'd never do that, that would be terrible, but what I'm saying is Robert would be about as good at painting as, as,' she searches around for an apt comparison, 'well, as a cat would be in the fire service. I mean, why would Robert do this?' She downs her coffee, pours another and gives her cup a distraught look. 'Have you anything stronger, Iris?'

'That's strong coffee.'

'I meant alcohol-wise.'

'Wine.'

'Yes,' Dee bobs her head rapidly, her frills jiggle, 'that would be good.'

My mother sighs and, after a pause, pulls a bottle of wine from the drinks cabinet.

'I think,' Dee looks at us both, 'that we should all go down to the police station and see what the story is. Maybe we can visit him.'

My mother is battling with the cork on the wine bottle when the doorbell rings, 'Get that, would you, Eve?'

I press the intercom. 'Hello?'

'Eve, hi, Robert!'

Dee gives a tiny gasp and clasps her hands tightly together in her lap. My mother freezes.

'Stupid fucking eejit, Robert?' I ask.

'Eve!' My mother exclaims as Dee titters.

'That'd be me,' Robert sounds quite chipper.

I get the apartment door open before Robert appears out of the lift and I spot him before he does me. His cheerful manner is obviously a feint because the Robert I see stepping out of the elevator looks stoop-shouldered and ever so slightly defeated, despite the natty grey suit.

'Hey!' I say and he flinches. As he turns to look at me, a wide smile creases his face.

'Hey, you!' he says back.

I walk halfway down the hall to meet him. 'We're dealing with a very stressed Dee in there,' I warn him, touching his sleeve, 'she thinks you're having a breakdown.'

'I had to do it, Evie,' Robert says seriously. 'It was all getting too messy. I told them I painted the painting, so they won't know it's you.'

'I was going to go down today.'

'I know. I had to get in first.'

'You didn't.' Then I enfold him in a big hug, loving this man who would gladly sacrifice himself for my mother and me.

'And don't you go confessing now,' he warns. 'It'll look ridiculous.'

'Robert!' Dee calls from the doorway. She stands, hands clenching and unclenching in front of her, her tousled sexy hair negating the awfulness of her attire. 'Hello.'

'Every cloud has a silver lining,' Robert gives me a small sad wink and, walking forward, holds out his arms to his ex-girlfriend, who gives a little gasp before letting him enfold her in a tight hug.

I leave them to it and walk back in to my mother, who is standing at the counter, a full wine glass in her hand. 'The best thing that Dee suggested was a drink,' she says holding out the bottle. 'D'you want to join us?'

I pass.

Ten minutes later, Robert is sitting down with Dee alongside him. He takes a deep breath and informs Dee that, yes, she was right, he does have something to tell her.

Dee nods encouragingly. Then she flicks her gaze to me and my mother. 'You both know what it is?' she asks.

We nod and take seats opposite him.

'Go on,' Dee says quietly, taking a large gulp of wine. 'It can't be worse than what I was imagining.'

Robert begins and stumbles through his tale. After he explained about the plan, he says, 'I posed as a Frenchman.'

'You posed as a Frenchman?' Dee repeats.

Robert nods. 'And I faked provenance documents.'

'Faked documents!' Dee flashes anxious looks at my mother and me. We can only shrug. Oh please let her understand, I pray for Robert's sake.

'And John, Iris's husband, helped me sell it.'

'He helped you sell it.' Dee gawks at my mother, who nods her head dejectedly.

'I think,' my mother says then, 'that things would go a lot quicker if you didn't keep repeating everything he says, Dee.'

'I keep repeating everything you say?' Dee looks astonished.

'You do,' Robert smiles affectionately at her.

'I do?' Dee stops, thinks, then giggles, 'Oh, I just did. Oh.'

I feel relief seeping through me; if she can laugh like that, then maybe she'll stick with him. Robert is crazy about her. And the fact that she's here now is testament to her feelings about him.

'And then,' Robert goes on, 'this guy came and bought it for ten million.'

'Ten—' Dee looks about and clamps her mouth shut and I have to snort back a laugh.

Then she giggles again, and her giggle is so girly that my mother and I start to smile. But then the seriousness of Robert's situation overtakes her and, touching him gently on the sleeve, she says softly, 'Oh, but it's not funny, Robert, you could go to jail.'

'I know,' Robert touches her hand and she entwines her fingers in his. They share a smile. Then looking around at us all, he says, 'But I had to confess. It's not good keeping secrets like that.'

There is a pause. Silently I agree. Keeping secrets is not good.

'And why didn't you tell me before this?' Dee asks him.

'I didn't want you to think less of me,' he answers.

'Did you think less of me when you found out that my great-grandfathers were both cattle thieves and that my great-aunt was up for murder?'

'That's different.'

'A little, maybe, but I could never think less of you Robert, that's what I'm saying.'

Robert looks like a man who's just been given his life back.

'You might as well tell her the rest,' I say then.

Robert pulls his gaze from Dee to me.

'The rest?' Dee exclaims in slight disbelief. 'There's more?'

Oops, maybe that wasn't the best suggestion.

'I think I'll have a shower,' my mother announces. 'My head is splitting.'

'It's not so much about Robert,' I rush to reassure Dee.

'Are you sure you want me to?' Robert asks me as my mother leaves.

'Well,' I manage a smile, 'it looks like the two of you are back together so you might as well tell her everything. Meanwhile, I'm going to go home to think about what to do next.'

Robert jumps up and clamps a hand on my arm. Quite forcefully, he says, 'You are going to do nothing. If that Della lady says anything, it's no harm admitting that you knew this Larry guy.'

'She knew Larry?' Dee says. Then pauses. 'Larry who? Do I know him?'

I suppress a smile. 'I leave you to it. Talk again.'

'Do nothing,' Robert says. 'I have it under control.'

'Bye, Mam,' I call out, ignoring Robert. 'I'll call you later.' Then, before he can follow me, I let myself out into the hallway and down to the foyer.

Paddy is at the desk. 'Well, hello you,' he beams as I walk by him. 'You sneaked in past me last night and I missed you so you better be storing up all those compliments for the next time. I'll really be expecting something good now.'

I laugh, then double back and stop beside his desk and he looks at me in surprise. Gently, I say, 'How are you doing? I'm sorry I never knew about your wife before.'

His smile slips slightly. 'Well, thank you for asking,' he replies, his voice a little unsteady, 'I'm doing as best I can, thank you very much.'

I pat his sleeve. 'Take care now.'

'She was a very special lady,' he says quietly, his eyes a little misty. 'You remind me of her because,' he pauses, 'well, because you make me laugh.'

The compliment catches me off guard. 'That's so nice of you to say.' I'm touched. 'Thanks.'

He shrugs and half-smiles and we look at each other for a second. 'See you soon, Paddy.'

'Oh, you will, you will.'

I leave the building, smiling, which is good considering the day that's in it.

40

Back in my own place at last, I look up the number of the hospital so that I can phone and ask after Della. Then I decide to ring Olivia first and ask her over. Flipping open my phone, I see that I've had three texts. Why is it that I seem to miss all my calls? I scroll through them.

Look at news. Is it true? L. That's from Laura.

Is that your Robert on the news? June.

And then a missed call from my mother. And a message telling me to ring her urgently. And just as I'm dialling her number, my phone rings and it's Robert. His first words are, 'They've caught the bastard!'

'What?'

'Larry, they've got him. They got him coming off the boat from England today.'

I'm so shocked I have to sit down. 'Larry? Are you sure it's him?'

'Well, they didn't name him, but you don't have to be a genius to work it out.'

Christ, I'm glad I slept well last night. This is turning out to be the day from hell. My personal Armageddon. Pieces of my world seem to be flaking off like paint in the sun. I keep the phone pressed to my ear as I flick on my radio. It's five to the hour so I should catch something soon.

'He didn't know what he was being arrested for, did you ever hear such, such rubbish!' Robert fumes.

'Don't stress,' Dee says in the background.

'Don't stress? Don't stress! I've confessed and that, that . . . ' Robert is not used to cursing people and, floundering for an apt description of Larry, he spits out, 'asshole gangster who stole all our money says he doesn't know what he's been arrested for! Of course I'm stressed.'

'Robert, Dee is right,' I say. 'There's no point. I think we should wait and see how it pans out. And if he gets arrested, the money will be no good to him now, will it?'

'Oh, so you think he stole it now, do you?'

'I don't know,' I say, 'but, by God, I'll find out.' An idea takes shape. A very ill-formed idea, but an idea nonetheless. 'I'll bloody well find out.'

'And how are you going—'

I hang up.

Better to just do rather than think about it, I decide. My phone rings but I ignore it. I run a hasty brush through my hair and, grabbing my canvas bag, which doesn't look the part but which will have to do, I leave my flat. If I make a mess of things, I'm past caring, but, by God, if I'm going to get caught then he's going down with me.

Hopping into my car, I flick on the radio and, sure enough, while Robert mightn't have made the lead item, Larry has. At least it has to be Larry.

'A man was detained by police in relation to the theft of a Van Gogh painting from the billionaire Derek Anderson. The man, whose identity has yet to be confirmed by police, was detained whilst disembarking from the Holyhead ferry last night. He expressed surprise when officers surrounded him and demanded to know what was happening. Officers say an anonymous tip-off led them to him. The man is being held at Pearse Street Garda Station for questioning. Ironically, last night a man, Professor of History, Robert Lynch, admitted to faking the painting at the centre of the search. The story continues to evolve.'

This man, who has to be Larry, is in Pearse Street. Well, at least I know where he is. And I'm about to find out what he has been up to, I hope.

*

I park my car, grab my bag and stride forcefully toward the garda station.

'Hey, Miss, you can't park there,' someone shouts after me.

'Sue me,' I shout back and my voice is strong and hard. I'm getting into character. The light summer breeze whips my hair back off my face and I realise with some surprise that, finally, I can walk in stilettos. Anger has made it possible. They click clack along the street and I barge on, gaze locked on the garda station, like the sights on a gun. I wipe my mind of anything other than getting what I want.

I march in. The place is a hive of activity with phones ringing and voices talking and unsavoury characters chewing gum and swearing. Up to the desk and I rap my nails impatiently along its wooden surface.

'Hello?' a young guard, probably about twenty, smiles agreeably at me. 'What can I do for you?'

'Larry McLoughlin please,' I rasp out.

He blinks. 'Larry McLoughlin? And who are you?'

'I am his solicitor. Can I see him now please?'

'He is refusing a solicitor. Says he's innocent.'

Well, bingo, at least I know it's him they have. I glare at the young man. 'Eve & Cole Solicitors. Just tell the man I'm here. Quickly now, I don't have all day.'

The young guard disappears off behind the desk and I hear murmurings. My phone rings. It's lodged in the depths of my bag. Still acting like I belong, just as Larry has advised, I fish it out. It's a withheld number.

'Hello?' I try to sound businesslike.

'Is this Eve?' A male voice, one I don't recognise.

'Yes, who's this?'

'Thank, God. I've been trying to get you all day. It's Clive. Larry says not to worry, it's in hand. Everything's good.' Then he clocks off.

I stare dumbly at the phone. Clive? It's in hand? Is this a joke? Maybe Clive doesn't know that Larry is in a police station. That Robert has confessed. That Della Sweeney has collapsed. In hand my backside, I think.

'Hello?' I'm startled as a more senior guard pokes a ponderously large face into mine. 'You're Larry's solicitor, eh? Well, that is amazing.' He stresses the 'amazing' as he moves back from me, big meaty hands placed firmly on the counter.

I say nothing. I don't think this is a man I can boss about.

'It's amazing because,' a pause, 'unusually for someone in his position, he hasn't requested one.'

I flush. 'Well, I am his solicitor just in case he does want one.' I wag a finger at the man. My confidence is ebbing away faster than a business in recession. So much for Larry saying that if I acted like I belonged I would.

'And what solicitors are you from?' the guard asks with a leer.

'Eve & Cole Solicitors.'

'That's what we thought,' the guard nods. 'And there is no such firm, is there?'

I flush. I was right. This was an ill-formed idea.

'Now,' big meaty arms are folded and the guard glares at me, 'I'm inclined to think that you're a reporter.' He nods sagely, 'And impersonating a solicitor is almost an offence, so I'd skedaddle if I were you.'

His patronising attitude annoys me. 'Well, just as well you're not me, isn't it?' I flash back, 'because I'm going nowhere.' And I sit down on a very suspect-looking chair and fold my own arms.

'It's a free country,' the guard says with a smirk, 'but you'll get no story here.' And he walks off.

'You're a fecking eejit,' the man beside me says. He's a particularly drugged-up young fella and he leers at me with his two remaining teeth, 'you must be the only person on the whole planet who wants to stay in a garda station!'

This causes him to wheeze with laughter.

I shift away a tad.

Three hours later, my backside is numb from sitting on the hard plastic chair. A succession of oddballs have come and gone, the underbelly of humanity in most cases. The guards behind the desk keep looking at me and laughing. Sometime in the afternoon, a real reporter comes in, gets some information and leaves.

'That's how it's done,' the big sergeant, or whatever he is, calls over to me. 'Honesty at all times.'

A guffaw of laugher.

I flush, all bravado knocked out of me, mainly by my high heels and the hard chair. I wonder if I will lose face if I leave, and then decide that I don't care. I stand up, and behind the desk, heads turn. People nudge each other. Feck it, I sit back down again.

Someone laughs.

The young guard, the guy who'd met me first, strolls over. 'Would you like a cup of tea?' he asks kindly. 'You look uncomfortable.'

I'm tempted to refuse but I can't. 'Thank you,' I say. Then add, 'Would you look up the number of a hospital for me while you're at it? I need to enquire about a friend.'

'I will.'

'Thank you.' I pause. Then as he turns to walk away, I add hastily, 'I didn't mean to be so stroppy earlier.'

He gawks at me. 'That wasn't stroppy. We hear a lot worse in here.'

More time passes and, eventually, he arrives with the tea and the phone number. 'Sorry it took so long, I was busy.'

I take the tea from him and say meekly, 'I'm sorry for pretending to be a solicitor.'

He grins. 'You look nothing like a solicitor, they're far scarier.' Then he winks at me and walks off.

I suddenly feel really lonely sitting there on my chair. The station has suddenly gone quiet and the officers, faced with some unexpected free time, are standing behind the counter, chatting to each another. I dial the hospital. Della Sweeney is stable. Some good news at least. I flip the phone closed and hold it close to my chest, thinking about what I should do. I know I have to stay here, to catch Larry. To keep an eye on him. To know where he is. To know what he's saying. If I leave, I will never know what happened to the money or my painting. I want to look at him one last time and see if he really did make a fool out of me.

41

At four o'clock, something starts to happen. At first, I'm not sure that it has anything to do with Larry, but an air of confusion seems to permeate the station. The sergeant starts calling out orders. Mostly, he asks people to try and confirm what has happened. I wonder what he's talking about. Has some great disaster befallen the city while I've been in here? With growing interest, I watch the hustle and bustle and toing and froing and I forget about the hard chair and the pain in my feet. This is all very interesting. I wonder if a big criminal is going to be marched in or if a bank robbery has taken place. Not that I want to be in the presence of a big criminal. If he came in, he'd probably think I was looking at him funny and have me shot. I'd have to keep my eyes down and not look him in the face.

Then the nice young guard passes me and says softly, 'You might get your story if you hang around for another while.'

'What story?' The only story I'm interested in is Larry's.

The guard draws a finger across his lips as if he's zipping them up.

I sigh and sit back down into my chair.

From behind the desk a young officer hangs up the phone and calls out, 'It's true, sir. I've just had it confirmed and RTÉ have confirmed it too.'

The sergeant stands up and shakes his head and says 'fuck' really loudly. Then he sighs and in a really pissed off voice says, 'OK, nothing for it but to let him go.'

Him? Larry?

I watch as another officer picks up the phone and makes a call and then the meaty, grumpy sergeant looks across at me and says, in a deeply sarcastic voice, 'Your client will be through momentarily.'

Everyone laughs, but he glowers at them and they shut up.

I wonder if the man is having me on, but he's turned away from me now and is already on the phone again and he's demanding to know what has happened. How could such a monumental cock-up have occurred?

I stand up, my feet protesting. Smoothing out the creases in my skirt, I wait eagerly for Larry to appear through the doors. I hope my expression is sufficiently menacing to stop him in his tracks when he sees me.

And then the door pushes open and there he is and, in a terrible cliché, time seems to freeze for an instant as I take in his dishevelled appearance. In one way, he is back to the Larry I knew before this mess began and a part of me breaks. We've both changed a lot, I think. We've lost a lot. Or maybe it's just me. I feel the hardened expression dissolve as the hurt of the past couple of weeks starts spreading right through me, in the way warmth spreads though frozen toes and fingers. I stand in his way and stare at him. I think I might cry but that would just be stupid, so I blink hard and straighten my shoulders. There's a flicker of something in his eyes and I'm not sure what it means, only that it lasts a micro-second before he averts his eyes from mine and veers out of the way.

'Did you not say hello to your solicitor, Larry?' the sergeant asks. 'She's been waiting all day to defend you.'

That man has really taken a dislike to me.

Larry ignores him as he signs for his bits and pieces.

'You can get your story now,' someone else says to me. 'Though by all accounts he has nothing to say.'

Larry glares at the guys behind the desk but remains silent. Then, with a quiet dignity, he gathers up a brown envelope, slips a watch over his wrist and strides past me without another glance.

'And not even a thank you,' the sergeant says.

I want so much to tell him to go get lost, but that might not be wise. Instead, trying to match Larry's composure, I hobble out of the station.

Larry is striding rapidly up the street towards Trinity College. Is he trying to get away from me? I open my mouth to call after him, then pause thinking that maybe it's not such a good idea. But I'll never catch him so I yell, at the top of my voice, 'Larry! Larry!'

He keeps going. Bastard.

'If you don't stop I'll—' I can't think of what I'll do. 'Larry!' I shout again.

Larry flinches as a camera goes off in his face. He pushes it away. I suddenly become aware that there are photographers all around us. Well, not all around, maybe three of them, but their lenses are all pointing in Larry's direction.

I watch in despair as he jogs out of sight, knowing I can't be pictured with him because it'll kill my mother. I wish I could scream really loudly, but obviously I can't. I've spent the best part of a day on a horrible chair being sneered at by the police and for what? To lose Larry along the street? I heave a huge sigh, wondering what I can do now. Well, the first thing I can do is pull those damned stilettos from my feet.

My feet ache more once the shoes are off and they have swollen so much there is no way the shoes will go back on again. I wiggle my toes and pain shoots through them, making me gasp.

'Do you know Larry McLoughlin?' A journalist is gaping at me, pen poised, notebook ready.

'No. I was just looking for an interview same as you,' I say and it's a testament to my lying skills that he believes me.

The man wanders away and I limp back to my car, which has been clamped.

Fantastic!

42

The call comes just as I've paid some moralising git the price of my week's shopping to unclamp my car. The man steps out of his big truck and shakes his head in despair. Then after some disappointed tut-tutting, he asks me, 'Can you not read?'

I know he isn't expecting a reply.

Pulling the tools from the back of his truck, he continues, 'This is a bus lane. You can't go parking in bus lanes. What would happen if the whole of Dublin decided to park in the bus lane?'

'Well, there'd be no traffic on the roads at all then would there?' I say back, 'so the bus would actually be on time for a change.'

He stares at me and allows himself a smile. 'You're not to park here any more, do you hear me?' With a clatter, my wheel is freed.

'Thanks.'

'You have a lovely day,' he says as he gathers up his tools.

My mobile rings and I pull it from my pocket. 'Hello?'

'What the fuck were you doing at the garda station?'

It's Larry. I pull the phone from my ear, stare at it and then have to sit into my car and take a deep breath before putting it to my ear again.

'Well?' he demands.

'I had to see you,' my voice shakes. 'Where is the—'

'I am in a coffee shop on North Earl Street, you can meet me here. I can only stay about ten minutes. Some bloody photographer is trying to follow me.'

'Oh, and I wonder why that is?' I say snottily.

Larry barks out the name of the coffee shop and is gone.

Ten minutes. That's not a long time. And I have a tight skirt and high shoes and a car to park. Well ditch that. 'Oy!' I call out to the clamper as he's starting his van up, 'can you clamp me again? Thanks.' I hop out of the car, my shoes in my hand, and start to run.

As I race up O'Connell Street, my phone rings again, vibrating against the lining of my jacket. I don't have time to answer it. I couldn't talk anyway as I'm so out of breath. People stare at me as I pound by them and, as in the way of Dubliners, some smart alecks decide to have a go.

'There's a toilet in the Kylemore Café,' is one of the cleaner ones.

'You'd want to run to Cork to shift that weight,' is one of the more insulting ones.

'I love a racy girl,' is one of the more pathetic attempts.

Most people though just look away as if I have some kind of a contagious disease they might catch.

I wish I had taken Larry up on the jogging though because, the more I run, the more I become convinced that I'm going to have a gigantic heart attack. My breath comes in great gulping wheezes and North Earl Street might as well be in Outer Mongolia rather than a short jaunt across the city. But I keep going, getting slower and slower like a twirling penny, until I'll eventually fall over. My feet ache as the tights I'd put on that morning are ripped to shreds on the concrete pavements. But eventually, after much heaving and panting, I hurtle past Ann Summers and Clerys and turn onto North Earl Street, spotting the sign for the coffee shop. I know now how people must feel when they near the summit at Everest. Only they'd be cold while I'm smelly and sweaty.

I stagger the last few feet towards the coffee shop and collapse in the door. Larry, sitting alone at the very back of the cafe, glances up in astonishment as I weave drunkenly towards him. In fact, the whole place gawps at me.

Larry, quietly furious, pulls out a chair for me. 'Coffee over here,' he says to the guy behind the counter. As I plonk down onto the chair, he hisses, 'Wow, I'm so glad you haven't drawn attention to us.'

'I am sick of your smart comments,' I hiss back. Taking a deep breath, I gasp out, 'You snake in the grass. What did you leave me hanging on like that for? Two bloody weeks. Where is my painting?' I fan myself with a paper napkin.

'Whoa!' Larry holds up his hand. 'Do I detect a certain frostiness?'

I am speechless. 'Do you know what has happened? Della Sweeney recognised you and she has collapsed. Robert has confessed to selling the painting as a fake.'

'Your coffee,' a man places a mug of coffee in front of me.

'Thanks.' I barely glance at him.

'Della Sweeney recognised me?' Larry looks confused. 'How? Sure she's never met me!'

'And she's in hospital now,' I say, unwilling to confess anything.

'Yeah, but how did she recognise me?' Larry quirks his eyebrows. 'Eve?'

'OK! From the bloody drawing I did of you in Florida!'

'Oh, for Jaysus sake!' His voice rises and a few people look disapprovingly over. 'Round of applause.'

'Yeah, well . . . ' my voice trails off. I suppose there is no excuse. 'She is scared,' I say then, 'scared because two people who she didn't know used her name in a fraud. The poor woman.'

'Tell her to watch the TV news and she won't be so scared,' Larry says.

'Oh, come on.'

'And Robert confessed! Well, well, well.' Larry laughs.

'It's not funny.'

'Well, you'll just have to tell the police he's barking mad, which, considering Robert, shouldn't be too hard.'

'How dare you! How dare you!'

'Aw, come on, Eve, it's funny.' A pause. He lowers his head towards mine. 'You haven't seen the news, have you?'

'I've seen more of the news than I want, thank you very much. I am sick of looking at the news. Any time I look at the news, I see someone I know on it.'

'No, it's good. I swear. Just—'

'Larry, you took my painting, you took my money and you sit there and laugh that people that I liked got hurt. You asked me to trust you and I did, and I defended you and what did you do? You somehow go free and my painting and money are missing.'

Larry's grin fades. The light goes from his eyes. Slowly he asks, 'Did Clive not ring you?'

'Yes, with some cock-arsed message that things were OK.'

'You go to the cops and convince them that Robert is crazy, you tell Della to watch the news and you, Eve, you get the facts straight before you go calling me a thief.' Then he stands up and walks out of the cafe.

I have the horrible feeling I'm the one in the wrong. 'I didn't call you a thief,' I say feebly after him.

His answer is a 'Ha!'

I watch him go and I know it's unforgivable, but people are staring and I feel stupid, so I yell, and there is no excuse for it, but I yell, 'Well, if you won't support our child then you are a thief!'

And, as a result, when I go to leave, the owner doesn't charge me for the coffee.

43

Robert has left three messages on my phone. My mother has left two. Robert's go from: 'They've released the bastard' to 'I'm finding this hard to believe, Eve, but he seems to have done it' to 'What am I to do now?'

My mother's are: 'They've released the bastard' to 'Eve, what's happening?' to 'It looks like Derek Anderson is issuing an apology.'

Oh, God, I am confused. As I pull a beer from my fridge, I ring my mother. 'What's happened?'

'Have you not seen the news?'

If one more person asks me that today, I think I'll cut my ears off. 'Not the latest episode, no.' I take a slug of beer and know that, tonight, I'll be getting drunk.

'Well, that man Derek Anderson was on, you know the man you stole the painting from?'

'Yes.' Though I don't really like admitting that I stole anything.

'And,' my mother says incredulously, 'he says it was a mix-up. That he has been paid for the painting and that Evelyn Coleman and Michael Shanagher were legitimate art collectors. And he has declined to comment on the fact that they were taken away in a police van. His solicitor and the art gallery owner are backing his story up. They say that everything was explained to them by Michael Shanagher and that he is not at liberty to disclose what was said. He says that he is sorry for wasting police time and that he will reimburse the force or take whatever penalty is handed out.'

'What?'

'I know!' She pauses. Then says sheepishly, 'Sorry for doubting Larry.'

She's not the only one. 'But why did he say that?'

'I don't know,' she laughs at the outrageousness of the idea. 'I thought you might.'

Whatever chance I stood of finding out is gone now. 'Nope.'

'Anyway, it's all fantastic. Well, it would be if Robert hadn't confessed but that's not Larry's fault,' she admits graciously. 'Tell him thank you when you see him.'

'Yeah,' I say dully, feeling guilty. 'I'll, I'll just ring Robert.'

Robert is stressed.

'I admitted to faking the painting,' he moans. 'What will I do now?'

I remember Larry's words. 'Maybe you could go into the station and convince them you were having a breakdown? Tell them you'd broken up with your girlfriend and it was your attempt to get her attention.'

'Oh, now. Oh, God, I couldn't do that. I'd look like an eejit.'

'I know,' I say weakly, 'but otherwise they might start to investigate.'

'I could lose my job over this.'

'Robert, I'm sorry. If you want, I'll go in with you. I'll tell them you were having a hard time.'

'Wasting police time is an offence, you know.'

'I know, but your best bet is to go in now and save them an investigation.'

He thinks about it. 'I'll bring your mother. She has an air of authority about her.' He pauses. 'You come too if you like.'

And so, for the second time that day, I'm on my way to a police station.

44

Most people, according to the policeman, plead insanity when a crime has been carried out, not when they confess to the crime. My mother does a tolerable job of describing how Robert was not himself while it was all off with his 'lady friend'.

'He whined a lot,' she says, her lip curling up with disdain.

'I did not!' Robert protests, then remembering that he's supposedly broken up, he cocks his head to one side and admits, 'Or maybe I did. I can't remember, my mind is a blank.' As if to emphasise the point, he gives an extravagant shrug of his shoulders.

'Sir, a file has been prepared and if there is nothing to your confession you'll be charged with wasting police time, but, in the meantime, we have to investigate the claims.'

'You'll waste a lot of money,' Robert blusters desperately.

The policeman shrugs, 'You were quite specific, sir, in what you told us, I doubt we'll waste that much money.'

There is not a lot the three of us can do. My mother puts her arm about Robert and leads him from the station. Once out in the street, Robert says, 'Well, that's me done for.'

'Oh don't say that,' I chide gently.

'Eve, they'll test the papers in the French archives and know they're fakes. They've much more sophisticated methods of detection now. We couldn't have got away with the fake Van Gogh if we produced it today.'

'I bet you could have,' I say, leading them towards a pub on the corner of the street. What Robert needs is a drink. 'At the time, everyone wanted to believe it was an undiscovered work, so you told them what they wanted to hear. That's a powerful thing to do. Objectivity gets sidelined.'

Robert considers this and then nods, 'You're probably right. Derek Anderson snapped it out of our hands like a dog after a bone. He was frantic to have it. Van Gogh was one of the few artists he didn't have in his collection. Asshole.' He collapses down onto a seat and asks me to get him a pint from the bar.

My mother sits in beside him. 'Now don't have too much to drink Robert. No point in getting drunk.'

'At this juncture, I see no point in staying sober,' Robert snorts.

My mother looks disapprovingly at him. 'I'm going to call Dee,' she says. 'I'm certainly not spending the evening looking after you. You're her responsibility now.' And as I cross to the bar, she whips out her mobile and makes the call.

Half an hour later, Dee rushes into the pub, looking as if she means business. Squishing in beside Robert, she takes the drink from his hands and says softly, 'Robert, if you're imprisoned for a hundred years, I'll still be here waiting for you when you come out.'

I rather doubt that this sentiment actually comforts Robert who's probably hoping that he'll avoid jail, but as Dee smiles up at him, her great glasses reflecting the image of his face back to him, he's certainly not complaining.

My mother and I glance at each other and take it as our cue to sneak away.

After I drop my mother home, I take my courage in hand and decide to go visit Della in hospital. I drop into a bookshop and buy a card and a good art magazine. Hopefully, she'll see me and, if not, well, I'll write her a letter or something. Even if she has me ejected from her hospital room in full view of everyone, I figure that there really is no way that this endless day can get any worse. It's seven thirty as I nervously approach the reception desk and visiting ends at eight, so I've half an hour to locate her.

'Della Sweeney please?' I ask timidly.

Without looking up, the receptionist says, 'Fifth floor. You can ask the nurse on duty if you can visit.'

I take the lift up and then begin the walk to the ward. Why is it on the fifth floor? Anyone with a heart condition would have a hard time running down the stairs in the event of a fire. Pushing open the doors to Della's ward, I'm stopped by a young nurse who looks enquiringly at me.

'I'd like to visit Della Sweeney?' Despite my resolve, my knees start to tremble. 'I rang earlier and they said she was stable and could have visitors.' Oh, God, I hope she won't react badly and have another heart attack.

'Della?' The nurse smiles. 'Oh, yes, she's doing much better. She'll be glad of some company.'

I have trouble clearing my throat. 'Maybe you might ask her if she'd like to see me first. I'm not too sure she will. I'm not family and well . . . ' my voice trails off under the half-amused gaze of the nurse. 'Just tell her Eve is here.' I hand the nurse the card and the magazine. 'And in case she decides not to see me, can you give her these and tell her to watch the news this evening? That's very important. Tell her to watch the news.'

The nurse's expression has gone to puzzled mode. 'O-kay. Well, wait there and I'll pop into her.'

I watch her walk away and I have to lean against the wall for support. Where has my uneventful but semi-fulfilling life gone? It's as if, before the revelation about the painting, I was living in a bubble and now it's popped and suddenly the whole world is rushing in on me at once.

From down the corridor the nurse smilingly beckons me forwards, and hardly daring to believe it, I walk slowly towards her.

'Now, Della,' the nurse says as I join her at the door, 'isn't this lovely? A visitor for you.' She gently pushes me inside and pads back up the corridor in her soft-soled shoes.

Della does not look like a woman who collapsed rather dramatically yesterday. She is in a standard-issue hospital gown, but her face isn't pale and it looks as if someone styled her hair that morning. There is a lump on the side of her head where she'd hit her head off the table, but other than that, she appears healthy.

'Hmm,' Della's bright eyes take me in. 'Hello, Eve.'

'I'm so glad you're OK,' I cross towards the bed. 'You gave me a fright.'

'As you did me.' Her tone is clipped.

So she remembers then. I glance at my feet, not willing to lie to defend myself or Larry. 'There was nothing sinister in it,' I say instead, and I'm sure she's wondering if I'm talking about the sketch of Larry she'd seen or the fact that two people half a world away had used her name. 'Watch the news tonight.'

'I have seen the news,' she says and despite her recent illness, her voice is strong. 'It's very puzzling but that Derek millionaire man has said that he doesn't recognise any pictures the police have shown him of that Larry person.'

'He said that?' Then I flush. 'Oh, I just haven't seen the news, my mother, eh, told me that Larry wasn't involved.'

Della pulls away from me, her eyes studying me hard and making me cringe. 'So, you know this man then?'

'Larry is . . . was a friend,' I say. 'He posed for that picture. I'm sorry if it gave you a fright.'

I don't think she believes me. She's a clever woman. Instead, she looks me up and down. 'You don't look all that dissimilar to the woman who was with this con man,' she says.

I don't respond. She can call the police if she wants. I deserve it after using her name.

'It was low blood pressure,' she says then. 'My heart is fine. But they're monitoring me for a few more days to be sure.'

'That's good news.'

'I have no family.'

'I know that.'

'I would like you to visit me,' she says then and she sounds almost shy as she adds, 'if you want to.'

I recognise this for the burying of the Larry subject that it is. I don't deserve it but I'm not going to let that stand in my way. 'I would really like that, Della.'

She smiles. 'And I think I'd like both your paintings.'

She drives a hard bargain. 'You can have them.'

'And you can buy me a nightdress for tomorrow. This thing,' she lifts up a flap of the gown, 'is hardly flattering.'

'OK.' I can't believe she's let me away with this. Does she know or not?

'Now, if you don't mind, I've some reading to do.' She holds up the magazine I bought for her.

'See you tomorrow, Della.'

She doesn't reply; her head is already stuck into the pages of the magazine.

Once I get home, I find it impossible to relax. All sorts of thoughts are swirling about in my head. Will Robert go to jail? Will I get my painting back? How come Derek Anderson did such a u-turn? Does Della know? Will Larry move back in beside me? Will we ever talk again? Can we go rekindle our friendship? Can we have something more? I doubt that somehow, but he might move back to the apartment because he has nowhere else to go. So far, though, there doesn't seem to be any sign of life from next door. But he only arrived back in the country yesterday and he was in a police station for most of that. I wonder why there are no reporters outside our building, waiting for Larry to come home. Do they not know where he lives?

I do a half-hearted clean up of the kitchen by dumping the half-drunk can of lager I opened earlier into the bin and taking another one from the fridge. My mother would be appalled if she saw the contents of my fridge. Ten cans of lager, some cheese and a pint of milk. Closing the door, the drink in my hand, my eye falls on my mobile phone and I suddenly remember that I haven't called Olivia. It's just as well she's not the sensitive type. Anyone else would have run out of patience ages ago. I dial her number and ask her over, only half-expecting her to come – after all I've fobbed her off for the last two weeks – but she says that of course she can come over and that she'll give Eric a call and cancel him.

'Thanks,' I say, touched.

'What are BFs for?' she asks, laughing before hanging up.

I wish I had planned it a bit better and had more in the way of food to offer her. Or even some half-decent wine. We're hardly going to have a nice cosy chat with some cheese and milk. Damn. I begin a hunt for a takeaway menu. I normally have about a hundred lying around.

Olivia arrives twenty minutes later, just as I've managed to find a menu for the Chinese down the road. Shrugging out of her long green velvet coat, she enfolds me in a hug. Then holds me away from her and nods. 'Yep. You're fine.'

She looks great as usual, her life running normally as always. Long legs in white trousers, feet with painted red toenails wearing red and white sandals and her top is a beautiful red and white silk blouse.

I have made no effort and look like a grungy secretary, my skirt and top having long lost their crisp sheen.

'Did you know,' she asks me, 'that Larry was a con man? When I heard that, I was even more scared for you. Did you know?'

In response, I hand her a can of lager and ask her to sit.

Eyeing my smelly sofa, then her white trousers, she says, 'On that?'

'You can sit on the floor if you like, I'll get you a blanket from my bed or bring in the bean bag.'

None of the options appeal to her so she gingerly sits on the edge of my sofa. I join her.

'Eve,' she says peering around at my unkempt apartment, 'you really have to get some new stuff for this place.'

'It's all been a bit mad,' I say. 'I haven't had a chance to clean up.'

'Well, yes,' she nods. Then she pauses, and says, 'Why didn't you return my calls? Did you get a shock when you found out he was a con man?'

'I slept with Larry,' I announce, wanting to get straight to the point but, unfortunately, she has just swallowed a whole mouthful of drink and it sprays out of her mouth, neatly avoiding her trousers and splashing instead all over my crappy sofa.

'Now, aren't you glad that's not new,' I joke feebly as we watch the drink seeping into the nasty brown cloth.

'You slept with con man Larry? When was this? Was it before he was arrested? Well, of course it was,' she answers her own question and looks at me. 'So, when? Florida?'

I nod. 'I really fell for him, Ol.'

She says nothing, just gives me a look as if I've just told her I have an incurable disease, which, without being corny, I feel I do.

'I'll tell you everything that happened over there,' I say. 'Just don't go feeling all sorry for me.'

Olivia's reaction to my tale makes me feel that my life hasn't been smashed to smithereens by a baseball bat. And I don't think she's pretending. She says that the whole plot was bold and daring and clever as nobody got hurt and the fact that Larry and I shared a night together makes it even better. As I draw towards the end, however, her expression darkens. 'Oh, Eve,' she places what has to be her third can onto my counter top and says, 'it's not just a laugh really, is it? Robert actually confessed and Della collapsed.'

'Uh-huh.'

'And Robert might go to jail.'

'I know.'

'That's awful.' Olivia chews her bottom lip. 'Like, you did the right thing. I see that now. If it was me and someone had sold something I'd unintentionally faked, well, I'd have to get it back too. My career would be over.'

'I know, that's how I felt; though, looking back, I'd hardly had what you would call a career.'

Insultingly, she agrees, and then asks, 'So where is the painting?'

I shrug. 'I don't know.'

'But I thought you went to Florida to get it back and get rid of it?'

'I did.'

'So get it back,' she says firmly. 'If no one sees that painting, they can't actually prove it was a fake, can they?'

'Exactly, but I don't know when I'm going to get it back. I'm half afraid to ask Larry now because he blew the top at me today.'

'You get it back,' Olivia says again. 'Take no shit from him, hurt feelings or not.' She glances at her watch. 'Oh look, it's almost eleven thirty, turn on the telly and we'll catch the late news. Let's see if there's any more on the story.'

I'm not sure I want to, but ignoring it won't make it go away. Olivia and I move to the floor in my studio and, locating the remote control, I flick on RTÉ. The ads are on. I take the opportunity to pluck two more cans from the fridge and, as we crack the tops off, the news begins. I hand her the takeaway menu.

'Too late to eat,' she says, handing it back.

'Derek Anderson denies that the painting he sold was a fake and challenges the mysterious buyers to return it if in doubt,' the newscaster announces under the drum roll. As the music fades out, footage of Derek standing on the steps of the gallery flanked by his solicitor are shown.

'He looks like an asshole,' Olivia remarks.

What does everyone see that I can't, I wonder?

'To the best of my knowledge *Man with Swollen Face* is not a fake painting,' Derek states firmly in his charming North American accent. 'I bought it in Ireland many years ago and I do not recognise this man who claims to have sold it to me.'

Olivia looks questioningly at me. 'Has Robert changed that much?'

'I don't think so.'

'And Mr Anderson, you still maintain that you have been paid for the painting by this mysterious Michael Shanagher and Evelyn Coleman?'

'That's you!' Olivia screeches.

I squirm.

'They were not mysterious. There was a huge misunderstanding between us which has been cleared up. I have been paid for the painting and all is fine. That's all I have to say. Thank you.'

The news moves to other things.

Olivia stares at me. 'Well, whatever happens to Robert, it looks like you got away with it, Eve.'

And a tiny part of me is beginning to believe that she is right.

But where the hell is the painting?

45

A thump on my door startles me awake the next morning. I've fallen asleep on my bean bag and am stiff and cold. Olivia left sometime around three. I would have asked her to stay the night only there was just one bed and I knew neither of us wanted to sleep on the sofa. And now, I somehow find myself on the bean bag. So she could have stayed.

The thump comes again.

I'm so exhausted that it doesn't alarm me to have someone knocking on my door. It's probably the Party People from downstairs because whoever it is has to live in the building otherwise I'd have had to buzz them up. Wearily I call out 'coming' and shamble from the bean bag to the door.

Clive and a guy who looks so like Larry that I am momentarily speechless are standing outside.

'Eve?' the Larry lookalike asks, and even his voice sounds the same. I can only nod as I realise that this is what I have lost.

'Hi, I'm Declan, Larry's brother.' He sticks out his hand.

'Yeah,' my voice is faint. I grasp his hand in mine and shake it. 'Yeah, I guessed that. You look like him.'

'Can we come in?' Clive asks. 'We won't stay long.'

'Sure.' I pull the door wider, hoping that today will not be a repeat of yesterday's rollercoaster. The two men enter. Both are dressed casually in jeans and sweatshirts.

'We have something for you,' Clive says with a small smile.

From behind his back he produces a long cylinder. 'Compliments of the boss.'

'My painting?' I ask, hardly daring to believe it. At Clive's nod, I take it from him almost wonderingly. Flipping the top of the cylinder open, I pull out the rolled-up canvas. Shaking it loose, it unravels and my *Man with Swollen Face* stares up at me in all his faked fabulousness.

Clive comes to stand alongside me. 'Isn't he an ugly-looking geezer?' he chortles.

The relief of having it in my possession is immense. It is here. In my place. It's as if I've been holding my breath for the past few months just for this moment. Tension seems to eke out through the balls of my feet. 'How long have you had it?' I ask, laying it on the floor and kneeling down to stare in more detail at it.

'Since Florida, about fifteen days.' Clive has made himself at home and filled up the kettle. Holding it aloft, he asks, 'D'you mind?'

'No, you can make me one while you're at it. I fell asleep here last night. You woke me up.' I run a hand through my tangled hair and think that I must look a mess.

Declan sits down on the sofa, not even giving it the suspicious once over that everyone else does. I like him immediately. 'Clive got it out through Canada. That's how Larry travelled too. They flew from there into Europe and travelled across by train to France. Larry got the boat to England and the others came in at Rosslare.'

I nod, my eyes raking Declan's face and rejoicing in its similarity to his brother's. If I can't see Larry, well, he is the next best thing.

'Well, thanks a lot, you guys. It means so much to me not to have this painting out there.'

'Thank Lar, he was the brains behind it,' Clive fills three cups with water and dunks in a tea bag. 'Milk anyone?'

We all take milk, so Clive pours a small measure into each cup. As he hands mine, I say, 'I think Larry is cross with me. I thought he'd done a runner.'

This admission is met with two quite horrified faces. Eventually his brother says, 'You said that to him?'

'As good as,' I admit glumly, wrapping my hands about my mug. 'If you see him can you tell him I'm sorry?'

Declan shrugs non-committedly. He doesn't look at all happy with me.

'I really am,' I press, desperate for him to believe me and tell Larry, 'But Declan, you have to understand, I didn't know what was happening. He never told me.' At their lack of response, I say, 'I mean, how come Derek Anderson dropped the charges and said that by reporting the crime that he'd wasted police time?'

Both men look at each other. Declan shrugs, though he smiles a little. 'Well, you know how Larry suspected that Derek knew the painting was a fake all along?'

I nod.

'Well, he was right, he's known it's a fake for the past year. So, when he took your deposit with the intention of selling it to you, he was committing a crime. He just had to be told that we knew this. It would not have looked good for him.'

Declan takes a sip of tea, and then asks me, 'Is there any bread?'

'Over there,' I point to the bread bin, 'though it might be a bit stale.'

'Hand us a slice, would you, Clive,' Declan asks and as Clive does so, he continues. 'Before we started the project, Larry wondered if your Derek Anderson had ever, in the ten years, had your painting tested, to see if it was a fake. He figured it was what most people would do eventually. Larry told Clive to look into it. Check if the painting had been tested and bingo, it had. We found out what company had done it – there are not a lot out there – and because we already knew it was a fake, we know they had to have discovered it. And Larry knew from Derek's reaction that night at the exhibition that he knew it was a fake. Said Derek almost shit himself.'

I vaguely remember Derek flinching at Larry's comment, but his reaction wasn't overboard. Larry must be really good at reading people, I think uneasily.

'So when we actually stole the painting, Derek had a choice. He could have laid low and said nothing, knowing that he was in the wrong or, in a desperate attempt to make the money back on the insurance, do what he did, go to the police and pretend it had been stolen, thinking he was never going to hear from us again. So, after Derek reported the painting missing, we just let him know, through some correspondence, that we would pay him eleven million if he retracted his statement about recognising Larry or you, and, if he didn't, we would go to the media to say that despite his millions, he was still trying to sell on a known fake. We told him we had copies of the results from the lab. Of course we didn't, we're not computer hackers or anything, but he fell for it. He can pay off the cops for his alleged time wasting, but he could never buy back his reputation. Asshole.' Declan takes a swig of tea.

Ingenious. For the first time, I think I'm getting an idea of how Larry operates. He's always one step ahead. 'But why did Derek try to sell it? Why didn't he just try and return it to my dad?'

'Probably figured he'd make more money selling it on. Probably paid the company money to suppress results.'

That makes sense. I wonder what Larry would have done though if Derek hadn't known it was a fake.

'He would have done exactly the same,' Declan seems to read my thoughts. 'Derek Anderson could never prove that he hadn't known it was a fake. And Larry would never have gone to jail because he was never out of the country.' He points to himself. 'It might have been messier, but they could never prove beyond a shadow of a doubt that it was him, plus Larry is not known for using accomplices so his modus operandi was not the same.'

'So, you lot have never been involved in a . . .' – I'm unsure what to call it, I settle for 'scam' – 'scam before?'

'Nah,' Clive shakes his head and sits on my kitchen table. He really does like to make himself at home, I think. 'Me and Lar go back to primary school. He got the bullies off my back. You wanna see what he did. Told them he'd set spiders on them because he figured out the lead guy was terrified of spiders by a chance remark in class one day.'

'And you?' I turn to Declan.

He shrugs. 'Larry brought me up,' he says matter-of-factly. 'I owe him big time.'

We're silent for a while.

'It's not like he planned to do this,' Declan says earnestly. 'When he got out of jail he wanted to just be normal. I mean, he'd had it hard,' he looks at me. 'Did he tell you about Libby?'

'His daughter? Yeah, he said he never sees her.'

Clive and Declan exchange glances. Clive turns and makes himself some more tea, Declan glances down at his hands. The silence can only be described as awkward. 'What?' I ask.

Declan meets my gaze. 'He never sees her because, well, she's dead.'

'What?' I think of the happy little face of the girl in Larry's bedside picture and I feel sick. 'Dead? His little girl?'

Declan nods. 'She was on holiday with Laura, her mother. Larry and Laura had split and things weren't too good between them, and Laura had taken Libby and herself on a holiday.' He pauses and looks at me, 'This is really for Larry to tell you,' he says.

And despite the fact I want to know, I think Declan is right. If Larry wants me to know, he'll tell me. If he feels I'm worth it, he'll tell me. 'You're right,' I agree. 'This isn't my business. If you see your brother, will you tell him that I'm sorry for doubting him? I was stressed out.'

'Larry is many things,' Clive says, sounding a little cross, 'but when he likes you, he won't let you down. You don't know him too well obviously.'

I flush. 'I did trust him,' I say. But I wish so much that I'd held firmer to those first instincts about him. If I had, I'd still have him around and Robert might not have confessed because I'd have defended Larry a lot better. 'Well, thank you both,' I say, a little more glumly than I would have thought. 'And if you see Larry, will you tell him to talk to me?' I glance down at the painting. 'I can never repay him for this.' My voice wobbles a little and I have to bite my bottom lip really hard.

The two lads, obviously not wanting to get stuck with an

emotional woman, hastily drain their cups and make a beeline for the door.

At the last minute, Declan turns to me. He pauses as if there's some internal battle going on in his head before he blurts out, 'If you want to talk to him yourself, he's fishing today, in Kilkenny.'

And then they are gone.

Once again, I glance at the painting and I realise suddenly that if I've lost Larry than it's been too high a price to pay.

46

My car is not really equipped for journeys longer than forty minutes. It's like an obese person who has quite suddenly decided to take up exercise. It's knackered after a short burst of speed. Nevertheless, my car and I chug along, infuriating other motorway drivers with our 'steady as she goes' approach to travel. Onto the Naas Road and the Red Cow roundabout which is, as usual, more confusing than a University Challenge question. Two endless hours later, after a few wrong turns, I arrive in Thomastown, park my car and realise that, in my haste to get going, I'd failed to pack any suitable footwear. I'm dressed in jeans and a white shirt and a pair of quite nice trainers. I look down at them in their shiny almost-newness and mentally make the sacrifice. They will be ruined, but if I get Larry back, even as a friend, it'll have been worth it.

Larry's car is parked opposite mine, so at least I'm in the right place. I'd had a sudden vision on the way down of there being other fishing spots in Kilkenny and of arriving here and it being wrong and having to drive all the way back. But there was no need to worry so, with a happy heart, I start walking in the direction we went the last time, up along the bank to the viaduct. It's not as dry as it was previously and the ground is slippery and marshy, and my feet are soon squelching along, sinking into soggy soil. After about twenty minutes, I spy a lone figure up ahead, tall, broad shouldered, but as I draw nearer I realise that it's not Larry. How far has he gone, I wonder in despair. If the ground underfoot gets any worse, I'll be forced to strip off and swim. Hmm, if he fancies me, that might be a good idea.

I decide to ask the man as I walk by. He's standing waist high in the middle of the river. 'Hey!' I call out, 'have you seen a man go by with—'

The fisherman turns to me and if looks could flatten, I'd be in middle earth. He doesn't answer, however.

'Excuse me!' I call. 'Can you hear me?'

'Jesus!' he slams his rod on to the surface of the water, causing ripples to fan out in every direction. Glowering at me, he hisses, 'Even the bloody fish under the water can hear you! Do you mind?'

Then he turns away and recasts.

Oops. I wonder if I should call out a sorry but feel that he might think I'm taking the piss. I turn away and trudge on.

And on.

My legs start to ache. Larry must have walked the whole of the country to fish today. Then I wonder if maybe he walked in the other direction, which means turning around and starting over. I decide that I will not allow that to be a possibility. Neither unfortunately will my legs. He has to be up here somewhere. Maybe I'll just sit down and wait for him to come back this way. That seems like a good idea. How long can a guy take? We were only there for a few hours the last time. So I gingerly find as dry a spot as I can and make myself comfortable.

Bees buzz. Birds chirp. The water laps gently against the shore. I bloody well wish I'd brought an iPod or a book. Sitting here is boring. I've never really been a country girl. I like noise; even when I paint, I like music playing in the background. I've never been one for solitude or contemplation. And the constant sound of water trickling and babbling does terrible things to a person's bladder. I try to tune it out, to think of other things, but it's no use. After about thirty minutes, I'm bursting. I'm definitely not a squat-in-the-bushes kind of person and so, reluctantly, conceding defeat, I stand up to leave.

I startle a man who's just coming to fish in the part of the river I'm leaving because he jumps. I must have been very well hidden on the bank.

'Sorry!' I call out and earn another glower.

What a grumpy lot these fishermen are.

I start walking back, shoes ruined, jeans ruined from sitting on the grass and then, the final indignity, a slip, a slide and skid and a desperate flailing of arms before a 'splat'. I hit the ground face first. If it had been hard, I'd have broken my nose, but as it is, my whole face lands straight down into the soft mud. I pull myself up onto my hands and knees and can feel the sensation of mud in my nose and on my eyes and it drips down from the front of my previously sparkling white shirt.

'Damn!' I yell loudly and I don't care how many fish are startled. It can't be any more traumatic than a huge hook catching them in the mouth.

I haul myself to standing and gaze down at my body. I'm like a mud monster. I can barely open my eyes and I figure that being wet is preferable to being covered in mud and so I cautiously wade into the river. Bloody thing is freezing. The shock of it makes my eyes pop wide open despite the mud and of course then they start to sting as the mud drips into them. This is a fecking nightmare. Frantically, I start sloshing water over my face to try to wash the slime off. Then I scrub my arms and within minutes I'm dripping wet and freezing cold. Even the light breeze feels like a severe arctic chill as it washes across my body.

I shake the excess water from my clothes and hair and begin a slow trot back to my car in a vain attempt to get warm. Coins jangle in my jeans pocket and I think that I might grab a cup of take-out tea somewhere and that might warm up my freezing hands.

I eventually reach the road and climb unsteadily up the bank towards my car. I valiantly ignore the curious stares and rude titters of passers-by. And then, even their titters fade into the background as my gaze is riveted by a tall figure coming out of the local pub. The girl who cooks there, I can't remember her name, has accompanied him to the front door, her hand lightly on his sleeve.

I freeze, mortified that he'd see me like this.

He says something to the girl, who throws her head back and laughs, exposing her throat. I'd read somewhere that that was a classic come on. If Larry is any sort of a credible body language reader, he should know that. He says goodbye and turns in my direction.

I nervously wait for him to draw closer.

He does but continues walking, obviously not recognising me. I hesitate, wondering if it's wise to draw attention to myself when I look so horrendously unattractive. I mean who could possibly win back the guy she fancies by being covered in mud? Again, maybe Cameron bloody Diaz. Still, I've come this far, I've endured this much and who knows when I might see him again? He might never move back into his apartment.

'Larry?' I call out with as much confidence as my appearance will allow.

He pauses as he scans the road before his gaze finally comes to rest on me.

'Eve?' He looks so confused that it's almost funny. 'That you?'

'Yes.' I straighten up. Water drips from the tips of my hair. 'I want to talk to you.' Damn, I sound like a teacher. 'Please?' I add as I wipe a hand across my face.

Larry moves towards me. 'What happened to you?'

'I fell when I was looking for you. I walked for miles along the bank.' Shit, now I sound petulant.

'I finished up for the day,' Larry says, not sounding sorry for me at all. He shoves his hands into his jacket pockets and, despite his casual stance, his tone is combative. 'I was having my dinner in the pub. What do you want to talk about?'

It hurts that he hasn't acknowledged my efforts to locate him, but, then again, I wasn't exactly enamoured with his efforts to get my painting back.

'I came because I owe you a massive apology,' I say as humbly as possible. 'I'm sorry I doubted you.'

He shrugs before nodding, 'Apology accepted.' Then he walks past me to get to his car.

I watch in disbelief as he unlocks his car and pulls his jacket off before throwing it on the back seat. Is that it? Is that all he's going to say?

'Larry?' I cross towards him, the squelching of my feet making me sound like a monster in a horror movie.

He looks up.

'Is that it?'

'Sorry?' He looks at me. 'I dunno—'

'I apologised,' I say.

'Yeah, and I accepted it.'

'But I came all the way down here for you.' I know I sound whiney but I feel like crying.

'Yeah, and I went all the way to Florida for you.'

Ouch. I open my mouth to say something but I can't. He's right. He's so right. I can't think of a thing to say.

Larry stands at his car, studying me. Then he lays his hands on the roof of the car and bows his head. When he lifts it again, he says, 'You don't trust me, Eve, you never will. I can't live like that.'

'I do trust you.' This can't be happening. He can't mean it. My mind is suddenly scrambling with the horrible thought that he won't be mine.

He has the nerve to scoff out a laugh.

That sets me off. He can reject me, but I can't let him laugh at me. 'You never told me what you were doing,' I say, drawing nearer to him. 'It was all a big mystery. I was confused, upset. I didn't know where the painting was. I didn't know—'

'I could have bought a genuine Van Gogh from that man along with your fake painting,' Larry interrupts me. 'Taking two paintings is the same as taking one. But I didn't because I am out of that game now. I thought that would make you understand.'

'Well, I'm sorry,' I say and I'm not, 'but that was too subtle a thing for me to see. Anyway,' I fold my mud-crusted arms, 'you fiddled cashiers left, right and centre across America. I know you did. I don't know how you did, but you did.'

Larry nods. 'Yeah, I fiddled them out of about a dollar each. It could have been fifty dollars if I'd wanted but it was only a dollar. I did it because I needed to keep on my toes. Altogether, I was in profit to the tune of ten dollars and I gave it to a collection box.'

Fuck. I think that word in massive letters. 'You never said,' is all I can manage.

'I didn't think I'd have to. You told me you trusted me.'

'Oh, bollocks to that,' I say, my language getting as bad as my mood, 'you're so self-bloody-righteous. Trust. Trust. Trust. What about actually telling me what you were doing?'

'You'd have ruined it if you knew. You would have been looking out for the lads to show up.'

'No I wouldn't.'

'Right!' Larry rolls his eyes. Then he pushes himself away from the car and comes to stand in front of me. If it wasn't for the stench of mud, I'm sure I would have been able to inhale his own delicious scent. 'Eve, I accept your apology, OK. Let's just leave it at that.'

'You never trusted me either,' the thought pops into my head quite suddenly and I make the statement without rancour. 'Did you?'

'What? I already said the reason I didn't tell you about the plan was—'

'You told me your dad left you.'

He takes a step back, dips his head. 'He did leave,' he mutters.

'And you never told me that your mother . . . ' I can't finish the sentence. He knows what I mean anyway.

There is a silence. Then his eyes meet mine. 'You never asked.'

'I did. I asked about your mother and you made a joke.'

'It's not something I really want to talk about.'

'Well, then you should have said.'

'Oh shut up, Eve.' And he turns about and stomps back to his car.

'No! No, I won't.' I run after him. 'You say I don't let people in. I let you in but, you, you never gave me a chance. And now you're pushing me away because you're afraid.'

He slams the door on me and fires the engine, then pulls away in a hail of dust.

Well, I think, that's that then.

When I'm in the safety of my car, I start to cry.

47

It's a week later and despite the heat that is slowly building as the month turns from July to August, I light a fire in my mother's apartment and together we watch as *Man with Swollen Face* slowly begins to burn. I feel no emotion as it blackens and starts to emit a weird sort of odour. As far as I'm concerned, that part of my life is over.

The new Eve is ready to start painting her own stuff. The new Eve is going to take a chance on people hating her work. The new Eve is ready to deliver her canvases to Della Sweeney when she comes out of hospital tomorrow. The new Eve is just going to have to cope with the fact that her next-door neighbour never raps on her patio door anymore. And on the odd occasion when they do bump into each other, he smiles and says 'hi' and then disappears back inside. The new Eve is tired of apologising.

A sudden tapping on my mother's door startles both of us. In truth, we've been on tenterhooks this past week because according to Robert, the cops are trawling through the French archives looking for his fictitious family. We keep expecting to hear he's been arrested. When the tapping comes again, my mother pales and indicates for me to answer.

Pulling the door open, I come face to face with Liam and the rest of the book club. He puts a finger to his lips and asks in a big dramatic whisper, 'Is she in?'

'Well, I hope so seeing as you lot are here.'

There is a lot of giggling and shushing and I call out, 'Mam, visitors!'

'Who? Who is it?'

'Only us! Book club!' one of her friends calls out cheerily.

'Oh,' my mother is naturally surprised. 'I didn't know we were doing that this week. I thought you all wanted a break and had enough of Liam's pretentious shite.' As she joins me, her mouth drops at the sight of Liam. Her face reddens and her mouth snaps shut.

A massive embarrassed silence greets her remark before a chorus of insincere, 'oh nos' and 'not at alls'.

'Oh,' my mother says gaily, 'maybe that was my other book club friends. There's a Liam in that too.'

Now a chorus of 'maybe' and 'bet it was' before they lapse into more silence and turn to gaze at Liam expectantly. I think the 'pretentious shite' comment has thrown him but, give him his due, he rallies admirably. 'We've all been reading *I Should Have Loved Him*, by Natasha Green,' he says.

My mother blinks. 'Oh, really? Well, that's my favourite book.'

'Well, apart from *Septus Siberius* it is,' Liam teases. 'You said you loved that.'

My mother laughs uneasily, 'Well, yes, yes, I did.'

'So, may we come in? I've bought cream cakes and some lovely sandwiches in the local cafe so you don't have to do a thing.'

'Well, that's very nice of you, Liam,' my mother says. 'Thank you.'

'And,' Liam pulls out some tickets from his breast pocket, 'I took the liberty of getting two tickets for the musical *Love in the Air* for tonight. Here,' he hands her the tickets. 'I thought you might enjoy it.'

My mother takes the tickets and looks at them. 'Oh, thanks. That's lovely.' She doesn't seem to know what to do with them. I'd advised Liam to buy them but the idea was that he was meant to ask my mother to accompany him.

'Well, I'm sure Eve would love to come,' my mother shows me the tickets.

Liam coughs. I glance at him. 'Or Liam,' I say hastily, 'he might like it.'

'I'd say he'd love it,' one of the women, whose name I can't remember, chimes in. 'A good old romantic thing. Take him away from all the dry shite he's used to.'

Liam flushes. 'I wouldn't call what I like "dry shite" exactly,' he says politely, 'but I take your point. It's an acquired taste. Like good wine.'

'Yeah, dry. And shite,' says one of the women whose name I've forgotten.

The others laugh. Liam smiles.

'Would you like to go with me, Liam?' my mother asks, sounding shy.

And I know suddenly, watching Liam frame his answer to my mother, just what I have to do. I know that if Liam can go and phone up all my mother's friends and tolerate them calling him a dry shite and still come back for more, then I can't just give up. I'd be a fool to let my chance of happiness pass me by just because I got turned down once.

Pushing past them, I say goodbye to my mother, who barely notices, she is so enraptured with Liam. I grab my keys and my coat and pound out of the apartment, down the stairs, into the foyer, and am brought to an abrupt halt by Paddy, who is standing in my way.

'Hello there!' he smiles.

'You, beautiful, beautiful man, get the hell out of my way!'

He chuckles and stands aside.

It's nice to see him laugh.

It's still early, just after midday, and I heave a sigh of relief as I hop into the shower. I hastily scrub myself all over and wash my hair. Forty minutes later, I look presentable.

I slick on some lipstick, run my fingers lightly through my hair and steel myself for another rejection.

I've just opened the door of my apartment when Larry comes out of his.

He looks like crap. Well, as crap as someone with killer looks can appear. He's unshaven, his hair is greasy but he has made a half-hearted attempt to dress well and my traitorous heart sings as I take in his black jeans and orange T-shirt. We both stop in front of each other.

'You look—'

'You look—'

I nod for him to go first; I know my trembling voice will give my nervousness away.

'You look nice,' he admits. 'Going out somewhere?'

And I chicken out. Bloody fool that I am I don't tell him that I've got all dressed up to call on him. Instead, I shrug and give a half-hearted nod.

He winces, looking a little defeated. 'Oh, I was, eh, going to knock in for you.'

'Oh.' And now, of course, I can't tell him that I was going to call in on him because that would look pathetic. 'Why the door?' I ask instead. 'You used to come onto my balcony.'

'In fairness, I never came on to your balcony.'

I cannot believe he's making a terrible joke right now.

'Sorry,' he grimaces. 'I do that when I'm nervous. Make stupid jokes.'

'What are you nervous about?' Now I'm nervous. And a little bit hopeful.

'Nothing,' he waves the question away. 'If you're going somewhere, that's cool. I'll see you later.' Is it my imagination, or does he sound relieved?

'No! No!' My desperate voice makes him jump. 'I was,' I gulp, 'well, I was going to call in to you too actually.'

'Yeah?'

This is it, I think. I will humiliate myself yet again and if it doesn't work this time, well, I've given it my best shot. 'Yeah.' I inhale deeply and then, my voice quivering, I say, 'I can't just let you go, Larry.'

He says nothing, just stares at me with an expression that I can't fathom. It's like he's trying to process what I mean. Then he raises a hand and rubs it across his eyes. Oh please don't cry, I think. With his thumbs pressed into his closed eyelids, he stays still for a second, before slowly taking his hand back down and fixing me with a gaze so soulful I have to restrain myself from touching him. 'I was coming in to tell you that when my da killed himself, I cried for four months solid.'

'Larry—'

He holds up his hand. 'I found him, see. Sent my world spinning, so that nothing made sense. I pulled my first scam soon after and the buzz it gave me made me forget for a while. Then me and Dec we were sent away because my mother couldn't mind us. She drank, blamed herself for Dad, I think. When she died, I didn't cry at all. When I was eighteen, I got Declan out of care and we moved into our parents' house and I made a lot of money for myself. None of it in a good way, but the thrill of maybe being caught kept my mind blank. I had a girlfriend, she had my daughter.' He pauses and swallows.

'And,' I press gently. I take his hand in mine.

'And we split up, we were a mistake. But Libby was love at first sight. Her hugs and kisses and just . . . ' he pauses, 'everything,' he finishes.

'You don't have to tell me all this just now,' I say.

'I should have told you in Florida.' Larry looks down at me and I experience such a rush of feeling for him that I can hardly breathe. 'You're right, I did get scared. I was scared all the time around you. Scared of how you made me feel.' He takes my other hand and continues softly, 'Laura took Libby and went back to live with her folks. They hated me. I don't blame them, I was a prick. We fought all the time on the phone. Then, probably to escape me, she took Libby on holiday with her parents and didn't tell me.' Another pause before he continues, his voice dipped so that I have to strain to hear it, 'And my Libby got pulled out by a freak wave as she was standing on the beach and Laura ran in after her and they both drowned. I found out in the fucking newspapers.' His voice cracks. 'No one told me. Not Laura's parents, not anyone. They have pictures of Libby that they won't even copy for me. I was a prick, but I loved my daughter.' A tear falls from his eyes and he hastily scrubs it away.

I don't know what to say. I'd wanted this but seeing him so upset is awful.

'I pulled the garage scam soon after. I guess I was on self-destruct. I didn't care if I got caught. If I hadn't been such an asshole, ducking and diving and making easy money, I might have seen more of my daughter. I find it hard to trust anyone except Clive and Dec. I am a messed-up opportunist who is trying his bloody hardest to be a good man. And then you came along,' he pauses, half smiles and runs his finger down my face, 'with your cute looks and cheeky comebacks and amazing bloody talent and I was like, I dunno,' he pauses, thinking, 'spellbound, I guess. And the only thing I'm good at is hustling, so I know I'll never ever match up to you so I pretended I liked classical music, which, incidentally, I hate, and then you told me your story about the painting and, hey presto, I found a way I could impress you, only I ruined it all by not trusting you and expecting you to trust me and then you pissed me off big time by—'

'I am a messed-up copycat artist who likes the easy life way too much,' I interrupt, laying a finger on his lips. 'I steer clear of challenges and have to be in control of every tragic aspect of my existence. My dad died, I took charge of everything. I played safe and painted what I knew I could do. For my part, when you walked into my life, I never knew lust could be such a powerful thing, only it wasn't lust at all. I told myself it was lust because I was too afraid of getting my heart broken. Too afraid of stepping outside my comfort zone and, when I did, it was like all the colour in 'Somewhere Over the Rainbow'. I fancied you rotten. I know that I can't let you go without a fight because everything will just go back to black and white. And I am so sorry about your little girl.'

Larry nods, his eyes still glued to my face. He catches my hand in his and kisses the finger pressed to his lips. His eyes close briefly.

'You saved Millie from drowning, you know.'

Larry smiles softly, a faint upward lift exposing white teeth, and I melt inside.

We stand, inches from each other. The air is fizzing.

'I swear I will let you in,' he says with intensity, lightly catching hold of my shoulders and bringing his forehead to tip off mine. 'I swear I will not break the law any more, unless you want me to. I swear I have missed you and that it's taken me this long to screw up my courage to ask you to forgive me for how I treated you that day in Kilkenny. Declan rowed with me over it. He said you were the best thing that has happened to me in ages. And when I stopped pushing against it, I knew it. But, you see, I can never quite believe it when someone wants to be with me and stay around. I swear Eve that this is me.'

'And I swear that I am crazy about you. I dream about you in those running shorts.'

He laughs a little, then pulls back and looks hopefully at me. I stand on my toes and kiss his lips. He pulls me to him, his hand easily encircling my waist. It's just perfect.

Clattering footsteps in the stairwell cause us to look around. Ed, from the party flat appears, takes one look at us and starts clapping. 'And about bloody time,' he chortles. 'We kept wondering how long it'd take.' He looks at Larry. 'For a guy that's meant to be a smooth talker you took your time.'

'Yeah, well, what's worth getting is worth waiting for,' Larry grins, his palm caressing my back and driving me wild.

Ed snorts, obviously not a guy for romantic declarations, and says, 'We're having a party tonight. You are invited. Or,' he says, with a letchy laugh, 'maybe you'll be having a private celebration, eh?' Then he disappears off and we can hear him chortling all the way back to his own place.

Larry turns back to me, grey eyes sparkling, 'Charming,' he grins, then asks, half-shyly, 'so, beautiful, what now?'

'I dunno,' I dig him in the ribs, 'Fancy a cuppa?'

'I'd prefer tea, ta.' And as I laugh at our old joke, he wraps his arms around me and pulls me into him. 'So,' he asks, winking, 'd'you love me yet?'

'Right now,' I touch his face, grinning, 'the lust is pretty strong.'

'Fantastic!' Laughing, he picks me up, making me squeal, and carries me into his apartment. Then, kicking the door closed, he goes to kiss me before pulling back and staring into my eyes, 'Just so you know,' he says and he sounds dead serious and sexy, 'you are the best thing I have ever caught and there is no way I'll be following any catch and release programme.'

And that suits me fine.

Epilogue

THE FULL IRISH!

A full Irish cast is expected to star in the upcoming movie My Fake Life which is based on a book of the same name by Mr Robert Lynch. Mr Lynch wrote the book whilst serving a year in prison for the defiling of French archives in order to provide provenance for a fake Van Gogh that he hoped to sell. While the painting has never been recovered, the archives were found to be contaminated and Mr Lynch was subsequently sentenced on the lesser charge.

His book, which he declares to be 'a mix of fact and fiction', is about the faking of provenance for a Van Gogh and its subsequent sale.

In the latest twist, Mr Larry McLoughlin, an ex-conman-turned-actor, who himself was implicated in the falsely reported theft of a Van Gogh last year, is tipped to play the part of the forger. He is described by his agent as an actor of rare talent, with an amazing screen presence.

Mr McLoughlin was not available for comment yesterday as he was visiting friends in England with his partner, artist, Eve Cole.

Mr Lynch is said to be very excited about the movie and is already working on his second book about the theft of a painting by a couple of con artists. He says it's loosely based on the Derek Anderson tale of a year ago.

Acknowledgements

Thanks to the following:

As usual my lovely family – Colm, Conor and Caoimhe.

My parents, siblings and extended family.

My agent Caroline Hardman for all her work on my behalf. It's appreciated so much.

My publishers for their faith in me and for allowing me to write for a living.

To the Van Gogh museum for their help in finding out about Van Gogh and his pictures.

To the fabulous websites I visited – www.vggallery.com and www.vangoghgallery.com

To Laney Salisbury and Aly Sujo for their book *The Conman* – the beginnings of my book were formed by reading this wonderful factual account of how one man fooled the art establishment for years.

To all the people whose websites I read on the psychology of the con man – fascinating reading.

And to the man who conned me into buying some 'original' paintings – all is forgiven, though if I ever see you again . . .

ABOUT THE AUTHOR

Inspired by Enid Blyton, Martina Reilly started writing when she was eight years old and hasn't stopped since. At eleven years of age, she started writing a series entitled *The Gang* for the amusement of her friends. Four years later, she found herself working on a novel based on a character from *The Gang: Book Four*. This book was published years later as *Livewire*, which won an International White Raven Award and was sold to Germany, Italy and France. More teenage books followed, including *Dirt Tracks* which won a Bisto Merit Award and was shortlisted for an RAI reading award.

Martina has been writing adult fiction for the past ten years. *Something Borrowed*, which tells the story of a woman trying to trace the father of her child, was long-listed for an Impact award. She enjoys writing for the stage too, and many of her plays have been performed by amateur dramatic groups. Martina is also a drama teacher and actress.

She lives in Kildare with her husband and their two children.

Follow Martina on Twitter at *@martinareilly*
Visit her website at www.martinareilly.info